Praise for

BOND OF BLOOD

"What do you get when you cross the Crusades, Texas, hot and steamy sex, and immortality? The first in a vampire romance trilogy by the master of erotic prose . . . [an] incredible, sensuous story." —*Booklist*

And the novels of Diane Whiteside

"A very interesting story related in prose so steamy that it fogs one's reading glasses." —*Booklist*

"Extremely titillating . . . an excellent and engrossing story. I know I couldn't put it down. I . . . eagerly look for more books by the amazing Diane Whiteside." —*The Best Reviews*

"Erotically thrilling and suspenseful story line keeps the reader riveted to the book. Diane Whiteside has created fascinating characters that turn an ordinary story into a work of sensual art . . . it's a scorcher." —*The Road to Romance*

"A devilishly erotic story . . . full of vivid imagery that sets your heart aflutter . . . a hero who will melt your heart and make your blood pressure rise at the same time." —*Affaire de Coeur*

"Hot and gritty, seething with passion and the aura of the Wild West, Whiteside's debut presents readers with a solid western as well as a highly erotic romance, and the combination is sizzling. Erotic romance fans have a tale to savor and an author to watch. SPICY." —*Romantic Times*

Bond
of Fire

DIANE WHITESIDE

BERKLEY SENSATION, NEW YORK

THE BERKLEY PUBLISHING GROUP
Published by the Penguin Group
Penguin Group (USA) Inc.
375 Hudson Street, New York, New York 10014, USA
Penguin Group (Canada), 90 Eglinton Avenue East, Suite 700, Toronto, Ontario M4P 2Y3, Canada
(a division of Pearson Penguin Canada Inc.)
Penguin Books Ltd., 80 Strand, London WC2R 0RL, England
Penguin Group Ireland, 25 St. Stephen's Green, Dublin 2, Ireland (a division of Penguin Books Ltd.)
Penguin Group (Australia), 250 Camberwell Road, Camberwell, Victoria 3124, Australia
(a division of Pearson Australia Group Pty. Ltd.)
Penguin Books India Pvt. Ltd., 11 Community Centre, Panchsheel Park, New Delhi—110 017, India
Penguin Group (NZ), 67 Apollo Drive, Rosedale, North Shore 0632, New Zealand
(a division of Pearson New Zealand Ltd.)
Penguin Books (South Africa) (Pty.) Ltd., 24 Sturdee Avenue, Rosebank, Johannesburg 2196, South Africa

Penguin Books Ltd., Registered Offices: 80 Strand, London WC2R 0RL, England

This book is an original publication of The Berkley Publishing Group.

This is a work of fiction. Names, characters, places, and incidents either are the product of the author's imagination or are used fictitiously, and any resemblance to actual persons, living or dead, business establishments, events, or locales is entirely coincidental. The publisher does not have any control over and does not assume any responsibility for author or third-party websites or their content.

First edition: January 2008

Library of Congress Cataloging-in-Publication Data

Whiteside, Diane.
    Bond of fire / Diane Whiteside.— 1st ed.
        p. cm.
    "A novel of Texas vampires."
    ISBN 978-0-425-21738-2 (trade pbk.)
    1. Vampires—Fiction. I. Title.

PS3623.H5848B665 2008
813'.6—dc22   2007035152

PRINTED IN THE UNITED STATES OF AMERICA

10 9 8 7 6 5 4 3 2 1

*This book is dedicated to
Reference Librarians everywhere, especially
Brynda in Texas,
Gillian in Maine,
and Pedro in Atlantia.*

The vocabulary for the Texas vampire universe is drawn from feudal Spain. That very special time and place, where Christians, Moslems, and Jews lived in a rich cultural synthesis, was also the origin of the *vaqueros'*—and later the cowboys'—cattle herding skills and specialized gear.

A detailed glossary explaining those words, plus any other non-English terms, is provided at the end of *Bond of Fire*.

Brief pronunciation guides to French and Spanish (with hints about Don Rafael's quirks) are available on my website, www .dianewhiteside.com.

PROLOGUE

LONDON, PRESENT DAY

Hélène examined the photo carefully, moving the lens steadily over the print the same way she'd done when she'd first learned to hunt for underground German bunkers. The wood paneling of the private club in Mayfair was centuries old and solid enough to dim any midsummer evening noise.

Someone swallowed hard behind her and was admonished with an elbow, making him grunt.

The photographer had shot from an elevated vantage point and an awkward angle, creating a picture more artistic than logical. Still, some things could be gleaned.

Late 1920s America, somewhere that understood high fashion—New Orleans, perhaps? A festive street scene, probably Mardi Gras, given the masks and costumes. Most of the faces in the crowd were turned away from the camera or out of focus, making them unidentifiable.

A man came into focus, and she recognized him immediately—Rodrigo Perez, a very polite fellow when she'd met him at Versailles two centuries ago, though he could also be obnoxiously arrogant.

He was poised on the balls of his feet, his shoulders tense. She could almost feel his eyes moving left and right, hunting for the hidden photographer.

She sniffed, silently cheering the fellow's success, and moved on.

Another face slid into focus beyond her hat's bizarre shadow.

She froze, her hand clenching the jeweler's loupe until her knuckles turned white.

A woman, the image of her mother. Family. After all these centuries, she was not alone.

Tears sprang into her eyes, and she blinked them back fiercely. Not here, not in this audience, would she show weakness.

Besides, how much had her masters known all these years—and chosen to keep from her? *Nom de Dieu*, she would have answers from them and, this time, she would not be polite about how she asked her questions.

Lord Simon set a snifter down beside her, and she gulped the fine cognac with scant regard for its high cost. *Mon Dieu*, if *la petite* was alive, answers must be demanded.

She shifted the loupe slightly to give herself time to think, ignoring Lord Simon's watchful bodyguards around her.

A man's face sprang out at her. Jean-Marie St. Just?

Her heart slammed to a stop, harder and faster than any time she'd fallen into hibernation as a *vampira*.

She almost knocked the lamp off the table before she could control herself.

Alive, alive, alive . . . Joy fizzed through her veins faster than any champagne.

Her heart began to beat again, echoing her determination to find him, and her fingertips instinctively ached, desperate to caress his mobile mouth. If he'd lived long enough to be recorded in this picture, surely God would not be so cruel as to separate them again.

PART ONE

REVOLUTION

ONE

Thomas Jefferson, ambassador of the young American republic, led Jean-Marie St. Just and Rodrigo Perez down the long hallways, Sara Perez radiant on his arm. Candlelight blazed from hundreds of candles, magnified and scattered through mirror after mirror, only to shine like freedom's torch on his red hair. The quartet cut through the throng like masters of their own fates, wearing their peacock attire as if it were no more than a diversion or camouflage—not a grab for attention or a naked declaration of unassailable power.

Chattering courtiers, sweating under their paint and powder, as gaudy in their brilliant silks as parakeets, circled and glided inside the palace's spectacular cage. Predators, barbed glances flashing like knives, stalked their prey.

The king and queen of France were displayed on gilded chairs in an alcove, arrayed in their finest clothes and surrounded by fawning, over-bred lackeys. The corpulent, unhappy excuse for kingly omnipotence looked like a peasant forced to sit on the throne. If there was any hope for the next generation's intelligence or energy, it came from the Austrian queen, whose flashing eyes captured every detail. Marie

Antoinette displayed her legendary sense of style by wearing a costly, amber silk dress, which turned everyone and everything else here into a backdrop for her glory.

Louis XVI looked the newcomers over coolly, obviously wishing to be anywhere else. His royal hand waggled in a languid sign of recognition.

Jean-Marie retained his impeccably pleased demeanor, despite the dirk in his heavily embroidered silk sleeve and the overwhelming urge to retch. After all, how many times had he been caned in this very palace for promoting republican ideals, rather than the divine right of kings?

Whatever else Father had been, he'd rarely been openly rude without a good reason. If he'd lived to see his great-great-grandson sit on the throne of France, there would have been hell to pay in the royal nurseries decades ago.

But that had nothing to do with tonight's visit.

Jean-Marie let his expression slide further into open sycophancy, masking his opinion of his many-times-removed nephew and his body's unease. His mouth tasted of smoke and ashes, and a demon was drilling spikes into both temples. It was hardly the first time these agonies had attacked him at Versailles.

Jefferson nodded formally, stopping just short of a bow. "Your Majesties, may I present Don Rodrigo Perez, one of General Washington's most trusted advisors?"

And spymaster, come here to personally verify for Washington that France was not an immediate threat.

Rodrigo bowed low and very smoothly, as befitted a man who'd mastered the skill while wearing eighty pounds of chain mail, sword, shield, and other knightly accoutrements.

"And Mister Jean-Marie St. Just, whose gallantry in action has been recognized by both General Washington and your own *Marquis* de la Fayette?"

Jefferson's Virginia drawl managed Jean-Marie's name quite well, including the tricky detail of pronouncing the *J*'s like the *s* in "measure."

Jean-Marie's bow matched Rodrigo's in depth, although he automatically added the flourishes appropriate to greeting a king. They were taught to every member of the royal brood, legitimate or not. No matter how many decades had passed since he'd been here, some things were never forgotten, even when the skill could cause comment.

"And Señorita Perez, Don Rodrigo's sister." Jefferson's Virginia drawl lingered over every syllable, caressing her name.

Sara sank into a deep curtsy. While she was not blood kin to Rodrigo, they'd endured long years of hard trials together, forging a bond closer than many brothers and sisters. Her eyes were shining now, and her color was very high, causing an almost audible groan of desire from their watchers. Even the king's eyes widened, despite his notorious disinterest in carnal congress.

Instinctively, Jean-Marie's fingers flexed, and he started to edge forward, moving to protect her.

Rodrigo's foot tapped his, once, briefly.

Jean-Marie stilled. The other man was as tense as he was, perhaps more so. But he was willing to allow Sara's eagerness to shine like a diamond amid the jaded courtiers. Her hunger was, after all, the official reason they'd come to Paris.

Jean-Marie relaxed slightly, resuming his original sycophant's posture. He would wait and watch, as Rodrigo did. If any of these fools lifted so much as a finger against her, they'd wish they were dead. There was no need to do anything more now.

She rose, sending her taffeta skirts sighing back into place like an houri's invitation to paradise. She cast her eyes down, teasing those around with a come-hither look that seemed meant for each one alone. Meaningful glances were exchanged, laden with coded messages.

By Jean-Marie's reckoning, she'd guaranteed at least one assignation before the courtiers remembered to watch their monarch again.

He clenched his teeth, refusing to react to another stomach-churning wave of dizziness.

The king yawned, having lost interest in Sara, and waved the newcomers away impatiently. "Yes, yes, I know. Come back again with whatever you wish to say, Jefferson. And these three are welcome to Us, too. Now go."

They hadn't gone more than two steps away from the king and queen before a fresh-faced young man, with a weak chin and slender build, asked Sara to join an *innocent* card game.

"Ooh, certainly, Monsieur Simenon, is it not?" she cooed, her middle-aged face softening with delight. "It would be a pleasure to spend time at *play* with you. You'll excuse me, Don Rodrigo, Mr. Jefferson."

The men murmured their regret and bowed, hemmed in on all sides by the throng of courtiers.

Sara departed, her hand resting on her new acquaintance's and her head tilted attentively up to his. He was already chatting to her, of course, and would almost certainly be in her bed before the night was out. He'd probably consider himself lucky, although she'd likely drop him within a week or so—once she had an eye to where the king's spymaster might be found. She loved having a focus for the game of seduction, and it had saved them all more than once.

With Sara gone, there was little to keep Jefferson around, and he soon disappeared with a few polite words of farewell. He'd visit them again, of course, to exchange more conversation about French intentions toward America—and to indulge his fascination with Sara.

Courtiers rustled, eager to advance on their monarchs. By unspoken agreement, Rodrigo and Jean-Marie moved to the next room, seeking fresher air. They found a comparatively cooler space in a window embrasure, Rodrigo's imposing height and formidable presence chasing off its previous occupants.

Jean-Marie claimed a pair of glasses from a passing lackey's tray and handed one to Rodrigo. He sipped it cautiously—and the champagne's cool refreshment eased his throat a bit. Before he could stop himself, he'd gulped the rest, sending bubbles jolting into his stomach.

Merde, that was stupid. This was not the time or the place to display any weakness.

His head came up warily, and he scanned for watchers. Nobody tossed back champagne like water, especially at court. Growing up in these halls had taught him to guard every move, every glance, every word at all times.

Rodrigo silently exchanged glasses, providing him with another round. Droplets of red swirled and dissipated within the champagne, changing it to a pale pink.

Jean-Marie stilled and directed a suspicious glare at his friend's hand.

Rodrigo casually rubbed his thumb over his fingertip, erasing the few traces of blood.

"You do not need to guard me from every disaster, *mon frère*," Jean-Marie snapped, well aware starvation was turning him foul-tempered.

"You should have let her feed you this morning, as she asked." A big shoulder lifted in a shrug. "I do not have so many friends that I find myself able to face the loss of even one with equanimity."

"I do not need it," Jean-Marie all but snarled.

"Your stubbornness makes a donkey look as flexible as a papal diplomat, *mi hermano*. Bend your pride enough to take extra blood for greater needs, such as tonight," Rodrigo hissed, stepping close enough to block the view of onlookers. Only another *vampiro* or a *compañero* like Jean-Marie, whose body had been altered by decades of drinking *vampiro* blood, could have heard him. "You'll have to make do with mine for a few hours, until she can feed you again."

Despite the rational explanation, Jean-Marie gritted his teeth, loathing yet another example of his enslavement.

Rodrigo's iron grip closed around his wrist under his cuff and tightened until Jean-Marie could feel tendons start to grind against bone. "It has been weeks since you fed. Even at that, you need more than blood."

"I swore I wouldn't take more from her when I learned the truth of what she'd done." Jean-Marie shot him a barbed glance.

Rodrigo snorted in disgust. "In that case, let the *wine* cool you and your temper for a few moments."

Jean-Marie seethed but nodded acquiescence, knowing all too

well the truth in Rodrigo's words. He'd nearly died a dozen times in Washington's army—never because of wounds or disease but rather, because he'd been separated from Sara, the mistress who held him literally in thrall.

If he went another day like this, he'd barely be able to speak. Three days, and he wouldn't be able to walk. A week longer—*eh bien*, that was as long as he'd ever been able to force himself to live without a taste of Sara. Much more than that and he'd die—very painfully.

He drank the second glass more slowly, letting the bubbles break against his tongue before diving down his throat.

A slow, rich warmth crept into his torso. His dizziness faded into the background, followed by the bitter headache. His roiling stomach settled back into position. The aches still lingered at the edge of his consciousness, like unwelcome houseguests. But he'd be able to function normally for a few hours more until he could claim Sara's blood.

Silence stretched between them, emphasized by the chattering fools around them and a seductive minuet dipping and gliding in the distance.

All the while, the less favored—younger brothers and sons, lower ranks, the purely ambitious, malcontents—plotted and planned and whispered while watching every passerby at this most brilliant and deadly of all Europe's courts. The one whose queen could lock the king out of her favorite bedroom, while lewd pictures of her with a legion of lovers were bought and sold in every city. The one whose greatest royal palace glittered like a diamond and reeked like a cesspool, thanks to the open latrines in the stairwells.

Beautiful, corrupt, and deadly—like its *vampiros'* reputation. Yet even here they respected certain fundamental tenets of *vampiro* society, such as the necessity for speaking Spanish. Charlemagne had brought to France Spanish translations of Arabic travelogues, including Spanish names for everything related to *vampiros*. Given that most *vampiros* were widely scattered and a quarrelsome lot at best, their lingua franca was the only thing that allowed any courtesy. Every young *vampiro*—or *cachorro*—therefore learned the Spanish terms, or was quickly destroyed by a testy older *vampiro* for bad manners.

So-called civilized Frenchmen could no more avoid the painful necessity of accepting Spanish terminology than they could hide their monarchy's decay.

Jean-Marie had not survived this long by ignoring bitter truths.

"I will go to her later this evening, after she's sated," he said abruptly. "The taste should be extremely—satisfying by then."

"*Sí*, her taste should completely heal you, given how rich it's likely to become," Rodrigo agreed.

Both men glanced across the room at her. Sara was barely visible in a card room, surrounded by a crowd of admirers, both men and women. She was usually considered lovely but quiet, with her dark hair and eyes and olive skin. Now she was glowing with all the radiance of a girl enjoying a long-promised treat, making her appear a great beauty. Her sultry looks promised pleasure and fulfillment to all those around her.

Even if she hadn't been a *vampira*, her vivacity would have been more than enough to capture the attention of any *prosaico*—or mortal—whose carnal favors she wanted to taste. As a *vampira* on the hunt, she was irresistible.

"She's chosen well for her first night here, since all of them appear very sensual. The morning should see her very replete," Rodrigo commented. He claimed two more glasses from a servant and gave one to Jean-Marie. "But, *sabe Dios*, I'd rather be in Texas, breathing the open air, than here amid all these courtiers . . ."

"High in the hills north of San Antonio?" Jean-Marie queried softly, remembering where he'd ridden half-wild horses with even rowdier Indians, and Rodrigo had spent days roaming the hills and rivers. But there'd been little peace between the Spanish settlers and the Indians, until finally the governor had eliminated all but a few heavily armed settlements. After that, their small household had headed north and east, their wanderings eventually leading them to Savannah and finally to Washington's army.

Rodrigo and Jean-Marie lifted their glasses in a silent toast to the one place they'd found on their travels that they'd both loved.

"It was worth exploring La Salle's survivors' fantastic tales, was it not? After all, not every story voiced in these halls can be completely false." Rodrigo twirled the fragile crystal goblet, sending shards of light dancing over their brilliantly embroidered suits.

Jean-Marie huffed in mock dudgeon, allowing himself to be teased out of his megrims. He stretched, subtly shifting his coat's fine silk across his shoulders and checking the position of his weapons. While his instincts hadn't warned him of any trouble near Sara tonight, there was still work to be done. "I'd best be going. Sara's already gathered a court and . . ."

Rodrigo's deep voice overrode his. "I'll make sure her suitors are acceptable."

Jean-Marie raised an eyebrow. He'd expected Rodrigo to be hunting here, too.

"I fed earlier—and well." Rodrigo almost purred the words, investing them with an entirely appropriate carnal significance.

Indeed? Jean-Marie considered the implications for his protector's duties. *Vampiros*, such as Rodrigo and Sara, fed on the emotional energy carried in blood. *Vampiros* who were pleasant companions enjoyed carnal energy and had spent every year of their long lives perfecting their techniques for granting the utmost sensual pleasure to their lucky partners. With five hundred years' experience to guide Rodrigo, his prey were uniformly fond of his company and sustained him very well.

Disgusting *vampiros*, on the other hand, fed on terror and death.

Even knowing Rodrigo was both free and capable, Jean-Marie had his own concerns, starting with Rodrigo's health. "It's my duty to guard her at all times."

"Tonight you're off duty and must enjoy yourself. *¿Comprendes?*" Rodrigo shrugged lazily, every inch the haughty grandee, whose word alone was more than enough justification for any action.

Jean-Marie hesitated before nodding his acceptance. Rodrigo loathed watching Sara feed. He'd likely be depressed and guilty tomorrow, ridden by old memories that only she shared and might be able to discuss with him. But there was no use arguing with him in this mood. He'd use a *vampiro*'s gifts of mind compulsion to gain his way or, more likely, his own remarkable ability to forge clever punishments no sane man wanted to repeat. "You are too kind, *mon frère*."

"I live to make my family happy." Rodrigo swept Jean-Marie a ridiculously ornate bow, and they both laughed at the absurdity of him ever behaving like an overanxious flunky. He slapped Jean-Marie lightly on the shoulder and strolled toward Sara and the card room, shaking out the lace under his cuffs. The crowd parted before him, most of them probably not even aware they were doing so.

Jean-Marie shook his head, wishing his best friend had more to occupy his mind than sacrificing his peace for his family's momentary comfort. He'd been far happier as Washington's spymaster in New York City, when he'd needed to continually juggle everything from Washington's desperate needs—and utter lack of funds—to the British perceptiveness and bloodthirstiness. He'd even managed to have Jean-Marie assigned as his courier, in order to feed discreetly from Sara. They'd done well after peace was signed, too, helping to rebuild America's cities and mercantile empires. Only Sara's increasingly rabid loathing of North American provincialism had made them leave for Europe.

Europe, with its bright lights and frivolous assemblies, intent only on pleasure. Europe, which expected the French court to show the way in art, music, and dance.

His intuition jostled him then, sending a frisson rippling through his spine. It was the irregular voice that had guided him through an unsettled childhood surrounded by enemies and sycophants, where he could speak freely to nobody and his only assets were what his grace and sweet speaking won from his father. It had told him when to speak or remain silent, when to move or remain still. It had always been right, even though it rarely spoke in words.

His oldest friend, other than Rodrigo, and his most trusted companion, although he could never predict when and how it would visit him.

He glanced around—and was rewarded with another nudge when he faced the ballroom. So be it.

He headed for the glittering room, enjoying a minuet's brilliant cascade of notes. He'd been trained in dancing from earliest childhood, part and parcel of learning swordplay and riding. A few minutes of that would fulfill his promise to Rodrigo, after which he could return to their rented Paris mansion.

The ballroom was as magnificent as anywhere else in Versailles, of course. Spectacular chandeliers, gilded mirrors, lavish paintings and murals, polished floors—all combined to form a setting of immense style and majesty. Yet here, the emphasis was entirely on the dance. An alcove at one end allowed the orchestra's music to pour over the dancers and through the halls beyond. A single row of gilded chairs circled the oval room, allowing the few spectators to gossip in comfort. The center of the room was filled with set after set of magnificently dressed men and women, all dancing the minuet.

The doorway was full of men, much more so than Jean-Marie would have expected for a dance while the king was still present.

Ah, here was a small puzzle to unravel!

He stepped forward, elbowing his way through the crowd. The throng swayed—and rebounded, refusing to move. Even more interesting.

He grew more determined and worked his way into the knot of people until he could see what drew them.

As was the pattern in minuets, a single couple had taken the center of each set and was dipping and turning, gliding and swaying together, in a pageantry so precise dance masters spent a lifetime studying it.

Yet one woman held everyone's eyes. The most graceful lady of all was centered under the finest chandelier, her jewelry making her sparkle like the sun. She was young, too, and slender, standing more than average height. She danced like a young Diana, as if the delight of the moment was more than enough reward for her, totally disregarding everyone and everything else.

Jean-Marie froze, his breath hanging in his throat. His heart forgot to beat. *Nom de Dieu*, she was the most beautiful woman he'd ever seen.

Her partner, a cavalry officer, was bowing and gliding as if he'd give his life to see the line of her ankle and foot displayed to their fullest advantage. He caught his dress sword on his coattails and stumbled.

Jean-Marie's hands started to close into fists, ready to snatch the clumsy fool away from her. He caught himself before he lunged, cursing himself for being an idiot.

The boy—a mature soldier, to give him his due—recovered and danced on, barely missing a beat.

Jean-Marie recklessly memorized her face—the perfect oval, the straight nose, the winged brows, the—God help him!—carnal mouth, and the green eyes like the deepest glade in a forest. Her long swan's neck, so well suited for tilting to look over her perfect shoulders at her partner. The sweet rise and fall of her breasts, inside the stiffly corseted blue dress.

What he wouldn't give to have her smile at him, while he unlaced her . . .

She and her partner backed into their side of the set. Another couple bowed and curtsied before gliding and dipping into their set's center, to begin another round.

Jean-Marie blinked. All around him, men shuffled their feet, the tension sighing out of them, and some left.

Fingers gripped his elbow, and a scent reached his nose.

Vampiro? But not Rodrigo or Sara. There was only a faint hint of *vampiro* here and no other *compañeros*, of course. Given the vast unpredictability of making a *compañero*, few *vampiros* cared to try it and fewer *prosaicos* were stupid enough to have been caught as easily as he'd been.

He glanced toward its source.

"This way, old friend." Donal O'Malley jerked his head at him. He was dressed expensively, but almost quietly, in dark green silk, and his few jewels were very fine. His arms-dealing business must be very profitable.

Jean-Marie threaded his way through to the Irish *vampiro*'s side. Together, they slipped along the wall until they found a gap among the spectators. Jean-Marie was still irresistibly drawn to watch the same woman, even though she was doing little more than occasionally curtsying to her partner or the gentleman next to her.

"Who is she?" Jean-Marie asked under his breath.

"The tall lady in blue? *Madame la marquise* d'Agelet. A very wealthy widow, as you can see by all the sharks circling around."

The marquise? "She should have family to guard her," Jean-Marie growled protectively, eyeing one greasy slob who was ogling her far too openly.

"They're back in the Vendée, at her grandfather's sickbed." O'Malley joined Jean-Marie in glaring at the clumsy predator.

The slovenly fool quickly retreated, clearly alarmed.

"Why is she here alone?"

"The late *marquis* was an explosives expert and a friend of Lavoisier. She's here to present his final work to the Gunpowder Administration and the Royal Academy, which aren't invitations easily refused." A soft Gaelic burr colored every word, despite almost two centuries away from western Ireland. "Even so, the stubborn, loyal lady managed to delay her arrival here for over a year, which is why she's not wearing mourning."

The four couples in each set glided forward and sank down courteously, the gentlemen bowing and the ladies curtsying, marking the dance's end.

Jean-Marie's mouth curled in anticipation.

Christ, but he was being foolish beyond belief even to consider feeding this attraction that was burning so fast, so hot, so bright—given all that had happened the last time he'd been tempted by a woman. But why not? After all, what the hell did he have left to lose?

"Will you introduce me?"

O'Malley's dark eyebrows arched. "What of Señorita Perez?"

"She is busy elsewhere." Jean-Marie shrugged, remembering all the other times she'd gone off to find her own amusements—as the Irishman knew very well.

The orchestra crashed into a long chord.

But if I could spend a few minutes with Hélène d'Agelet, I could pretend I was unattached. Maybe dance with her and simply enjoy being alive, as I had when I was young and foolish in this place . . .

"You have my word, my intentions toward *madame la marquise* are entirely honorable," he added harshly, half-wishing he could say he wanted more.

O'Malley searched his face for a long moment but nodded abruptly. "This way."

Hélène nodded politely, glad nobody expected her to have enough wits to think about anything more important than a glass of wine. Otherwise, she might have had to pay attention to the conversation around her, instead of longing for the musicians to finish their break and start playing again. She fanned herself, wishing that the wood and silk concoction was actually a steel-tipped pole long enough to give her a respite from importunate fools. She'd been prepared for fortune hunters, even for throngs of them clamoring for attention from all sides. *Cher* Bernard and she had discussed how to handle them many times, since she was almost certain to outlive him.

But she hadn't anticipated their female relatives and allies, buzzing around her like hornets. Those were by far the worst since no place was safe from them. No form of shopping, of course. But church? And surely a retiring room should be a sanctuary, if nowhere else. But it hadn't proven to be.

Returning home couldn't happen too soon, if she was to see *Grandpère* again while he was still alive. Frivolously, she also had mountains of new clothes for Celeste, her younger sister, to enchant her beloved Raoul with. Plus, there were books for *Maman* and two stallions for Papa, to help rebuild the family horse farm. It had been famous throughout France before *Grandpère* decided that success as a breeder of horses granted him equal brilliance at cards. Only *Grandpère*'s stroke and her own marriage to *cher* Bernard had salvaged their estates, land that had been held by her ancestors for almost four hundred years.

She'd married *cher* Bernard straight from the convent and counted herself lucky. He'd been courteous and considerate, interested in what she thought and felt despite the years between them. Certain that she'd never betray him, he'd even been able to laugh over her occasional flushes of admiration for young men. She had never been unfaithful. She'd never truly been seriously tempted to.

A fortune hunter's female ally was talking now, the nasal rasp of her voice destroying any possible pleasure in her effusive praise for her nephew.

Hélène allowed her gaze to drift toward the door where the musicians had disappeared. Not a crack in a panel, no liveried musicians bearing gilded instruments, nothing.

She considered the men around her, never letting her eyes rest on anyone for very long. A wide variety, certainly, but mostly fops—and every one of them turning alert and eager when her glance passed over them. Dependent on her for a good time. What she wouldn't do for someone who didn't care about her money . . .

Two men approached, tall enough to be glimpsed over the others' heads, even between the ladies' high-piled marvels of the hairdresser's art. Somehow a path opened before them, revealing *cher* Bernard's Irish business associate, Donal O'Malley.

The other man was young, looking little more than her own age, yet he bore himself with the assurance of a much older man. He was very handsome, too, and almost pretty with his light brown hair and brilliant blue eyes, like a free-running river on a hot summer day. He didn't just walk—he prowled, as unselfconsciously graceful and deadly as a lion she'd once seen in a private zoo.

Hélène's fan stilled, matching her startled heartbeat. What woman wouldn't kill to have him worshipping her?

The nasal voice fatuously compared her relative to Zeus—and the five-foot-tall dolt preened.

A wonderfully genuine smile danced through the stranger's eyes. His sensual mouth curved, drawing attention to its potential for sin.

Her eyes caught his, and they shared the joke.

A matching grin surged forward but she bit it back, desperate not to be publicly rude. She whipped her fan into action, pretending to be slightly overcome by heat. Would she have longed to flirt with the stranger so much if Bernard were still alive?

"*Ma chère madame.*" O'Malley bowed and kissed her hand, casually displaying their long acquaintance by addressing her only as a dear lady, not *the* marquise.

She twinkled at him, enjoying their old joke. He'd begun it when he found her enveloped in coif and apron like a maid, while helping her husband experiment with black powder. "What a pleasure to see you again, *Monsieur* O'Malley."

"May I present to you a very old and trusted friend, Jean-Marie St. Just, recently arrived from New York?" He indicated his friend. "You asked earlier about their unusual political structure, and he can answer you."

"*Enchanté, madame la marquise,*" St. Just bowed over her hand with all the grace of a dance master or a master swordsman, his tongue easily uttering the formal greeting.

She sank into a curtsy, deeper than protocol demanded, her brain spinning. He was an American—and so graceful? She'd met Ambassador Jefferson, of course. But somehow she'd thought of him as the exception, with the others as barbarians, incapable of managing court attire's full-skirted coats and dress swords.

The would-be suitors and their allies muttered their disapproval. Skirts rustled, heels tapped—and violin strings sawed.

The musicians had returned for the *contredanses*, the openly seductive half of the evening. Anyone present could simply find themselves a partner, form into a line with other couples, and begin to dance. Each dance's steps were usually very simple and designed to allow a great deal of flirting.

Recognizing their opportunity, the horde of men around her surged forward.

Hélène instinctively flinched, and St. Just's fingers, which had started to release hers, tightened. Perhaps she was crazy, but she thought she heard him growl.

"May I have the honor of a dance, madame?"

"*Certainement*, Monsieur St. Just." She granted him a regal smile.

"I would be delighted to help celebrate your visit from such a distant shore."

St. Just inclined his head and tucked her hand protectively into the crook of his elbow.

She tilted her chin up, trying to look as if her pulse wasn't racing a little too fast, and glanced around. "Please excuse us, ladies, gentlemen."

Edged glares were shot at him, but everyone moved back, giving them room. St. Just calmly guided her into the set, treating everyone other than the musicians as moving—but unimportant—obstacles. O'Malley blew her a kiss from the palm of his hand and quickly gained a lady.

Others found partners and moved into the dance with them, jostling to be close by. Skirts slapped against each other in the hurly-burly, sending ruffles shaking like leaves in a storm. Men clamped down on their swords' hilts, yet the masculine trinkets still slapped their legs and bounced against other people.

She frowned slightly, considering the tumult, and St. Just drew closer. "Is it always like this?"

"The king and queen probably retired some time ago." He glanced down at her, visibly considering how much to say. "That makes this ballroom one of the better opportunities to find company for the rest of the night, if you haven't done so already."

She opened and closed her mouth, shocked by both his frank words and her body's enthusiastic response.

"Please relax, I know you're a virtuous widow." He patted her hand. "I only wish to dance."

The musicians swept into the first chord before she could recover from being openly called a *virtuous* widow. Did she want that appellation? Or would she rather be wicked? She curtsied to him automatically, her mind spinning through possible explanations for his behavior and her own.

The music moved to the next measure, a familiar dance, and a step she mercifully knew exactly how to perform. She took both of his hands and stepped forward. An instant later, she realized her mistake.

Their arms crossed, and her face was only a few inches from his body—his hard, very masculine body.

She gulped.

They stepped away, spinning and uncrossing their arms. Somewhere down the line, a dancer was laughing with the rich, unmistakable certainty of imminent carnal satisfaction.

Hélène's gaze shot up to St. Just.

His mouth wore a bitter curve.

The next time the dance brought her toward him, he made sure she finished at an all-too-respectable distance from him.

But why? Why was he the only man here who didn't hunt her?

Two

CHÂTEAU DE SAINTE-PAZANNE
(a day's ride inland from the west coast of France)
THE VENDÉE, FRANCE, APRIL 1787

Celeste de Sainte-Pazanne shielded her eyes against the harsh sun, looking for the most beloved figure in the world. It was a brilliantly sunny day, and the air shimmered with heat, sending little swirls of dust above the road below.

Forests rippled over the surrounding hills, now quiet and waiting for nightfall. The small river, which gave Sainte-Pazanne its name and prosperity, flowed patiently toward the Atlantic, one of the few local rivers which didn't feed into the Loire. Its mother spring had never run dry, even in a drought as severe as this one. Wheat fields whispered in the light breeze, while cattle slept under ancient oaks.

If she saw him first, they could always take their time returning to the château—and pretend his horse had thrown a shoe or something similarly silly. Papa and *Maman* had always grumbled good naturedly over her thinner excuses, knowing they could trust Raoul's honor, but had never punished her too severely. Surely today they'd be even more lenient, since he would return to the academy tomorrow.

She'd worked so hard on preparing to see him this time, starting with the prettiest dress *chère* Hélène had sent her. But while she'd been having her hair pinned up in the latest fashion, her clumsy, clumsy maid had scorched her dress. She'd had her thoroughly whipped, of course, until all the girl could do was cry about not being able to sit down. Idiot! As if that mattered next to damaging her perfect dress.

Thankfully, *Maman*'s maid had fixed everything with a clever bit of embroidery, so all was well now.

She'd probably have another maid soon, her third this year.

There! His chestnut gelding Samson was just cresting the ridge to enter the small valley.

She waved her hat wildly, its long ribbons whipping like banners.

Raoul stood in his stirrups and swung his own hat like a semaphore. He dropped back into the saddle and kicked Samson into a gallop. They charged toward her down the well-tended road like immortals, or a knight of old come to carry his lady off. Other horses, which had been idly grazing in the green pastures, flung up their heads to watch. Some neighed and came down to the stone walls to race beside him, forming a cavalcade.

She laughed for sheer joy and spun, hugging herself. Dearest, dearest Raoul. Normally such a sober young cadet, but he'd remembered her longing for a romantic display on her nineteenth birthday.

She ran to join him, leaving her mare tethered by the small roadside shrine.

Raoul jumped off Samson a few feet away from her, tossing his reins over the well-trained horse's head to bring him to an immediate stop.

They flung themselves at each other in a pool of blazing sunlight, as if all the saints blessed their love.

"Raoul, *mon amour*!"

She had no words after that, because he was kissing her too fiercely, his arms locked around her, and her feet dangling off the ground. She sank her hands into his hair and set about the delightful task of convincing him his sentiments were returned in full.

Some minutes passed before either of them formed a sentence. Raoul was the first to do so, of course.

"Do your parents know you're here? Anyone could see you. Promise me you'll be more careful in the future."

Dearest Raoul, always so concerned about her reputation.

"I'm sure they do, but I promise to be good next time." She pretended to dust off his hat, while watching him straighten his cravat.

Raoul de Beynac came from a long line of soldiers, famed for honor, courage, intelligence—and lack of money. He was a natural with horses and the sword and a deadly shot from a remarkably young age. His dark eyes were normally calm, but he could trip up a liar within moments—or make her heart sing. Even Papa had admitted Raoul had the quickest brain of any young man in the Vendée and the bravest heart. At barely twenty, he was still filling out his long-limbed frame with muscle.

Someday, she'd be able to see everything that lay underneath his coat. Someday . . .

"*Maman* told me to take flowers to the Blessed Virgin's shrine. She had to know you'd be arriving on the same road from your sister Louise's house."

"*Très bien.*" His crisp voice gave his approval such a martial air, she almost swooned.

Ah well, her parents were glad she had such an honorable lover, even if she wasn't always so certain of the benefits. She was sure if she'd been pregnant, *chère* Hélène would have given her a large enough dowry for them to marry. Instead, they had to wait for him to graduate from the cavalry school at Saumur and take up his commission from the king.

Raoul clapped his hat back on his head, and they strolled together, hand-in-hand, toward the patient Samson.

"How do you think I look?" she asked, a trifle nervously. This was the first time in years he hadn't immediately complimented her on something about her appearance.

There was a pause.

Celeste stared up at him, shocked and hurt. Hélène had sent her new outfit by special courier from Paris, saying it was all the rage. The tightly fitted peach satin jacket flattered her bosom and tiny waist, while the creamy muslin skirts hinted at her long legs. The pure white fichu at her throat would hopefully inspire a man to consider removing it. She'd thought when she'd donned it she looked quite fetching, and hopefully irresistible.

"Celeste, *mon ange*, remember never to fear me! I would give my life not to hurt you."

She did so enjoy hearing him call her an angel.

He caught up her hands and kissed them extravagantly. "You are far too beautiful for me to describe. You are ravishing, incredible, a goddess come to earth, a . . ."

She peeped up at him through her eyelashes, her sore heart eased somewhat. "But?" she prompted.

"You should be wearing honest French silk and thereby supporting our starving weavers in Lyons." He kissed her fingertips, eyeing her a bit sternly. "Instead of flaunting imported Hapsburg muslin from Austria."

Oh, was his problem as simple as that?

"Dearest Raoul, you are always considering other people's welfare. Just as you stand up for peasants against noblemen's mischief or the clergy's abuses. Or argue the merits of the Americans' republic, because it allows ordinary citizens to protect themselves."

He spread his hands, clearly recognizing the litany of arguments he'd had with her father. He'd never backed down, although he'd always been very respectful to a retired soldier.

"You will be a splendid officer, always looking out for your men—and your wife." She kissed him on the cheek.

"Are you certain you wish to marry me?" A greater seriousness sharpened his voice and deepened his eyes.

A breeze whispered down the road, making the dust dance around her ankles like demons. Samson tossed up his head, snorting nervously.

Celeste stiffened her spine, determined to fight as well as any man for the only joy she'd ever truly dreamed of. "Have you changed your mind?"

"Never that, Celeste, never. Count me faithful beyond death as

I have sworn before, as I will swear again." Fierce devotion blazed from his countenance. "But you are young and have never left Sainte-Pazanne. You could meet another . . ."

"Not like you!" Truth rang through the valley.

His lips curved warmly, as though he wished to kiss her. She leaned forward hopefully, but he continued speaking relentlessly.

"Or I could be killed. I am a soldier, Celeste. I could lie in my grave long years before you come to meet me."

Leaves rustled somewhere deep in the forest, like a foretaste of a hollow future.

"That doesn't matter. That has never mattered." She gripped him by the arms, as desperately as she'd follow him across France and Europe given the chance. Her throat was very tight, and she fought to utter the words that would make him understand.

"Celeste, my heart . . ." Their gazes locked, his as passionate as hers. His strong hands wrapped around her wrists, tying them together.

"I have loved you for as long as I can remember, and I will love you until the day I die," she choked out.

"If I go first, Celeste, above all else I want you to be happy."

She shook her head fiercely, the tears on her eyelashes haloing him in light until he seemed an angel come to earth.

"You are everything that makes my life worth living, Raoul. If I ever offer myself to another, may the good Lord strike me dead!"

"My love!" Raoul fiercely snatched her to him, and their lips met, sealing the eternal pledge.

PROVENCE, JULY 1787

"This way, I believe," St. Just's fine tenor announced their next turn.

Hélène obediently nodded, more conscious of his leg brushing hers through her silk skirts than any logic involved in deciphering the labyrinth. Truth be told, she cared very little whether or not they found the center or not, so long as she was with him.

Hundreds of miles away, Paris was stiflingly hot, broiling in an inferno of dust, disease, and starvation. There had been no rain since February, only the brutal sun hammering everyone and everything. Little food could be grown, and only the wealthiest could buy what tidbits could be found. The desperate poor took to the streets in riots to demand salvation from their monarch, while the rich and powerful argued over who wouldn't have to pay to save France. At night, it seemed the city's stones radiated heat back to the uncaring stars, together with the dying screams of those unwary enough to risk their lives by going out.

But here, all was quiet, filled with hot sunlight, lavender, and anticipation. After five months amid stone walls and angry crowds where St. Just was the only one who spoke sense to her, she'd followed him here to compel action between them.

After months of seeing each other almost every day, of dancing and riding together, of shared books and idle chatter, of laughing together and sometimes finishing each other's sentences.

Of sitting side by side at long musicales or salons, of their fingers entwined between them, hidden by her skirts, before they'd clapped for the performer.

Of tendrils of heat flushing over her skin when he read poetry in a salon, his voice deepening and slowing over phrases of a man yearning for the woman he could not have.

Of his eyes searching for her the minute he entered a room and joy leaping into his gaze before he quickly reined it in.

Of their hands and arms brushing each other in a dance, the fine silks and muslin whispering past when they moved slower and closer than a dance master would recommend.

But never touching each other above the elbow.

She needed to resolve looks, and voices that fell away during phrases into something, something that matched the leap of her heart whenever he watched her, or she dreamed of him at night.

She'd accepted an invitation to this château for a week, well aware that neither her parents nor her confessor would approve of the deeds done there. A discreet purchase of a filthy painting from her host's collection had gotten her into an isolated suite, with a very private entrance. She could spend as much time as she chose with any man present, and no other guest need know.

Rodrigo Perez, Mademoiselle Perez, and St. Just had arrived the day after she did. Mademoiselle Perez had already established her claim on several of the party's members, which suited Hélène very well. Surely they'd keep her far away from St. Just.

The labyrinth Hélène strolled through with him was made of boxwood, clipped taller than even *Monsieur* Perez. The scent of lavender, hot and rich as her unfulfilled hunger for the man beside her, rolled into her nostrils from the hillsides above. The most beautiful man in the world, in mind and body—she wished she understood why he wouldn't make advances to her, even though she'd felt his hand linger on hers a little too long during a dance, been scorched by his gaze when he saw her in a new dress . . .

She'd even considered him as a husband.

It didn't matter now whether he had any money or not, since she had more than enough for two. Bernard's family had always been comfortably established, but he'd made a fortune with his explosives inventions after he retired from the artillery. He'd left his nephew a substantial sum to protect the marquisate, and he'd also been extremely generous to her. She could marry anyone she wanted to, especially since her birth—to be brutally honest, as well as snobbish—was haughty enough to allow her a great deal of eccentricity anyway.

Including bestowing her favors on a man whose social position was undefined. He carried himself like a prince, yet he was clearly the junior member of a very secretive household.

She truly didn't understand why he traveled with *Monsieur* Perez and Mademoiselle Perez. *Monsieur* Perez was a tall, strong man, carrying such a formidable aura that she'd seen members of the king's Swiss Guard snap to attention upon his approach. Yet he looked only a few years older than St. Just and might be considered handsome, if one appreciated Roman features marked by a wicked scar across the forehead. Certainly his dark eyes were very fine and had set more than one lady—and gentleman!—sighing after him at this corrupt court. He'd bestowed notable attentions on none of them.

Mademoiselle Perez, on the other hand, was a middle-aged female of considerable beauty, when she was in good spirits. Upon her arrival in France, she had quickly joined a private club notorious for its unbounded lechery—although they did not prey upon anyone outside the group, nor indulge in any sins other than lust. All of which made it one of the more disciplined clubs here at court.

"Are you certain you've never been trained in rhetoric?" St. Just asked, his thumb rubbing sensually over her hand in a manner totally in contrast to his words. "The way you had the Royal Academy scientists in the palm of your hand, they'd have voted you a member."

Hélène blushed and laughed. "Truly, you are too kind. I simply read what *Monsieur le marquis* had written."

"You answered the questions, did you not?" His eyes lingered on her mouth.

"True, but . . ." Somehow she couldn't readily assemble her words into sentences. Perhaps if they stepped into one of the small alcoves in the labyrinth or found the center quickly. If they reached it before the other couples, surely they could steal a kiss or two.

He yanked himself away, seeming to breathe a little faster.

She frowned slightly. Surely she was starting to have an effect. All she had to do was continue to stay close . . .

"Very detailed questions they were, too." His voice seemed slightly breathless. "The one comparing the results of electrical ignition to lighting it with a standard slow match." He shook his head. "None of that was in your husband's paper."

"That was my specialty." Despite her immediate goals, she beamed at the intellectual interest in his eyes. "*Monsieur le marquis* thought fire was old-fashioned so he wasn't interested in it, unlike electricity. I did all of the experimentation with slow matches."

"As well as laying powder trails . . ." Jean-Marie mused. He turned her hand over. "My deepest congratulations, madame. You are a very brave woman."

His thumb rubbed the inside of her wrist for a moment before he kissed it. The warmth of his lips, the slight brush with his strong teeth, all combined to send an electric shock jolting through her.

Their gazes met. She was wide-eyed, breathing too fast—and he looked as unsettled.

He all but dropped her hand before returning it to the previous very proper position on his arm. She flexed her fingers slightly, testing the strength of his muscles—and her own self-discipline.

A moment passed before they began walking again. They rounded one more corner—and stopped in their tracks.

Hélène took a second, long incredulous look at the labyrinth's center. An octagon, it held the requisite marble statue, in this case, an obelisk rising from a smoothly carved rose granite block of shoulder height to most men. An equally traditional marble bench stood in the center. The occupants of the bench were, however, extremely untraditional.

The *vicomte* de Saint-Gabriel—whom she'd always considered a foolish young cavalryman—was seated on the bench facing them, his head thrown back, his breeches around his ankles, and an expression of the utmost rapture upon his face. His coat was scattered across the grass, his shirt spread across his chest, and one arm free.

Mademoiselle Perez sat beside and behind him, skillfully milking his cock like a dairymaid, and—drinking?—from his neck where he arched it over her arm, her cheeks hollowing and her throat muscles moving in unison with her hand. Echoed by his shuddering groans of delight.

A pencil-thin line of crimson slowly trickled over his collarbone and down his chest to his nipple.

Hélène could not believe her eyes. And yet she could not deny them.

A vampire? Impossible.

Hélène shrieked her denial, as scientific reasoning utterly failed her.

St. Just clamped his hand over her mouth and stepped behind her, pulling her against him to control her with his body.

Mademoiselle Perez promptly stopped and lifted her head, triumph flitting across her face. "Oh dear, what a surprise," she said mendaciously.

"Shut up and help me clean up this mess," St. Just hissed. "If Don Rodrigo finds her here . . ."

"Why should I protect *her*?" Mademoiselle Perez spat, neatly expressing her low opinion of Hélène.

Voices were raised in the distance, muffled by the tall hedges.

Saint-Gabriel moaned and nuzzled Mademoiselle Perez, clearly seeking more of what had been denied him. Blood dripped slowly from his throat.

Hélène struggled desperately against St. Just. *Mon Dieu*, what was happening here? If she ran or screamed or fainted or . . .

Monsieur Perez ran into the enclosed space, hand clapped to his sword, and cast an all-encompassing look around. Hélène shivered when his icy gaze rested on her.

"Don Rodrigo," Mademoiselle Perez whined.

"Is Saint-Gabriel your creature?"

"Of course, but—"

"*Silencio*, Sara. Say nothing more until we are alone." Hélène did not blame her for flinching at his tone.

"Saint-Gabriel." The young soldier leaped to his feet, in response to an officer's sharp summons, his lust-dulled eyes clearing a bit. "The only thing saving your life is your blood bond with Mademoiselle Perez. Pull up your breeches and leave, taking your clothes with you. Do not be seen or suspected by anyone until you are completely recovered. You will never discuss any aspect of this incident with anyone. Understand?"

"*Oui, monsieur.*" Saint-Gabriel bowed, managing to look obedient and aristocratic despite his disheveled condition. He disappeared an instant later between two files of boxwood, clutching his clothes.

St. Just's hand still had not relaxed over Hélène's mouth. Breathing was difficult, but not as much of an effort as believing any of these events.

Monsieur Perez looked back at Mademoiselle Perez, his features harsher than if they'd been carved in stone.

"If you had not guaranteed he would not be harmed by giving you his blood regularly, Sara, that boy would be dead now. You should not have used him as bait for this trap."

"Wh-what trap?" She came to her feet, straightening her clothes like a bourgeois matron. "I was only sitting here, feeding on a strong young man, as is my right since Jean-Marie denies me."

St. Just growled, deep and low. His body seemed to vibrate with rage.

"Why here? Why not in your room, where you are guaranteed privacy?" *Monsieur* Perez stalked the woman. She took a step back and another and another until the obelisk blocked her.

"No, you had to have him here, didn't you?" St. Just accused her. "Knowing I'd be the first to find the labyrinth's center, since I can't resist a puzzle even when I have a beautiful woman on my arm. A lovely lady whom you hate and fear."

"What of it?" Her face twisted between fear and rage, and she glanced rapidly from one man to the other. "What of it? She is young, and you cannot stop looking at her, no matter how much blood I drink to become more vibrant. Why wouldn't I want to make her stumble and fall?"

"I will kill you for this," St. Just snarled and moved toward her, his hand falling away from Hélène's mouth.

"You're a vampire," Hélène whispered. "A bloodsucking vampire."

"Damn you! Damn you, Sara!" Jean-Marie cursed. "Now you've signed her death warrant, since she's admitted *vampiros* exist."

"*Madre de Dios*, Sara, are you so jealous that you must destroy an innocent?" *Monsieur* Perez's voice was etched in grief. "Do you not remember the agony of losing your own innocence?"

"I saved your life many times when we were prisoners in The Syrian's dungeon. How can I forget those days—unless you do?"

Monsieur Perez flung up a hand in acknowledgment, his eyes suddenly decades older.

Hélène squirmed, trying to duck out of St. Just's hold and run for the château, while the others were arguing. His arms tightened ruthlessly hard around her until she gasped.

Don Rodrigo turned to face her and St. Just, his expression sober as an executioner's.

"There is no need to invoke *vampiro* custom against her," St. Just said, his voice's calm agonizingly different from how his fingers gripped her wrists.

Vampiro customs? But if they would help her in this hour of need, Hélène prayed for his success.

"How else can we protect Sara, as you've sworn to do?" *Monsieur* Perez countered, his dark eyes now once again coldly considering Hélène. "She knows Sara is a *vampiro* and will probably tell others, making her a threat to all of us should she send a mob into a panic."

How could he speak so calmly about killing her? Why wasn't anyone else coming to help? Admittedly, this was the most difficult labyrinth in Provence, but even so!

"You are reading too much into this," St. Just argued. "*La marquise* is a logical woman. Even so, it's unlikely her few words could cause a mob to form in the streets."

"Everywhere you look, France is sliding into chaos, *mi hermano*." Don Rodrigo spread his hands in disgust. "Our safety, especially Sara's, argues *la marquise* d'Agelet can never be allowed to talk. Even if it means killing her."

Hélène's knees melted. She managed to hold herself erect and somehow keep breathing.

"No," St. Just said flatly. "If you want to kill her, you'll have to come through me."

"Jean-Marie!" Mademoiselle Perez gasped, her hand flying to her throat.

But did St. Just speak from love or honor? Hélène was very much afraid only honor inspired his words. But no matter what his motivations were, he was her sole protector.

"You have seen *vampiros* die because *prosaicos* learned of them. You have seen Señorita Perez cowering and half-dead from fear, while hiding from riots. You swore to protect her, *mi hermano*. Will you risk her life because of a woman's loose tongue?" *Monsieur* Perez's rich voice offered the question like a duellist's sword, gleaming with sharp edges.

God help her, St. Just hesitated.

Hélène shuddered and prayed she'd live another five minutes. She entered the fray on her own behalf, even though she didn't know all the stakes or the weapons.

"I would never say a word," she insisted, staring at the man whose harsh features had shifted not at all while he discussed her death.

"Never is a very long time, madame," *Monsieur* Perez pointed out, as calmly as though they discussed Voltaire. "Even if it meant saving your mother's life? Or your sister's? What then?"

She closed the mouth she'd opened to hotly deny his reasoning. He was entirely correct: She'd sell anyone and everyone here to rescue her little sister or her mother.

His lips curved into a bitter, mirthless smile. He bowed slightly, the winning fencer accepting the loser's capitulation.

"You can't negotiate with her about it!" Mademoiselle Perez interjected. "She is only a *prosaica* and has no rights in this."

"Sara, be still!" *Monsieur* Perez shot back. "You trapped her into this, thereby losing any say in the matter. I can choose to mete out any justice I please, as a *vampiro mayor*."

Hélène blinked, not understanding the logic. She didn't question it, either, since she didn't trust Mademoiselle Perez's intentions for her future.

"You could wipe her memories of this place," St. Just suggested.

Erase her memories? What kind of demon could do that?

"I can read your thoughts very easily. Shall I prove it?" *Monsieur* Perez's bittersweet gaze dwelt on hers, ancient and unfathomable.

She shrugged as haughtily as possible, unwilling to admit anything even without words.

"What shall I say that is not too embarrassing for you, in front of these others?" he mused, holding her eyes with his.

She frowned but refused to draw back.

"You've been slightly concerned about whether your heel might catch on the worn edge of the carpet in your boudoir."

She stared at him incredulously. He couldn't possibly have seen the small tear. Could he really see inside her head? And if so, how horrible! Would she ever have any privacy again?

"Do you wish me to detail where it is located?"

"No, certainly not. That won't be necessary," she stammered quickly.

He bowed without a trace of mockery, enraging her. "The king will catch and punish you if you harm me," she snapped, blustering to cover her distrust.

"Indeed, madame?" Don Rodrigo raised an eyebrow. "Please be so good as to explain to me how you will accomplish this miraculous intervention—when none of your fellow guests have yet sounded the alarm or come to investigate your shrieks."

She stomped her foot in pure frustration. St. Just touched her hand lightly, a subtle gesture of warning.

She pursed her lips, tapped her toe, and contented herself by visibly fuming.

"I will not permit you to kill her," St. Just reiterated, squaring his shoulders.

Don Rodrigo arched an eyebrow, clearly surprised. "You cannot stop me."

"You do not wish to murder a defenseless woman."

For the first time, she saw the big man flinch, but he rallied quickly. "I will, if I deem it necessary to protect Sara. I have done far worse than that."

"I won't tell anyone," Hélène repeated desperately, clutching St. Just's arm. "I swear by Our Lady."

The hooded dark gaze shifted to her.

She held her breath, terrified that she was closer to death now than when she'd lit gunpowder hour after hour.

"Enforce her vow," St. Just suggested abruptly. "You have the strength and the skill to do so. Set a compulsion in her head that she can never speak of tonight—except to the three of us here. We'll be able to learn if anyone's been pressing her to learn about it."

A compulsion? Have *Monsieur* Perez walk through her head, with Mademoiselle Perez to enforce it? But if it kept her alive, could she argue?

"I won't tell anyone, ever—but I'd permit you to lock my tongue on the subject." She managed a polite smile, wishing she could fry him like a capon.

Monsieur Perez studied her, his expression as detached as any butcher. He finally nodded.

"Very well. Be aware, madame, that the ban applies to all forms of communication and is enforced by your own body. If you believe you have broken it, then you will die without any of us having to find you or kill you."

"What if another *vampiro* speaks to her? She might need to be able to argue freely against him." Jean-Marie was poised lightly on his feet, as warily as if he fenced with a great master. "Even her *prosaica* sense of smell would instinctively recognize a *vampiro* now."

How many more *vampiros* were there? Hordes—or just a few, each more deadly than the last? *Nom de dieu*, which alternative was worse?

"Very well—but only if that *vampiro* first speaks of *vampiros* to her." Monsieur Perez glanced at his sister. "Are you ready to leave, Sara?"

"She'd look better in her grave—"

"Sara . . ." warned *Monsieur* Perez.

She rolled her eyes. "Yes, of course, I'm ready—but you'll both regret this day's work."

"Is that it?" Hélène choked. "Don't you have to do something more . . ." She waved her hands, at a loss for words. Tears welled up in her eyes again, surely due only to exhaustion.

"Visible? Emphatic?" He lifted an arrogant eyebrow. "No. As your escort said, I have the skill to do whatever I wish inside your skull. You've already been limited, madame, and may only discuss tonight with the three of us."

Hélène turned and buried her face in St. Just's chest, shuddering, her knees buckling under her. More than anything else in the world, she never wanted to think about this afternoon's events again.

He choked, wrapped his arm around her waist, and half-carried, half-walked her out of the labyrinth.

THREE

By following the hedges of the labyrinth, the herb garden, and finally the rose garden, they managed to reach the château unseen by any guests. The only servants they saw immediately behaved as if a fainting woman upheld by a man was so normal as to cause no notice, thus bearing out the demesne's licentious reputation.

He stopped at the guest wing and shifted his grip, preparing to free her. God knows holding her like this was dangerous to his heart, as well as damned improper.

Her grip instantly tightened on him ferociously. "*Non!* Do not release me! You are my only defender!"

His chest swelled with pride and something more personal, something he dared not look at too closely. He was sworn to protect Sara, and he could not live without her. While he hadn't warmed Sara's bed once he'd learned how cruelly she'd tricked him, he also hadn't been a monk. But he'd never dared let himself dream of the softer emotions with a woman, of doting fondness, soft glances, and passion that could last beyond the loved one's presence. Doing so would doom him—and possibly the lady—to hell on earth.

He glanced down at her. The tears on her face and her quivering lip sent a pang shooting through his heart. Poor darling, she was trying so hard to be brave. She'd had far too much to endure tonight—a *vampiro mayor* ready to kill her?

Jean-Marie shook his head, wondering if he'd ever completely understand his friend. Rodrigo's first instincts were always to protect women, but equally ferocious was the need to defend those under his care.

"Would you like me to carry you to your room?"

She nodded quickly, her green eyes enormous, and laid her head back against his shoulder. Trustingly, dammit.

"Left," she murmured at the top of the broad marble staircase, her flowered silk skirts floating over his arms.

He would be a gentleman and not think about her exquisitely embroidered white petticoat framed so enchantingly—and fashionably—in front. Most importantly, he would not look down to see if her fragile white fichu, transparent enough to display her dress's bright flowers, also permitted a glimpse of her bosom.

He spun on his heel, cursing himself as ten times an idiot. He was committed elsewhere, mind and body. Hélène d'Agelet deserved far better than a man like him.

Her delicate fingers brushed the nape of his neck, under his hair, and her breath brushed his cheek.

His heart slammed against his ribs, sending shards of something stronger and sweeter than lust lancing through his flesh. Its force made his lungs seize, and he broke stride. "Madame . . ." he muttered, scarcely able to think.

"Turn left again. My room is at the end of the hall."

Merde, she was caressing his neck, even though her ribs were still shaking from withheld sobs. His chest was tight, his blood running hotter and faster.

"Madame." He tried to restore some decorum to their situation.

"Call me Hélène, *s'il vous plaît*," she murmured. "Surely we can move beyond formality to friendship, after surviving this afternoon's disturbances together."

Her great eyes lifted to his, full of sincerity and—need. Possibly hunger, or even lust, two emotions he knew very well. He could not allow himself to believe it was anything more, even though they'd known each other for almost five months.

Even so, words leapt out of his throat to answer her, without consulting his brain. "If you will call me Jean-Marie."

"My pleasure, Jean-Marie." She lingered over his simple name, like a delectable bonbon. A brilliant smile lit her face.

He shouldered open the door to her room, cursing his cock for swelling in response. He needed to leave before he leapt on her like a wild animal.

Sunlight flowed over everything within, bringing it to life.

Hélène's boudoir was a miracle of feminine simplicity, like the marquise herself. Bas-reliefs of goddesses and flowers swept around the walls. Great alcoves, where rich green silk flowed from gilded rods, marked the multiple windows of the corner room. A great cabinet, taller than a man, carved and painted to match the bas-reliefs, stood ready in one corner to yield her beautiful wardrobe. A small, elegant desk, its tambour lid neatly shut to preserve her privacy, and a matching bench, waited to serve her, as did a pair of fragile chairs. Beautifully inlaid parquet floors and scattered soft rugs were silent testimony to feminine delight in elegance.

But Jean-Marie paid little attention to any of that fashionable nonsense. The bed drew his entire attention, nestled as it was in an alcove with silk draperies sweeping from the ceiling to veil it. The embroidered dark green coverlet had been turned back to invitingly offer pristine white pillows and sheets.

Ah, to see Hélène stretched out across the silk, her hair as golden as the willingness in her eyes . . .

His mouth dried, and a heavy pulse began to beat slowly, demandingly through his veins.

"Hélène," he rumbled, his voice as deep and harsh as his emotions, the need to use the bed, remove her clothes, find pleasure for them both . . .

A single finger tapped his cheek, then a second.

He glanced down.

Naked desperation and yearning gleamed in her eyes.

"Do not let me think too much, *je vous en prie*."

Everything masculine within him roared its demand to protect her. Nothing and no one should be allowed to make a proud lady like Hélène d'Agelet beg.

"Hélène—" he began.

She caught his face in her hands, pulled it down, and kissed him full on the mouth. It was the move of an experienced woman who knew what she wanted and how to take it.

He met her more than halfway, pouring his own hunger into the kiss—a night's pleasure with a beautiful, willing woman. But surely not for someone who cared more about him, than what they needed.

She moaned softly, sweetly, into his mouth, her fingers caressing his head. She turned in his arms to face him, pressing herself against him. The busk, that damned stiff strip of ivory running up the center of her stays to support her breasts, tugged at one of his coat's buttons. It forcibly reminded that the delights of undressing were yet to come and should be undertaken soon, lest he start tearing impatiently at the fabric like a beast.

He set her on the bed, following her to kiss her again—to adore her face, her throat, her fingers with his mouth. To whisper sweet words of her beauty and grace and charm. But not love words, like *mon coeur* or *mon ange*, my heart or my angel. Not those, never those, not in this lifetime.

She purred under him, threading her fingers through his hair and teasing the long strands free. Her legs rippled against him between the layers of cloth, whispering of her eagerness.

Jean-Marie leaned up on one elbow, dropping kisses on her forehead, her eyelids, the top of her head. She chuckled and closed her eyes, exactly the response he'd wanted.

He slipped his free hand inside her fichu, resting it across her breast. Ah, *mon Dieu*, her skin was soft as the finest silk.

She moaned and twisted closer.

His thumb brushed her nipple, modestly hiding just below the top of her rigidly boned stays.

"Ah, mais oui!" She arched up to meet him, tossing her head back. "Ah, Jean-Marie!"

Hot fumes of lust, rich and spicy, rose into his brain.

He rumbled approval of her hunger and kissed her again, fondling her, rubbing her nipple again and again until it stood tall and stiff and aching, continually teased by either him or her stays through the silk. He shifted and adored her other breast the same way, rousing her until she was a writhing, sobbing woman under him.

But it wasn't enough. Oh no, even though he, too, was breathing hard and fast, his skin flushed as if they stood in the Sahara desert.

He lifted her waist up and untied her fichu in the back, drawing the long, pretty streamers forward. It was the work of a moment to tug it free from her neck and toss it aside. Its mate, which had been tucked into her bodice, was already so disarrayed and dislodged that it gaped prettily for him, offering a superb frame for her delights.

While most men certainly enjoyed breasts, they were not the inspiration for poets or the subject of much conversation. But he'd swear Hélène was lovely enough to make even the most blind beg for a chance to worship her. Hélène, who was even more beautiful than a goddess of old.

"Jean-Marie . . ." Her hands moved convulsively and fell back.

"You're so lovely, you take my breath away."

"Ah, *mon bébé*," she crooned approvingly—and he caught the last syllable with his mouth. Her affection was delightful beyond belief, especially a silly endearment like "baby" since it didn't threaten his commitments elsewhere.

Mapping the perfection of her breasts' blue veins led inexorably to the concealed seam down the front of her dress. He muttered his acclaim for her fashion sense and unhooked her dress.

"Stand up, please."

"If you will take off your coat?" She kneaded his shoulders gently, emphasizing the layers of fabric. "And maybe more?"

"Of course, Hélène." He kissed her fingertips and nodded.

He drew her dress off and set it aside. He turned back and stopped dead, savage lust racking his bones.

Her blonde curls were tumbling from her once precise coiffure, yet she still wore a *marquise*'s eye-catching earrings, the three pearls stroking her neck like a lover. Her gold silk corset was another jewel enhancing her skin's creamy beauty, while her embroidered white petticoat floated over her legs and ankles from her hoops. Beautifully embroidered silk stockings led to a pair of delicate shoes offering her feet for worship.

Her green eyes were dark with lust under heavy lids, her mouth swollen and hungry. His *concubino compañero* sense of smell told him clearly she was melting with lust, her sweet petals unfolding and cream flowing in welcome.

His lover, dammit, hot and willing. His for tonight, if no longer than that.

She took a step toward him and another—and snatched his lapels. Their lips met, passion running between them like the finest cognac. His cock was hard-pressed against his breeches, wildness thrumming in it.

He could toss her across the bed, flip her skirts out of the way, and be in her within moments.

No. He'd promised her something. But what was worth delaying their mutual delight?

"Jean-Marie, *mon bébé*." She sighed into his mouth, their tongues dancing together more enticingly than any *contredanse*. She kneaded his shoulders, her nails pricking him through the silk.

Clothes. His clothes, to be precise.

"*Chérie*," he muttered against her cheek. *Merde*, but he sounded hoarse and out of control. He tried again. "*Chère* Hélène, I too need to disrobe—as you asked."

She blinked up at him and ran her tongue over her lips.

Passion ripped through him, firing white-hot darts from his lungs through his heart and cock. He jerked himself up short before he could slam her up against a wall.

"Stand back, *chérie*, please." *Before I act like a rutting boar . . .*

She did so, her bosom heaving above her stays. Her hand crept up to her mouth when he yanked off his coat. Her eyes grew enormous when he started to tear off his waistcoat. She murmured something about his poor buttons but his glare silenced her.

He tugged hard on his cravat. She squeaked, he lifted an eyebrow, and she nipped her finger. A total disregard for his valet's sensibilities brought the rest of it quickly off his neck.

She was flushed, restless, her legs twisting against each other. She glanced down, back up to the bulge of his cock against his breeches, and down again. Shy and hungry? Lord help them both, feasting on each other visually had fired them both up for the banquet that was to come.

He unbuttoned his shirt as fast as possible and pulled it over his head.

Her gasp echoed across the room.

"Ah, *oui*," she sighed, her eyes roaming over him. "You are very finely made."

He could not stop himself from strutting but he did keep it to only a step or two.

"*Ma chère* Hélène." He kissed her shoulder, licking and nibbling her collarbone until she moaned his name and her head fell sideways, allowing him free access. "You are a bonbon *extraordinaire*, made to tempt a man into madness."

"Hmm." A single emerald eye considered him before her golden lashes veiled it again.

He kissed the nape of her neck.

He untied her petticoat, pushed it off her hoops, and let it fall to the floor, never pausing in his attentions to her throat and shoulders.

She moaned something about the mountaintop being higher when it took longer to reach. He smiled privately, his body throbbing with both agreement and impatience, and moved to explore the best way to tease her delectable spine, to delight her back, to lift her breasts from their cocoon in her stays and plump them in his hands.

All of which demanded that he unlace her stays, of course. Which gave his hands access to her waist and ribs, from underneath her hoops. More pleasure for her hidden areas, those restricted places that had been shut away from the world since early childhood, yet were so close to her center.

She writhed restlessly, her hips twisting and turning. Her head lay against his shoulder, her soft hair teasing his skin, while her expression tore his heart with her need for release. Her soft pleas rippled through the room, each one diving into his blood and flashing straight into his balls, heating his seed.

He untied her stays' shoulder straps and lifted it over her head. *Nom de Dieu*, her silk chemise was almost transparent. He gulped, every drop of blood heading south.

Even so, he was slightly incredulous when his hands shook while they untied her hoops. How many times had he done this before? And yet . . . She moaned again, and he had to bite his lip until blood flowed before he could continue.

She began to jerk her chemise over her head.

Fire jolted through, demanding fulfillment, from his spine, through his balls, to his cock. By the time her chemise joined her hoops and petticoats on the floor, his breeches were in the same untidy heap as his coat and waistcoat.

He lifted her onto the bed, pausing only to kick off his shoes and drop hers onto the floor.

He cast a single possessive glance at *his* lover—her green eyes dark with passion, her golden curls tumbling across the white sheets, her swollen mouth, supple tongue. Her taut breasts lifting toward him, her narrow waist begging for admiration. Her curving hips and sweet rump, which he hadn't *yet* explored the wonders of. Her long legs gleaming in their silken stockings, leading to her beautiful golden delta, her plump feminine folds, creamy now with lust and welcome for him.

His dream.

"Jean-Marie, *mon bébé*." She lifted her arms toward him.

His wits dropped into his cock, and he joined her, logic gone.

Her hand closed around him, pumping his cock gently.

He threw his head back, groaning like ten kinds of fool. He knelt between her legs and gathered her up to him, slipping his arms under her shoulders.

She delicately stroked his balls, and he all but howled.

He found her entrance easily, gliding in on the warmest of welcomes. She was scalding hot, glove tight, and oh so very, very wet. Perfection.

He forgot to breathe.

She tightened herself around him, pulling him in, and locked her arms around his hips. "Ah, yes . . ."

Heaven, heaven on earth.

He thrust again, in . . . and out. In . . . and out. Faster and faster. Every stroke matched by her, her body arching to meet his, her core reaching out to hold him longer. Eager, desperate, as he was.

Red touched his vision. He could see little, feel little except her and the blood pounding through him, the seed rising from his balls into his cock to fill her, the hard drumbeat of desire in his muscles and bones. Nothing except this mattered.

She shifted under him—and his cock slipped deeper inside her. She jerked, and her nails scored his back, drawing blood for the first time. The salty, sweet smell filled the air—and he raced helplessly into orgasm.

She screamed and bit down on his neck. Climax rocked unmistakably through her and her channel rippled around him.

He jetted again and again, locked in an orgasmic dance with her. Every spasm, every pleasure that ran through one was given back to the other, spinning him through a galaxy of stars.

She gasped, one last pulse running through her, and collapsed back onto the bed.

The last stars burst behind Jean-Marie's eyes, and his eyelids closed tight, bringing welcome sleep.

At least Hélène wouldn't think of the night's events for a time.

Hélène pointed her toes under the sheet and wiggled them. An hour or two, perhaps three, past dawn, and surely it was time to start a new life.

It was amazing how being sore and tender in so many places, both inside and out, could make one feel so marvelous. *Cher—cher?* What a joy to be able to say that again!—Jean-Marie had kept her so delightfully busy last night, she'd scarce had time to sleep. But it was no hardship, not when he'd shown her time and again by his tenderness how much he cared for her.

Surely she must mean something to him, else he wouldn't have stood up for her against *Monsieur* Perez.

She sniffed. The arrogant, high-handed brute—to think he could dictate exactly how those around him should live. She'd file a complaint against him this morning and see him thrown out of France immediately.

The door into the small dressing room opened silently, revealing Jean-Marie, immaculate except for his coat and waistcoat, which he carried over his arm. He bowed politely to her. "*Bonjour*, madame."

Hélène jolted upright in the bed, clutching the sheet to her. A formal greeting after last night's passion? She tried to return to the intimacy they'd agreed upon after those—*vampiros* had appeared. "*Salut*, Jean-Marie."

"I do not believe it wise for you to address me in that fashion, madame." His expression was forbidding above his fingers, fastening his waistcoat as if they closed off both his body and any relationship from her. "Pray do not do so again."

"But—but we agreed!" She rose from the bed, wrapping the sheet around her.

"That was yesterday." An ice flow would have been warmer than his voice. "I am departing now, and nothing like last night will ever happen again."

Perhaps she'd been naive to place so much faith in the first man she'd given her body to, other than the marriage arranged upon her exit from a convent. But she'd lived in the world for ten years, run a marquis's estate, kept accounts, judged men's verity. She was no child to be fooled by a pretty face. She could not believe she'd been entirely wrong in everything she'd read in Jean-Marie's attendance upon her these past five months—and the sweetness of his attentions last night. Surely there was something more, something worth fighting for.

"Will you come back with me to the Vendée?" She pushed her hair back from her face so she could see him better. She ground her pride ruthlessly into the dust for the one man who'd interested her since *cher* Bernard's death. "Leave the court's corruption behind and the *vampiros*, for the countryside's purity? I have a manor at Sainte Marie des Fleurs near the coast, which is very beautiful. Or we could build something larger, if you'd prefer . . ."

"What?" He paused, staring at her. He shook his head violently and resumed shrugging himself into his coat. "You must be insane."

"Why not, Jean-Marie?" She pressed herself against him, letting the sheet droop to offer what had so excited him last night. His eyes traveled downward before jerking back up to her face, glittering like steel. His expression closed into an icy mask.

Merde.

She gambled on another asset, one every other man had found irresistible.

"Do you have a personal fortune greater than mine? I also have monies flowing in from the marquis's inventions. We could live very, very well anywhere you like."

"No." The refusal was as emphatic as a mine's detonation. He pushed her away from him by the shoulders before stepping back.

For an instant, she thought she saw grief and a ravaging loneliness pass through his eyes. But his words erased the impression.

"There can be nothing more between us, ever, madame. If you wish a husband—or a lover—look elsewhere."

Jealousy gripped her. Lover? Did he have someone else? Ah yes, of course!

"You're returning to that Spanish woman! All I've been to you was a momentary diversion, a way to make her jealous while she played so freely with other men at court."

Almost gibbering with rage, she swung for him. But his hand shot up and caught hers, just before it reached his cheek. "Do not try that again."

She glared at him, chin high. "Brute! You deserve the hatred of every woman for treating me so."

He inclined his head, his expression completely unreadable.

She sniffed and yanked at her hand, praying her sheet would maintain her decency with its one-handed fastening. It was bad enough to know one had been used to make a Spanish woman jealous. But for a Frenchwoman to appear maladroit would be truly appalling.

He finally released her, white marks on her wrist from his fingers' grasp. She refused to rub them, knowing she'd be bruised for days to come. Terrified she'd nurse the marks and long for their maker.

His eyes lingered on them for a moment, a bitter curve to his mouth. He bowed again and turned to leave, his shoes striking with a cold finality on the wood parquet.

"I will tell the king about your *vampiro* friends!" Hélène flung after him.

He glanced over his shoulder, one hand on the doorknob.

"I pray that you will have a surgeon close at hand if so, madame." His face was utterly, chillingly serious. "Death will come all too quickly in that event."

The door closed softly and finally behind him.

Hélène collapsed onto the bed in tears, where her maid found her a few minutes later.

"Madame? Madame, what is wrong?"

Hélène drew herself up, determined to set one thing right according to rational and scientific principles. She had to tell the authorities about the *vampiros*.

"I need to report . . ."

Her throat tightened.

What? She hadn't said anything of note yet. A small voice whispered that *Monsieur* Perez had instructed her not to mention *anything* about last night's attack.

Even so, she had a duty as a citizen.

"Madame, what are you trying to say?"

"I . . . need." *Mon Dieu*, every word was an effort. "To . . ."

She clutched at her throat, completely unable to breathe.

"Madame?" Her maid shook her. "Madame!"

Hélène's vision grayed, and her heart pounded in her chest. Her maid's screeches were coming from farther and farther away.

Report . . . Report . . .

She was dying. If she told anyone, her own body would strangle her.

Damn *Monsieur* Perez. If she never saw the man again, it would be too soon. If she never saw another *vampiro* again, it would definitely be too soon.

"Talking isn't worth dying for."

"Madame? Ah, thank God!" Her maid dropped to her knees beside the bed, weeping and kissing her rosary.

Hélène managed to pat her on the shoulder before closing her eyes.

Jean-Marie's face swam before her.

Oh no. Oh no, no, no.

If the Lord was very good to her, he'd send her someone else to dream about.

Maybe.

FOUR

Jean-Marie slammed his fist against the mansion's front door. There was a kitchen door somewhere, but he couldn't remember exactly. He sure as hell was not about to enter Rodrigo's house through a window. He barked with laughter at the thought of how fast he'd be caught and punished.

Assuming Rodrigo was still alive and well, unlike Paris's *vampiros*. Every *esfera* in town, the territories whose possession was the subject of so much dueling and spite by *vampiros*, but which had always been hidden from *prosaicos*—all of them were gone, destroyed by the Parisian mob. After the common people had captured the Bastille, the fortress which symbolized royal tyranny, they'd lost themselves in an orgy of drunken slaughter that had extended across much of the Parisian slums. Anyone caught unaware, especially during daylight, was dead meat— and the *vampiros* had been the most hapless prey of all, either sound asleep when their former victims turned on them or collapsing into dust under the first rays of sunlight. Their vaunted mental and physical powers hadn't saved them from the hordes coming against them, happy to find someone, anyone, to slake their bloodlust on.

Nom de dieu, how the hot summer days and nights had echoed with screams, reverberating through the city's stone walls and along the cobblestone streets . . .

Only *vampiros* like Rodrigo and Sara, who lived far from the slums and with a strong *comitiva*'s protection, had survived. Even so, most of them had fled to the countryside, trading a steady supply of food for the hope of a longer life.

God willing Rodrigo was still here, simply keeping his doors and shutters well locked. No respectable man tolerated trespassers, or allowed bullies of any kind onto his property. And as for the thought of rioters charging into his home, intent on destroying his wife . . .

Impossible to imagine in a civilized country. And yet . . .

Jean-Marie doubled over yet again, his stomach knotting like an anaconda. The innumerable bloodstains on his coat had dulled the once glossy silk into a dull black, concealing their mates on his waistcoat. His breeches and boots weren't fit for a pigsty. He'd ripped off his shirt cuffs hours ago—or was it days? Probably hours, since they'd gone to cover the eyes of that young Swiss who'd . . .

His stomach clenched again.

The door opened.

"*Gracias a Dios*, you're home, Jean-Marie!" Rodrigo yanked him inside.

It was a magnificent house, a true mansion, built for use in Paris by one of France's great families. Rodrigo had bought it upon their arrival two years ago and cared for it well, adding to its glories from increased wealth wherever he visited.

Jean-Marie noticed none of that.

But when Rodrigo hugged him—the strong, simple embrace of masculine friendship—he returned the clasp as warmly. "*Mon frère*," he murmured, his throat tight, "I must reek."

"You do," Rodrigo agreed. He released him, unabashedly displaying the tears on his face, and cuffed him lightly on the shoulder. "Which means I now have someone to play piquet with again."

Jean-Marie managed a smile as he was intended to do.

"Any wounds?" Rodrigo asked, his dark eyes fiercely cataloguing every inch of Jean-Marie.

"All small and well within a *compañero*'s ability to heal. Most of this is from other men."

"Jean-Marie!" Sara raced into the vestibule and stopped on the threshold. She swallowed hard and fanned herself rapidly. "You look . . . You smell . . ." she tried again. She turned away slightly. "Of course, I'm glad you're home," she finished in a rush.

He bowed in acknowledgment, a cynical smile touching his mouth.

Rodrigo signaled to a hovering servant and drew Jean-Marie into the drawing room, a painted and carved ode to French craftsmanship, and handed him a brimming goblet of Burgundy.

Jean-Marie poured it down, savoring for once the rich taste of Rodrigo's mighty *vampiro mayor* blood, forgetting how long he'd craved such sustenance. Its power kicked him harder than a tankard of illegal apple brandy, screaming like fire through his bones and veins faster than cannonballs across a battlefield. His knees buckled, and he would have sagged except for Rodrigo's quick grab.

"Easy there, easy, *mi hermano*." He eased Jean-Marie into a chair, ignoring Sara's brief squawk of protest over damage to the upholstery. "You'll still need to feed and drink deep when you do. But this will keep you on your feet for another hour or so while you wash. The servants are preparing everything now."

"And tell you what happened."

"If you wish to and are ready." Their eyes met, and Jean-Marie saw a battle-hardened commander's bone-deep, bitter experience there. Rodrigo would give him time—but only while silence endangered no one else.

"You need to know." His body tightened again at the thought of reliving, even through retelling, that horror. He tried to think of a gentle, elegant summation and failed. He settled for bald facts.

"The Paris mob's womenfolk have captured the royal family at Versailles and brought them back to be immured."

"That's impossible! What about their bodyguards? Or the Swiss Guards?" Sara demanded.

Jean-Marie shuddered, a thousand horrific images whipping before his eyes.

"Slaughtered." He didn't recognize his own voice. "All of them butchered. The mob fought over the pieces of their bodies and tossed the shreds about for trophies."

"And you?" Rodrigo's steadiness was a lifeline.

"Early last night—after I delivered Sara's message to her, the *vicomtesse* asked me to wait while she composed a reply. I couldn't sleep and was visiting some of my childhood haunts in the palace."

He rose and began to pace, unable to sit still even now though the battle had ended.

"The howling crowd attacked unexpectedly in the dead of night. I heard them coming—so damn fast!—and took the dauphin to safety through the old secret passages. I found the king wandering aimlessly afterward and managed to get both of them to Marie Antoinette."

He inspected the bottom of the goblet, decided he wouldn't ask for any more of Rodrigo's blood, and drank the dregs.

"After that, I went back to the guards but there was nothing . . . Even so, I tried. But all I could do was give them a decent burial." Would he ever stop seeing their broken, scattered bodies? Or his childhood home, bloody and defiled?

Fire crackled on the hearth.

"The mob found the Royal Family hours later, when their bloodlust had been sated. They're bringing them back to Paris. I doubt they'll ever leave alive." He studied his goblet again, before he headed for the wine. Rodrigo's hand pressed down on his shoulder, and he reluctantly settled back into his chair. The big Spaniard refilled Jean-Marie's glass and placed the bottle at his elbow.

Jean-Marie thanked him silently and gulped the wine greedily, even though it wouldn't blur his *compañero* senses enough to make him forget. But it did bring him to the next step, understanding the implications for France—and by extension, his adopted family. "The monarchy is gone."

"The break truly happened in July when the Bastille—that great prison—fell to the mob, because the governor lacked the *machismo* to shoot them." Rodrigo's big shoulders lifted in a shrug.

"And nobody else, either the monarchy or the elected representatives in the National Assembly, called them to task for killing men in the public streets and parading them like barbarians. Today's events only confirmed it." Jean-Marie couldn't keep his bitterness out of his voice. Or his longing for his father's iron hand, even with the sure knowledge that his father's time was long gone.

"Society left Paris afterward, leaving only the queen's dearest friends and the legislators." Sara shook out her skirts with a snap. "Now your *belle amie* will surely never return to the capital, Jean-Marie, even though we've lingered here for two years. You can return to me."

"Never! I will never share your bed again!" He sprang to his feet with a roar of denial. "A century ago, I was a foolish young man, vulnerable to anyone who'd speak softly and at least half-truthfully to me. You lured me into your arms with lies, saying that you cared about only me, not my father's wealth and power. Telling me it would be for a few nights, not for decades and centuries to come."

Rodrigo watched them warily from beside the fireplace, clearly ready to take action on a moment's notice.

"Every word was true! I wanted you since the day Rodrigo showed you to me in his prison cell," she snapped back, coming to her feet to face Jean-Marie, a febrile glitter in her eyes. "You belonged to me then, and you will be mine again."

"All you have ever thought about was yourself. Of having a *concubino compañero* eternally at hand, eager to provide you with carnal pleasure. So that you would need no one and nothing else ever again for the emotion and blood you need to live on. Isn't it?" He dragged Sara up out of the chair by her shoulders and shook her. "Isn't it?"

"Of course! Why not? My life has been bitter. Why shouldn't I have what I need and desire?" She glared at him defiantly.

"Even when it destroys a young man's life?" Rodrigo slapped the carved marble with a force that set portraits shaking on nearby walls.

"Rodrigo, *por favor* . . ." Sara shrank from his rare open display of wrath, as Jean-Marie released her, turning to open another bottle of Burgundy rather than maul her again.

"France's armies could have used him decades ago, and she needs him more today. Yet you have tied him so completely to your apron strings that he must travel wherever you go or die within a few weeks." Rodrigo towered over her, his dark eyes flashing. "I thought our long captivity had left you too much of a child to ever deliberately destroy someone else. I have cared for you, protected you, and been glad to see your wits return. But I will do so no more."

"Rodrigo, what do you mean?" She caught at his arm.

He regarded Jean-Marie, completely ignoring her. "*Amigo*, there is one other alternative to being her *concubino compañero*."

"You've never mentioned that before." Jean-Marie's head came up, and he stopped uncorking the wine.

"*Compañeros* are very rare outside of Asia, *concubinos compañeros* even rarer, and those whose *vampira primera* is a *vampira mayora* are possibly the rarest of all. Something I suspect Sara was counting on to protect herself." Rodrigo's voice gained the slick deadliness of a Toledo blade. "Am I not correct?"

She made a rude gesture more suitable to a gutter than a fine mansion and flounced out the door, silently confirming his story's truth.

"What is the option?"

"I doubt you will like it."

"What is my other choice?" Jean-Marie repeated, ready to lunge at his old friend.

Rodrigo's dark eyes were troubled but honest under the brutal scar.

"I, too, am a *vampiro mayor* and a century older than Sara, which makes my blood more potent than hers."

"As I already know. You've saved my life more than once with its ability to heal." Jean-Marie shrugged impatiently. "What of it?"

"You've probably also noticed that I—enjoy the company of both women and men."

"As does every other *vampiro* I've met. But you linger with none of them, and you're always careful of their pleasure, no matter what their gender." Jean-Marie rolled his eyes, wondering when the Spaniard would get to the point. "Why are you telling me the obvious?"

"A *compañero*'s addiction to one *vampiro* can be overwhelmed by an addiction to another, older *vampiro*."

"You?" Jean-Marie all but dropped the wine bottle.

"Myself." Rodrigo inclined his head. "However, since you're a *concubino compañero*, whose bond was originally based on blood and sex, any new bond would have to include both elements."

"Take you as a lover?" Jean-Marie's legs were suddenly very unsteady. He'd always, only thought of himself as an admirer of women.

"For the rest of your life, although I would, of course, never be a demanding one, *amigo*." Anger flared briefly in Rodrigo's voice before being pushed back.

"No, you wouldn't. You're too much of a friend to force yourself where you weren't invited." Jean-Marie smiled briefly, his brain whirling.

"*Gracias.*" The other's face lightened.

Jean-Marie tried to think clearly. If he agreed to Rodrigo's offer, he'd be tied to a friend, who'd support him in his interests. Who wouldn't be petulant, irrational, jealous, drag him away from places he loved and things he cared about doing . . .

But he'd have to have sex regularly with another man. He'd never done that, ever. Not when he'd been a young boy or even during some of the more extravagant orgies he'd attended. Always, something inside him had jerked him away.

He knew very well that in *vampiro* society, the odds of survival increased rapidly with the ability to find willing, sensual partners to enjoy sex with, starting with those of the opposite gender. Refusing Rodrigo could shorten his life span, given how much more often these dizzy spells were starting to occur.

But he couldn't do it. He'd rather be in bed with a woman, preferably someone like Hélène d'Agelet.

"I'm sorry—but no." He shook his head. "I appreciate your offer but . . ."

"All you can see are the ladies, and a particular one at that?" Faint humor lit Rodrigo's eyes. "As you wish, *amigo*. But the offer remains open. If you ever change your mind, all you have to do is say so."

"I will never . . ."

Rodrigo held up his hand in warning. "Do not tempt the Almighty, *amigo*," he said entirely seriously. "He has a remarkable way of persuading one to follow paths one would never have thought possible."

"I'm as likely to become your *vampiro* as your *concubino compañero*," Jean-Marie sniffed.

Rodrigo laughed outright at that, having vowed never to become any *vampiro*'s *creador*. They hugged, the tension broken.

"Do you wish more blood before you go upstairs? The servants should have water heated for your bath by now."

"No." Jean-Marie stretched, rubbing the back of his neck. "I'm strong enough to sleep now and go to Sara in the morning, when she'll be more generous."

"*Bien.* We'll leave Paris for London tomorrow afternoon, if you're ready." Rodrigo's eyes searched his for a reaction.

And abandon hope of seeing Hélène d'Agelet again, at least anytime soon. But—how much hope had he really had?

"I'll be ready."

CHÂTEAU DE SAINTE-PAZANNE, THE VENDÉE, FEBRUARY 1793

"Raoul de Beynac is a soldier fighting France's enemies!" Celeste slapped the table, making her wine dance in its glass. She was very good at that, gained by arguing with her father for so many years.

"He is a traitor to his king and a regicide!" roared their father, the *comte* de Sainte-Pazanne, the setting sun pouring crimson over his hair through the windows. "If he truly honored his oath, he'd have resigned when those foul beasts in Paris executed the King last month."

"How could he when there are Austrian and Prussian armies on our frontiers? When he has already fought—and won!—one victory against them?"

"France has a new king, Louis XVII, the young boy who needs every brave man's help to escape his stinking prison and bring peace."

Their voices set the crystals rattling below the sconces, and Hélène winced reflexively. If only the footmen were still standing watch, Papa and Celeste's argument might not have gotten out of hand.

The servants still served the Sainte-Pazannes out of love, unlike many other aristocratic households after feudal rights had collapsed. But *Maman* had excused them as soon as Papa had mentioned politics, of course, knowing the conversation would quickly become heated.

Like the dining room's combination of clamorous argument echoing against the silence from absent servants, its light was now a shifting mix of shadows and fiery streaks of crimson. The family had lingered in the dining room so long the candles weren't even lit.

"Raoul is the best of men, and you loved him before the Revolution. You read how bravely he fought at Valmy and all you hate is his politics." Celeste threw her napkin onto the table, tears standing in her eyes. "Please let me marry him. If you do, I will leave this house, and you will never hear from me again."

Maman's breath hissed in, and her eyes met Hélène's across the table. Hélène suspected hers were as wide and appalled as her mother's were. But could Papa truly keep clever, stubborn Celeste here if she didn't wish to stay?

In these terrifying times, nobody traveled anywhere unless forced by necessity. Hélène had moved back to Sainte-Pazanne under the pretext of caring for her mother, after her nephew by marriage had tried to rob her of her widow's portion at gunpoint. She'd talked her way past him, but she'd practiced ever since then with guns and black powder.

"No." Papa's voice was completely cold, that of a patriarch whose family had dictated the law for more than six centuries. "You are my youngest daughter, and I will not abdicate my responsibilities toward you. When de Beynac comes to his senses and agrees to serve the King, I will gladly give you to him. Until then, I will protect you as best as I know how."

"But . . ."

A single eyebrow lifted, quelling even Celeste. She inclined her head after a long moment, tears running down her cheeks. Sobs shook her chest, another and another, ripping into her throat, until finally she hid her face in her napkin.

"*Petite*," coaxed *Maman*, putting her hand over her youngest daughter's.

The weak winter sunlight was fading faster and faster now, disappearing from the room's windows. A great candelabrum stood ready on the table to light their repast, its candles high above their heads to avoid dazzling their eyes, as did several of its smaller mates on the side tables.

Celeste shoved everything away, including her mother's touch and her plate. She buried her face in her arms and wailed.

Maman shot a glance at her husband, clearly torn between her duty to support his definition of honor and her need to comfort her daughter.

Papa harrumphed, but his fork hung in midair, lacking the single-minded force he'd displayed earlier. He nodded to his wife, and they silently left the room, their usual practice for dealing with Celeste's hysterics over things which would not be changed.

Hélène hurried around the table to her sister, wishing yet again the four of them were united as a whole as they'd been for so long. The three women singing in harmony, while Papa played his violin. Or cheering on Papa's latest racehorse. Or fussing over Celeste's newest dress . . .

"Celeste," she cooed and rubbed her sister's shoulder.

La petite continued sobbing, but at least she didn't shrug away from the contact.

"All will be well, sweetheart. They have your best interests at heart," Hélène tried to reassure her. Logic had never worked well with her sister, but it always was worth a try.

"Nobody has ever loved anyone the way Raoul and I love each other." Celeste's voice was so choked with tears as to be almost indistinguishable. "I don't know why he begrudges me such a love."

"Perhaps he believes you already have the love." Hélène leapt on the opportunity to divert her sister. "But marriage is a different matter. He is generous enough not to have forced you to break the betrothal with de Beynac, after all."

"But how can I wait, knowing he could be killed any day?" Her voice broke.

"There are other men . . ."

"Haven't you ever known one man is special?" Her tear-filled eyes met Hélène's. "So unique that everyone else is completely invisible next to him? So perfect that only he, and he alone, will do for you?"

Hélène hesitated, thinking of Jean-Marie St. Just. Remembering the months of laughter and dancing. The chess games, the conversations about politics, the jokes about trivialities. And, God help her, the candlelight gleaming on his naked body . . .

"You do know what I mean! You *have* met such an individual." Celeste grabbed Hélène's hands. "Do you deny it?"

"*Mon Dieu*, I wish I could," Hélène sighed, as much to herself as to Celeste. "But I'll never have him. I don't even know where he is."

"That is why I, too, will not settle for second best. Why having my love, I must also have marriage with him or go to my grave unwed." She pulled the thin gold chain out from around her neck with Raoul's grandmother's ring and held it out. "Ah, Hélène, it is Raoul de Beynac for me and no one else in this world."

It had been more than five years since she had seen Jean-Marie, yet no other man had so much as made her pulse twitch. Still, Celeste could have her Raoul if she but waited.

Hélène steeled herself for a storm of disappointment. "You must be patient, *petite*."

Sheer disbelief stormed through Celeste's dark eyes and she clutched Raoul's small gold ring like a talisman. "Don't *you* understand? He is a soldier, and he could be killed any day. I want to have him *now*!"

Tears welled up and over, spilling down Celeste's cheeks. She pointed a finger at her sister. "Go away and promise me I won't see you again until tomorrow." She squeezed her eyes shut, sobbing, twisting, and tugging on the thin gold chain, as if she was holding her lover's hand.

"I promise," Hélène agreed, recognizing their old promise. She backed out of the room, hoping this bout of hysterics would end quickly. There'd be no approaching *la petite* until it did.

A sharp POP! sounded just after she'd passed the doors.

"No!" screamed Celeste.

Hélène whirled and peeked into the dining room, wondering what else could have gone wrong.

The thin gold chain was slipping from Celeste's neck in a single long thread. A bell-like tone announced the ring's leap onto the wooden floor. It rolled, flashed once in the sun's dying light, and disappeared under the sideboard.

"No!" screeched Celeste, diving to find it. She pulled up short, baffled by the darkness under the massive piece of furniture. Finally she began to crawl along the floor, methodically shoving her hand into every opening under the sideboard and cursing.

Hélène took a step into the room and stopped. She couldn't see where the ring was, given the darkness, although it should be easy to find—if there was light in the dining room. On the other hand, she'd given her word to *la petite* they wouldn't meet again until morning.

If only one of the candelabrum on the side table was lit, it would be enough to help her.

Could she do so from the door?

She'd always been mesmerized by fires, from harvest bonfires' great leaping flames to a single candle's delicate flicker—and terrified by her own fascination. But still, she couldn't stop herself from staring into their blazing hearts and wishing she could shape the power there.

True, she'd heard family legends of *Maman*'s Breton ancestors, women who'd been able to accomplish intriguing feats with their mastery of ordinary objects. But those tales had always seemed more fantasy than reality, stories from a time before Christianity, here on France's western coast where great carved stones hinted at powers beyond mortal understanding. Even *Maman*'s account of how her great-great-great-grandmother had lit a lantern to warn her husband of an ambush, even though she was bound and gagged—had seemed a story more mythical than real.

Cher Bernard, on the other hand, treated fire with extreme caution and studied it the way warriors eyed their greatest enemy. He fought to eliminate it and its dangers from men's lives with his electrical igniter, all the while knowing that one false move in his laboratory would let fire claim his life in a single massive explosion. As it had in the end.

Never openly admitting his fear, he'd taught her all he knew of fire's science until much of her unreasoning terror was gone. She was still very, very wary of it but seemed to have reached an accommodation with the power residing inside the flames, if one could call it that. Welcoming her greater comfort with "old-fashioned methods," as *cher* Bernard called matches and fuses, her husband had encouraged her to take full responsibility for that aspect of his experiments.

She'd once set fire to slow matches, those lengths of slow-burning fuse used to light gunpowder, without using a candle or another lighted length of slow match. She'd been alone in Bernard's laboratories, and confident she fully understood slow matches and gunpowder. She simply hadn't known she didn't need to physically touch them and had lit it from less than a foot away, while wishing it would light quickly so she could check on Bernard's unaccustomed silence behind the screen.

Nobody could have been more surprised than she was when the slow match started smoldering. It had been all she could do not to drop her fuse and run shrieking from the room. Instead, she'd decorously snuffed her fuse while her heart slammed rapidly around her ribcage, announced the countdown for the slow match—and never told anyone else what had happened.

Could she do as well with a candle from a few feet away?

Hélène turned quietly until she could see the side candelabrum in the knife's polished silver.

Three candles, all beeswax, all with linen candlewicks, all well made. Everything could burst into flame quickly and brilliantly when excited, as *cher* Bernard, the master chemist, had taught her. Deep down inside, they were like a bow spinning into dry wood: Turn it very quickly until a spark came, and fan that spark.

She closed her eyes and focused on making the candles' linen candlewicks revolve more and more rapidly where nobody except a chemist could see. Faster and faster, spinning more and more . . .

A flame snapped into being on the center candle, rather as if it had always been there. An instant later, the second candle and the third also burned brightly.

Hélène gulped and closed her mouth before anyone could comment on one particularly well-lit corner. God help her, but she'd actually lit a candle. Three of them, in fact.

She also seemed to have ignited a brutal headache behind her eyes, and the question was who she really was. That hadn't mattered in the friendly confines of *cher* Bernard's laboratory where anything and everything could be explored if it might help France. But here?

She wouldn't try such an experiment again.

Celeste smacked her hand down on the ring and began to back away from the sideboard, chortling over her success.

Her older sister smiled privately. She'd have to light a candle to the Virgin tomorrow—undoubtedly with a match—to say thank you.

VIENNA, MAY 1793

"The Vendée has risen en masse against Paris." Rodrigo dropped the stack of newspapers onto the table. Knowing the latest tidings from everywhere in Europe was a necessity for the proprietors of the Austrian capital's most fashionable—and exclusive—gambling den. It wasn't a profession Jean-Marie had ever expected to find the proud Spaniard engaged in, but its profits were a definite benefit.

Jean-Marie immediately set aside his coffee and began sorting through the sheets with almost indecent haste. He'd been glad to leave London almost two years ago, with its citizens' stubborn insistence on treating Americans as recalcitrant toddlers who'd run back to their king after another, better "spanking." Coming to Europe's center was almost a relief, especially since he could aid its continual opposition to the French revolutionaries. After all, their princess was the French queen who'd just been butchered.

But none of that, or his avoidance of Sara as much as possible, had kept his mind away from Hélène d'Agelet. It was purest folly, to be obsessed with a woman, whom he'd only known for five months and left five years ago. Yet his hands were shaking as he hunted for mentions of her, her family, or their lands.

"London papers," Rodrigo commented, settling into his chair and throwing back his head, scents from the finest English tea teasing their nostrils.

"Ah!" Jean-Marie yanked the slim page to the top and began reading the few, cryptic words. Sara was sleeping off a night's debauchery, so he could say what he pleased afterward.

"If Brittany and Normandy also rise up . . ." He fixed his stare on Rodrigo, who'd once sat on a crown prince's war council.

"Hmm," was the noncommittal answer.

"Why not?" he demanded. "Paris is loathed in the provinces, and the Vendeans are excellent soldiers."

"Paris is terrified and has an army." Rodrigo's face shifted, his eyes turning abstract. "I am not sure the Vendeans will believe how much evil their enemies are capable of."

"Evil?" Jean-Marie stiffened, watching his friend with growing alarm. "What vision are you seeing, Rodrigo?"

Rodrigo's visions came rarely but were always accurate. They were usually of great events, such as an immense storm, and occasionally of a happening in a friend's life.

"Blood." The dark chocolate eyes turned inward at images not granted to others. "Streams of blood, filling the streets and the rivers. Killing everyone—from the oldest to the youngest, even the beasts in the field. Fire rising to the sky from every corner of the farms, towns, and the woods . . . All by the order of their distant masters."

He shook his head, black hair flying forward to cover his appalling scar.

"I must go to her." Jean-Marie sprang to his feet.

Rodrigo's fingers locked on his wrist. "You cannot help her."

"I do not believe you."

"You do more good here, helping me run an outpost of the British Secret Service."

"You're joking." Jean-Marie stared at him.

"Would I on that subject? Would you have helped me if I'd asked your permission?"

Recent events combined with old experiences to form a pattern.

"All the unusual visitors, the gamblers with their truly unusual bets—they were passing messages!"

Rodrigo bowed.

But spying meant little, next to her.

"Even so, Hélène needs me. I must go to her."

"You know as well as I that you will die before you reach her," Rodrigo snapped. "Besides, you have greatly shortened your life by your foolish insistence on not tasting Sara's carnal juices. I will not allow you to commit suicide."

Jean-Marie threw a salt cellar at him, which Rodrigo caught and set down without losing his soldier's wariness.

"Someday a woman will shatter your inviolable calm, Rodrigo, and you too will beg for her survival," Jean-Marie growled.

A muscle ticked in his friend's jaw. "The only lady with that power sings in an angels' choir, *mi hermano*."

Jean-Marie threw up his hands and turned away. He took out his rage on an inanimate object, pounding his fists against the wall.

"How long?" he asked, without looking at his brother of the heart.

"I don't know. This vision only lets me see blood and fire, not even the time of year." Rodrigo shuddered.

THE VENDÉE, THE MONTH NIVÔSE OF THE YEAR II, JANUARY 1794

Raoul de Beynac considered his orders again, the plan of *total destruction* as the Committee of Public Safety called it. They'd defeated the rebel army a few weeks ago at Savenay, and now it was time to stamp out the fire of rebellion with a bonfire of their own.

All of it necessary to frighten rebels elsewhere in France away from the foreign jackals—to keep the northwest from the Austrians and English, the northeast from the Prussians, the southwest from the Spanish. France had not faced so many foreign armies in centuries, and she needed to be united, or they would all die. A harsh lesson, but sometimes fools needed that.

As for himself, he was fighting for Celeste and their future together. That she and their children would know peace and never see anything like the mobs he'd watched destroy Paris. He needed to know she could walk down the streets safely, holding their sons and daughters by the hand, could laugh over a new dress because no bandits would rob her house. If he had to kill, and kill again, to provide that for her—then he would do so gladly and without a second thought.

Any penalty he might pay, even the ultimate, meant less than nothing to him, if it brought her another second of happiness. After all, there would be no Heaven for him without his angel Celeste.

He could do a great deal in the coming campaign, thankfully. Thanks to his efforts at Savenay, he'd been given his choice of routes for his "infernal column" to follow on its mission of total destruction.

If his sister had been able to stay in touch with dearest, dearest Celeste, he'd find her within the next few weeks, no matter how well that rebel leader of a father had hidden her.

He dipped his pen into the ink and began to write,

"*Ma chère* Louise . . ."

SOMEWHERE IN THE VENDÉE, FEBRUARY 1794

"We can rest here in the woods," Papa said. "Nobody can see us amidst the trees."

Celeste shouldered off her pack and sank to the ground gratefully, while Hélène helped *Maman* do the same.

Papa stayed alert, listening for any followers. He was one of the very, very few Royalist leaders who'd escaped Savenay. The Blues, the Republican army, wanted to catch him more than they wanted to fight the English.

She understood their feelings perfectly: He was an unfeeling tyrant, who understood nothing of reason and honor. Especially honor as it pertained to a seven-year-old betrothal. At twenty-six years of age, she had not yet married the man whose only fault was his differing views on France's future. Even her father admitted Raoul de Beynac was a patriot.

But what could she hope for now, after the rebellion? Like many other women, they'd followed Papa and the army. *Parbleu*, how she'd hated it, although she'd probably have enjoyed it in Raoul's company. Her family had fled after the crushing defeat at Savenay, but they'd never been caught by any of the Blues.

If they had, she'd have shown them Raoul's letters, including the special one telling anyone who read it that she was a friend of the Republic. And hours after that, she knew she'd finally have been in Raoul's arms. Forever. Finally to taste the full splendor of love with him and bear his child.

It was all she asked. All she'd prayed for, all her life. Only Papa stood in the way.

She shot another glare at his back and sipped her watered wine. He still somehow had enough friends to keep them supplied but surely they couldn't stay on the run forever.

Papa crouched down before *Maman* and took her hands. Her eyes searched his, dark and enormous, even in the twilight.

"We're very close to Sainte Marie des Fleurs, *ma chère*."

Every nerve in Celeste's body came to quivering alert.

"If it remains quiet, I will take you through the woods to Hélène's manor just before dawn. You will be safe there, from what I have heard."

"*I* will be safe? What of you, Henri?" *Maman* was biting her lip. Hélène was pacing up and down the narrow forest track, trying to keep watch. Celeste came to her feet, tense—and oddly hopeful.

"I draw the Blues the way honey draws bees, and you do not deserve to be stung, my sweet." He rubbed his thumb over her hand. "So I will remove myself elsewhere for a few days."

"A few days?" Celeste burst out.

"*Mais oui*. In two days, the English will come for me and my family with the quarter moon. And all of us shall wake up safe on the third day in England, *ma chère*." The *comte* kissed his wife's hand.

England? Away from Raoul? If that happened, she would never see Raoul again until peace was declared. Who knew when that would happen or if he would live that long? No and no and no!

She had to do something to stop this monstrous plot, but what? Moving jerkily, she began to pace in the opposite direction from Hélène, pretending she too was standing watch.

She couldn't escape. If she knew anything about Papa, he would certainly make Hélène and *Maman* swear to protect her in his absence. They'd never allow her to sneak off. She'd already experienced that last summer, during the rebellion.

Louise, Raoul's sister, lived an hour's walk away from Sainte Marie des Fleurs. If she could send a message to her, telling what Papa planned, surely Louise would ensure Raoul would rescue her from being carted off to England like a cow.

But she'd need to tell her how quickly Raoul would have to act, which meant saying when Papa would return. Raoul could choose to arrive when Papa was there—and capture him, for delivery to the guillotine and his death.

Celeste blanched.

But Papa was an aristocrat, a protector of feudalism, which had cost so many people so much. The government in Paris had put a price on his head, and they would choose whether or not to kill him.

Surely it would not be her responsibility if ill befell him. Surely . . .

FIVE

SAINTE MARIE DES FLEURS, TWO NIGHTS LATER

Safely concealed behind the barn door, Raoul de Beynac surveyed the small manor. Barely the size of a typical manor, only its excellent construction, broad herb garden, and superb livestock set it apart from its kindred. The cattle and most of the horses were in the pastures, with only a few of the better mounts still in the barn.

A river marked its southern border, rising beyond the dense eastern woods and flowing placidly through its rich green pastures before tumbling wildly down a steep cliff to meet the ocean only a few leagues away. The view there was considered magnificent, with a terrace and gardens built as observation points—all on the opposite side of the house from the barn.

The manor house had two stories, of course, with steeper roofs than usual, implying large attics full of stores. The harvest here, as elsewhere in the Vendée, had been unusully good, leaving the loft overflowing with hay.

The house, barn, and many of the outbuildings were built of stone, while the courtyard itself was paved with flagstone, shimmering under the moonlight like a lake. Anyone moving across it would be instantly visible, which was why he kept watch from here.

The roads and pastures were still sodden from strong rains last night and this morning, forcing him to leave most of his incendiaries at the village he'd destroyed yesterday. He should still have enough to torch this manor. But it wouldn't go up as quickly as he'd like, even with the stiff breeze blowing from the woods toward the ocean. He'd scattered his men around the buildings, ordering them to stay hidden until he gave the signal.

He smiled faintly. In the end, everything would burn to the ground—after Celeste was safely in his arms, of course. There'd been a few lights inside the house earlier but none in the last hour or two. His heart told him she watched for him.

It was past midnight now, but the *comte* had not yet arrived.

"Can you see him yet?" Celeste whispered.

"Not yet." Hélène shook her head, holding the curtain barely wide enough to view the courtyard from inside the attic. It was an excellent location to watch for approaching enemies, even if she couldn't see their faces very well.

Caught by a premonition she couldn't shake, she'd dismissed every servant in the manor immediately after sunset. Given the tales of murder, looting, and destruction by the Revolution armies, they'd chosen to spend the night deep in the woods at the Blessed Virgin's shrine.

"We *can* see the entire courtyard." The far shorter Celeste peeped under Hélène's arm, edging her away from the window. She was almost vibrating with nerves.

"Except for the herb garden gate, but *Maman* is waiting there. We'll go down as soon as he comes." She put her arm around her younger sister and gave her an affectionate squeeze. "All will be well, *ma petite*."

"God willing."

*   *   *

The quality of the silence changed into something heavier and more ominous. A frisson ran over Raoul's skin under his woolen uniform and settled into his stomach, bringing the still clarity of combat readiness. His sword settled into his hand.

Even so, he was unprepared to see the *comte* de Sainte-Pazanne appear in the courtyard without any preliminaries, his golden hair looking like a crown atop a man of his height and proud bearing. The *comte* glanced around the courtyard, wary as any proud stag.

Raoul started to shout a demand to surrender.

A woman suddenly burst out of the garden and ran toward the aristocrat, her dark hair touched with gray spilling from under her cap. "Henri! Oh, *mon amour*, you have come at last!"

"Desirée!" The *comte* spun on his heel, joy transforming his face.

A soldier simultaneously stepped out from behind the barn and shot the lady through her chest. She tumbled forward, blood spurting across the shining stones, her body shaking.

For the first time, Raoul saw her face.

Mon Dieu, it was Celeste's mother. His man had killed the living image of what Celeste would look like in a few more years.

Blessed Virgin, what had he done? What had he been doing for all these weeks?

All the other women and children his men had killed . . . No, murdered.

Deus meus, *forgive me for what I have done.*

The *comte* ran her murderer through with his sword before the trooper could reload.

Duty sank its claws into Raoul and yanked him back to the present. No matter what else happened, the *comte* had to be captured for having led a rebellion against the Republic.

He raced out of the barn into the courtyard, the act of contrition running through his heart for the first time in far too long.

> *O my God, I am heartily sorry*
> *for having offended Thee,*
> *and I detest all my sins . . .*

"No!" Hélène shouted, the roar coming up from her depths like a volcano's rage. "No, not *Maman*!"

Celeste gasped, one hand flying up to her throat.

Hélène ignored her sister, too angry to stand still. She slammed the window open, breaking the inoffensive latch, and leaned out.

The Blues leader ran forward, shouting at Papa to surrender. But why should he, when they'd already proved what treacherous, loathsome dogs they were?

More soldiers began to appear, from the barn and through the gates, their bayonets ready. Wisps of hay clung to them.

Murderers, ready to kill Papa and Celeste, as they'd killed *Maman*.

No, and no, and no. Not if she could help it.

Papa spun to face the Blues leader, lifting up his dripping sword in an unmistakable demand for a fight. The officer had a wickedly disfiguring scar across half of his face, making him into an image of Satan.

Hélène growled like a wolf and bared her teeth. Anything would burst into flames if it spun fast enough deep inside. Bits of hay resembled slender bits of fuses.

But there was so much of it. The most she'd ever lit before were those three candles at dinner.

Celeste crowded into the window with her, almost as if she wanted to leap onto the ledge running the roof's periphery and from thence onto another roof and into the courtyard. Hélène flung an arm around her and held on desperately.

"Let me go, Hélène!" Celeste demanded, yanking away.

"No! You will only distract him!" Hélène gripped her harder, using her greater height and strength.

"Ahhh." Celeste made an inarticulate murmur of pure agony and shuddered, gripping the window frame as tightly as any smith holding the steel ready for the forge.

The Revolutionary officer was trying to argue with Papa, who seemed to be sneering at him. The earlier breeze had become a wind now, shaking the trees in the orchard and rattling branches against the roof. She couldn't hear what they were saying.

Mon Dieu, she couldn't just stand here. If she considered all the hay in the hayloft as a single mass, rather than individual strands, maybe she could make it burn at once, rather than bit by bit.

Papa suddenly produced a pistol and pointed it at the officer. The word *Murderer!* cut through a brief lull in the wind to reach their ears.

An instant later, a half dozen muskets fired, and Papa fell across *Maman*'s body, as united in death as they'd been in life.

"Noooo!" Hélène screamed, her agony ripping out her lungs and her heart. Her arms tightened around her only remaining family and she closed her eyes. "Die, damn you, die!"

Burn, bits of hay. Burn, you devils, burn . . .

BOOM! Light and heat blasted across the courtyard, shaking the house and knocking Hélène and Celeste back into the attic. Windows shattered, in a high-pitched staccato complaint. Horses screamed in panic, matched by the other animals.

Shaken, half-deafened, Hélène staggered back to look out.

The hayloft was on fire, flames shooting out of every opening and black smoke pouring into the sky. Pieces of hay spun through the air, burning furiously on the wind and setting alight anything they touched.

Three still figures lay in the courtyard's center: Papa and *Maman*, plus the Blues officer. His skull had been crushed by a wooden block blown out from the hayloft. Even as she watched, burning hay began to drift onto their clothes. Other floating firebrands landed on the house's rooftops.

Most of the Blues lay motionless in the courtyard. A few were slowly climbing to their feet, dazed and bleeding, covered with raw red and black streaks from the fire.

Celeste came up alongside her.

"Ah, *mon Dieu*!" Her hands clenched into fists, tears streaming silently down her face. "Someone will pay for this."

"Exactly so, *ma petite*," Hélène purred, in perfect agreement.

The animals were getting louder, led by the horses pounding on their stalls. With a loud neigh, the first one broke out, quickly followed by another and another. They bolted out of the barn in a long stream, rearing and kicking at the few foolish men who tried to catch them. They quickly found the gates the soldiers had used and disappeared into the pastures and the night beyond. At least they were safe, as her head groom had no doubt hoped.

Fire was licking at the barn's beams and onto the roof. She and Celeste would have to leave soon before it reached the house. There was no safety nearby, either, since they, too, were condemned to death for being members of a rebel leader's family. She didn't know how to contact the English, a trick Papa had kept to himself for security. But somehow she'd find a way for them to escape.

At least there were enough flaming doorways and windows to keep those murderous Blues from looting the house.

"Come along, Celeste, we must go now." Hélène grabbed her sister's hand.

"No!" She dug her heels in, obstinate as ever.

"We have to go now before we're caught." Hélène tugged hard, ignoring her headache, and dragged Celeste into movement.

"But how can we leave them behind?" Celeste was clearly appealing to sentiment, her usual tactic. "We must see them properly buried."

"What is there to stay for?" Impatient and desperate, Hélène brutally told the truth. "The Blues will only rape and kill us, if we do."

"Rape? But . . ." All the fight seemed to go out of her at once. Tears choked her voice for the first time. "Of course."

They ran out of the attic and down the hidden servants' stair to the root cellar. A concealed door allowed them to exit unobserved into the herb garden.

Hélène paused on the terrace above the river, looking out over the road and pastures at her departing enemies, marching back to their headquarters and a good night's sleep—before they destroyed somebody else's life tomorrow.

Damn them, damn them, damn them.

Burning hay spiraled out of the sky and onto the long, pointed horns of her cattle in the pastures. A bull bellowed and tossed his head. But the impertinent wisp lingered like a tiny pitchfork. More came until most of the cattle's horns were decked with the fiery ornaments and all of the beasts were snorting and pawing in anger and fright.

A bull charged and broke out of its pen onto the road, followed by other cattle. Funneled by the stone walls, they bore straight down upon the Blues, roaring like demons from millennia gone by, the ground shaking under their hooves.

The soldiers looked back, flung up their hands, and scattered their weapons to the winds. They ran for their lives and jumped off the road into the fields toward the north, away from the woods and the great beasts thundering at their heels like the wrath of God.

The great fire crackled and sparked behind Hélène and Celeste, pouring out enough black smoke to obscure the moon as it devoured the beautiful little manor house and barn. It was a Viking funeral pyre for her parents and that Blues officer, with all their possessions around them.

Hélène's lips curled in a faint, pitiless smile. She had no regrets, whatsoever, for any of it.

If she could ever do anything, at all, to stop the Blues' so-called revolution that only killed innocent people, she would. No matter what it cost her—except for Celeste's life—she would pay it, although she could wish she'd see Jean-Marie again.

"Come, Celeste." She touched her sister's arm.

Celeste was staring at the manor, clutching the chain around her neck, her lips moving continuously in a silent mutter. She nodded, keeping her face averted from her sister.

Hélène could understand the need to make vows, which were best not overheard. Many of the things she'd like to do to the Blues were nothing she wanted to explain to her virginal sister.

She turned toward the steep cliff down to the river, Celeste following at her heels.

"Madame la marquise?"

Their heads came up to face the newcomer.

"Hé, connarde, you're late," she snarled.

Celeste gasped at the crudity but Hélène refused to apologize for calling an Englishman an idiot, even if he had recognized her. Especially when her parents would be alive if he'd arrived an hour ago.

"A thousand pardons, my lady. The wind delayed us." He bowed deeply, the fire illuminating his face. He might be considered handsome, if you liked big brutes with excellent manners. She found nothing appealing, especially since he didn't even have blue eyes to remind her of Jean-Marie. "I am Sir Andrew ffoulkes."

She tapped her foot impatiently.

"Please excuse my sister, *m'sieu*," Celeste cooed, batting her eyes quite winsomely. "The evening has been long and difficult for us."

Hélène tried not to blink. What the devil was Celeste doing, flirting with someone other than Raoul de Beynac? Had she finally given up on that revolutionary?

The man promptly softened, as males always did for Celeste. Hélène refrained from rolling her eyes. In some ways, this small reminder of normal life was very reassuring after so much horror.

"Of course, mademoiselle." He bowed, just a shade more deeply than strictly necessary to a *comte*'s unmarried youngest daughter. At least she hadn't needed to provide formal introductions to Celeste, which would have been incongruous under these circumstances.

His voice gentled, dropping into genuine consideration. "May I inquire as to the *comte* and *comtesse* de Sainte-Pazanne?"

"They have gone to join their ancestors," Hélène forced out from a suddenly tight throat. Would this ever become easy to discuss or remember?

"My deepest sympathies, madame, mademoiselle." He bowed again, seemingly with great sincerity.

Both Hélène and Celeste acknowledged him silently.

"May I offer you and your sister safe passage to England, madame?"

"Thank you." She had very little money in England, since Bernard had not chosen to place his investments with France's sworn enemy. But perhaps her knowledge of explosives might earn them a little money.

"This way, my ladies. A boat awaits us on the river."

Hélène paused for a last look before the cliff blocked all view of the house, although Celeste hastened down. She needed the reminder of what she'd lost, and learned, and why she'd fight to the death for revenge, burning it into her brain through her headache's raw agony.

The house roared its fury, destroying all traces of their parents. Flames leapt to the skies, competing with the black smoke. Sparks swirled across the landscape like demons, seeking to destroy the unwary. The heat was like a living enemy, pushing them away from everything she'd loved. And the smell—of burning sweet hay, of crisp wood, charred meat, sweet flowers, and the mustiness of old books and older furniture . . .

The flames hammered at the barn's roof, ripping through sections of it. With a great whoosh and crackle of sparks, the entire thatched expanse slowly fell in upon itself. The walls swayed, battered by the wind, and tumbled toward the house—into the courtyard, onto her family's bodies.

Now her parents' remains were beyond their enemies' most twisted notions of revenge, together with the Blues officer.

Hélène crossed herself and turned away, her lungs and heart seared.

DOVER, TWO DAYS LATER

"Good morning, madame. A word alone, if I may?" Sir Andrew ffoulkes bowed politely.

It was a very direct approach from a man she'd already learned favored indirect tactics whenever possible. Even so, she could agree to it, since Celeste was out walking with their hostess and a young naval lieutenant.

"Certainly, Sir Andrew. Please sit down."

He did so with his usual grace, and Hélène poured him a cup of coffee, reflecting on the differences a few hours had made. She was clean, well fed, as well rested as her nerves would allow, and certainly quite safe under the roof of a retired general. She'd cried but not much, possibly because she was still vibrating with rage at how her parents had died.

Her clothes were the only oddity. She and Celeste were both now wearing new and very fashionable garments, although wholly suitable for full mourning. When she'd attempted to demur, her hostess had waved off the subject, saying something about Hélène's protection and necessities coming from the Crown.

It was probably a misunderstanding. Someone was being kind because of Papa's valor.

She considered Sir Andrew over her coffee cup's rim. He had something of Donal O'Malley's restrained lethality, although she didn't think he would ever dominate a room as well as *Monsieur* Perez could. He certainly had nothing of Jean-Marie's elegance, or the lurking laughter living side by side with the ability to whip a blade up against a bully's throat.

She bit back a sigh and waited, calling upon all of her training as Bernard's hostess to conceal her thinking.

Sir Andrew briefly lifted an eyebrow but said nothing. She had the strange notion he might have caught her thoughts, which was impossible.

"Madame," he began sweetly enough, "have you considered what you will do next?"

"As the *marquis* d'Agelet's widow," she began, concealing her surprise at his frontal attack, "I have some expertise in explosives, vouched for by my lectures to the Royal Academy and the Gunpowder Administration. I had hoped the British Crown might find my skills useful."

"So you'd be willing to risk your life, even kill your fellow countrymen?"

Hélène lifted an eyebrow at his idiotic question. Did he think explosives experts grew flowers? How did he imagine Bernard had died so abruptly—falling into a pond while throwing bread to ducks? She snorted privately.

"Of course I would. The revolutionaries killed my parents. I will risk everything, to make sure no one else goes through the same agony."

"What else would you do?" He leaned forward.

"*M'sieu?*" Her gut tightened, bringing her alert as it always had before a key discovery. He was too intent, making this interview very tricky.

"At Sainte Marie des Fleurs, the wood was very wet since it had been raining for several days. Yet it managed to catch fire and blaze very quickly." He leaned forward, watching her intently and speaking intimately.

"So? The Blues brought incendiaries, as they always did." Hélène watched him placidly, refusing to be drawn into any trap. Firestarting without any visible aids would be considered witchcraft in most places, making one liable to be hanged or worse.

He drummed his fingers for a moment on the arm of his chair, watching her face very closely, before he spoke again much more softly.

"What if Shakespeare spoke the truth when Hamlet said there are more things in heaven and earth than are dreamed of in your philosophy? What if there are firestarters—and vampires. Or, more properly, *vampiros?*"

Hélène's eyes widened. Memories flashed past, of a summer day and a man groaning in delight while a woman drank from his neck.

"Do you believe in firestarters, madame?" Sir Andrew's voice was very soft, scarcely loud enough to be heard two paces away.

"Why are you asking?" she parried, recovering some of her nerve.

"Because explosives experts are easier to find than firestarters. I didn't see all of the fight at Sainte Marie des Fleurs, but I saw you start the fire."

She turned pale, her skin rapidly flashing hot and cold.

"And I'm damned glad you did because otherwise you and your sister wouldn't have lived. Please believe me. You know those troops would have searched the house and killed you both, long after you'd started begging them to grant you mercy."

She flinched, but gritted her teeth and nodded.

"You could fight Paris far better as a firestarter, madame," he coaxed.

She snorted with disgust at the unlikely role. "What, torch the entire Committee of Public Safety?"

"Unlikely. They have their own guards, who are very powerful. But we play our own nasty games on them."

Mon Dieu, he sounded completely serious. Perhaps she could probe for a few of his plans. "Such as?"

"You could become more powerful. Mind powers, like firestarting, increase when someone becomes a *vampiro*."

She set her coffee cup down so abruptly, she completely missed the saucer, and it landed in the tray. "*Vampiro*? Me become a vampire?"

"So you have seen them before," he purred triumphantly.

She nodded distractedly, a thousand possibilities chasing themselves through her mind—mixed with relief at finally being able to speak freely. "But how could I do that? I'd have to drink blood for the rest of my life!"

"We live on the emotional energy carried in the blood, not the blood itself. The more powerful the emotion, the less often we need to feed."

"Carnal pleasure." As in the passion on the *vicomte*'s face.

"It's one of the greatest. But so is death and terror."

She sprang out of her chair. "I would never do that!"

"Nor have I, nor will you be asked to. Please calm yourself, madame, and return to your seat. We have much to discuss."

"Will you swear to me that I will never kill for food?"

For the first time, he allowed his mask of indolent good humor to slip and show the steel underneath. His gray eyes were very hard above his strong jaw.

"You have my most solemn oath. The first emotion a *vampiro* tastes is the emotion they must feed upon for the rest of their lives. Should you agree, you would not be taught to feed upon death or terror—since the British Crown would never trust a *vampiro* who required such meals."

She propped her fists on her hips and hooted with cynical laughter. "So very pragmatic of you. Very well, I believe you now and I will listen to the rest of your proposal."

She sat back down with all the elegance of a *marquise*, who'd been born to the ancient régime's oldest and proudest class of nobility.

"You would also live forever," he added.

"Years and years as a servant of the *British* Crown? No!" Better to die now.

"It's a powerful gift and takes long, difficult training." Granite was more flexible than his countenance. "A suitable period of service must be given in recompense."

"Such as?" Why was she considering this?

"As long as you're a 'creature of the night' who must avoid sunlight at all costs, without considering twilight. I myself have never been able to see twilight since I became a *vampiro*."

"How long would I have to serve, in years?" Did he think Frenchwomen were so foolish as to be tricked by pretty words from *Englishmen*? Dolt. She poured herself a fresh cup of coffee.

"Approximately two hundred years."

"That's far too long!" Twenty decades sworn to a foreign king?

"As one, you would be able to start a fire so quickly and precisely you could kill a *vampiro* before he took a step. That's faster than a cannonball can leave the gun's muzzle."

Hélène shot him a sideways glance and stirred more cream into her coffee. "Impossible."

"No." The very flatness of his response made it believable—and tempting.

"I would be your *creador*, unless you object to me."

"My *creator*? Is the bond very intimate?"

"More than you can imagine." His eyes danced briefly, unsettling her stomach. "My loyalty to the British Crown is absolute, and your loyalty to me, as your *creador*, would also be certain."

She whistled unhappily but said nothing.

"Exactly," he agreed. "Our branch of the Secret Service is deeply hidden but we are controlled from the very top."

On the other hand, who else did she know in England since she'd never been here before? He had brought her out of France, and he'd always been very kind to her and Celeste. "Your handlers are trying to be generous to me."

He shrugged, a small splotch of color appearing high on his cheekbones.

"They truly must want me." She probed a little harder.

"Very much so." His tone was extremely dry and she laughed for the first time in days.

"Will they pay me well?"

"Excuse me, ma'am?" She'd obviously shocked him out of his British sangfroid.

"No war between Britain and France has ever lasted for two full centuries. Besides, I can hardly believe that those Parisian donkeys are competent enough to provide for an army that long," she announced haughtily, testing the limits of her newfound influence. "So I will need some diversions, which means fashionable clothing for every season. I am a Frenchwoman, after all."

He gaped at her. Excellent; she'd managed to completely knock him off balance. She needed at least one victory in this sea of newness and uncertainties.

"And my sister . . ."

"Has already accepted the same offer."

Hélène glared, catching his momentary smugness. "How dare you seduce an innocent like Celeste?"

"Mind powers run in families, and we need every possible advantage in this war. Besides, she is twenty-six, madame."

On the other hand, *la petite* was distraught from seeing her parents' murder. Hélène had noticed she'd seemed calmer this morning. Perhaps Sir Andrew's body had provided some comfort. Hélène could hardly deny her sister the right to find healing wherever she found it—and revenge, as well.

Even so, as her older sister, she did need to keep an eye out for her.

"If you hurt her, I will gladly kill you. Slowly," she warned him.

"Understood." He bowed slightly. "She has also received one last warning: Very, very few females' sanity passes intact through *El*

Abrazo, the process of becoming a *vampira*. The worst will be *La Lujuria*, the lechery at the beginning."

"Oh, I will survive your *El Abrazo*, Sir Andrew," Hélène assured him. "It will be a pleasure to do so, in order to protect my sister and avenge my parents."

She had no doubts at all.

OXFORD, JUNE 1795

Celeste revolved slowly, examining herself critically in the mirror from every possible angle.

The peignoir and nightgown were both made of the finest silk, trimmed with exquisite Valenciennes lace and fluttering ribbons. The entire ensemble was dyed black and slightly transparent, to remind Andrew she'd been his lover for months. The neckline exposed her breasts, which fascinated him—the masculine idiot!—and also allowed free access to her neck.

She would have worn something far less revealing with fewer ribbons for Raoul, of course. White and virginal, to celebrate the perfection of her life and the hope of a child. Displaying the beloved ring he'd given her, the one she'd been forced to destroy, lest its implication of a lover be questioned.

Her eyes closed in agony.

"Ma'am?" the maid questioned cautiously.

"Go!" Celeste waved her off, for once not throwing something at the clumsy bitch.

All Englishwomen were bitches; it was an article of faith. She had to believe that, if she was to have revenge on the entire race for Raoul's death.

The latch clicked shut.

Celeste turned away from the mirror, silk whispering around her feet.

She had only one goal now: revenge for Raoul's death. On the English spies for arranging the ambush, and on Hélène for killing him.

She intended to destroy every English agent she possibly could, to carry on the work Raoul had left behind.

Her hands curled into claws, and she slashed at the air. Ah, if she could tear her so-called loving sister's eyes out! But no, she had to smile and coo and pretend that she was grieving solely for their parents. And that she loved Hélène. Bah!

She'd wondered a thousand times how Hélène had forced that barn to burst into flames. But there were only two possible killers—the Blues soldiers or Hélène. After a summer and fall spent following an army, Celeste had known exactly what soldiers did to cause fires, whether accidentally or deliberately.

On that bitter night, she'd had an excellent view of the barn and its surroundings from the attic. But she'd seen nothing, heard nothing, smelled nothing to indicate any military cause for that great explosion of flames. No shouted orders, no continuous spiral of smoke from a fuse, no stench of sulphur from a match, no clatter of hooves or creak of wheels to indicate a wagonload of black powder being pulled stealthily into position.

The only one who'd done anything whatsoever was Hélène. Celeste had heard her chanting under her breath, felt her tenseness—seen the fire start with her own eyes.

Heard her scream, "Die, damn you, die!"

For that alone, the bitch deserved destruction.

When the ordinary was ruled out, only the extraordinary remained, no matter what the means were. Celeste had no doubts left. Witchcraft or not, Hélène had caused it to burn and thereby knowingly murdered Raoul.

Therefore, Hélène must die.

When all the English spies were gone and Hélène—who'd been foolish enough to join them—knew herself alone, as Celeste was now . . . Ah, then and only then, would Celeste kill her. It was a very simple plan and would be easy to carry out, since Hélène suspected nothing. Their protectors wouldn't watch Celeste, since men always thought with their dicks around willing women.

She'd seduced Andrew as quickly as possible. It had been easier after he'd sworn he couldn't give her children, swearing he was a *vampiro*.

He'd offered to make her one of the same half-mythical beings as himself, and she'd promptly agreed. Whether or not it was true, he believed it. If it wasn't real, turning over a madman to Paris would be easier. If it was true, becoming someone so powerful would make it that much easier to destroy the British Secret Service from the inside.

She hadn't expected he'd make Hélène the same offer, damn him, or that Whitehall would insist Hélène become a *vampira* first. The murderess had been one for more than a year now. They'd said they needed her powers desperately, not Celeste's skills as a seductress, which was where even Andrew agreed her talents lay. And the bitch had been one of the rare females who'd made it through *La Lujuria* smoothly, keeping her sanity intact.

Ces salopards! She'd show the bastards who laughed last.

She hoisted a brandy decanter over her head by its neck but stopped herself in mid-swing.

She needed to regain her discipline.

She could hardly explain why she'd broken it when she was supposed to be eagerly anticipating Andrew's embrace and becoming his *hija*, the *vampira* he sired.

She laughed at herself.

That was no hardship. The true pain—the agony that was tearing her heart—was the certainty she needed to stop thinking of Raoul.

She couldn't permit Andrew to know she plotted revenge on England, not on the revolutionaries in Paris—and all because of her lover's death, not her parents'.

Andrew had warned her he could read every thought in her head once she drank his blood and he became her *creador*. He'd honored her grief before now and stayed out of her mind. But the blood bond between *creador* and *hija* would not permit him to do so afterward.

It felt like the worst form of adultery. Yet it was necessity and must last for years. If nothing else, revenge for Raoul would surely give her the emotional focus Andrew insisted she needed if she was to survive *El Abrazo*.

But to tear Raoul—dearest, most beloved Raoul, the light of her life for as long as she could remember—out of her heart?

She whimpered, hiding her face in her hands.

"My dear Celeste! If I had known you were so nervous, I would have knocked first."

"Andrew!" Celeste whirled to face him, forcing a tremulous smile. "*Mon cher*, it is nothing—only a silly girl's vapors at finally gaining what she wants." *That at least is the truth.*

"There's no need to rush, my dear." He was holding a bouquet of red roses, dew still beaded on their petals. But his eyes were searching her face, and he wasn't eagerly kissing her hand or another portion of her anatomy, as he usually did.

No need to rush? She would not wait another minute, if she had any choice.

Raoul, please forgive me. You are, and will always be, my angel. But you cannot accompany me on the paths I must walk now. Please forgive me.

She mentally closed a door on her memories, locked it, and forbade herself to open it again.

"Andrew, my pet." Was that a properly saccharine British endearment? It seemed to be, judging by how he straightened up. She walked her fingers up his chest. "Please forgive me a silly girl's nerves. I'm somewhat overwhelmed by the thought of finally becoming completely yours." She traced his lower lip with a single finger. "Can you ever forgive me?"

"Of course." He was still eyeing her cautiously, dammit.

She needed something more, something to keep her mind away from Raoul and Andrew's thoughts far from her motives. What games had they enjoyed the most during the past year?

Something to sharpen the senses, with a bright edge of pain.

"Or should I call you my lord now?"

His eyes lit, recognizing their codeword, before he veiled them. "Those games are too risky at this time, Celeste. Your first taste of emotion sets the stage for all following drinks. To have it colored by pain . . ."

"Is it so bad if I enjoy it?" She cupped his face between her hands.

He was watching her mouth. His tongue slid over his lips, showing his fangs for an instant.

"If it takes us both to the heights?" She sharply twisted his earlobe and quickly released it.

He arched up onto his toes and grabbed her, his cock thrusting hard against her belly. "Bitch!"

His mouth crushed down on hers, his teeth ravaging her lips. She yielded immediately, drunk on pain and her management of him.

The great bouquet fell unnoticed to the floor. The scent of crushed roses slid into the room, no more noticed by its occupants than vanished memories or destroyed promises.

PART TWO

WAR

Six

GENEVA, AUGUST 1808

Jean-Marie took another sip of Turkish coffee and slowly perused the latest issue of *The Monitor*, looking for the latest news from Paris about important aristocrats. This was, after all, part of his job as a British spy, even if nobody had asked him to look for the *marquise* d'Agelet. Beside him, a proper English breakfast of eggs, bacon, and buttered toast with strawberry jam steamed gently in the morning air.

The bacon and jam had been expensively smuggled in from Britain, using funds gained from playing cards with recuperating French officers at this lakeside resort in the Alps. No matter what government ruled in Paris—the Committee of Public Safety, the Directorate, and now the *Emperor* Napoleon, hah!—their servants still preferred to heal here.

He'd done well at last night's game, enough to indulge himself with the ostentatious treat, although he was doing so out here on the terrace overlooking the lovely Alpine lake, rather than inside where his *vampiro* housemates slept.

Here at the crossroads of Europe, almost anything was acceptable, so long as one was discreet and paid the necessary bribes. Their business of operating a letter drop for the British Secret Service had gone very well, especially with their gambling and frequent amours to cloak the presence of strangers. Rodrigo had also, of course, managed to find at least a dozen other more respectable ways to make money.

The big Spaniard appeared in the doorway, as if conjured up by Jean-Marie's thoughts. His skin lacked its usual golden glow, and his mouth was very tight, with white lines bracketing it.

Jean-Marie began to carefully fold his newspaper. If Rodrigo was disturbed, any sane man would be sharpening a sword. He chose the gentlest greeting possible. "Good morning, *mon frère*. Would you care for some coffee?"

The dark chocolate eyes broke away from the placid waters and snowcapped peaks to consider him. "I—yes, thank you."

A chill ran down his spine. Rodrigo, talking in broken sentences?

Jean-Marie poured a cup of black coffee and set it down across the table.

"Will you look at these accounts for me, please? I'm not sure if I've tallied them up correctly." His friend handed Jean-Marie a piece of paper and folded himself into a chair.

Double-check that Rodrigo had accurately deciphered the latest message from London? What the hell was Whitehall asking them to do, to have upset him so much? *Nom de Dieu*, if those British pigs wanted them to turn traitor against the United States . . .

"It's only a matter of accounts, Jean-Marie, although it does make me wish I was back in Texas, where Englishmen never come." Rodrigo's fingers slowly released their abruptly gained, brutally tight grasp of Jean-Marie's wrist. "If you would, please?"

"At once, *mon frère*." He abandoned his bacon and strawberry jam without a backward glance.

He encountered Sara, her peignoir falling off her shoulders, as soon as he reentered the house. "Coffee? Isn't there any tea?"

"Sara, hush." He jerked his head toward the terrace.

"*Mierda.*" She bit her lip, studying Rodrigo. "I was hoping never to see that expression on his face again."

She was worried enough about Rodrigo to stop thinking about herself?

"Do you know what's wrong?"

"No, not yet. I'm about to find out."

"I will wait with him until you return." She patted him on the shoulder—reassuringly? *Mon Dieu*, that was a change in their relationship.

"Don't be too frightened. As long as he turns to one of us for help, he hasn't let his darker memories overwhelm him."

Jean-Marie nodded his understanding and went to the library. Ten minutes later, he'd deciphered the message twice. Pursing his lips, he burned the *en clair* version and strolled back to the terrace.

Sara was sitting beside Rodrigo, her hands wrapped about his arm and their glossy heads close together. They were speaking very softly—far too quietly for even him to hear—and their attitude resonated of years of trust and shared experiences. Not equals or lovers, but dear friends.

Rodrigo's shoulders had even lost some of their previous tautness, and his mouth curved a little.

No matter how much Jean-Marie loathed Sara for what she'd done to him, he had to admit that he himself could not reach Rodrigo during the nightmares. Only she could, because the same agony touched her.

Five hundred years ago, Rodrigo had been captured and forced to become a *vampiro*. When a century of torture had failed to break him, his brutal master had purchased a young Jewish slave girl—Sara—planning to make Rodrigo watch her being tortured. A century later, neither Rodrigo nor Sara had shattered from the continuing horror. Instead, Rodrigo had managed to kill their master and escape with Sara.

Sara had privately told the story to Jean-Marie in fragments, confiding few details and none whatsoever from before her time in captivity. But sometimes, she or Rodrigo would have nightmares. Then the other one would offer comfort, speaking in whispers like now.

Curious though he was about almost everything, Jean-Marie wasn't sure he wanted to know what they said.

*   *   *

Rodrigo's head snapped up at the all-too-deliberate thud of a boot heel. Jean-Marie was far too graceful a dancer and too experienced a spy to have accidentally announced his presence. He must be giving them time to compose themselves. *Dios mío*, had he allowed so much of his alarm to show that his young *hermano* would try to protect him?

He quickly rearranged his features into a more social mask. "You've studied it, *amigo*?"

"The orange and lemon harvest in Spain this year needs looking into." Jean-Marie tossed the sheet onto the table, with its three neat columns of figures, and sat down.

At least they could talk freely in front of the servants who were blood-bonded to himself and Sara. They came from Turkish families who'd spent generations serving in *comitivas*, a *vampiro*'s retinue, and considered it a special honor to serve *vampiros mayores* like himself and Sara. They knew their lives and family honor were forfeit if they were anything less than completely loyal and discreet. Their term of service was ten years, after which they'd return home to be replaced. Even so, he excused the butler, signaling him to keep watch.

"Not surprising there'd be some upheaval after the Spanish trampled that French army at Bailén," Jean-Marie added, pouring a fresh cup of coffee.

"We're going to Spain?" hissed Sara, sounding horrified.

"Madrid," confirmed Rodrigo in only slightly happier tones.

"Surely you can refuse?"

"Why?" He disentangled himself and sat up straight, his face a stony mask. "We serve the cause of peace and liberty. How can I invoke sentimental reasons for not returning to my native land, especially when nobody in my family is still alive?"

"But the pain and the nightmares . . ." She shook her head. "You haven't been back in over five hundred years."

Rodrigo refused to allow himself to flinch. Rape, being forced to become a *vampiro*, and two hundred years of torture and captivity provided ample fuel for terrors in the night. A simple journey would not make him run.

"It does mention they have few experienced Spaniards for this role," Jean-Marie said quietly. Ever the trained soldier and diplomat, who could couch military necessity in the sweetest of terms.

May he never learn that the older brother he loved so well was a knight who'd committed mortal sin after mortal sin, in order to stay alive long enough for revenge. Who barely tolerated those memories now and had never taken them into a confessional. Or had walked into a church since he'd been rescued.

"Bah!" Sara spat fiercely on the carpet. "Who cares what London does or does not want, has or can get? They can find somebody else!"

"Sara, *mi dulce*, we have aided them—flawlessly—for almost twenty years since the first bloodshed in Paris." Rodrigo took her hands, forcing her to look into his eyes. "If they demand my presence now—someone senior, in such a difficult, important location—it probably means they're about to send an army there."

"So they want the best help possible, of course. But they shouldn't risk you, especially when I need you."

Jean-Marie rolled his eyes.

"I must go." Rodrigo's voice was very harsh. He would not let his fears rule him and keep him from his duty.

"We will all go," Sara dictated.

Risk the only family he had left? "No! You two can stay here."

"Never!" Sara and Jean-Marie shouted simultaneously—and stared at each other, shocked by their first unforced agreement on anything. United, they turned to glare at Rodrigo.

Rodrigo gaped. Those two, who fought viciously over anything and everything—except how to seduce information out of unsuspecting fools—*both* wanted to accompany him into danger?

"You'll be safer here." *Sabe Dios*, it was the truth.

"Don't be absurd." Sara sniffed loudly, fluffing up her silk ruffles until she looked like an empress in coronation regalia.

"You're the leader of our family, and we're a team. We stay together," Jean-Marie declared, linking hands with Sara. "If you leave without us, we'll follow on the next ship."

Rodrigo muttered disgustedly but couldn't bring himself to destroy Jean-Marie and Sara's rare unity. They'd be at each other's throats if he left them behind. Matters would be much worse if Jean-Marie suddenly started to age.

A chill draft brushed the nape of his neck but he shrugged it off. Jean-Marie was over a century old, but he'd lived well, even if he'd done so without the carnal emotions a *concubino compañero* craved. Surely there'd be no problems any time soon.

Even so, it would be best to keep together their team of three, who had done so well together for so long.

"*Bien.* I wouldn't be happy without my family." He rose, holding out his arms, and they embraced.

He spared one last prayer to the Savior who'd rescued him and kept him safe for so long. *But may I not have to visit the northwest and my wife's tomb . . .*

THE CORPUS CHRISTI CHAPEL IN THE CATHEDRAL OF TOLEDO, SPAIN, SEPTEMBER 29, 1808

Rodrigo slipped into the back of the small chapel, wondering yet again why he'd spent a day journeying from Madrid to Spain's ancient capital. Why had he come to the church where he'd last seen his beloved wife—and on the day she'd always kept vigil for him during the long years she'd waited for him?

The small chapel was crowded, many people having come to ask for San Rafael Arcángel's protection for their escape or for the healing of their loved ones, who'd been wounded fighting the invaders. Yet Rodrigo was isolated, as if an invisible shell kept the others away from him where he stood beside a pillar.

He automatically crossed himself, the beauty of the ancient Mozarabic rite embracing him. Only six parishes in all of Spain still celebrated this version of the Catholic rite daily, with this chapel as its center.

How many centuries since he'd heard this most Spanish of Christian rites, which had survived and flourished under the Muslim conquest? The rite which sang the most eloquently of the *Santísima Virgen*, the Mother of God and Lady whose purity makes all men better?

The congregation answered the priest, their voices ringing out lovingly and trustingly, certain that the Lord and San Rafael Arcángel would bring their loved ones home safe and sound.

For the first time, Rodrigo wondered if healing might be possible, instead of always carrying scars and doing penance.

Touched by their faith, he bowed his head and prayed harder than he had in years.

San Rafael Arcángel, I have returned to Spain, as my lady wife asked. I am a sinner who deserves nothing. But if aught remains undone, please answer her prayers, she who was the best of all women. Amen.

The priest elevated the Host, sunlight striking the golden chalice until it seemed to rise up to Heaven. Everyone was utterly silent, transformed by the moment's power.

A single strand of golden light danced off the high altar and fell squarely on Rodrigo's forehead, soothing the great scar like holy oil.

MADRID, LATE OCTOBER 1808

Jean-Marie cursed everyone calling themselves a servant of George III *and* intelligent. He set about deciphering the message again.

"Well?" Sara demanded, hanging over him. "Are they still idiots or merely forgetful?"

"Probably idiots." He flipped open the marine dictionary and started counting pages, looking for the first one listed in the ciphered message.

"Let me bring you some more light. You will go blind, sitting here in the dark, reading those scribbles."

"But—"

"We don't need to maintain a romantic atmosphere. I've already had a nice tumble with Señor Garcia, who believes deep growls and sweet talk make every woman want to fall into his arms."

Despite the decades they'd been together and all the seduction techniques he'd seen and heard, Jean-Marie still leaned back and stared at her. "You're joking, *oui?*"

"Hardly." She shrugged, setting a candelabrum down on the table. "Of course, almost any phrase and setting can be amorous if the tone and glances accompanying it are."

He shook his head, well aware they were chattering to distract themselves until Rodrigo came home.

Last spring, the Spanish people had spontaneously risen up against their French occupiers, climaxing with their startling defeat of a large French army at Bailén. Napoleon hadn't risen from nowhere to emperor by ignoring barefaced challenges to his rule, especially when the puppet Spanish king was his brother. Now rumors were running rampant that Napoleon himself was lurking at the border, ready to invade Spain with his Grande Army.

Nobody knew what had become of the small British army, who'd landed in Portugal last summer and defeated its French invaders.

Or at least, he and Sara hadn't known until this message had arrived a few minutes ago.

The last candle caught fire. It leapt high briefly before settling down, bringing a circle of surprisingly bright light into the small library.

Sara's breath hissed out. "Oh no . . ."

He stiffened, wondering what she'd seen in his hair.

The front door opened and shut, slamming back into place against the bitter weather outside. Not in living memory had anyone seen such a winter.

"Sara? Jean-Marie?" Rodrigo was home at last.

Jean-Marie immediately set down his pencil and shoved back his chair.

She stared at him, her eyes wide and staring. Her hand covered her mouth for a moment before she patted him on the cheek and ran into the hallway. "We are here, dearest Rodrigo."

Why the hell had she done that? Sara was never affectionate with him unless she hoped for sex.

In the foyer of their small town house, Sara was clasping Rodrigo fiercely, totally disregarding his snow-splattered greatcoat in a startling need for comfort. He was hugging her and crooning to her protectively. But he held out a hand to Jean-Marie, to equalize their circle as he always did. *"Mi hermano."*

He entered the embrace gladly, clinging to the only family he'd ever known. For all its faults, it was the one who'd welcomed him and sheltered him. Long minutes passed before they were gathered around the library table.

Massive shutters and heavy velvet curtains muffled the storm's sounds, while the massive bookcases filled with gilded leather-bound books lent the conversation a spurious air of relaxation. A heavy desk offered space for writing or impressing visitors.

The fire hissed and sparked on the hearth. Given Madrid's chaos, Rodrigo had felt it best to adopt a bourgeois level of comfort, not their usual lavish opulence.

"What does the new message from London say?" Rodrigo asked, leaning back in his chair and sipping a glass of sherry. Ever since they'd arrived in Spain, he'd taken great delight in drinking only Spanish wines, especially the finest sherries.

"Go to Galicia, in the northwest, and help the British navy supply the Galician and Asturian Juntas. There's a big port there called . . ." Jean-Marie looked for the exact name.

"La Coruña, in Spanish. Or Corunna, in English," Rodrigo supplied. A muscle ticked rapidly in his jaw.

"Correct. They want it done immediately, of course."

"Is it ever anything else?" Sara muttered and perched on the arm of Rodrigo's armchair.

"Has anyone picked up the other message?" Rodrigo queried.

"Where we must give the proper messenger the code book and the message?" Jean-Marie shook his head. "Nobody has arrived with the password."

"They've placed a very tight lock on that one." Rodrigo kissed

Sara on the cheek and rose, drumming his fingers on a bookcase. "It must be very important."

"Or the courier is."

They both looked askance at her, and she shrugged. "There can be more than one explanation!"

"True, which makes it all the more vital one of us remains here in the capital to deliver it." Rodrigo lightly slapped the table. "I will do so, and you two will go to Galicia."

"Don't be absurd, Rodrigo. You're Galician. You have to go so you can speak the local language—Gallego, *oui*?—to the Galicians."

"I will not leave you here in Madrid."

"As a native, your *Gallego* is far better than mine." Jean-Marie didn't mention the years they'd used that language as a form of code. He also kept his tone level, striving to remain casual. If he let his family think about his proposal, they'd object—and they'd be the ones risking their lives, not him. He wouldn't, couldn't allow that.

Rodrigo hesitated. "Surely the British must arrive soon and claim their message. Perhaps if you came within a week, it would work."

"No! Rodrigo, look at his hair!"

"What are you talking about?" Jean-Marie stared at her and started to rise.

Rodrigo's eyes narrowed. His hand came down on Jean-Marie's shoulder, forcing him back into his seat. He gently brushed back the strands at Jean-Marie's temples before stepping back. His harsh features were graven harder than stone, except for a single tear touching one eye. "*Madre de Dios,*" he groaned.

"You see it, too." Her voice was tight and hoarse.

Rodrigo nodded. "There is no doubt."

"Will you two tell me what the hell is going on here?" Jean-Marie roared, coming out of his seat to pound on the table.

Rodrigo hitched himself onto the desk's edge. "*Compañeros* have a long life but are not immortal." His voice was darker than his eyes.

Jean-Marie's stomach promptly knotted. This conversation did not sound promising.

"They can die of mortal causes, with death coming very quickly after it first approaches. You have lived for more than a century, always looking the same age you did when you first tasted Sara's blood. Now . . ." He swallowed hard before continuing. "Silver touches your hair. You have very little time left."

Jean-Marie vehemently shook his head, but Rodrigo nodded, inflexible certainty written across his face. "I am sure of this, *mi hermano*. Would that I was not!"

And Rodrigo never, never lied.

Jean-Marie turned away to the window. Dying? Dead? Surely Rodrigo must be wrong, and yet, he was growing slower, less interested in blood or carnal excitement. Were those signs his bond to Sara— and the long life he'd gained through that bond—were finally slipping away from him?

No, Rodrigo had to be wrong. He wasn't going to die, dammit, not like this. Not when he'd dreamed for so long of outliving the war and finding Hélène d'Agelet again. He'd gone back to Sainte-Pazanne, her family home, during the false peace and learned she'd survived the first year of the Reign of Terror—but hadn't been seen since. He'd allowed himself to hope somewhere, somehow, they'd be reunited, and this time, he wouldn't be stupid enough to walk away from her for her own sake.

He was going to fight, even if he had to play dice with fate.

He leaned back against the shutters and studied his friend.

"How long do you think I have?"

"Based on what I learned as a sex slave in the eastern *vampiro* courts?"

"Out with it, *mon frère*." Jean-Marie waved his hand, encouraging Rodrigo to talk.

"Three months, six at the most, if you spend the entire time in bed with a *vampiro mayor*."

Jean-Marie grimaced despite himself. *Too damn soon. But Rodrigo had to be wrong—at least this once.*

"In that case, I'm staying in Madrid." The first necessity was to get them to safety.

"No!" they shouted in unison.

Mon Dieu, they meant so much to him—even Sara. He couldn't let them be trapped here, on his account. The risks were too great to chance anyone else's life.

"Be reasonable." He slapped his thigh, demanding they accept his logic. "If—when—the French army comes, I am a Frenchman and can be accepted as a French officer. But I can also pass muster as a Castilian."

"Barely," Rodrigo muttered.

"But enough—more than you can say for your grasp of French military protocol, Rodrigo. I am the only one of us who can do both. I'll stay here and wait for that so-important British messenger." Who would surely come soon. After all, he was supposed to have been here last week.

Rodrigo growled something under his breath but didn't openly disagree.

"You're the best for speaking *Gallego* to a Galician, Rodrigo. Sara will go with you."

"Nooo," she moaned, sinking back into her own chair. "You're mine. I can't let you go like this."

"There is no other choice."

"You could turn him into a *vampiro*, Rodrigo, or he could become your lover?"

Jean-Marie stared at her, knowing damn well his horror was more than equaled by his friend's.

"You of all people should understand why I wish no *hijos* of my own, after how our *creador* tore our sanity apart when he gave us *El Abrazo*," Rodrigo protested.

"You're a far better man than he was, Rodrigo," she countered. "Your *hijos* would be cherished and protected."

"I will not take the chance on destroying the sanity of anyone I care about by giving them *El Abrazo*. He would be better off dead than insane for all eternity."

"And I—while I care for Rodrigo as a brother, I do not wish him as my lover." Jean-Marie came to stand beside him. "Even if I did, it would only gain me a few more months." It was an easier option to refuse than Rodrigo's vehement rejection of siring *vampiros*. Rodrigo's *hijo* would have an eternity to find Hélène, if she still lived.

"Perhaps if you used force, Rodrigo?" Sara suggested hopefully.

"Never."

Even Sara went no further down a path slammed shut in that tone of voice.

Rodrigo took a turn around the room before he planted his feet and faced them squarely. Jean-Marie had never seen him so stern, or look so much a leader of men.

"Very well. Sara and I will depart for Galicia. There are rumors part of Napoleon's army is clearing the way for him to its east. After we fulfill our mission—or if we cannot because matters are in worse shape than we've heard—we will go to my ancestral lands in San Leandro. They are so remote, no invading army should disturb them. You can rejoin us there, a day's walk north of Lugo, the old Roman capital."

"I will do so." Jean-Marie committed the names to memory. He'd leave for Galicia once he delivered the message. Even if gray hair was dangerous for him, surely nothing would change that quickly. Or if it did, he might slow it down by spending a little time—not too much, please God!—in Sara's bed.

"We will also leave blood for you, in bottles of wine." Rodrigo glanced down at Sara, who vigorously nodded. "A month, perhaps two months' supply."

"*Merci bien!*" He ground his teeth at his overenthusiasm.

"It is not much, not nearly enough." Rodrigo shrugged. "Only blood and sex with a *vampiro* would help you live longer. But there are no *vampiros* left in Madrid, its few natives having been slaughtered by the mob during the spring uprising. The closest are in Andalusia, the opposite direction from Galicia."

"One could almost wish mobs weren't so very prone to slaughtering *vampiros*," Sara commented. "If even one survived, we could compel it to feed Jean-Marie."

The intended beneficiary shuddered.

"But he'd be a most untrustworthy protector," Rodrigo pointed out.

"True." She sighed. "What a pity, since he makes such a deliciously scented *concubino compañero.*"

Nom de Dieu, much as he loathed her description of himself, he had to admit she was right: He'd need to be very careful. After a century as a *compañero,* his body was very well attuned to *vampiro* blood and emotion, something *vampiros* found almost as attractive as feeding on one of themselves.

"Jean-Marie will do better relying on his wits and his speed, which are as great or greater than those of any young *vampiro,*" Rodrigo countered, "even with the French army coming back—and bringing their own *vampiros* with them."

"I'll watch for them," Jean-Marie promised dryly. "And I'll do my best to join you as quickly as possible."

THE VALENCIA ROAD EAST OF MADRID,
EARLY DECEMBER 1808

Hélène d'Agelet took another step and another, straining to lift her feet out of the mud rather than slogging through it. The weather was worse than appalling, changing from snow to rain and back again with the frequency of a drunken madman intent on causing the most misery possible. Her team had ridden mules until yesterday, horses being nearly impossible to find in this war-torn land. After painfully learning even that much wealth made them far too conspicuous, they'd chosen to walk instead, keeping only one mule for their baggage.

Snow tumbled down from the sky, promising a wretched end to a dreadful journey. She batted it off yet again from her widow's heavy black veil, trying not to let her *vampira* strength inadvertently tear the fragile silken layers protecting her from suspicious watchers.

On every side, hordes of strangers—on foot or in carts—shoved and pushed against her, desperate to escape the victorious French. Progress was slow, motion accomplished by facing forward or edging sideways. And always fighting the smothering cloth for every breath of air.

She wanted to tear it from her face. Or fall into bed and sleep. Or simply be held in the arms of a strong man who'd loved her long and well. Not that she'd experienced that simple delight since her time with Jean-Marie St. Just.

Celeste, on the other hand, could turn ripping her veil into a seductive prelude for a good feeding, an art Hélène had never mastered. Instead, she went on prearranged rendezvous with gentlemen sent by the British Secret Service. Sometimes she even saw the same man twice, but it still seemed calculated, especially since they always watched her out of the corners of their eyes. Worried, no doubt, she might lose her temper and incinerate them.

Which was probably why the veteran spy Harry Wade was up in front with Celeste and Sir Andrew. He apparently felt his presence was necessary to make sure *la petite*'s eye-catching femininity could distract any Frenchman who might become suspicious of them.

He was not walking with her, which would have ensured the team's "secret weapon" remained safe. As a *prosaico*, he was the only one who could protect her, since he alone could walk the streets at all hours of day or night.

Hélène sighed and reminded herself not to be jealous. She should look after her younger sister, even if she did sometimes long for the attention their *creador* seemed to shower on Celeste. Hélène had managed to survive without it, although dreams of Jean-Marie St. Just occupied far too many of her nights.

She drew her cloak around her, ducked her head, and hauled herself up another steep slope, the night's bitter misery destroying any lingering pleasure from heated dreams.

A bell began to ring sweetly in the distance, from high atop a hill. It was probably the monastery of Our Lady of the Angels at Cerro de los œngeles, just south of Madrid. It sounded like angels singing.

Similar little things would have pleased *Maman* and Papa during the Vendée's rebellion. Papa would smile at *Maman*, from where he led his troops along a muddy road, and their expressions would say so much of shared love and trust.

Hélène's eyes misted. For a moment, she thought she saw *Maman* and Papa walking hand in hand along the side of this abominable highway, although it didn't resemble the Vendée's wooded roads in the least. They were strong and healthy, dressed in the same sturdy, honest clothing they'd worn throughout that summer.

They looked back at her over their shoulders, just as they had then, and beckoned to her.

Instinctively, she sidled closer to them. The chaotic horde somehow made way for her, and the ground was firmer under her feet.

Her parents smiled, and Papa began to whistle a march, very softly. She hummed it under her breath, dreaming she was a child again when he would keep her safe from all dangers.

The road slanted downward, changing the pressure on the back of her legs. Her brain stirred, turning away from days long past and reluctantly reacquainting itself with icy mud.

She was now marching straight ahead with nobody bumping against either of her shoulders. In fact, there was only a narrow file hurrying past on the opposite side of the road—and a mere scattering of people ahead of her.

She came to a complete halt and stared.

Celeste? Wade? Sir Andrew?

Surely she should be able to see two tall men and one small female.

Ahead of her, the wide road stretched to the outskirts of the city less than a league away, under the clear sky. Even with the night's darkness, her *vampiro* eyesight allowed her to be certain there were only a few unmistakably short, impoverished beings.

Nom de Dieu . . .

She spun around and ran the few steps back up to the crest of the hill. A long look to the east reluctantly convinced her no one there answered her team's description.

Worse, the eastern sky was starting to lighten. If she didn't take cover before the first ray of dawn, she'd die—whether or not she found her sister and her *creador*.

Merde.

She'd have to use the backup plan: find someplace on her own to hide. She'd make her way later to pick up the message, which only she and Sir Andrew knew how to read.

She'd need to feed, too, and very soon. She'd only been a *vampira* for fifteen years, so she still needed sweet emotion and blood every day. Wade was supposed to have taken care of her this morning.

Still cursing under her breath, she hastened toward Madrid, plotting where to go, using gossip she'd overheard during the journey from the port. It was probably a far better guide than anything their London lecturer had said weeks ago.

God willing, the French wouldn't seize her companions before they were reunited. The tactics of Napoleon's police minister, to break *vampiros* and British spies, would begin with the stuff of nightmares.

To have *la petite* subjected to that? Best pray for a swift death.

Hélène shuddered and crossed herself.

SEVEN

A DAY'S RIDE NORTH OF LUGO,
THE PROVINCIAL CAPITAL OF GALICIA, THE SAME DAY

Despite his best efforts, Rodrigo could not stop himself from leaning forward every time the road rounded another bend to commit another set of changes to memory. His knight's sword, forged from the finest Toledo steel and given to him over five centuries ago by the king of Castile, thumped his horse's flank regularly, reminding him of what he'd sworn to defend and how he'd failed.

New shrines and chapels, a farm here and there, or a bridge. And always the sights and sounds of the land fed his soul, soothing aches he'd tried to forget. Crystalline webs of ice, willow trees arching down to the river under a gust of wind only to spring back, a golden eagle spiraling overhead, a roe-deer springing away through the ferns, the music of the many rivers singing over the rocks . . .

"Do you think there are any French around here?" Sara asked, casting an uneasy glance at a small church's bell tower, starkly prominent atop a knoll.

"Perhaps, since a sentry could see for miles from the church tower. These mountains are why Galicia was one of the first kingdoms the Moors left. But it's unlikely since we're too far from the coast or a main road." He didn't point out that anyone traveling hard and fast from Madrid to Corunna, especially in a foul winter like this one, was hardly likely to want to visit San Leandro.

She shuddered, visibly fighting not to clutch at her horse's reins. He eyed her warily, ready to rescue the patient mare yet again.

"All I'm certain of is that these mountains will keep us from any form of civilized entertainment." She did not, quite, pout. Even she had agreed they needed to leave the Galician Junta's arrogance and idiocy behind before Napoleon arrived, even if it meant retreating to a distant village for the winter.

Thankfully, as *vampiros mayores*, they required very little blood to survive. San Leandro should be more than large enough to support the two of them.

"My latest lover—you remember, that cabinetmaker in Lugo?— said San Leandro is a very prosperous little town, thanks to San Rafael Arcángel's church."

A chapel dedicated to San Rafael Arcángel? *To whom my beloved wife prayed for healing and a safe return for me?*

"Many people are healed there, even though it's a very difficult journey climaxed by crossing a narrow bridge. Apparently there's also a convent, hospital, and a couple of good inns," she chattered on, casting a considering glance at him. "Don Fernando Perez, the local grandee, is so well-off that he sent his wife and family off to England, while he's in Seville with the Junta Central."

"Flourishing, indeed," Rodrigo agreed, finding it hard to speak past his throat's tightness. *Gracias a Dios*, his prayers for all these long years had been answered.

"Enough people"—Sara's voice dropped to the softest of whispers— "You could give *El Abrazo* to someone."

"Sara, no!" Rodrigo roared. His mount shied violently, nearly tossing him out of the saddle and onto the road. Sara's horse reared, whinnying its alarm. Their servants' mules brayed their alarm, and some tried to buck off their packs.

By the time peace was restored, Rodrigo had sworn he would never allow the subject to be raised again. He would also remain completely disciplined, no matter what happened when they reached his birthplace.

Even so, he still unconsciously drew rein at the top of the pass leading into San Leandro, his heart leaping with joy.

It was nestled in a high mountain valley, as it had always been, surrounded by great peaks which took the brunt of the worst weather and turned it into soft flowing rivers. The town itself was full of golden buildings, stucco sweeping over sturdy stone, with warm red tile roofs and stone chimneys. The church's graceful arches and spires lifted to the skies, as if reaching up in prayer.

In the distance, an old, square watchtower stood guard on the mountainside over the only pass where a northern enemy could approach. *Por Dios*, how many times had he paced that tower, dreaming he was a warrior grown?

Two men approached, driving a half dozen fat blond cattle with the ancient local breed's curving horns. The senior was a tall man of more than thirty years, with dark hair, olive skin, and dark brown eyes. The other was his teenaged counterpart, dressed in the same sturdy, though not rich, clothing. The adult looked them over curiously, assessing their obviously Spanish clothes and equipment, and nodded politely.

"*Bon día, señor,*" Rodrigo greeted him, automatically falling back into his native tongue despite centuries away.

The other's face lit up. "*Bon dia! Benvido a San Leandro!*"

Rodrigo grinned back. Welcome to San Leandro, indeed.

Rodrigo, Sara whispered, using the mind link they shared as *hijos* of the same *creador, he could be your older brother.*

I know. Rodrigo's throat was as dry as dust. *Madre de Dios*, how completely had his family established themselves in this mountain fastness?

"You haven't seen anyone else?" Sir Andrew asked quietly.

"No, sir," Jean-Marie answered for the third time, keeping well back in the shadows. His intuition was kicking him like an angry mule, insisting he leave immediately.

Behind them rose the great *Mudéjar* tower, its square bulk marking a medieval Spanish church built on a mosque's foundations. Before them, a narrow street led to a broad avenue in the distance, every inch of it overlooked by layers of balconies.

Why the devil were they still standing about, chattering like friends in a London club? Madrid was a lawless city, only barely controlled by its new French masters. If any French soldier or sympathizer happened to overhear a whispered conversation in *English*, there'd be hell to pay.

Even more damning, there were four of them here: himself, Sir Andrew, Wade—his second and a *prosaico*, plus Celeste, a young *vampira*.

Sir Andrew was still silent, one finger tapping the small, leather-bound marine dictionary. It was the British code book, which Jean-Marie had only delivered after a series of challenges and counter-challenges. Its owner would be able to read British Secret Service messages throughout Spain and Portugal. Jean-Marie heartily admired how closely Sir Andrew held it.

What he didn't understand—or approve of—were Sir Andrew's companions.

Jean-Marie scanned his surroundings once again with all his senses, this time letting them linger on Sir Andrew's companions.

Sir Andrew was an impressive man, who looked fully capable of living up to his legend as one of the longest-living, British *vampiro* field agents. Yet he was accompanied by a *prosaico*—the embodiment of clumsiness compared to a *vampiro*, no matter how competent—to this meeting, when the utmost secrecy and speed were required.

He'd also brought a *vampira*, a female who reeked of men's lust, as if they'd spent days doing nothing but enjoying her carnal favors. Despite that—despite her heavy eyes, swollen mouth, and the odors of stale musk and sweat rising from her flesh—she still eyed them hungrily, gliding her tongue over her lip and flashing a bit of teeth in a *vampira*'s invitation to party. No wonder the *prosaico* sported an erection which made him walk stiff-legged!

Worst of all, Sir Andrew leered at her, too—staring at her mouth or her breasts when she let her cloak fall open. Every time she stretched or arched her back, he'd lose his thread of thought and have to begin again.

He'd introduced her as his *hija*. As her *creador*, she should be helplessly in thrall to him—*not* the other way around.

Jean-Marie shifted, ready to slip away. Thankfully, the *vampira* had paid no attention to him after her initial inspection. Perhaps there was something good to be said for his hair turning salt-and-pepper in the past two weeks, no matter how bleak it made his future. Obviously, appearing forty had removed him from her list of eligible men.

The *vampira* and *prosaico* obviously came to the same conclusion and began to walk off, their heads close together to enable a whispered conversation.

Sir Andrew's gaze returned to Jean-Marie. "London's orders are to carry out our mission immediately, regardless of anything else. How much longer will you remain here?"

"Sir?" The unusual question flummoxed him. Frankly, it was none of the man's business.

"We're missing one of our team." For the first time, Sir Andrew's voice was crisp and professional, albeit edged with worry.

How the hell had one of his people disappeared? Was that a euphemism for a worse fate?

"I don't believe Hélène's dead."

Hélène? Could it be his Hélène? No, surely there had to be more than one Hélène. He had to stop coming on guard every time anyone mentioned a woman named Hélène.

"The French would be more likely to try to capture—and turn her."

"Her?" Jean-Marie came alert, instinctively sliding his dirk into his palm. A woman in danger from the French? Or the French sympathizers, who'd be more vicious?

"A *vampira*—and a firestarter." Sir Andrew's voice was softer than an owl's wing, relying on Jean-Marie's *compañero* hearing to catch it—and keep it from *prosaico* eavesdroppers.

Merde, the greatest of all weapons that could be employed against *vampiros*, especially in wartime. A firestarter could light gunpowder as easily as any artilleryman—or incinerate a *vampiro* with a thought. Only they could act faster than a *vampiro* could move, which made her the only truly terrifying opponent.

His lips tightened, pulling back into a snarl. She had to be found, and quickly, before the French destroyed her.

But could his Hélène have become a *vampira*? No, that would be too much to ask for, to have her gain such a long life.

"I'm glad you recognize her importance," Sir Andrew commented dryly. "We had to dodge some French sentries, on the Valencia road just outside Madrid. We didn't see her when we took shelter, and we haven't seen her since. I don't believe they have her—but I don't know where she is."

"Any ideas?" His throat was sandpaper dry.

"Hélène knows how to contact you, since she too can read the message. I argued against it, but my superiors insisted."

Indeed? Both of Jean-Marie's eyebrows flew up. She wasn't just a weapon—she was considered smart and tough enough to be trusted with codes and contact information. Quite remarkable.

"Or she may be hiding from the sun. She's only a year older than Celeste as a *vampira*—and not as well fed." Regret flitted through his voice.

Jean-Marie's hands clenched into fists. The selfish fool had been enjoying himself, while not seeing to the health of his best asset? How the hell could such an idiot call himself a professional?

"Poor Celeste. She's been very brave and hasn't said a word about it." Sir Andrew watched his lover's hips sway invitingly beside Wade's, highlighted in a patch of moonlight. He swallowed before going on. "We've tried to distract her, of course."

"Excuse me?" Why would the slut feel any need to be brave?

"You don't know? Well, of course I haven't mentioned their full names."

A frisson sparked through Jean-Marie's skin, painful as an electrical charge. Hélène? Surely it couldn't be . . .

"Celeste de Sainte-Pazanne is the younger sister of the *Marquise* Hélène d'Agelet."

Hélène d'Agelet? Here—and possibly captured by the French? Jean-Marie's core promptly slammed itself into a lava pool, hotter than all the fires of hell and more painful than a sword thrust through his gut. He gritted his teeth, forcing himself to regain control. Nobody else would help her if he didn't.

"Thank you." Sir Andrew squeezed his shoulder. "I won't mention this to Celeste; don't want to bring the darling's hopes up too high, lest they be dashed."

Darling? The bitch had shown no signs of being interested in anything except men and pleasure. Something rang false, very false in any expressions of concern, given her behavior.

May God help this mission, because the Devil certainly seemed to be enjoying himself among it.

"Good luck."

"And to you, sir."

They shook hands before Sir Andrew loped after his team members.

Jean-Marie turned his back on them without a second thought.

London had arranged two methods for contacting him. Sir Andrew had used the first—and more cautious—approach, which could only be initiated during daylight. The other was for crises and assumed the contact point was constantly manned.

He stepped back into the shadows, counted to thirty, lest they'd been watched, and took off. He'd plotted a dozen routes between the two points months ago, as soon as they'd reached Madrid, just in case something like this happened.

Even as he kept watch for the unusual, a back corner of his mind considered the worst case. The Valencia road came in from the southeast. He needed to plan how to search it tomorrow, if he didn't find her tonight.

He'd meant to leave tomorrow for Galicia, after delivering this message. He'd have to wait, even though he was growing old far faster than he'd hoped.

*   *   *

Hélène shrank deeper back into the shredded shrubbery, away from a French sentry's crisp tread, while the lights of Madrid shimmered invitingly far below. If the London idiots had paid more attention to the actual conditions in Spain, she would not have needed to hide herself in the midst of French fortifications.

Arranging the alternate meeting point for the public gardens at Buen Retiro, near the Observatory, might have seemed a good plan for a city at peace, especially when it was so close to the Valencia road's end. It was a damn risky one when the buildings and grounds had clearly been torn apart by professional troops. She hoped the city's people would see it return to its former glory, when all these piles of rubble and shattered trees stood tall and proud again.

Even more, she prayed her contact would see the chalk marks she'd left on the designated convent wall and come quickly, even though it was now hours later. It was also two days, almost three, since she'd last tasted the life-giving cocktail of blood and emotion. She was starting to stagger, even though she'd slept undisturbed yesterday in the abandoned wine cellar.

She'd actually considered sidling up to a drunken muleteer she'd seen, hideous thought! Thankfully, no man was handsome when compared to Jean-Marie St. Just, and she'd turned away.

But, *parbleu*, the fellow's bulging muscles had almost made him look acceptable . . .

She shuddered and rubbed her forehead, trying to force her abominable headache away, along with any chance she might actually carry out such an ill-advised, humiliating activity.

"Hélène!" A sibilant whisper reached her ears. A man and unmistakably French, even familiar. Jean-Marie? Could her exhaustion and loneliness be making her fantasize?

"Hélène." Callused fingertips brushed her arm as lightly as swan's-down.

"Jean-Marie!" Totally ignoring any need for stealth and uncaring what had brought him here, she flung herself at him. His arms closed hard around her, bringing her breathtakingly close to a solid masculine chest. She clung, most satisfactorily cozy.

He rubbed his cheek against the top of her head, caressing her hair. She sniffled happily, glad she'd stuffed the damn veil into her pack.

"We need to leave. Where are your things?"

"Only this leather pack." She pointed at it, forgetting he probably couldn't see anything in the dark. Although his scent wasn't exactly like any other *prosaico* she'd ever met.

He picked it up without so much as a fumble.

She gawked but told herself he must have spotted it in a patch of moonlight or starlight.

He caught her by the hand and guided her from the thicket, carefully leading her past the worst of the ensnaring branches and twigs. Within minutes, they were weaving through Madrid's archaic warren of streets, rarely stopping even to catch their breath.

Celeste stumbled and fell to the ground. The stupid Wade was on her in a moment to help her up—but she'd already seen what she needed: two horsemen watching them from a distance, with moonlight glinting on a spyglass.

In an impoverished land whose people could barely afford donkeys, much less mules, horses were a great rarity and usually had to be imported. But even at this hour and upwind from the beasts, she could tell the difference between horses and mules.

They were French soldiers or sympathizers, it didn't matter which. Nobody else would have the arrogance to display such valuable beasts so close to Madrid, when open war was about to break out between the so-called *Patriots* and Napoleon.

But why the devil had they shown themselves?

She stretched her memory back, struggling to remember her French master's hasty words during those few snatched minutes back in Portsmouth.

There were only two of them, both men, with no sign of a woman.

Merde! The fools hadn't captured Hélène. The self-righteous bitch who always succeeded in every mission, just as she'd killed Raoul with little more effort than snapping her fingers.

Celeste ground her teeth, fighting not to scream out loud. How could they have been so inept? She'd walked Hélène straight past their ambush. All they'd had to do was have their powerful *vampiro* bind her mind and grab her. Then take her back to France for questioning, which would end up with her alive and in the service of the Emperor—or dead.

Celeste truly didn't care which. The first would relieve her of the sin of fratricide, something she wasn't sure she could explain to Raoul in the hereafter. It might even stop her from ever seeing Raoul again, in this life or the next. But the second would be the proper penalty for Hélène's murder of Raoul.

Her fingers curled into claws, longing to rip out her sister's throat. She forced them to relax, one by one, and went back to considering the horsemen.

What would they say—they hadn't seen her in the darkness? She snorted in disgust and quickly covered it with a bout of coughing.

Now what?

Mercifully, she'd managed to cloak her true feelings for her sister well enough that Hélène still believed they both thought of each other as family. Celeste had given the excuse she didn't like to think or talk about any reminders of life in France.

Protocol dictated missing team members would rendezvous with the others at predetermined points. The first one was in Salamanca, northwest of Madrid and past the tall Guadarrama mountains. Hélène, the noble bitch—and murderess—would no doubt make every effort to rejoin them there.

Celeste would have to let her French masters know somehow. There should be something in those signs they'd taught her.

She'd have to keep Sir Andrew from suspecting anything. Given his propensity for thinking with his dick, the wonder would be if he had a coherent thought on any subject!

She snickered privately.

Maybe she could even lift that codebook Sir Andrew was clutching so closely and slip it to her friends soon.

Hélène hesitated when Jean-Marie opened the side gate into an elegant house's garden. "Yours?"

"Yes, of course. Don't worry—you'll be safe here." His hand tightened on hers, urging her forward.

"But will you be?" She fumbled for words to describe his danger, without saying she was a spy.

"Hélène." To her shock, he chuckled slightly. "I'm sorry, I forgot we haven't been properly introduced yet."

He released her, gave her a neat bow, and declaimed,

> "*And did those feet in ancient time*
> *Walk upon England's mountain green?*"

He waited expectantly, one eyebrow visibly arched in the light from the kitchen window.

She stared at him, her jaw dropping open. Him? Jean-Marie was the brilliant, long-lasting, British spy resident in Madrid? How had he swallowed his distaste for the Hanoverian kings and their minions long enough to serve them? Quite possibly for the same reasons she had.

She managed to recover herself, curtsy, and respond with the correct countersign, also taken from Milton.

> "*And was the holy Lamb of God*
> *On England's pleasant pastures seen?*"

Jean-Marie threw back his shoulders and cleared his throat.

> "*I will not cease from Mental Fight,*
> *Nor shall my Sword sleep in my hand,*
> *Till we have built Jerusalem . . .*"

He cocked an eyebrow at her.

"In England's green and pleasant land."

She finished for them both, feeling definitely stunned. He was definitely the British spy she'd been seeking.

"Now will you come inside? Perhaps I should have mentioned I've already met Sir Andrew and his companions. They're all quite well, by the way, but have already followed their orders and left town."

"Orders? Left town?" *Mon Dieu*, how she'd hoped to be reunited with her sister and *creador*.

"Very clear and emphatic orders." He sounded completely sympathetic to her discouragement. His hand rested on the small of her back, gently urging her up the stairs to the kitchen. He rapped lightly and swung the door open. Two servants were revealed, an older but still vigorous couple, who promptly swung into action, fussing over her as if she was a lady of the house.

An hour later, Hélène belted the dressing gown closer around her, muttering possible conversational gambits to toss at Jean-Marie. She'd bathed in hot, gardenia-scented water and knew herself clean from head to foot, even if she wore only this soft velvet and the thin silk nightgown underneath. The maid had carried off her clothes to be washed, clucking over their condition, a summary with which she could hardly argue—even if it did leave her at a disadvantage in facing her host.

At least the dressing gown and nightgown were a lovely deep gold, superbly made from the finest fabric, and long enough to fit her well. They couldn't belong to Mademoiselle Perez, who barely reached Hélène's shoulder, and Hélène refused to speculate about anyone else. Not tonight, not when she was warm and safe—and nervous about a multitude of other things.

Mulling over how best to apologize for her hasty judgment and quick temper at their last meeting, she stepped out of the bathroom without checking her surroundings.

A cough brought her up short.

Her heart stopped beating. Her eyes widened, striving to take in the astonishing sight.

She stood in a small bedroom, furnished with only a few, very finely made items—a carved bed whose four posts were as solid as her waist, a sea chest, a small table next to the bed, and a chair. Rich curtains offered glimpses of the typical Spanish ironbound shutters, capable of blocking all sunlight. A dozen flaming candles burned in a great candelabrum on the small bedside table, revealing the room's true surprise—her host.

Jean-Marie watched her arrogantly, legs spread in the confident stance of a ruler. Candlelight caressed him, emphasizing his strong jaw and high cheekbones, the deep-set blue eyes with their intense emotions, the salt-and-pepper hair glinting in the light. Even worse for her skittering pulse, he wore only a simple linen shirt and wool trousers, the shirt unbuttoned to show his strong muscles, the steady rise and fall of his chest, the pulse beating in his neck.

Hélène's throat dried, and her tongue cleaved to the top of her mouth. *Mon Dieu*, but he was beautiful beyond belief.

"Cognac or a kiss, Hélène?" Jean-Marie lifted a crystal decanter, flames dancing within its golden depths.

"Eh?" she stammered, trying to retrieve her brain from purely carnal spheres. From this angle, she could see the strong muscles in his thighs, the ones he'd use to ride his lover . . .

"What do you want first—cognac or a kiss?" His tempting mouth quirked briefly but grew stern again. "Answer me, Hélène."

The growled order rippled through her like a wave of molten lava, leaving every inch hot and aching. She somehow dragged her gaze up to his eyes. "Do you mean talk or make love?"

He inclined his head, his expression mildly encouraging.

"But . . ." She blinked, fighting for logic in this unfamiliar landscape. So few steps separated them, yet he was unreachable until she understood him. Baffled and too famished to think of pretty words, she fell back on the truth. "I'm a *vampira* and a firestarter, Jean-Marie. You can't want to kiss me."

"Why not?"

"I could drain you dry. Or burn you to a crisp." Those were the nightmares walking through all of her lovers' eyes, even her *creador*'s.

"I am disappointed in you, Hélène." He clucked his tongue. "Perhaps I enjoy playing with fire."

She gaped at him.

"How shall I punish you for your lack of faith in yourself? Shall I tie you up and make you wait for fulfillment?"

An image of herself, bound in soft leather and completely helpless under his skillful mouth, flashed through her head. Hunger jolted through her, shaking her knees and sending cream floating onto her thighs. She bit back a startled moan. "No, please, Jean-Marie."

"Perhaps I should heat your lovely derrière with my hand until your clit enjoys every touch?"

She pressed her legs together, fighting a desire to fondle herself. How had he known, when she had not, that those words would trigger such a hungry response in her?

"Hélène, your words say one thing, but your body declares quite another." He pulled a few items from the bedside table and prowled toward her, graceful and deadly as a big cat. "Must I force the two halves of you to reach agreement?"

She fought for breath, but her feet wouldn't run away, mesmerized by a man so confident in himself a dangerous lover was seen purely as a woman.

"Are such drastic measures the only way to ensure you believe at least one man doesn't give a damn you're a firestarter?" Jean-Marie whispered in her ear. He knotted a twist of leather around one of her wrists with the ease of long practice and quickly secured the other as well, leaving a few inches between them.

She stared at him, gasping for breath, wondering why her nightgown's delicate silk suddenly felt so harsh against her aching nipples. Her breasts were taut and far too hot underneath her clothing.

"Excellent. You're starting to look more pliable, Hélène."

"This is insane," she whispered.

"Not if it will teach you to trust, *chérie*."

He unfastened her dressing gown but didn't immediately remove it. Instead he kissed her throat and breasts, and fondled her hips and ass with those wicked hands. Ah, *le bon Dieu*, how fire leapt through her veins in response! She twisted closer, writhing against his leg, shamelessly throwing back her head so he could suckle her breasts through her nightgown's fragile silk. With her hands bound, she could do little to tempt him, but she tried, stroking his arm and his shoulder, moaning with hunger, and sobbing with delight every time another strong tug on her nipple sent a spear of desire into her womb.

When she was about to go mad if he didn't finish her, he abruptly sat down on the sea chest and pulled her down across his lap. Despite her keen awareness his cock was burningly hard against her hip through their clothes, he put his full attention to arranging her dressing gown and nightgown in order to give him full access to her derrière.

"Jean-Marie?" Her voice quavered but perhaps he wouldn't notice her desperation.

"Hmm?" His big hand rested on her rump, easily spanning more than half of it. He rubbed her curves gently, clearly measuring his grip.

"Jean-Marie, would you please . . ." She wriggled, uneasy about his intentions and wishing he'd return to his previous activities.

"What, *chérie*?" He changed his grip, slipping his fingers between her legs to test—but not tease—her clit.

"Jean-Marie!" To her absolute shock, her core heated faster and hotter than it had from his attention to her breasts. Her folds swelled, achingly conscious of every detail of his hand—down to the placement of every joint in his finger.

His hand remained completely still for a moment before leaving.

"Jean-Marie, no! Don't spank me!" Not when cream was rushing out to greet him.

"Yes." He smacked her very lightly. "You must learn that a man can desire you for yourself. If that means punishing you for your lack of faith in me, then so be it."

He swatted her again, catching her in a magical spot which sent sparks of bright-edged delight through her core and into her clit.

Hélène moaned helplessly.

He swatted her again on the same spot in exactly the same way. Pleasure blurred her senses, and she writhed on his lap, seeking more from his all-knowing touch.

He spanked her on the other side, the mirror image of the first swat. Heat swirled through her core, inviting stronger fires.

Hélène gasped, wondering if she could walk away after his idea of punishment.

Was he playing with her or punishing her? She couldn't tell, nor did she much care. His touch was sometimes teasing, sometimes hard as iron—but always irresistible. Sometimes he swatted her, or stroked her derrière or thighs or hips. But at other times, his fingers delved deep between her legs—playing with her folds, teasing her clit. Or sliding into her channel, ruthlessly stretching her for the cock so close and yet so sternly locked away.

Her skin was tight, stretched tight over the bonfire blazing within her. Nothing mattered except being with him again.

"Jean-Marie, I'll do anything if you'll take me!"

He pulled back to look down at her, his eyes glittering in a harsh-edged mask. Hunger dwelt there, twice as strong for being bitterly leashed. A slow smile of pure masculine triumph turned his mouth into the carnal temptation she remembered.

"Please . . ." she whispered.

He rose and tumbled her onto the bed, quickly covering her and rolling her. He freed himself from his breeches with a few harsh twists of his hands, just enough to unleash his cock. Barely a minute later, she lay on top of him, her bound wrists wrapped around his neck.

He claimed her mouth, hot and passionate. She kissed him back desperately, half-blind with frustrated lust and love.

He growled and roughly gripped her hips, shoving her legs apart and lifting her over him. His cock eagerly nudged at her pussy and entered, thanks to an expert twist of his hips. He began to rock, driving himself in and out of her. Stoking her fires higher and higher.

She moaned, still reluctant to feed. Not Jean-Marie, not the man she'd dreamed of for so long.

He rubbed her clit, perfectly matching the pulse of imminent orgasm, and pressed down.

She howled. Her fangs descended, and she bit into his neck, perfectly finding his jugular. Rich, spicy blood flowed—sweet as honey, with no taint of caution or mistrust, only passion and complete trust.

She drank, filling her empty soul.

"Ah, finally, Hélène, finally!" He pulled her hips down hard onto him, shouting his satisfaction when he climaxed, extravagantly jetting his seed into her.

She gripped his shoulders and clung closer. Stars swirled, blinding her in the most joyous meal she'd had as a *vampira*.

EIGHT

Jean-Marie caressed Hélène's back, enjoying the aftershocks still shaking her body and delightfully making his cock twitch deep inside her. If he'd been stronger—or younger—he'd still be spilling his seed like a twenty-year-old. As it was, he savored the slow glide down from the best orgasm he'd enjoyed in years.

Thank God he had enough blood left from Rodrigo and Sara to keep propelling him forward; otherwise, he wouldn't be able to feed Hélène while she was here. *Prosaico* food might keep his body alive and create enough blood to feed a young *vampira*. But without Rodrigo or Sara's blood, he was a dullard who could scarcely think or move past the demons drilling spikes into his skull. Even with their blood, the physical changes in him were coming more and more rapidly.

Although Rodrigo had said drinking a *vampira*'s blood would keep him going for a time . . .

Hélène happily muttered something and buried her face against his shoulder, her arms still around his neck.

He kissed the top of her head and disengaged himself, carefully settling her beside him on the bed. It was a moment's work to take a dagger from the bedside table's drawer and slice the leather off her wrists. His heart swelled with pride and something softer when she never flinched at the sharp blade, simply twisted her arms to allow him better access.

He disposed of the scraps and turned away.

"What? Where are you going?" She blinked at him, all tousled golden hair and flushed creamy skin.

"One moment, *chérie*." He kissed his fingers and touched them to her lips. She grumbled but didn't loudly complain.

He returned a minute later to find her trying to sit up in the bed.

"Let me wash you first, Hélène, and you'll be more comfortable." He set the basin and towel down on the chair. "As a *vampira*, you've already healed from the spanking, so you can choose whether to sit up or lie down."

She blushed furiously—and enchantingly. "I'll lie down," she said gruffly and flopped onto her stomach, a position that hid her face from him. It also showed him a great deal of her most intimate delights while he cleaned her.

What he wouldn't do to bring her up on her knees and ride her . . .

Relaxed and sated, all Hélène wanted to do was be his lover. Yet they desperately needed to talk after so long a separation—and with the shadow of war hanging over them. She steeled herself, glad she was lying on the coverlet rather than between the sheets. If she'd been half-asleep in his arms, she doubted she'd have had the strength to do anything more than memorize every blissful second.

First came the apology, of course. "I'm sorry I importuned you in Provence. I saw you as a toy who could be rearranged to suit my world, not as a man with plans of your own. It was none of my business how you spend your life, and I was very rude."

He glanced at her, surprised. She forced herself to meet his eyes, even though she was lying on her stomach.

"Hélène, how could you have known what life among *vampiros* was like? You made a mistake born of ignorance, leaving nothing to forgive." He shrugged off the old insult and moved the basin and towel onto the table.

"You speak like a diplomat." She came up to face him, suddenly unwilling to let him escape this conversation with any of his well-polished word games.

"*Vraiment?*" He raised a haughty eyebrow and straightened up, totally ignoring his dishabille of sweaty shirt and trousers. *Mon Dieu*, Louis XVI had never looked as regal.

"Who are you?" she whispered, her eyes going very wide. "You sound and move like a prince, yet you live with Spanish adventurers."

His face hardened into a mask, but unfathomable thoughts wheeled behind his eyes. He blew out a long breath before speaking, every syllable precisely placed.

"My mother was known as the Jeweled Butterfly."

Her breath flew out of her lungs. In any place, at any other time, she might have collapsed into a faint. She came to her feet, facing him, too agitated to stay still.

"Marie-Louise de Montpazier?" The ancient name rang through the small room like an exotic cymbal. "But she was Louise de La Vallière's great rival for the Sun King's affections."

Jean-Marie bowed in acknowledgment. "First rival," he corrected her. "The great rival—and the victor—was Madame de Montespan."

Her vision grayed slightly, her lungs still unable to find air. She fought to think logically. He lived among *vampiros*, although he was a *prosaico*. He could be old enough, if he was a *compañero*. But royalty?

He was intelligent, beautiful, and proud enough.

Her heart began to beat steadily again.

"The poets still sing of the Jeweled Butterfly's beauty. You must resemble her a great deal."

He shrugged off an obviously boring comment. "As my arrogance came directly from my father."

Her eyes flashed. "And your grace."

He flushed, startled by a compliment delivered so directly as to seem a statement of purest fact.

"But not the legendary de Montpazier greed, which forced the Jeweled Butterfly into banishment after a bribery scandal. Yes, yes, I've heard the old gossip." Hélène impatiently waved her hand, still staring at him.

A wry smile twisted his mouth at the obituary for his mother.

She put the rest of the puzzle together, hunting for his true name.

"But—but that would make you the Duc de—"

"Enough, Hélène!" He gripped her hand, stopping her voice. "That man is dead—and even here, the walls may have ears."

She cocked her head for a moment and studied him, finding the pain behind that all-too-fast denial. She wished she could help heal him. But it was easy enough to promise never to call him that.

"Still, you are a prince," she whispered.

"But I cannot inherit the throne and am no threat to Louis XVIII, or the other Orleanist heirs."

"What happened?"

"You should ask instead, what am I?" He laughed, unable to keep the bitterness entirely out of his voice even after all these years.

She blinked, caught completely off-balance by his tone.

"I am a *concubino compañero*."

"A *prosaico* who drinks *vampiro* blood—but not enough to become a *vampiro*?" She frowned. "They're very rare, aren't they? I'd heard of them but hadn't met one."

"That's a *compañero*. But a *concubino compañero* is also bound by carnal ties."

"Do you mean blood and emotion, like a *vampiro*? Or more precisely, blood and sex like some *vampiros*?" He was looking more and more tense.

"Correct."

Poor darling, his hand was shaking. How hard on him would this be?

"A *concubino compañero* is very dependent on their *vampiro primero* or *vampira primera*."

Dependent? Her proud Jean-Marie *dependent* on anyone? How appalling! But if so, it would have to be on . . .

She gasped, her eyes rounding. "Mademoiselle Perez?"

"Correct."

"That's why you stay with her—you need her blood." Her hand covered her mouth. Oh, how she had misjudged their relationship if he needed the woman only in order to survive.

He nodded, his body rigid and his face unreadable.

Or might there have once been an emotional tie between them?

"Did you—did you ask to become her *concubino compañero*?" Hélène's voice was very soft.

"*Merede*, no!"

Thank God! Hélène beamed at him.

He gawked at her.

She swallowed and decided to take the chance of openly displaying her hopes. "Could you consider—coming to care for somebody else?"

"*Mais oui, chérie.* I have loved you since the day we met at Versailles."

She flung herself into his arms, barely giving him time to put their wine aside before their lips met. He kissed her passionately, for the first time letting loose all of his joy, all of his need for her. She clung, kissing him just as desperately, their tongues dueling to tell the other who'd longed the most.

Was it forever or was it seconds before he lifted his head and caressed her cheek? She kissed his fingers and rubbed her cheek against him, pleased that they were now ensconced together once again on the bed.

"If you need Mademoiselle Perez," she said slowly, choosing every word with great care, "shouldn't she be close at hand?"

Jean-Marie flinched but drew himself up. "She's in Galicia with Don Rodrigo. I'm supposed to join them as soon as I deliver the message to your team."

"But that's days away from here." Hélène lifted her head to look down at him from her perch stretched atop him. "Can you travel that far? Shouldn't *compañeros* receive blood more often than that?"

"I have blood mixed with wine," he answered stiffly.

"Is that enough?"

He was silent.

"What goes wrong if it isn't?" She stroked his cheek and slid her hand into his hair—his almost entirely *gray* hair. *"Mon amour,"* she whispered, "you look twenty years older than when we met last. I thought *compañeros* never aged."

"I have lived for more than a century as a *compañero*, Hélène. Death is approaching quickly."

Death? To keep him alive, she'd shove him into Mademoiselle Perez's bed every night. She would not lose him now. "They shouldn't have left you behind!"

"I couldn't let them risk their lives when mine is already forfeit, Hélène." His expression and voice were implacable.

"I can't lose you now, not when I've just found you. I've had years full of imaginary conversations with you—exclaiming over new sights, mulling over acquaintances, sharing good books, just as we did in Paris. How can I lose the comfort of your presence and the joy of your mind?"

His eyes offered her no hope.

She buried her face against him with an inarticulate sob, and he hugged her close.

"I don't know how soon it will happen, *chérie.* But we can spend all our time together, *oui?* Frequently making love and sharing our blood?"

Her arms tightened around his neck, and she wiggled closer. He wasn't looking at her while he spoke, and she didn't want to see how much truth he was telling, even in that seductive tone.

"I will accompany you on your mission, Hélène." His voice strengthened to a warrior's note. "I am as strong and fast as most *cachorros*, the newborn *vampiros*, and my senses are as good. Together we can do much."

She sniffled. His voice was so husky, painfully unlike his usual smoothness.

"Plus, a *compañero*, who is well-provided with *prosaico* food, can easily take care of a *vampira.* I swear, you will not lack."

"But will you, *mon amour?*" She braced herself to kneel over him. "If accompanying me risked your life in any way, brought you closer to dying by taking you farther from the blood that will keep you alive . . ."

His gaze softened, and he possessively rubbed her shoulders and back.

"I adore you, Hélène. I would far rather spend what time I have with you, fighting Bonaparte's tyranny, than doing anything else in the world." The words rang through the quiet like a vow.

"Then we shall go to war together, my love." A brave smile quavered on her lips.

They met halfway, sealing their love with a kiss both sweet and fiery hot.

SAN LEANDRO, GALICIA, THE NEXT DAY

Rodrigo exited San Rafael Arcángel and set his hat on his head, preparing for yet another snowstorm. He automatically considered the peasants around him as they too departed morning mass. He personally hadn't taken communion, of course, simply attended the service— his second visit to a church in the past five centuries.

There were far too many men here, reflecting the migrant laborers' return from other parts of the Iberian Peninsula. Yet on the whole, San Leandro was a peaceful, prosperous town with men and women receiving the priests' blessing before bustling off to the day's chores. Many of them were tall and blond, clearly descended from the Celts and Visigoths who'd originally conquered these mountains. Their clothing was stark black, enhancing the warmth of the sunshine and the smiles when they greeted the priests. Here, unlike so many other places in Europe, the clergy were obviously deeply trusted.

The younger priest, one of the very strict Capuchin Franciscan, was a stout fellow deeply involved with their lives. Every woman and most of the men paused to talk with him, not just receive a quick blessing. Some obviously promised to return later, while the nuns clearly enjoyed his company. He was apparently the senior priest, given the congregants' fondness for him and that he'd been the one to celebrate mass.

The older priest was taller, thinner, and quieter—except when small children scampered past. Also a Capuchin Franciscan, he had a knack for dropping to one knee and speaking to them in a way which brought chortles and rapt attention. Mothers and grandmothers chuckled and lingered, letting their priest practice his halting *Gallego* on their offspring for a few minutes.

The people were well fed, thanks to the rich green pastures of the Costa Verde and these natural mountain fortresses high above it. Here they had plenty of beef, pork, and chicken, as well as wheat—so long as no grasping landlord or provincial government stole it. They'd been hit hard by those scourges but not destroyed, probably thanks to their isolation—especially the sheer difficulty of reaching San Leandro over the famous bridge.

Centuries ago, Rodrigo's father and grandfather had drilled him and his brothers in how to protect their people, how to husband the land and enrich it, how to build for the ages. As a knight, he'd sworn to protect his people and his lands—but his captivity had torn him completely away from those obligations. He couldn't have walked in daylight to see what needed to be done, and he'd closed his mind to the responsibilities—and the joys—he'd been denied.

He could live with how he'd kept his personal duties as a Christian alive—of prayer and confession. But how much he'd failed others? Those were the worst nightmares, the sins that locked him in the church's outermost reaches.

They'd also kept him from visiting his wife's tomb within San Rafael Arcángel.

But now with war approaching . . . Now he found himself wondering if those three men sitting under the oak tree would make a good work party to repair the section of road in front of the baker's. Part of the wall holding back the hillside near the bridge needed some work, too. But it would be better done by more men. He could also ask the women to make more cheese and sausage for food. Of course, if he hired some of the boys to bring water, it would spread money to more households . . .

Two little boys raced past him to join their mothers, their scarlet caps blazing against the stone walls.

"Ah, God bless them," the older priest commented from behind him in English. "Surely children are the grace that keeps us all alive."

Rodrigo whipped around, startled he hadn't heard the man approach.

"Father Michael." He bowed as was proper—before realizing that he'd answered in the same language, the first time he'd used it publicly in San Leandro.

The priest made a graceful sign of the cross over him in response, the first he'd received in so very long. Light brushed his cheek but faded under the dark scudding clouds.

"Welcome to San Leandro, my son." Surprisingly bright blue eyes in a seamed brown face saw far too much without probing. He watched the children and the parishioners disappear around a corner, leaving them alone. Even the other priest and the nuns had departed.

"Thank you, Father. Your voice has the soft cadence of Ireland." He cautiously opened a conversation, offering his knowledge of the other's accent.

"I was born and raised in County Wicklow, within a few miles of Dublin, but I spent many years in the west near Galway." His face lit up with joy at finding someone to share memories with.

"One of my dearest friends is an O'Malley."

"Famed for their fighting men—and their pirate queen."

Rodrigo laughed. "He made very sure I could pronounce her name properly. Graw-nya O'Malley."

"Or Grace, as the English translate it."

"What brings you here to Spain?" Rodrigo asked casually, ready to withdraw the question at the slightest hint of constraint.

"Galicia is at the other end of the great smuggling route to Ireland." Father Michael's eyebrows went up. "Traveling here is very easy."

Rodrigo blinked, having considered those sailing routes very little while he was growing up.

"This land is as green but far more mountainous than Ireland," he said neutrally.

"Here the children play amid gardens of stone, while we are certain that the French will come." The priest's voice turned as leaden as the skies, his dark brown habit whipping against his legs. "Eleven years ago, the French didn't come to Ireland where the children hid and the men stood tall among fields of green."

"The '97 Rising!"

"Aye. I'd been a hedge priest, serving my God and my countrymen by hiding in thickets to bring Holy Communion and teach Catechism in open fields to the music of birdsong—because the Protestant English forbade all other celebration. When my people chose to fight—believing the French would help—I went with them."

"As a priest."

"I didn't expect my principal duties to consist of giving the Last Rites—and running for my own life, lest my presence destroy others." Agony scored his face, an expression Rodrigo knew far too well. He pressed his hands together in an attitude of prayer and closed his eyes, breathing hard.

Rodrigo started to edge away, so the old priest could grieve in private.

"Forgive me if I have disturbed you." The Franciscan glanced at the other man from under his level silver brows. "It is still painful to remember. Having someone to speak to in English seems to have opened deeper floodgates than I expected."

"I, too, have bitter memories, Father, which I hope to heal." Rodrigo shrugged a disclaimer, denying any awkwardness.

"That's what the vicar-general said when he sent me here. He hoped San Rafael Arcángel would heal me, the traveler."

They smiled wryly at each other in perfect accord.

Wind ruffled their hair, raw-edged with the threat of snow and touched with wood smoke's warmth.

Both men immediately, instinctively measured the distance to their lodgings. But Rodrigo hesitated, caught on the verge of saying a polite and very secular farewell. Would the Lord think he deserved even this much of a favor?

"Father—will you bless me before I go?"

"Of course, my son." Father Michael's face softened and became almost transfigured.

Rodrigo knelt on the cold, wet stones, removed his hat, and bowed his head.

Father Michael lifted his hand.

"The blessing of Mary and the blessing of God,
The blessing of the sun and the moon on their road,
Of the man in the east and the man in the west,
And my blessing with thee and be thou blest.
In the name of the Father, and the Son, and the Holy Spirit. Amen."

He made the sign of the Holy Cross above Rodrigo.

The ancient words settled around Rodrigo like a cloak, protecting him from harm. Tears touched his eyes and he crossed himself before rising.

"God, Mary, and St. Patrick be with you, Father."

Father Michael brightened even more, recognizing the traditional Irish response to his blessing.

They smiled at each other, understanding far more than they could put into words of why they both needed that blessing.

MADRID, THAT AFTERNOON

Hélène drummed her fingers, ready to hurl the marine dictionary across the room. No matter how often she decoded the message, it still said the same thing. The same set of words, which evoked the same set of appalling memories.

"D'you think frowning will change the answer?" Jean-Marie set a glass of wine down in front of her on the library table.

"No." She poured the extremely expensive port down her throat without regard for its quality. She'd learned very quickly *vampiros* were immune to becoming drunkards, although they usually savored the taste of fine drink as a substitute for eating.

He raised an eyebrow but refilled her glass without a word.

"Are you sure we can trust the servants?" she asked abruptly.

"Completely," he replied and returned to his chair.

She lifted an eyebrow at the extremely succinct answer—and accepted it. If a man who saw life in shades of gray was certain of something, then it was completely true.

Since Jean-Marie was accompanying her, he deserved to know what they'd be doing.

"We are instructed to do everything possible," she mimicked the tone of a haughty bureaucrat, "to protect the British army's supply lines to the major western ports."

He considered, his long legs stretched in front of him. "In other words—Lisbon, Oporto, Vigo, and Corunna. Lisbon is the Portugese capital—and Bonaparte's target after Madrid."

"Are you sure?"

"Capturing it would feed *la gloire*, the glory of France—and the legend of Napoleon." Jean-Marie's eyes were very cynical. "The British fleet is also there, supplying the British army."

"It sounds—crowded. And obvious."

"Very. Especially when it is in the southwest, and all of Napoleon's troops are in the north and northeast."

She set the paper down and rested her chin on her hands, watching every flicker crossing his face for a clue to his thoughts. He had far more experience at divining a leader's intentions than anyone else she'd ever met. "Don't you think he'll march that far? His troops are famous for moving swiftly."

"But Sir John Moore, with the British army, is in the west. If he can move quickly enough against the French army at the *perfect* moment, he could snap Napoleon's attention away from the south. He'd save Lisbon and Portugal, plus all of southern Spain."

"But his army is a fraction of Napoleon's army's size!" Hélène objected instinctively, imagining thousands of British soldiers slaughtered on a wintry field in the same way the Austrians and Russians had been at Austerlitz.

Jean-Marie shrugged. "Did I say it would be easy or safe? It's the move of a master chess player and a great gambler. His port, in that case, would be Corunna," he added. "And to help him, we'd have to race both him and Napoleon across Old Castile to the northern mountains."

She shuddered.

He sipped his wine and waited.

Despite her horror at the potential cost of one alternative, she had to admit it held a certain logic. She nibbled on her fingernail. "You believe we only need to protect two supply routes—the one to Lisbon, in the southwest, and the other to Corunna, in the northwest."

"Exactly."

"Did Sir Andrew say which direction he'd be going?"

"No."

She'd never had to make a decision like this before.

"In that case, we'll go to Corunna."

"Excellent."

But his voice wasn't quite as surprised as she'd expected.

She tilted her head. "Jean-Marie, what would you have done if I'd said Lisbon?"

"Deceived you into taking the Corunna road." A slow wicked smile curled his lips.

"Wretch!" She ran at him and pretended to pummel him.

He caught her hands, laughing, and pulled her down into his lap for a kiss which closed out the world.

"I don't know why I love you so much," she whispered a very long time later. "You are arrogant, impossible . . ."

"Always willing to go off on mad adventures with you?"

"The best man in the world." For as long as I have you.

NINE

OLD CASTILE, A WEEK LATER

Hélène moodily considered the sullen landscape spread out beneath her. Primarily built from flat plains cut by a single great river and its tributaries, Old Castile was notable for the great hills scattered across the landscape, most of them crowned by ruined castles. Seen in the fading moonlight, they seemed the work of lost kings and kingdoms, for whom the land itself mourned.

The peasants lived in villages, huddled by the fields and watercourses, deep within the shadows of those past glories. But they, too, remembered—and they hated invaders.

They'd refused to talk to her with her French accent, unless she used her most forceful forms of *vampira* mind persuasion on them. But they'd chatter to Jean-Marie, with his Spanish clothing and polite manners toward the women and clergy. He'd even spoken to some roaming bands of men in a familiar-sounding language called Gallego, which he'd learned years before from *Monsieur* Perez. She couldn't stop her moue of distaste at the man's name and Jean-Marie had abruptly ended the conversation.

They had an excellent idea of where they were and had only once been bothered by bandits and guerillas. She'd tossed a burning brand at the bandit leader's hands, scaring off him and his followers. Jean-Marie and their two excellent riding mules were still well fed, compared to the world around them. The mules had even accepted her very well, probably because *Monsieur* Perez had previously accustomed them to *vampiros*.

His servants had remained in Madrid and planned to journey south away from the fighting. As members of an ancient *comitiva* family who'd served *vampiros* for generations, they had connections who'd help them find shelter.

She still hadn't seen Celeste or the others, even though they'd traveled as fast as they could. They hadn't heard any rumors of their capture, either, which was small comfort when her imagination was starting to stir up nightmares.

Such as now. She was standing atop what had once been a castle, but had since been reduced to a single watchtower and a wall. It was surprisingly sturdy, even if its gaping holes did make it resemble a bell tower more than a fortification. But she was high enough to see for miles, giving her a chance to spot any pursuers—or the people she followed. Their riding mules waited patiently below, the two sentries who kept watch during the day.

An isolated fire burned in the distance, close to what Jean-Marie had said was a road. A hut? Perhaps. But it cast much more light than she'd expect to see from the typical airless hovel.

A branch crackled.

She smiled faintly, recognizing Jean-Marie's signal and his scent. He'd warned her in the beginning that *compañeros* had the strength and senses of *cachorros*, the very young *vampiros*. A week's traveling had taught her he'd barely sketched out his knowledge and talents.

"Any news?" She held out her hand for him without turning around.

"Moore has made his move. The British army thrust hard toward Napoleon's supply lines." He wrapped his arms around her, lending her the comfort of his body. He'd put on a little weight, and his eyes weren't as guarded.

"He must have stirred up a hornet's nest. He at least saved Portugal and probably southern Spain."

"Indeed. Napoleon's charged out of Madrid, chasing Moore like a schoolboy who's had his name turned into the latest playground taunt."

"You're not impressed," she observed mildly. The distant fire was still burning, still isolated, and still surprisingly bright.

"Napoleon has ten times as many troops as Moore—even though he has to use most of them to keep the local civilians in check. On the other hand, if he doesn't destroy Moore here and now, he loses his reputation for invincibility."

"And the rest of Europe takes heart and begins to tear him apart, every chance they get."

"Exactly." He kissed her hair.

She leaned her head back, savoring his steady heartbeat, which meant safety and homecoming.

"Napoleon must stop Moore before he reaches Benavente, where the Corunna road starts climbing into the truly nasty mountains and a handful of men could hold off a division," Jean-Marie said quietly. "I'd wager Napoleon has also ordered Soult's forces to head due west and cut off the British."

"A race for Benavente," she summarized, wondering why he was spending so much time talking, instead of riding. It was less than an hour until first light, and they should be taking shelter soon.

"Correct. We'll have to get there first, of course, but we're ahead of Moore on the Corunna road, as is Sir Andrew."

"Excellent." She let the silence linger for a moment. "What's the other news?"

He chuckled. "Will you ever let me bring up something diplomatically?"

"Perhaps," she murmured tactfully.

"Sir Andrew and the others have, if anything, lengthened their lead."

"What!" She pulled herself out of his arms and whipped around to face him. "*Mon Dieu*, he must be driving them like beasts of the field. How can we rejoin them?"

"There is worse news, *chérie*." He watched her steadily, his voice darker and deeper.

"Go on." She drew herself up.

"Roaming patrols of Napoleon's beloved Chasseurs à Cheval cavalry, his 'favored children' from the Imperial Guard, have been seen in this area."

She froze, chilled to the bone. "Oh no . . ."

"Interestingly, they are not patrolling in our direction—but where Sir Andrew and his team must be."

"Celeste . . ." Her hand flew to her throat. No, she couldn't lose *la petite*. Not her only family. "We must warn them immediately, lest they be captured during the day."

"Only a mind link will work for that, *mon coeur*—and a very strong one."

She'd only been able to reach Celeste mind-to-mind very briefly, even using the channel they shared as *hijas* of the same *creador*.

Celeste! She frantically pictured her sister—the dark hair and eyes, laughing over a joke. *Celeste!*

Nothing. She could faintly hear Jean-Marie's thoughts, sternly withdrawn to allow her to focus. She could even catch snatches of a few local peasants' thoughts just starting to rise for the morning chores, less than a mile away beside the small river. But not a hint of *la petite*'s, even though the distance was small enough she should have been able to reach her.

Jean-Marie cleared his throat. "Try Sir Andrew."

"I should be able to reach my sister much more easily." Why was he suggesting her *creador*, whom she only had the most formal relationship with? The bond should be stronger with her sister.

"What can it hurt to try talking to your *creador*? Perhaps Celeste is distracted in some way and not listening." His words were so carefully chosen as to be unreadable, like his face and voice. What was he driving at? But she had no time to worry about such details, not with sunrise approaching.

She straightened her shoulders, assuming a *marquise*'s posture, that of a lady born and bred to the nobility of the sword, the proudest nobility in France.

Sir Andrew, may I have a word with you, please?

A very faint buzzing, as if he was distracted.

She tried again, forcing herself to shout.

Andrew threw down his greatcoat and looked around the meager shepherd's hut yet again, extending every sense he had. The mules were in the excuse for a stable, peacefully eating the grain he'd bought in Valladolid. It had taken them days to accept *vampiros* as passengers, not surprising since most animals were extremely wary of the unfamiliar scent.

In the hayloft, Wade had just finished feeding Celeste—or should he say that Celeste had just drained Wade dry yet again? In any event, Wade was snoring loudly, and there'd be no waking him for hours to come.

There weren't many shadows to search, given that they'd lit two candles. Normally they went without any light, since this was enemy territory. But Celeste had begged for the special treat, saying it was almost Christmas, and she wanted to see her men. He'd agreed, thinking the hut was sturdy enough to conceal them.

Linen rustled and hay crackled. Celeste must be rolling over. She preferred to sleep next to her partners when they traveled in harm's way, although not back home in England. There she had more—adventurous notions of how to sport in a bed.

A slow smile brought the corners of his mouth up, echoed by his cock's anticipatory surge. He ignored them both.

Where the devil was the marine dictionary, the codebook that would decipher any message he—and every other British spy in the Iberian Peninsula—sent? It had to be here. He'd made sure it was in his coat when they'd first arrived but he hadn't seen it since.

It was a small book, leather bound and designed to survive in the worst sort of weather. This was a tiny hut, and there were very few places it could have disappeared into.

Sir Andrew? Hélène's voice intruded.

Thank God you're alive! Give me five minutes, and I'll talk to you.

But . . .

He broke the link, enforcing it with a brutal order to be silent. Even though he was delighted to know she was alive, the codebook was far more important than any sentimental reunion.

He sniffed, choosing to hunt by scent instead of sight. The book's binding held traces of its past owners, who'd all been *prosaicos* and therefore rather odiferous to a *vampiro*'s acute senses. *Vampiros*, however, smelled quite differently than *prosaicos*, and their scent faded with age, even as their ability to detect it grew. In the end, only a *vampiro* of his own age—or older—could have found Andrew, although he could readily locate any *vampiro* younger than himself.

His coat bore strong traces of the codebook.

He sniffed again, catching a vagrant draft through the door. *What the hell?*

Totally disregarding the abominably cold weather, he whipped the door open, drew in a deep breath—and went completely still.

An instant later, he grabbed the codebook from its hiding place under the frozen watering trough and dove for cover in the stable.

A heavy musket ball thudded into the wood, barely missing his head.

The book reeked of Celeste. She must have stolen it from his coat and taken it outside when she'd relieved herself.

Christ, how could he have been such a fool not to have noticed that all the agents who died did so after missions she went on or evenings when he chatted about what old friends were doing now?

A pistol shot rang out from inside. He cursed, knowing it meant Wade's death.

"God dammit, Celeste, I will kill you for this!" he shouted. A dozen *prosaico* cavalrymen had little chance against a *vampiro*. He'd start by stampeding their horses . . .

She had the effrontery to laugh at him from inside the hut. "Did you truly believe that I'd turned against my country? Take a deeper breath of the night air, you fool, and then tell me what you think of your chances."

His skin prickled at her tone. The horsemen were staying farther away than they should for a night action, barely within musket range. What else was wrong?

He crawled to the end of the water trough and tasted the wind, where it flowed unhindered by haystacks or low hills.

A very, very faint but unmistakable scent reached him, one whose like he'd encountered before in London. A *vampiro mayor*, far faster than he was and well able to hunt by daylight—when he'd be forced to seek shelter indoors lest he be turned into ashes by the sun.

It was the perfect trap. Worst of all, the French would have the codebook, the nearly impossible to destroy volume.

Celeste smashed through the small window in the hayloft. She thudded to the ground and ran for the closest French cavalryman, ice and snow crackling under her feet.

Dammit, why had he broken his own rules and not kept a pistol to hand at all times? He could have done at least one thing right and destroyed the treacherous bitch.

Celeste dropped into a walk a few feet away, smirking when no bullet clipped her skirts. The foolish Englishman was still so enamored of her he couldn't bear to kill her? Well, he'd learn differently in a few more minutes, once the Emperor's men caught him.

She began to hum one of the tunes she'd danced to with Raoul, allowing herself to remember a little of her only joy.

A cold, dry wind softly brushed her cheek, totally unlike the ice-edged storms that came from the north. *Run, Celeste.*

The ghostly voice sounded like Raoul's. Impossible. She dipped and swayed, her hand lifting to an imaginary partner. There was plenty of time to celebrate her triumph over the clumsy English.

A gust of wind swirled the snow around her, building it into a pillar. *Celeste, run!* Raoul shouted in her ear and shoved her hard, spurring her into movement. *You'll die if you linger.*

She recognized his voice with an instinct owing nothing to logic. She was two steps away before she looked back.

Raoul was watching her, wearing his old revolutionary uniform, his body outlined in blue and silver against the tattered hut. The appalling scar he'd gained at the Battle of Valmy, marking his heroism, tore from his face the youthful beauty he'd once had. Dear God, how she wanted to caress it, kiss him, reassure herself he was here, with her.

She slowed and started to turn back. For him, she would brave Hell or the fires of Purgatory.

He raised his hand to her, warning her off.

A fierce wind slammed into her, staggering her. Snow swirled around him, dissolving his outline.

"No! Nooo!" The wind ripped away her cry and stripped the tears from her eyes.

A strong man ripped her away and swung her up before him, without checking his horse. A single glance over her shoulder confirmed Raoul's ghost had vanished.

Tears blurred her eyes.

Sir Andrew? Hélène was speaking again. *There are French Chasseurs à Cheval from the Imperial Guard nearby . . .*

Hélène. He smiled grimly. His little firestarter. Damned if he'd ever valued her gift quite so much before.

They're already here, my dear. Napoleon sent the best cavalrymen in his army. Where are you?

On top of the ruined castle about a day's journey back. St. Just is leaving now . . .

There's no time for that. The French were circling the hut, closing off his avenues of escape although disinclined to come too close. Smart lads.

He slipped into the stables and untied the mules, giving them the freedom to run as he could not.

How close do you have to be in order to set something on fire? He cursed the sexual folly that had kept him in a woman's bed, rather than overseeing his *hija*'s training. His *hija* who was Britain's greatest weapon.

Within eyesight. But you know my accuracy decreases with distance, sir. I'd be likely to burn everything within a couple of yards. Her voice wavered before she brought it back under rigid control. *Who else is with you?*

Wade is dead. He made a quick decision. *The French destroyed Celeste, too.*

No *creador* could directly lie to an *hija* in the mind link, although they could stretch the truth. His words weren't enough of a lie to poison the link. After all, the vicious immoralities of the Revolution and Napoleon's empire were what had destroyed Celeste's oaths to the British Crown.

Hélène's answering scream was soundless and heart-wrenching.

He gritted his teeth, praying the Lord would bring Hélène safely home without encountering her treacherous sister and the French army. At least he'd kept Hélène from hunting for Celeste and getting herself captured.

Thankfully, an *hija* couldn't forcibly question her *creador* through the mind link, so she'd never know how much he hadn't told her.

You have to set this hut on fire, he ordered.

I can't kill you! She was almost sobbing for breath but somehow coherent. Damn fine fighter, she was, to rally her thoughts after these shocks.

Better my death than having Boney's lads get their hands on this codebook—along with every other British spy in Spain and Portugal.

She continued to hesitate. *But . . . But . . .*

The wind changed, bringing a new reminder of his greatest danger. Metal clanked, and a horse whickered softly. The French *vampiro mayor* had started to move in.

You must. He sharpened his tone, desperate to bring this to a quick end. *It is the only way to ensure the marine dictionary—the all-important codebook—is completely destroyed. Do not think of anything except the book.*

She was silent, agony roiling her thoughts.

Hélène! As your creador, *I command you to set fire to the book!* He slammed his will into her, weighting it with memories of all the oaths she'd sworn, all the deaths which had driven her to pledging her own life.

Her breath caught, and he sensed strength flowing into her from someone else. St. Just, of course; good man.

I can't see the book with my eyes, sir, she said with a return to her usual crisp logic, *not with the village and trees in the way.*

He would have preferred them to be properly green English trees instead. But he'd always known, as Charles II had warned him, he was unlikely to find rest on the western side of the Channel. He blew out his breath and shoved away memories of swans floating on the River Avon under the verdant willow trees.

Use my eyes instead. I'll return to the front of the hut and hold up my arm.

Very well.

He prayed God would see Hélène and St. Just safely home. *On the count of three, then.*

God be with you, sir.

And with you, little one. I wish I'd done better by you.

We'll stick it to Boney for you, she assured him stoutly.

Despite himself, he laughed at her unusual vulgarity. *Three, two, one . . .*

Andrew jackknifed to his feet, holding his hand aloft with the codebook. He stared at it, picturing every detail for her as they'd taught him in that very secret spy school. Bullets thudded into the hut and tore at his greatcoat, trying to tear him down quickly before he could complete the image.

For King and country . . .

Light blazed, more brilliant than the sun, and he knew nothing more.

CASTRO SANCHEZ, EAST OF BENAVENTE, TWO DAYS LATER

Jean-Marie and Hélène were studying the bridge at Castro Sanchez, east of Benavente. The weather was abominable, with either snow and ice covering the roads or torrents of rain falling to turn the execrable tracks into bottomless troughs of mud. Jean-Marie almost envied those who lacked money and had to remain close to home.

Hélène had walked in a rigid haze ever since her sister and *creador* had died, where sobbing and brooding over revenge were her only true emotions. Even feeding seemed to be done by rote.

They'd searched the hut's ruins, but found nothing except charred ashes and a man's skeleton. They'd had Wade properly buried in the local cemetery, of course, and said their own prayers over everything else. *Vampiros* left nothing behind but fine powder, so there was no point in looking for any remains belonging to Sir Andrew or Celeste.

He regretted Sir Andrew's death but hardly Celeste's, not that he'd ever say so to Hélène, of course. A small voice in the back of his head wondered if the little slut had actually done anything so convenient as to perish.

Jean-Marie smiled wryly and focused the spyglass yet again on the bridge.

He and Hélène had already studied the impressive stone structure, looking for the best spots to attack it. She'd been well trained by both her husband and the British in how to use munitions. But this job looked trickier than most, thanks to the very narrow, deep gorge and two massive piers rising from the riverbed far below. A sturdy tower rose on one side, flanked by the old medieval town, emphasizing the imposing mountain behind them. Unless executed properly, any explosion could be magnified by the chasm into unpredictably larger effects.

Napoleon's vanguard was no more than a day away, giving them little time to carry out the attack. It also brought the risks of being captured or killed—and possibly finding out if Celeste had truly been destroyed.

Hélène was pacing the room behind him, far enough away from

the window that the dawn's first light would illuminate the bridge, not herself. They'd rented an apartment on the top floor of a wool warehouse, giving them a sturdy and well-locked building. The rooms were very private with a few pieces of old-fashioned, well-made furniture. Every window had strong iron shutters, of course.

"What do you think of it?" She paused, tapping her toe.

"It's very promising." He swung his spyglass again, checking a few last details. "This bridge is on the main road, cuts through a deep gorge with no convenient alternate routes, and it's overlooked by a sturdy tower. Is that where you plan to get the gunpowder from?" He swung around to look at her.

She nodded. "The warden is very old, and I've already teased his mind into telling me the sentries' schedule. He truly wants to be relieved of any responsibility before the professional armies arrive." She silently ticked items off on her fingers. "Can you pick the locks here?"

"Oh yes. Oh yes, indeed." He smiled at the prospect.

"Naughty boy."

His smile deepened to a totally unrepentant grin. Damn but he liked seeing her come alive again, even if it was for destroying things. "Do you want to demolish only the roadbed or the arches, too?"

"If we destroy just the roadbed, Boney can have it back in use within days, correct?"

"Or hours, for infantry."

"That won't do!" She glared at him, her hands on her hips. "We'll blow up everything we can."

"Now you're starting to sound like a man." He managed to sound heartily approving.

"I was not!" Sheer horror washed over her face.

"Of course you were."

"Was not!" She was behaving like a woman again.

"Perhaps I need to look more closely—at your hands and your throat—to be certain." He lounged against the desk and considered her, lingering on her feminine assets, concealed though they were under layers of widow's clothing. The weather was so nasty she could almost go out in daylight, given the amount of clothes she wore. "Or those skirts could be hiding a great deal, which would warrant a detailed investigation by my tongue . . ."

His voice deepened into a purr.

Realization of how she was being teased began to dawn. She blinked, a multitude of expressions rapidly crossing her face from bafflement to anticipation, before cautiously settling on flirtation.

He concealed a hopeful grin, never having seen that particular gleam in her eyes before.

"Indeed?" She pursed her lips and looked him over thoroughly, lingering on his groin.

His blood stirred eagerly.

"Can I be certain that any man as blind as you are has a mouth capable of discernment?" She sniffed and tilted her nose up in the air. The effect would have been more dismissive if the tip of her tongue hadn't swept out across her lips. "But, since we're to be members of a *team*, I suppose a little *mutual* exploration might be beneficial."

"Mutual? My dear partner, I am the one who called into question your identity." He lifted her chin with a single finger. "After all, you could be a captain—or a colonel—of engineers, given the way you discuss gunpowder so expertly."

She gaped at him for a moment before breaking into peals of laughter.

He silenced her by the simple expedient of kissing her thoroughly. She flung her arms around his neck and returned the salute, her mouth opening immediately so their tongues could twine together.

Long moments passed before he lifted his head. He caressed her cheek, sliding her veil back from her hair. "Hélène, *chérie*, if we closed the shutters, we could satisfy our curiosity in a much more direct fashion."

"You're trying to distract me, *mon cher*." She played with his cravat's knot, her slender fingers teasing the sensitive nerves and muscles in his neck.

His breath caught, and he had to swallow before he could speak. "Would I do such a thing, when we are two servants on a mission?"

"Of course," she answered simply. The linen strip fell away, opening his throat to her touch. She delicately rubbed the back of her finger up and down the long muscle on one side.

He tilted his head happily, trying not to purr.

Fair was fair, though.

He bent his head farther and kissed her neck, tasting the small patch of skin below her ear and above her dress's high collar.

She moaned sharply and surged up to meet him. He nuzzled and licked, lavishing attention on both her ear and the pulse hidden behind it until she lay shaking against his shoulder.

"Perhaps another kiss, *chérie*—to your wrist? Or to that most intriguingly hidden zone above your boots?"

"Jean-Marie . . ." Her luminous green eyes blinked, trying to focus.

He put a stop to that nonsense by lifting her onto the immensely sturdy dining table.

He pressed a kiss into her palm and lightly scraped his teeth over her wrist, teasing her senses in the fashion he'd learned would drive her wild.

"Jean-Marie!"

His breath hitched at the passion in her voice. Her free hand wrapped around his head and pulled him close, her fingers tangling in his hair.

He needed to pause for a moment until he recovered a little discipline. She didn't help him by caressing his head and whispering his name. Nobody had ever made those simple syllables sound exotic before.

He licked the delicate skin, sensitizing it. He kissed and nibbled— and blew lightly.

She moaned, her head arching back.

A hunter's smile of masculine triumph touched his lips. His chest tightened, and his heart beat faster, but he forced his body's demands back. Not yet, not yet.

He gathered her other hand in his and courted it, as he had the first.

She swayed, moaning softly, her eyes heavy-lidded with lust. Good; she wasn't thinking about yesterday's losses or the coming night's dangers.

Unable to stop himself, he kissed her sweet mouth again, savoring every delicious thrust and parry of their tongues as they tangled to taste more and more of each other. She pushed at his coat and somehow it vanished, together with his waistcoat.

He laid her backward onto the table. Hélène, *chère* Hélène, the most adored, the most perfect of all women. The one who made his heart sing and his breath rasp in his throat, until the frustration in his cock at being locked behind his trousers meant nothing compared to her pleasure.

Her legs opened, her woolen skirts tumbling across the glossy wood. He eased them farther upward, letting his fingers brush her stockings—so fragile compared to her heavy outer garments!

"Ah, *mon coeur.*" She gasped and writhed against him, sobbing his name when he fondled her knee.

He would not take her like a boar rutting in the fields. She would have her pleasure first. He had made himself that promise, and he would carry it out. He gritted his teeth yet again and wondered if there had ever been a vow more difficult to carry out.

His thumb stroked the inside of her thigh—and she moaned, a sound coming from deep within her soul.

He smiled tightly, hooked his foot around a chair, and pulled it up.

An instant later, he sat down and drew her hips to him, posing her on the edge of the table.

"Hmmph?"

The sound was barely a question, and he chose not to answer it with words, just as he refused to yield to the heat sparkling through his body. He caressed the inside of her other thigh, and she promptly tightened her legs around his hand.

Bien. Very, very good indeed.

He folded her skirts back and nuzzled her leg. A long, gentle lick brought her hips rolling to meet him, her folds dripping with cream.

Lovely, perfectly lovely—and the most intoxicating taste in the world, fully capable of driving a man insane.

His pulse speeded up, driving into every cell of his body until it made even his fingers tremble.

He tasted more, nibbling, teasing, stretching her sweet folds like the beautiful flower they were. Writing her lovely name with his tongue onto her wildly sensitive muscles, while his own skin leapt with a matching fire.

She was the finest banquet in the world, the richest and the spiciest delight ever to enrapture him. He could have spent hours or days finding new ways to lift her to the heights, while his body throbbed with anticipation.

Until finally he lifted her hips up a little more with a subtle twist and fine pressure on her mound—just so!—to urge her clit closer to his mouth.

And, ah, *mon Dieu*, did she howl with delight! She writhed and she moaned, she surged to meet him and she ground herself down on his fingers. She poured cream over his hand and she begged for more.

He was half-blind with lust. His cock was leaking pre-come, his trousers clearly having been unbuttoned by his mindless fingers at some point. Thinking about anything was nearly impossible—but he knew she had to be lifted into ecstasy, and left sated.

She cursed him again, frantic at being denied. Her fingernails sank into his shoulders, ripping through his shirt and stabbing his skin with a *vampira*'s strength.

He flung back his head, startled. His breath seized, and his cock jerked, demanding everything. Sanity fled.

He knocked the chair over in his hurry and came down on her.

"Take me now, *mon prince*!" she ordered, locking herself around him with both arms and legs, her green eyes closing in anticipation.

No one had ever called him that before with love.

He entered her in a single clean stroke, aroused beyond endurance. She tightened herself around him in welcome, her channel caressing his cock.

He pulled out and slid back, trying to make the moment last, while she rippled around him. Again, and again, and again, impending orgasm building deep within his spine and groin.

She bit his shoulders, sending the familiar bright burst of *vampiro* pleasure wheeling through him.

He stiffened and howled. Climax poured over and through him like a geyser, blasting up out of his spine and through his cock, pummeling his sanity as much as it shook him to the bone.

CASTRO SANCHEZ, BEFORE DAWN THE NEXT DAY

Hélène edged farther uphill along the slippery path, the old castle rising solidly at her back. The river foamed and frothed below her, laden with mud and boulders after the sudden thaw and a day of heavy rains. Bringing down the bridge would send fragments downriver past Napoleon's engineers' ability to recover them.

She could see remarkably well, though, the rain having yielded to a brilliant moon, which reflected off the river and the town. To her *vampira* eyesight, it was almost as bright as day. She could certainly discern the barrels of gunpowder she and Jean-Marie had laboriously wrestled into place under the pier closest to the tower. Destroy that, and the structure it supported would collapse in a cloud of stone and dust.

But if she miscalculated, the explosion could take out the tower, as well as some of the town and the mountain.

Jean-Marie cautiously pulled himself over the bridge and onto the road. There were still a few passersby at this hour, mostly a few ill-equipped soldiers serving the local junta at the castle. Many had already disappeared into the mountains to become guerillas, knowing full well their odds of defeating the tens of thousands of Frenchmen who'd arrive tomorrow were nonexistent. Plus, the English cavalry were rumored to be only hours behind the French but on the other side of the river.

He vanished into the shadows and reappeared beside her on the path. Scarcely wider than a goat trail and hanging perilously close to the cliff edge, it must have originally been an escape route for the castle's garrison. It was certainly the only spot from which she could see the ledge holding the gunpowder under the pier, given the restricted choices of bridge pier, wide ledge for gunpowder barrels, and a high enough sill to keep the fuse dry.

Unfortunately, this vantage point was almost completely exposed to any blast effects. They could knock her off her feet—and there wasn't a parapet here to protect her from sliding into the river, as there was beside the road.

Jean-Marie kissed her lightly on the mouth, a sweet but risky salutation, given their rather public location. She shook her head at him in mock dudgeon, which he completely ignored, of course. Instead, he threaded his fingers through hers, and they held hands, quietly enjoying each other's company.

"The monastery is holding Vigils tonight," he whispered.

"Prayer service?" She blinked. People were *moving* about the old city tonight?

He nodded grimly.

"How many are attending it?"

"At least two dozen, some of whom probably came from the other side of the river."

She bit back a curse. "Do we know how long the service will last?"

"Do you want to take the responsibility for guessing?" he countered.

She blew out a breath and shook her head. The priest could add extra prayers or psalms to extend the service until matins. Or simply send his congregants home early.

"I'll go down to beyond the bridge portal, where the statue of Saint Peter is," he said firmly.

"I can see it." The *downstream* side of the bridge? Chills ran through her that had nothing to do with the weather or the wind. If the blast went wrong, he could be hit by the portal.

"I'll signal you when the road is clear, so you can light the fuse. We don't have much time, after all, not with the British cavalry likely to arrive at dawn."

"Of course," she echoed faintly. She tried to think of an alternative but couldn't. Of course, they couldn't let innocent people die—and there was no other spot where someone could watch the church and signal her.

She nodded briskly, pushing her fears aside.

"Hélène . . ." He cupped her face in his hands. His fingers were long, callused, and shaking slightly. "Give me a kiss for luck, *chérie*."

She blinked at him, a little startled by his unusual seriousness, but leaned up to him. He caught her close in a passionate kiss, as if he wanted to devour her into his memories. An instant later, he released her abruptly and turned away, immediately vanishing into the shadows.

He reappeared when he reached the bridge portal, raising his hand in a startling echo of Saint Peter's protective watchfulness over his flock.

She waved back at him reassuringly. Her bruised lips were already healing from his kiss.

Church music stirred the night.

A quick glance reassured her she could still see the gunpowder, lurking under the bridge like an oncoming thundercloud.

Jean-Marie moved farther downstream along the road, his gray hair turning silver in the moonlight. She dug her nails into her palms, fighting not to scream at him to stay closer to her.

He braced himself beside the parapet, facing the church, and scanned the small plaza.

Calm swept over her, extending time into long steady beats. She and Jean-Marie were the perfect team, two halves of one whole, acting together to execute a single thought.

He came alert, poised on the balls of his feet like a dancer—or a brilliant swordsman.

The gunpowder barrel was as easy to see as if it stood next to her. A bit of slow match curled on the sill above it, dry as a cat on a winter's night.

Jean-Marie brought his hand up—and slashed it down, as if slicing through an opponent with his saber.

She pushed the slow match, shoving into motion the small things inside that couldn't be seen. Flame leaped into being on the fuse and sped toward the gunpowder.

What the devil? The slow match was burning much faster than she'd expected.

Hélène ran toward the road with its protective parapet. Jean-Marie raced toward her but he was far, too far away.

With an ear-shattering roar, the gunpowder blew up, shattering the night with its thunder. Flames leapt upward, stabbing through roiling clouds of black smoke. The deep, narrow gorge had increased the explosion into a beast of incalculable strength, rather than a neat shove at a single pile of stone.

The ground tried to tear itself apart under her feet, dropping Hélène to her knees onto the slick, muddy slope.

Windows shattered throughout the town in a heavy staccato torrent. Chunks of roadbed flew into the sky like birds and rained down in an avalanche, chipping chunks of stone the size of men's heads out of the tower. The great bridge portal swayed, its immense columns teetering as if drunk.

Hélène started to slide toward the river and grabbed for an ancient rosebush, sturdy enough to climb several stories up the castle.

Jean-Marie flung himself up the road toward Hélène. Debris rained down around him, and cracks opened in the cobblestones under his feet.

Something groaned, long and loud. Jean-Marie hesitated but quickly redoubled his speed, ignoring the huge pieces of stone dropping from the sky.

With a great crack, the portal's columns ripped out of the cliff nearest the town, taking Jean-Marie with them, as if a giant had thrown them. They fell into the river, followed by the bridge's few remaining pieces.

"Nooo!" Hélène screamed. "No!"

She caught the rosebush and brought herself up with a yank, her feet dangling over the precipice. A crack formed in the tower and another, as chunks began to slowly drop off it.

The church's great bell was ringing madly. Ignoring her own peril, Hélène changed her grip on the thorny, icy shrub until she could peer into the river.

Everything below was thundering white waves, pounding against chunks of rock the size of horses. For an instant, she could see Jean-Marie's head, but he wasn't moving.

One of the columns rolled over him, and he went under, not to be seen again.

"Jean-Marie!" she screamed. "Jean-Marie!"

A crooked gap formed around the bush's roots, and it slid toward the river. The tower groaned like a dying soul.

Was she going into the water, too? Did it matter? Did anything truly matter now? Sobs ripped at her heart.

"Hold on, ma'am. We've got you. Uh, *señora, por favor*," a very Welsh accent coaxed, and a man's arm reached out from the unstable slope.

She reluctantly let him catch her.

TEN

"Ma'am, there's no sign of anyone washed up below the castle."

Hélène closed her eyes, glad her heavy veils concealed the signs of still more tears. The major had led the squadron of British Hussars who'd stormed into Castro Sanchez in the explosion's wake and rescued her from the cliff edge. He was also well enough trained that he'd recognized her as a spy, after they'd exchanged passwords. He'd guarded her very closely, of course, keeping her out of town in the British camp and away from the French army. She doubted many, if any, of the local townsfolk had caught a glimpse of her since the patrol had brought her down off the tower.

"Thank you for looking, major. I'm sure you searched very thoroughly."

At least her voice was completely composed, as befitted a Sainte-Pazanne or a d'Agelet. Without Jean-Marie at her side, she had only her family pride to uphold her, after all, throughout the long lonely years—centuries!—ahead.

Not that it would help her to forget him.

Her visitor lingered, and she waited to learn the reason why.

"If you don't mind, ma'am, the colonel would like to leave within the hour."

"Very well." She rose, shaking out her skirts. She'd sponged out the worst of the mud after they'd brought her safely off that cliff.

"If you'll tell us where your luggage is, I'll send a man to fetch it."

Her stomach knotted, and she fought the need to wrap her arms around herself and keen her grief. Go back to the rooms where she'd last shared love with Jean-Marie? And relive those last happy moments? No!

"Ma'am? If you don't have any luggage, I'm sure General Moore's chief exploring officer can provide you with some clothes." Despite the major's evident caution in dealing with her, at least he was clever enough to know General Moore's chief spy had the resources and the knowledge to cope.

"I have no baggage worth reclaiming, major." Let the honest landlord have their clothing, whenever he decided to search the rooms. "I am ready to depart whenever you wish."

"As you wish, ma'am."

CASTRO SANCHEZ, THREE DAYS LATER

Jean-Marie turned his back on the devastated plaza after two days of searching and refused to scream—or curse God. Either would have been satisfying. Neither would have solved anything.

He'd managed to grab a large beam, part of the roadbed's supports, and hold on to it during a wild ride downstream. Water, stone, and mud had all done their best to batter him into pieces—but that was nothing compared to arriving back here and learning nobody knew what had happened to his gentle lady. They'd all seen the bridge destroyed and the tower nearly shattered. But they hadn't seen any survivors.

The French had killed her, as surely as if they'd put a gun to her head.

He smiled mirthlessly. And for that, he'd carry out her work as her memorial. It was the least he could do for her.

Hélène, his only love. He'd become a *vampiro* for her.

Une éternité d'amour ne paraîtrait jamais que passagère. Loving you forever doesn't seem like long enough.

He had to reach San Leandro, despite two warring armies on the main road and impassable winter snows in the northern mountains. He started walking north, his pack on his back.

Barely an hour later, he slipped and fell into the river again, the waves tumbling him like a child's toy. He staggered out of the water and collapsed, gasping for breath but bitterly determined.

A dozen Spaniards, very roughly dressed, thin but still showing signs of strength, watched him warily. Taller than most on the Iberian Peninsula. More than one had blue eyes, while several had blond hair. A small fire burned behind them, half-hidden among the willow trees.

Hands returned to pockets, evidence they now considered him a threat rather than someone to be rescued.

Jean-Marie blinked and shook his head, clearing the water from his face. Swaying slightly, he took a chance on the language Rodrigo had taught him for very private conversations.

"Bon día, señores. ¿Comos está?" he greeted them politely in *Gallego*.

Their faces immediately brightened, and they overwhelmed him with a flood of the same language.

He damn near collapsed in relief.

Thanks be to God, he'd found a group of migrant Galician workers returning to their homes in the northwest. They were probably delayed by dodging provincial juntas who wanted to draft them into local armies. They'd recognized him as another stranger in a strange land and welcomed him.

Strong arms helped him to the fire, while others built it higher.

"Do you know where San Leandro is?"

"Of course, grandfather," they assured him. "We are taking the smugglers' road to the coast, then the old pilgrims' route to Santiago. We will pass by San Leandro and can take you there."

Grandfather? *Nom de Dieu*, had his hair turned that gray so quickly? He laughed—and spluttered on an unexpected mouthful of water.

Someone shoved a cup of thin soup into his hand, somebody else draped a blanket over his shoulder, and two men began to strip his boots off his feet.

This should work—as long as the winter snows didn't turn brutal before they could cross the high northern mountains to safety, the route all the armies had already deemed impossible.

SAN LEANDRO, THAT NIGHT

Rodrigo's heart was pounding in his ears, and his breath rasped through his throat. Overhead, feet shuffled softly as nuns prepared the church for evening services, their voices a muted river of timeless customs retold.

Simple iron candelabra swung from the ceiling, illuminating the glory of vaulted stone whose beauty could make cathedrals take flight. Behind Rodrigo burned the banks of votive candles he and others had lighted to lift their prayers to heaven.

He was alone in San Rafael Arcángel's crypt—except for the tombs of his wife and children.

Blanche, his heart's delight. The unknown carver had honored her as a daughter of the church, placing her in an attitude of eternal prayer with her hands pressed firmly together. He'd faithfully shown her habit as a married sister of Santiago, the warrior monks whose order Rodrigo had joined as a novice five hundred years ago.

Somehow he'd also recreated her alertness and warmth, the vibrancy which had made her the light of Rodrigo's life from the moment he first saw her.

Rodrigo almost expected her to sit up and start talking to him. Perhaps it was because he'd spent years recounting to himself every second of their few short years together, until every shining note of her laughter was as clear to him now as the day he'd first heard it. Or the wry patience behind her wise words, or the anticipatory gleam in her eyes when she waited to go upstairs with him at night . . .

He missed all of that and more with a bone-chilling ache the centuries had done little to ease.

For family. Someone like Inez, the daughter he'd never seen walk this earth, although her effigy lay within a few paces. Or Fernando, the son who'd been a famous warrior and beloved patron of these lands. Or Beatriz, whose beauty and compassion were legendary as far south as Toledo. All the grandchildren he'd prayed would find health and prosperity, and their children.

His gut twisted, tearing him apart worse than anything he'd experienced during his centuries of captivity.

He dropped to his knees and prayed for peace, for a new beginning. For something more than what he had. For what he couldn't have clearly said . . .

Hours—or minutes—later, boots thudded on the stone, bringing him onto his feet to face the newcomer. He flushed slightly, embarrassed for having overreacted in these sacred precincts. "Señor Alvarez."

"Please forgive me for having disturbed you," Luis Alvarez apologized from the foot of the stairwell. He twisted his hat, straightening an already immaculate brim. "I can return later if you'd prefer."

"No, there is no need for that," Rodrigo spread his hands. "There is more than enough grace here for both of us."

Alvarez nodded acceptance. "My daughter is expecting my first grandchild," he explained, coming forward into the light. "It's tradition to light candles and ask *Doña* Blanche to watch over her."

Rodrigo blinked. His darling had never had an easy time in childbirth.

"It is a woman's custom." Alvarez shrugged, flashing his easy smile. "More men than not honor it as well—but we do it when we won't be seen."

"I won't speak of it to anyone," Rodrigo assured him, "if you'll tell me the origins." He joined the other, looking across the quiet space filled with his sleeping children.

"*Doña* Blanche was the matriarch of a very large family. Only three children—but thirty-one grandchildren and more than seventy great-grandchildren, every one healthy and happy. All of us here carry their blood in our veins. Who would not wish that for their children?"

"Who indeed?" Rodrigo muttered, remembering all the hours he'd spent on his knees in that stinking cell in his captor's castle, praying his descendants be given the joy and health he was denied. *Dios*, no wonder Luis looked like him—he'd have to be some sort of great-great-grandson.

"*Doña* Blanche was a holy woman, who spent as much time doing good deeds for the people as she did for her own family."

Rodrigo nodded, remembering how often she'd blistered his ears for paying more attention to politics than the common folk.

"Her passage into heaven was graced by the archbishop and bishop's prayers. All of her children were there, as well as her grandchildren and great-grandchildren. It is said so many priests and nuns sang, that the angels themselves wept." Alvarez's eyes unashamedly glimmered with tears. "Her last words were of her husband, of course. She told her children not to mourn, since he'd come again to San Leandro."

"What?" Rodrigo croaked. He swayed and caught himself against the wall, unsteady atop knees that suddenly seemed to be made of straw.

"*Sí, Doña* Blanche was deeply in love with Don Rodrigo, the great knight who went away on crusade."

"*Great* knight?"

"The battles he fought? And the tournament against the French champion? Parry left, thrust right!" Grinning, Alvarez mimed the moves exactly—to Rodrigo's startled fascination. "The stories of his life have been passed down through the generations, exactly as *Doña* Blanche first told them. It would take an entire winter to recount all the great songs and the poetry written about him."

Rodrigo gaped, unable to form words. Just as he'd retold himself every minute of his life with her in order to keep her alive in his heart, Blanche had ensured he'd be remembered here.

"Even now, we know Don Rodrigo is *our* knight, and he lives somewhere. The legend promises he will return when his people's need is the greatest."

¡Imposible! Yet Alvarez's expression was as steadfast as when he drove cattle across a stream and through a muddy field.

"Do you believe all of that?" Rodrigo asked, his voice fading to a whisper.

"I believe there is more than the good doctor can readily explain from his leather-bound books. I believe a good woman's love and faith can work miracles beyond a man's understanding. I will not turn my back on something I have not seen disproven." Alvarez's eyes met his, dark and quite serious.

"Alvarez, *amigo*, no mortal man can live five centuries."

"I have told you this as one Perez to another." The other clapped him on the shoulder, eyes boring into his from the same level. "You resemble Don Rodrigo, as many of us do—since we are descendants of his children."

"No," Rodrigo denied instinctively. Had he guessed Rodrigo truly was *Doña* Blanche's husband?

"His blood runs true, *amigo*, even in distant cousins. Have faith—and trust God will answer a good woman's prayers when He deems the time is right."

When Rodrigo didn't answer, Alvarez shook his head compassionately. "There's no need to talk more about this today. I will return later to say my prayers."

Rodrigo lifted his hand in farewell, deliberately ignoring the last unbelievable words. A prophecy saying he would return to save these people? He, the knight who'd chosen to let damsels die? Admittedly, it was while his *creador* was trying to break him during those centuries of torture. He'd given Rodrigo the brutal choice: Become an assassin, murdering anyone and everyone ordered to—or watch another damsel die. Rodrigo had believed it the lesser of two evils to watch the ladies pass into the next life, rather than become a killer for all eternity.

Even so, their blood still stained his hands, no matter how often he prayed for their souls or had masses said for them. He was not worthy of saving anyone, since he'd failed the basic oath to protect women and virgins!

No, he could not be the one whose return was foretold.

Far, far better to ponder the incredible gift his beloved darling had given him.

"*Blanche,*" Rodrigo whispered. He dropped to his knees before his lady's tomb. *You gave me a family. A small town full of people, carrying my blood, many of them bearing my likeness. Because of you—and the stories you left behind—they welcome me as one of their own.*

Family.

Giddiness welled up deep inside him, as when his darling had first told him she was carrying their child.

He threw back his head and flung out his arms, embracing his wife and children—and the family beyond.

His, by the grace of God and his wife's love.

ALONG THE RIVER ESLA IN LEÓN, THE SAME NIGHT

The squalid Spanish village dozed uneasily under the midnight sky, too full of French boots and muskets to openly fret. Couriers trotted briskly up and down the steps of the largest house, saddlebags slung over their shoulders. French cavalrymen from the Imperial Guard, the Emperor's "Favored Children," stood watch in the plaza. Their cynical eyes and well-oiled weapons announced they'd earned their gorgeous uniforms by being the best in battle.

Too many men and too many guards for a single regiment or even a corps, judging by what Celeste had been told in Britain. Who then?

She shot her escort a considering look but continued to follow him meekly into the house. Nobody ever lived to argue twice with a *vampiro mayor*. She was damned lucky he hadn't killed her for not bringing the codebook when she escaped Sir Andrew.

She'd told them everything she knew. The only remaining question was what would happen to her next. She couldn't always be used against British spies, since those devils would sooner or later realize she'd changed sides—even if Sir Andrew didn't make it back to England.

Did she want to work as a spy somewhere else in Europe? Russia perhaps or Austria?

She pulled a face and swept her skirts safely away from another soldier's boots. Ragged peasant's clothing, in tatters like her plans for destroying Hélène. She'd prefer to rest and regain her composure—perhaps even enjoy the finer things in life again, which had been wrongfully denied to her for so long. But how?

The upper hallway displayed half a dozen men, all garbed in still more glamorous uniforms and bustling about carrying neat leather portfolios, full of papers. Another edged past her, carefully holding a covered silver tray surmounted by an eagle.

An *imperial* eagle.

Napoleon was here? Why on earth did he want to see her? Did she care?

A guard quickly opened the final door for the servant, grinning at a shared joke. As soon as the door closed, his tanned face swiftly solidified into a suspicious visage again, underlined by the crooked scar splitting his forehead.

Despite herself, Celeste shivered. The penalties for failure would be dealt quickly and ruthlessly in these quarters.

Her escort marched directly up to the same guard, who looked only slightly friendlier than his cohort. A whispered conversation ensued, throughout which the guards eyed her with all the enthusiasm of butchers considering hogs in a marketplace. As if whispering would keep her from hearing anything she chose!

Finally they knocked and opened the door, in response to a growled reply.

"Celeste de Sainte-Pazanne, as you requested, Your Majesty." The *vampiro mayor* bowed deeply.

Dark eyes swept over her like a thunderbolt. Why, he was just a *prosaico*! Uncommonly charismatic with those eyes and the force of will blazing out of him. Raoul had always set maidens sighing, but this fellow never would, if you concealed his eyes. Even so, he was a man—and fond of bedtime diversions by all accounts.

Perhaps if she always had a lover to protect her, life would improve. And who better than the Emperor?

"Your majesty." She sank into her lowest curtsy, her eyes sweeping over him lasciviously before her lashes veiled them. She focused her power as tightly as she could, gambling nobody else would hear her.

Desire me, she commanded the Emperor of the French. *Desire me* . . .

A chair was shoved back against the wall. Celeste kept her eyes modestly lowered and her smirk completely private. A well-kept hand lifted her up.

"My dear lady." Napoleon patted her hand. "Welcome home. We thank you for your great services to us and to France."

His passionate eyes swept boldly over her.

She allowed herself to smile. Encouragingly, of course.

SAN LEANDRO, JANUARY 1809

Sunset touched the high peaks, gilding a few bits of snow but utterly failing to penetrate the forests or warm the great granite massif.

From high atop the ancient watchtower, Rodrigo measured it and the passing of time, wondering yet again if he should hire men to guard the bridge into San Leandro. Few strangers would travel that road in the dark, with a howling wind in their face. This fortress guarded the northern road, with its coastal trade and seaborne raiders in ages past. He'd rented the house attached to it, even though it was almost a mile outside the town proper.

Days had passed since the last refugees had passed through, fleeing the desperate British army and the pursuing French.

They'd told horrible tales of battles conducted amid the mountains, with men and beasts dying of exhaustion as much as wounds. Any civilians caught in their paths could be destroyed by battle—or demands for food, supplies, and shelter. Most frightening of all, the French made a practice of doing so, backing up their voracious appetite with murder and rapine.

But none of those horrors had touched San Leandro. *Gracias a Dios*, no French raiding party had reached this valley, even though they were in Lugo a day's walk away.

Rodrigo had Seen the French coming to San Leandro but not by which road or exactly when. That was the damnable thing about his gift—it was most useful about disasters for his people. But it didn't foretell specifics, and it said less and less the closer events came to him or those he loved.

He'd spent his time doing what he could for the people, even though he'd only be here a few months. He'd hired men to improve the roads and rebuild walls. Women had made cheeses and sausages, storing them deep in caves to last through the winter. He now had mobility and provisions, a military commander's prerequisites for waging war.

If he used those roads and provisions to build an army, he'd be usurping the rights and honor of this land's rightful lord. Yet if he didn't, the ones he'd come to love could be destroyed. Alvarez, with his wife and three lovely daughters. Emilio, Alvarez's son-in-law with his blatant adoration for his heavily expectant wife. Father Michael's delight in little children, and old Sanchez the baker's ability to know every man and woman in town . . .

Rodrigo slapped the old parapet, cursing with a Galician's easy fluidity. There were too many people who might be injured if he failed yet again.

Life would be easier if he could adopt Sara's insouciance. She'd quickly found a dozen or so individuals willing to engage in discreet, carnal pleasures and rotated her time among them. She appeared quite happy and healthy—unless someone happened to mention Jean-Marie. Her conversation would come stuttering to a halt, her eyes going wide and anguished.

He was little better. A thousand demons stabbed his heart whenever he counted the days since Jean-Marie had last drunk *vampiro* blood. If his best friend was still alive this long after the blood-laced wine had run out, it would be a miracle. *Por Dios*, how he had prayed to see Jean-Marie again in the flesh!

No wonder he and Sara had an unspoken agreement to change the subject, whenever their conversation fell upon Jean-Marie.

Rodrigo eyed the western mountains yet again. There were rumors a great battle had been fought between the British and the French at Corunna, the seaport. If so, the French would need supplies for the winter, and those murdering locusts would steal from anywhere and everyone.

Simply organizing sentries against such a pestilence would not be enough. Those insects would have to be fought—which could be done successfully here in San Leandro, a natural fortress with few entrances.

If he ground Don Fernando Perez's pride beneath his boot heel, that is.

He grimaced. Even if Don Fernando hadn't been the direct descendant of his own Fernando, he'd have hated to deal another man such a blow. As it was—the mere thought was almost insufferable.

He turned toward the stairs, his cape swinging around him. Maybe if he put sentries on the bridge . . .

Hooves plodded along the northern road, harder and more distinct by some trick of sound than a man's footsteps might have been. A mule's hooves—not cattle, nor donkey, nor horse.

A frisson ran up the back of Rodrigo's neck, and he ran to the opposite side of the watchtower where he could see the road more clearly.

A small party of men emerged into a patch of light, trudging wearily like those who have already traveled far and expect to walk at least as far again. They were roughly dressed but warmly, in heavy cloaks with the hoods pulled up against the coming storm. One of them rode a bony mule, who seemed slightly better off than his master, given how the man swayed in the saddle. Another traveler walked beside them, clearly ready to lend a hand if needed.

Obviously sensing a watcher, the rider looked up. His cape's thick wool fell back to reveal white hair, brilliantly blue eyes—and Jean-Marie's face. His teeth flashed in an enormous grin. *"¡Hola, Rodrigo!"* Jean-Marie rasped, barely audible even to *vampiro* ears.

Rodrigo's heart came alive with joy, hurling itself over the ancient stone parapet to his best friend. He flung himself down the stairs, tugging hard on the bell's rope as he passed. Its sweet cry rang through the small vale, telling of welcome guests.

He ran out onto the road, and Jean-Marie's companions quickly made way for him, murmuring greetings. He acknowledged them with a bare nod, all his attention on the *compañero*—who should not be alive, given the days without *vampiro* blood.

Jean-Marie's mouth quirked with something of the old insouciance, the smirk of a boy who knows more than his schoolteacher.

Rodrigo's frantic heartbeat eased from a panicked gallop to a more controlled canter. He'd at least have time to talk to his old friend, even if so much pure white hair meant that death was due within days. It was at least far longer than his original guess of mere hours.

He lifted Jean-Marie off the mule, thinking he was prepared to face any change after his years of exposure to *compañeros* at the eastern *vampiro* courts. Underneath the cloak, where Jean-Marie would once have been strong-limbed enough to wrench a recalcitrant horse into submission—now he was as fragile as a sparrow, hunched over in his saddle with skin barely glossing over his bones. Even the stench of long travel and few baths meant nothing compared to that horror.

Rodrigo's breath caught in his throat, cold terror slashing through his veins. He might have known for decades he'd lose Jean-Marie's company one day—but this physical reality drove home the coming sorrow as nothing else ever had. He quickly slid his arm around Jean-Marie's waist, taking the other's full weight.

"I can walk, old man," the younger fellow demurred, in a barely audible croak, and fought to free himself.

"Then do me a favor and don't struggle," Rodrigo retorted, sotto voce.

Sara and the servants spilled out of the house, their eyes wide with surprise.

Certain she would provide the necessary hospitality, Rodrigo half-carried, half-swept Jean-Marie inside. Sara's hooded eyes followed them, but she neither asked for—nor did he offer—any explanation.

Jean-Marie's boots skidded on the heavily polished floor, sending him sliding toward the floor like a marionette with slashed strings.

Rodrigo caught him in both arms, his throat tightening. Never had he seen such appalling clumsiness in his friend—nor lifted him so easily, even after allowing for his own *vampiro* strength. Sunset was coming all too quickly into this *compañero*'s life.

"Have I lost that much weight?" Jean-Marie's voice was a very thin whisper.

"*Sí*—a surprising amount." Rodrigo gave him the truth, as he always had. As he always would, no matter how bitter.

"Damn. I was hoping their shock over how fast my hair turned gray was because they didn't know *compañeros*." His French accent was more marked than usual, returning him to the young prince from Versailles. The body had burned away, leaving only the purest of flames—its spirit.

Rodrigo gritted his teeth and quickly changed his hold to his earlier, more casual grip. He'd honor his friend's pride by only supporting him with one arm around his waist, rather than providing all the support he needed. He eased his feelings by violently kicking the library door shut behind them. He guided Jean-Marie onto the settee, bitterly aware the other's breathing was growing harsh and faint.

"Beautiful room," Jean-Marie wheezed, fighting to keep his eyes open.

Social conversation about a sitting room suitable for the Paris of fifty years ago? How many hundreds of times had either of them ignored gilded furniture underneath painted walls, ornate little statues, and collections of music boxes?

A muscle ticked hard in Rodrigo's jaw. Dammit, must a century of friendship end like this? Not while he had breath.

He rapidly unbuttoned his cloak and let it drop onto the floor. He sat down and shifted Jean-Marie firmly into the crook of his arm. He shook back the ruffles on one sleeve, opened his vein with a single frantic slash, and brought his wrist to Jean-Marie's mouth.

Pure *vampiro major* blood, suffused with passionate concern and undiluted by wine, should have an immediate salutary effect. The only way to gain a stronger effect would be to feed his friend from Rodrigo's jugular, if Jean-Marie was close to dying—but doing so would grant him *El Abrazo*.

Blue eyes came alive, the only color in that parchment face.

"Do you mean to fight me, *amigo?*" Rodrigo asked warily, remembering all the times Jean-Marie had objected to prolonging his existence as a *compañero*. He didn't want to force him to drink the blood—but he would, at least this time.

"Not at all, *mon frère*." A singularly determined smile touched the other's lips. "Please give me as much blood as you can."

Dios mío, what the devil had changed? But he could worry about that later.

Before Rodrigo could proffer his wrist politely as he'd been taught too damn well, Jean-Marie snatched up Rodrigo's arm and brought the bleeding wound to his mouth. He set his lips to the gash and sucked hard.

A current of living crimson flowed between them.

Rodrigo's heartbeat strengthened, and warmth crept over his skin, like standing near a fireplace on a cold day. He murmured wordless reassurance and awkwardly stroked the other's hair.

Jean-Marie swallowed again, matching Rodrigo's pulse. And again, in perfect rhythm with Rodrigo's heartbeat.

Rodrigo rumbled approbation and drew his friend closer, settling him into a more comfortable position.

Jean-Marie drank, taking Rodrigo's blood almost like a babe taking his mother's milk. Peace suffused Rodrigo.

Jean-Marie's pace slowed to only a few drops at a time, licking delicately at Rodrigo's skin before he lay back against the settee, eyes half shut.

Rodrigo watched him lazily, no longer wondering why those eastern *vampiros mayores* had chosen to surround themselves with *compañeros*. This hadn't been the blinding rapture of sharing blood with another *vampiro*, but he'd nonetheless enjoyed himself. He was also damn glad he'd fed very well for the past few days—indeed for the

past few weeks. He still had enough blood left to work wonders—
shapeshift, fight a duel with another *vampiro*, grant *El Abrazo* . . .

"You need a more powerful entourage in these deadly times."
Jean-Marie stretched as elegantly as a cat, clearly recovered from his
journey, and reassembled himself into a sitting position.

"Probably. The French are in Lugo and have been patrolling very
close to us." Rodrigo considered the distance to the wine decanters but
decided against moving immediately. "What do you have in mind?"

"I want to become a *vampiro*."

What the hell? Jean-Marie who hated being a *compañero*—now
wanted to become a *vampiro*? "What the devil are you talking
about?"

"Why do you think I came back here, when I could have died with
the British army fighting Napoleon?" Brilliantly alert blue eyes met
his. "I intend to live for at least a few more years."

"That's an absurd reason to become a *vampiro*!"

"Hélène d'Agelet died fighting Napoleon's troops. I have sworn to
carry on her work."

¡Ay, mierda! This news changed everything. To fulfill an oath to
the woman he loved, Jean-Marie would probably dare anything—
including become a *vampiro*. As a *compañero*, he'd be dead within
days. His only chance of survival was as a *vampiro*.

Even so, Rodrigo's stomach heaved when he remembered how his
mind and body had been flayed for years by the agony of becoming
a *vampiro*. The months and years of thinking of nothing else except
blood and sex, craving it until he'd begged even the foulest brutes
for more—anyone except his hated *creador* and Diego. He could not,
would not, put anyone else through that. It was too appalling a life
for even the strongest.

He would never force anyone into *El Abrazo* as he had been forced,
and he would do his best to talk any candidate out of their decision.

"If I grant you *El Abrazo*, you would become my lover—utterly
enslaved to me sexually for at least two years, possibly nine."

"And I'd run those imperial brutes ragged from one end of Spain to
the other." Jean-Marie's eyes were as inflexible as the tip of a sword.

"You would also become my servant, completely obedient to me—and nobody else." The more polite warnings hadn't worked; now it was time for the bone-deep one.

"Not just the few months of the rut, during *La Lujuria*?" For the first time, Jean-Marie seemed startled. Of course, Rodrigo wouldn't be following *vampiro* custom in this. "Rodrigo—"

"Hear me out, Jean-Marie! I killed my *creador*."

"Impossible!"

"I decapitated him—and I won't permit even the slightest chance any *hijo* of mine would ever do the same to me. I will therefore be my *hijo*'s only blood source as long as he is physically immature—a *cachorro*."

Jean-Marie stared at him, measuring his resolution.

Rodrigo looked back, absolutely immovable. He had spent too many years in too much agony: Whether it was logical or not, he would not risk meeting the same end he'd dealt to his *creador*. The only guarantee of complete control over an *hijo* was to be his only blood source, while he was a *cachorro*.

Jean-Marie gulped hard, silently yielding the point. He rose and walked to the sideboard.

"Sara can't provide me any blood?" he asked, turning back to face Rodrigo.

"Other blood sources would weaken the bond to the *creador*. I had many blood sources, so I was able to ignore my *creador*'s commands." He'd felt his need to obey decrease every time he'd found another blood source. Disgusting as many of them had been—much as he'd hated to prostitute himself—he'd still been as promiscuous as possible, hoping to regain his freedom of action. It had worked in the end.

Jean-Marie tapped on the sideboard, beating out an erratic rhythm and looking at something far away.

Rodrigo remained quiet, hoping his friend would see reason and stop talking about becoming a *vampiro*.

"Would I still be tied to Sara, as I am now?" Jean-Marie's face was hidden, and Rodrigo couldn't read his voice.

"No. Your loyalties as a *compañero* would be dissolved, leaving behind only those of a *vampiro* to his *creador*." That was an easy answer. The link between *creador* and *hijo* overwhelmed everything else, except the *conyugal* bond—which was so rare as to not warrant any discussion.

"But still . . ." Jean-Marie was very pale. He jerked himself into motion and began to pace the room, his expression a study in horror.

Rodrigo relaxed slightly, careful to keep his own opinions concealed. Those weren't all of his objections, of course—only the ones most likely to weigh with Jean-Marie, the man so completely focused on women.

"Very well." Jean-Marie spun around and drew himself to attention. "I agree."

"To?" Rodrigo raised the haughtiest eyebrow he could.

"To all of your terms. I will be your lover." To give his courage full credit, Jean-Marie's voice barely wavered when he described his future activities. "And you will be my only blood source so long as I am a *cachorro*, which will give you complete command over me for the rest of my life."

Madre de Dios, his independent friend was willing to completely yield himself? "You trust me that far?"

"With my life and soul," Jean-Marie said simply.

With his *soul*? Unaccustomed joy rang through Rodrigo. But what if he betrayed it? What if Jean-Marie experienced the same shattering agony of mind and body Rodrigo had when he became a *vampiro*? Could either of them survive that horror?

He took a deep breath, grasping for space to regain his footing. "It's too soon for you to be certain."

"Rodrigo, there is nothing else in my world." Jean-Marie frowned at him.

"You may find another reason to live!"

Jean-Marie huffed out a breath, visibly leashing the words quivering on his tongue.

"Take a few days to think it over, while you regain your strength." Rodrigo shoved his hair impatiently away from his face and picked up his cloak. "I'm going to pray privately at the Blessed Virgin's shrine, a mile north of here. I'll give you blood again later tonight and tomorrow."

"I won't change my mind," Jean-Marie warned, his fingers twitching as if eager to demand Rodrigo's immediate acquiescence.

"Probably not—but grant me the time to think, too." Rodrigo managed a tight smile. "I have never wished to become a *creador*." Only a simple family man with my darling Blanche and our children at my side.

ELEVEN

Rodrigo knelt before the shrine to the *Santísima Virgen*. For some ridiculously sentimental reason, he had his knightly sword strapped to his back, as if he was on a vigil—even though explaining its presence would be nearly impossible. He might even have to resort to *vampiro* tricks. Even so, he'd brought it along because his inner eye had Seen him leaving the house with it tonight.

He shrugged the folly away, together with any discomfort caused by the great weapon's presence. He'd spent too many years traveling and fighting alongside this blade for it to be anything other than an extension of himself. He was free to pray and meditate, as he'd come here to do.

And watch to see if this was the night and the road that the French would arrive by.

There'd been a shrine here as long as he could remember, but it had always been very small—a roof large enough to protect two people, a stone floor for them to kneel on, and stone walls on three sides. The beauty was all in the simple statue of the Blessed Virgin and her son, looking out on the wild grace of the surrounding forest and mountain.

Here was peace and simplicity, just as there had been five centuries ago when he had been a boy. And the only time he'd brought Blanche here to meet his family.

He'd kept vigil here the night before he'd left for Toledo to join the king's court. He'd had so many ambitions then—to be a great knight, to become a member of the Order of Santiago, to be famous in battle, to gain great lands and protect his people from all enemies . . .

He'd even wished to conquer a lovely lady's heart.

He'd done some of that. He'd been knighted by a king, he'd served a great prince, he'd become a novice in the Order of Santiago, he'd been loved by the sweetest of all ladies.

But had he been truly worthy of her? Would she have approved when he'd let those maidens die in his *creador*'s torture pits, rather than become another of his *creador*'s assassins? Perhaps.

Would Blanche understand why he hesitated to give Jean-Marie a chance at avenging his lady, even if it meant giving him *El Abrazo*?

He winced. Probably not. She'd always had a very blunt, pragmatic outlook toward others' love affairs, even though she rarely interfered.

Would she have gathered up her household and wandered the world with him all these years? Or would she have sought to help and protect their small ones somewhere along the way? Would she have built a fortress to keep the night's dangers away from them?

Santa Madre de Dios. Rodrigo's hands curled into fists, and he pounded them against each other. Blanche had always fought to protect others. She might have traveled the world with him—but she'd have had her charities and her causes at every stop.

If she'd been with him, he'd have built her a home long before now, just to protect her and those she guarded. It would have been part of his knightly vows—the part he hadn't done much of all these years, the command to protect the weak.

He closed his eyes and crossed himself. Then he began to pray for forgiveness and the strength to do better.

*   *   *

Luis hummed softly while he strolled to Vespers at the church, happily listening to his wife and daughter's eternal chatter about her pregnancy. One might think nobody had ever had a baby before, the way his wife fussed over the imminent arrival of her first grandchild. But he was almost as bad, especially since Emilio, Inez's husband, was his oldest friend's son.

Bianca, his second daughter, would be married in the spring, while his youngest had her eye on a boy from another village. He knew they were fine lads, and his wife assured him they'd make good husbands, although he wasn't entirely sure of that. Even so, there were a few things he could do to test them before the knots were tied and his darlings left his protection.

Light sparked from the hillside and was gone in an instant, leaving black spots in his eyes and chills pattering down his back.

He frowned. He rolled his shoulders, willing the shivers to leave his spine. He was a prosperous farmer and well dressed for this weather. He should not, could not, be cold.

He counted up his beloved ladies, determined to distract himself. Beatriz, his wife, still as slim and lithe as when he'd married her. Inez, their eldest, ready to give birth within the next few weeks. Bianca, tall and dark as himself—a good girl, *gracias a Dios*, but her laughter drew men the way flowers lured bees. And little Ana, quiet, hardworking, and beautiful beyond belief.

They stepped from the cobblestone plaza into the colonnade bordering San Rafael Arcángel. More of their friends greeted them and began to exchange scraps of gossip in the last few minutes before entering church.

Luis caught sight of his godfather, Carlos Alvarez—the *alcalde* and San Leandro's most important official—talking earnestly to two other men. Lacking any instructions from Don Fernando Perez, the local grandee, *Tío Carlos* hadn't even been able to decide whether they should hide more of their livestock and food. The lines in his face were deep set, almost engraved into his skin, making him appear as fragile as an ice bridge.

If *Tío Carlos* proved too sick, Luis would have to lead the next town council meeting, since he was second to *Tío Carlos*. In that case, he'd be the one to answer his neighbors' questions and make the decisions.

However grievous their concerns were, they were all subjects that had been discussed many times before and did not have to be reconsidered tonight.

Surely, here—on sacred ground!—he could ignore how his hair prickled under his collar and the iciness of his palms inside his good gloves. Instead, he could fill his eyes with his beautiful family. God had blessed him beyond anything he had ever prayed for.

Luis relaxed and resolved to make an extra donation to the poor box.

A bugle rang out, the long, angry note ripping apart the valley's peace. Horses' hooves pounded over the cobblestones, metal clanging and rattling with every beat. Men shouted and swore in the distance, echoes rising up and beating against each other in a cacophony of terror.

Children flung themselves against their mothers' knees. Women screamed or turned pale. Men stared at each other. A few turned to run.

The horses galloped into the plaza, as dreadfully as any plague ever foretold. Their riders were ragged, armed to the teeth—and French. In an instant, every exit was blocked by a soldier with a leveled gun.

Predatory eyes marked the location of every woman.

Inez gasped—and wrapped her arms protectively around her enormous belly. Glaring, Emilio placed himself between the intruders and his wife. Cursing softly, Beatriz gathered her two youngest daughters to her.

Overhead, the great tocsin bell began to ring out the alarm.

Tío Carlos drew himself up and strode forward to demand an explanation, magnificent in his dignity but showing every one of his eighty years.

His heart in his throat, Luis crossed himself, silently yielded his family to God's protection, and fell into step with his *alcalde*.

* * *

Jean-Marie came down the stairs to the landing, chuckling softly. Given good food, hot baths, and clean clothes, his Galician friends had managed to fully enjoy them all. Now they slept in the attic, their faces as innocently relaxed as babes despite their hard lives.

Perhaps he could persuade them to rest here tomorrow but probably not. They were all eager to reach their homes as quickly as possible.

Horses' hooves clattered on the courtyard's cobblestones. French, of course—and he was the only armed man in the household, since Rodrigo was at the shrine.

He crossed himself and asked for God's help.

Someone demanded admittance in clumsy Spanish.

"Niquez vos mères!" he shouted and pulled out his pistols.

The extremely vulgar insult to their mothers, given in French by a Frenchman, brought an instant of stunned silence.

He locked the door to the upstairs, which would keep his friends safe for a few minutes. They were good brawlers, but they'd never last against professional soldiers.

A bell began to ring madly in the distance—the town's tocsin bell, calling desperately for aid.

Jean-Marie's mouth tightened, and he made sure he could draw his saber quickly. Thank God Rodrigo kept an arsenal here and had encouraged him to take what he wished. The sights he'd seen on his journey had made him go armed, even indoors.

A muffled chant, a solid weight hit the door—and it burst open, disgorging filthy, ragged French soldiers into the room. There were at least a dozen of them, more dangerous than rabid wolves—and a nasty contrast to the house's quiet elegance.

If only he'd had time to regain his *compañero* speed and strength, instead of only a *prosaico*'s. But with luck, he could fight them off long enough for Rodrigo to return and save Sara and his friends.

He'd be able to see Hélène once again in the next world.

One of the Frenchmen leveled his musket, but Jean-Marie's shot took him first.

Another waved a sword, ordering the others on—and Jean-Marie brought the leader down with his last bullet.

He thrust his pistols into his belt, knowing he wouldn't have time to reload them. But they'd be useful as clubs, should his sword fail him.

He drew his saber and smiled at his enemies.

"Come along, lads, who wants to be the first to die? You know as well as I that your muskets are ancient—and less accurate than a drunken pissing contest. Your chances of killing me are pitiful from down there—so you'll have to come up here to dance with me."

They eyed him warily, obviously trying to gauge how well he could fight.

His grin grew broader. They'd have to pass him to reach the valuables in the bedrooms—and Napoleon's soldiers could never resist looting. He just needed to buy time for Rodrigo.

Two of them charged him.

The bell's notes ripped into Rodrigo, snatching him away from his prayers. For an instant, he didn't know whether he stood in the thirteenth century or the nineteenth.

But his body didn't care about which century it was, and it jerked him to his feet. Invaders had come, and a knight's duty was to protect. To fight enemies.

He crossed himself. Then he ran—with all of his *vampiro* speed.

His home was on the way to San Leandro. He would stop there first.

Sara woke slowly, blinking and confused. She loathed moving around in daylight, and greeting Jean-Marie's friends earlier that day had left her sleepy and irritable.

Her coffin was familiar territory, small and dark, infinitely comfortable with its satin cushions and fine woods. It was the only sanctuary her *creador* had allowed her, and nobody had ever troubled her there in the years since. She hated bestirring herself, but something was wrong in the world beyond.

Her beloved coffin vibrated again, shaking her to the bones.

A bell was ringing, frequently and loudly. The tocsin bell from the village?

She pushed the lid off, sending it slamming onto the floor.

Jean-Marie was taunting someone on the landing, his voice ragged with exhaustion and pain.

No! He'd been hers and Rodrigo's ever since she'd first seen him in Rodrigo's vision, back in their *creador*'s dungeon. She'd taken him as soon as she'd met him, of course. Why bother with discussion, when she knew they were fated to be together? She would not let him be hurt now.

She erupted from her nest, her hair trailing down her back, and ran to the door, still clad in her frothy lace and silk nightgown. She flung it open, only to be met by a horrific sight.

Jean-Marie was surrounded by dead and wounded soldiers—but he was bleeding as much as or more than any of them. One side of his face was covered in blood, while his right arm hung uselessly at his side. He favored one leg, but his sword's point was still high, however much it wavered.

"Why are you standing there? Come on, you cowards—or don't you want to join your fellows in Hell?" He coughed—and choked on blood.

Someone growled and charged, bayonet lowered. How could his sword parry that?

Jean-Marie's face hardened.

Sara shrieked one of her *creador*'s favorite curses and hurled herself into the fight.

Sword drawn, Rodrigo raced into the courtyard, startling a handful of gaunt horses. French military horses.

The terror gripping him throughout his mad run tightened its hold on his throat. If he lost Sara or Jean-Marie because he hadn't been here to protect them . . .

He shoved past the unhappy beasts, all his attention on the swinging door and the reek of blood and death from within.

An abattoir awaited him, not the gracious room he'd left with gilded furniture, floral rugs, and painted walls. Now more than a dozen men lay dead or dying in his foyer, on the stairs, and on the landing beyond. Some had been killed by *prosaico* means—with a bullet or a sword. But a few had been almost ripped apart, and none would be alive for more than a few minutes more.

Men were pounding on the door to the attic bedroom, demanding to be set free. Since they were obviously alive and healthy, they could be ignored for now.

What the hell had happened? Jean-Marie had not had the strength to kill so many.

Rodrigo leapt up the stairs, barely managing not to step on any bodies.

Gracias a Dios, Jean-Marie was slumped against the wall, his face white as parchment under a coating of blood. His hands were clasped over his belly, a foul seepage oozing under his fingers. The door to Sara's room was open, showing an empty coffin.

A wordless prayer formed itself in Rodrigo's heart.

"Jean-Marie." He dropped to his knees and unbuttoned his cloak.

"Rodrigo." His friend blinked slowly. Agony was braided into every muscle of his face and throat. Death lurked behind his eyes. "Thank God. You must go . . . to the village."

"Not yet." He tore open his cravat, the broken linen sounding like a gunshot. Buttons popped on his coat and waistcoat.

"Every minute counts." Jean-Marie's voice strengthened into a lecture.

"So does your life. Where's Sara?"

Jean-Marie tilted his head slightly, indicating a corner of the landing.

Dios! White silk lay across a pair of the largest, most heavily armed soldiers, as if preventing them from attacking.

"She killed many of them . . . But the last one shot her in the heart, and she turned into dust. I will have to thank her for sacrificing herself for me."

She'd finally given back something to Jean-Marie, in recompense for the life she'd stolen from him? He would have to say the Viddui for her, the traditional prayer her Jewish people said at the time of death. Thank God, she'd found that much grace to light her way home to her people and to Heaven. *Hear O Israel, the Lord our God, the Lord is One* . . .

"Not in heaven, *amigo*. You're about to become a *vampiro*." Rodrigo tugged his cravat and coat away from his neck, baring his throat. Blood from his jugular was the richest, giving it the best chance of saving Jean-Marie's life. *Gracias a Dios*, he'd fed so well for the past few days. He had more than enough strength for this—and to meet other trials.

"It's too late—I'm dying. They gutted me."

"All the better," Rodrigo assured him, infusing his voice with a confidence he didn't entirely feel. "The weaker you are, the faster the *vampiro* elixir will seize you and heal your wounds."

Jean-Marie's gaze sharpened. "I'll kill more Imperial bastards."

"Exactly! Now center your mind on a single thought." The eastern courts always said there were two keys to *cachorro* survival: willingness to become a *vampiro* and concentration on a single thought during *El Abrazo*. God send they were right.

"Hélène at Versailles, the first time I saw her and blazing like a star under the candles, in the mirrors' reflections." Jean-Marie smiled beatifically, his gaze turned somewhere Rodrigo couldn't follow.

"Perfect." At least his old friend was focused. "Are you still certain? You could go insane or die when you awake."

"Don't be a damn fool," Jean-Marie snapped, glaring at him. "I will serve you with all my heart when I awaken."

Rodrigo smiled humorlessly, wishing he'd done this once before— so he could be certain that Jean-Marie would awake the next night, not too appallingly insane. But all was in God's hands. If Jean-Marie was to live, he needed to become Rodrigo's *hijo*.

By all the Saints, Rodrigo would be the finest *creador* ever known, to protect his best friend.

He lightly touched Jean-Marie's mind, washing away the pain but not reading any of the memories. Rodrigo gently carried Jean-Marie into his bedroom, setting him down on the bed that had been prepared for him so long ago. He lay down beside him and drew him close, his heart beating faster than the first time he'd ridden into combat.

Dios mediante, this would work.

"Thank you for granting me *El Abrazo*, Rodrigo." Jean-Marie smiled at him, his blue eyes completely untroubled in the scant light from the hallway.

His breathing ground to a halt. *Thanks?* For the first time, he truly believed his oldest friend was at peace with what was to come.

"*Mi amigo.*" He stroked Jean-Marie's cheek—and slashed open his jugular.

Jean-Marie feebly lunged for it, his gaze avid.

"Think of your lady, *mi hijo!*" Rodrigo commanded and lifted his friend's head onto his shoulder. Jean-Marie's mouth clamped down on Rodrigo's neck and sucked fiercely.

Rodrigo cradled him close, praying to the Blessed Mother he'd survive.

And San Leandro would not be too greatly injured when he reached it . . .

Luis tested his bonds once again, tears and blood caked on his face. He was tied to one of the pillars inside the church, where the French had tried to make him tell where the town's treasure was. But there was no gold in San Leandro, and they'd soon used Luis only for sport. *Dios*, what they'd done to his hands—the pain burned through his arms and into his lungs until he could no longer control his screams.

He could have forgiven them that, just as he could have forgiven them eating every scrap of food to be found—and drinking every drop of wine. But if they'd been beasts before, the wine had made them a hundred times worse. They'd hunted and stolen every chalice, every plate, every gift given to the church over the centuries.

He could have ignored that, too—but not what they were doing to his people. Not what his eyes and ears and nose told him.

Howls of agony tore at his ears, and the church reeked of foulness. Torches shook in the drafts, while candles burned and wept in their sconces.

The French bastards were raping every woman in town, even using the high altar to defile the nuns. Many of the men were dead, starting with *Tío Carlos*, and the others were either bound or broken. Emilio had been shot down for bravely—futilely—trying to protect his wife. Sweet Ana had been slaughtered before Luis's eyes, the last of his beautiful darlings to die. Beatriz, Inez, Bianca, Ana—all dying in agony and horror, the sights and sounds and stench burned into his memory.

Damn the French bastards, damn them! No matter what it took, or how long it took, he would find revenge. There would be no peace for him as long as he remembered his darlings' murders.

He clenched his fists, sending bone grinding against bone. He flung his head back and howled in frustration.

The soldiers were so damn confident now that they'd laid aside their weapons. Some were laughing almost continuously while they drank and urged each other on. If he had his pitchfork—or his scythe, which he'd sharpened yesterday—he could destroy many of them. If, if, if . . .

Luis wasn't sure he still believed in miracles, but he knew mortal men could offer them no aid. The church was dedicated to San Rafael Arcángel, patron saint of travelers and healers. Perhaps the archangel would send a traveler to cleanse his church and heal them.

Behind him, tied to the other side of the same pillar, he could hear the Irish priest praying continuously in his own language, his voice harsh from hard usage.

The great tocsin bell rang, probably because the soldiers were mocking it again. A woman screamed, only to be cut off abruptly.

The great doors slammed open, reverberating against the wall. Cold air washed through the room, bringing the forest's crisp scent. A man roared in fury.

Luis's eyes flashed open, allowing him to once again witness what was happening.

A tall man stood in the church door, his broad shoulders and swirl-ing cape blocking sight of the plaza beyond. He carried a great sword in his hands—and his harsh features were those of the knight awaited by *Doña* Blanche.

The soldiers gawked at him. Someone snickered. None bothered to leave their perversions.

"By all that is holy, you shall not foul this church," the knight shouted. He leapt forward, swinging his sword as if it were a featherweight—and beheaded the rapist closest to the door. In the same superbly smooth move, he killed a second Frenchman—and a third.

"Santiago y cierra España!" He bellowed the Knights of Santia-go's ancient battle cry: St. James and close in Spain! He contemptu-ously kicked one brute so hard that he flew off Ana's best friend and slammed against a wall, never to move again.

Luis echoed his rescuer in the war-cry that had terrified invaders for centuries, giving all the support he could. Other villagers lifted their voices, even a few women.

Gracias a Dios, Don Rodrigo—or his near kin—had returned to save them in their hour of greatest need, even as the legend foretold.

Luis laughed mirthlessly for not previously realizing the mysteri-ous newcomer was their long-awaited paladin. But perhaps his foolish eyes had needed the flashing sword to melt the scales.

Time slowed to a crawl—or did Don Rodrigo move so quickly the soldiers couldn't move fast enough to harm him? Their drunkenness and lack of loaded guns left them clumsy and vulnerable, falling to Don Rodrigo all too easily despite their greater numbers. None could do more than stagger to his feet and point an unloaded weapon before he too was slain.

Was Don Rodrigo a magical being or a mortal man? Who cared? Not when he walked safely in church and fought to cleanse it from its desecrators.

Luis's hands closed, disregarding any agony. Here at last was a fighter, someone to follow—unlike their absent grandee or their dithering—and now dead—*alcalde*.

*   *   *

Jean-Marie's heartbeat throbbed again, faint but very steady. *Gracias a Dios*, the *vampiro* elixir had taken him. He was fast asleep, and his wounds had already started to heal. With luck, he would awaken tonight with some trace of sanity besides the lust for blood and emotion.

Rodrigo stood up and stretched, relieving the aches caused by his cramped position. Measuring a pulse took unusually long when it was measured in beats per hour, not per minute.

Here at his house, he'd scattered Sara's few ashes in the sleeping rose garden and prayed for her. She'd ruined Jean-Marie's life when she'd grabbed him away from his role as prince of the Blood—but he'd never have met his Hélène if she hadn't. And at the end, she'd fought to save him. God knows, she'd done much to save Rodrigo's life time after time. *Sabe Dios*, she'd found peace at last.

He sighed and left the room, closing the door quietly behind him. It was time to go downstairs and help his own household.

Jean-Marie had not yet awoken as a *cachorro*, of course, but he should do so tonight. Rodrigo would be there to greet him—and give him that all-important first taste of blood and emotion. The emotion for which he would hunger as a *vampiro*. It would not be terror, the powerful—and all-too-typical—emotion that sustained most *vampiros*. No, it would be carnal passion, equally strong but far harder to create and sustain in pure form when faced with a crazed *cachorro* who wanted only to feed.

As for himself—when he'd heard the screams and realized last night what those *hijos de la gran puta* were doing—*Santa Madre de Dios*, in the church!—all he'd wanted to do was kill. And so he had.

He'd destroyed every one of those foul brutes. The smoke carrying their ashes to Heaven teased his nostrils now, even though it was distant and well disguised by fragrant pine boughs. He'd suggested the locals dispose of their remains on a single pyre, since the ground was frozen iron-hard. It would be difficult enough to provide proper burials for their own beloved dead—like Luis Alvarez's ladies.

He pounded his fist into his palm, wishing yet again he could have stopped the attack from happening. An impossibility since he was not the local grandee—but he was a trained warrior and a leader! He could have kept the French out and could still prevent them from returning, if San Leandro wished to fight. Because the French would be back, bringing the same flood of terror they'd perfected in the Vendée to terrify innocent people into cooperating with tyrants.

Yet it was entirely likely that the good people of San Leandro would believe *he* was the monster and refuse to listen to him, given the unnatural speed and strength with which he'd destroyed the foreign despoilers. *¡Ay, mierda!*

At least he'd killed every one of the French soldiers last night. It wouldn't bring back San Leandro's dead or dry the survivors' tears. But he had bought them some time to find a new leader, since their *alcalde* was dead. He'd also helped clean up and comforted the injured as much as he could, including the women.

He ground his teeth, biting back a snarl. Nobody would hurt those people again, not while he was around—even if he had to sneak around in the dark.

The doorbell rang, a surprisingly polite interruption in the bloodstained foyer.

Rodrigo's eyebrows rose, but he opened the door without waiting for his servants.

A careworn Father Michael touched his hat in greeting. A young boy hovered behind him, holding a mule's reins. What on earth was the priest doing here, when he must have a thousand things to do in town after last night's tragedy?

"Welcome to my home, Father." Rodrigo bowed formally, careful to mask his surprise. "Please come inside where it is warm. Your servant can take the mule around to the back, where there is refreshment for both."

"Good day, my son." The good priest seemed to have aged a decade in one night, which wasn't surprising. He nodded to his servant and followed Rodrigo inside, his expression calm.

"Would you care for coffee, wine, or other refreshments?" He led the way into the formal sitting room, furnished with the same music-box gilded extravagance of everything else in the house.

"No, thank you. I came to talk to you." He took a seat, glancing around with a connoisseur's eye.

Rodrigo waited, curious—and a little concerned. Had he displayed so much of the *vampiro* that he'd frightened the priest? But he'd only done so to protect the people!

A brook sang from within the forest. Peace settled into the room.

"I came to thank you for aiding my people last night," Father Michael said finally, looking straight at his host. "You rescued them when no one else could."

Rodrigo bowed, his throat very tight at the unexpected—and complete—acceptance. "I am honored to have been of service, Father."

"If there is anything I can do to help you, in this world or the next, you have only to ask, my son." Gray eyes, startlingly perceptive as ever, watched him—demanding nothing.

Rodrigo swallowed. How could he ask for what he'd never been able to voice even to himself?

A breeze caressed the trees outside, making the branches bend. Could he be as flexible? Could he rededicate himself to serving the Lord and protecting the weak, as in his knightly oaths?

Father Michael studied how the curtain's silk fringe stirred in a draft.

Rodrigo gambled, betting the Irishman would understand the difficult balance Rodrigo had tried to find. "Will you hear my confession, Father?"

"Of course, my son. May the Lord be in your heart and upon your lips that you may truly and humbly confess your sins, in the name of the Father, and the Son, and the Holy Ghost. Amen."

Rodrigo knelt, an aching peace sifting into his bones. "Bless me, Father, for I have sinned. It has been years since my last confession. Last night," he began. *Dios mío*, but he sounded as nervous as any *escudero* who hoped to one day become a *caballero*! "Last night, I drew steel and killed men in the Lord's house . . ."

The litany of sins fell smoothly from his tongue, and the priest listened to him compassionately.

"May our Lord Jesus Christ absolve you; and by His authority I absolve you from every bond of excommunication and interdict, so far as my power allows and your needs require," Father Michael said. He slowly made the Sign of the Cross over Rodrigo. "Therefore, I absolve you of your sins in the name of the Father, and the Son, and the Holy Ghost. Amen."

Oh, dear Lord, what joy to be freed of those burdens.

"May the Passion of Our Lord Jesus Christ, the merits of the Blessed Virgin Mary and of all the saints obtain for you that whatever good you do or whatever evil you bear might merit for you the remission of your sins, the increase of grace, and the reward of everlasting life."

"I am deeply grateful, Father." Rodrigo was unashamed of the tears on his cheeks. "I have lived a long and brutal life, performing deeds that should not be discussed in polite company."

"Actions which prepared you for last night?" the priest queried sharply.

Startled, Rodrigo inclined his head in agreement.

"In that case, I see no reason to be ashamed."

"Even so, I have not frequented churches much, as you may have guessed."

Father Michael harrumphed.

"I may need to fight again and it would—comfort me to be blessed."

"Ah." Hordes of meanings dwelt in that syllable. The devout Franciscan propped his chin on his fist.

Terror froze Rodrigo's veins like glaciers. "But if I'm not acceptable . . ."

"Why not?" Father Michael raised an eyebrow.

"I am not an ordinary man, Father." How could he tell him about *vampiros*?

"It is true that few men could have done what you did. But God did not slay you for besmirching his house, even though your methods might be called—unusual."

"You are generous," Rodrigo forced past a tight throat.

The priest shrugged. "I am old and have seen prejudice destroy many things but also much gained through love. Did you know that only Protestants can own property in Ireland?"

Rodrigo nodded, startled by the apparent non sequitur.

"When I was young, my brother converted—to save the land for our family and people. But I left Ireland to study, only to return and live in the open fields while I served as a priest. I could not have done what he did, yet we both served God and the people in our own ways, out of love."

"Flexibility." Rodrigo understood both men's bittersweet choices all too well.

"Aye."

They smiled at each other in perfect understanding.

"Please kneel for your blessing, Rodrigo."

Rodrigo went to his knees and bowed his head.

"May the God of the misty dawn awaken you,
May the God of the rising sun stir you up,
May the God of the morning sky send you on your way,
May the God of noonday stillness renew your strength."

Joy poured over his skin and through his veins like molten gold with every word, couched in terms of light—so rare and precious to a *vampiro*.

"May the God of afternoon bring you home,
May the God of sunset delight your eye,
May the God of twilight calm your nerves,
May the God of dusk bring you peace."

He was reborn as a child of the Church again, healed as Blanche had prayed.

"Father, will you baptize me? I wish to take a new name to commemorate this day."

"Certainly, my son. How do you wish to be called?"

"For the saint who protects travelers and heals even the most grievous of wounds—Rafael."

"Don Raf-fael?" His majordomo stumbled slightly over the new name.

Rafael nodded encouragingly but didn't bother to look up. He was cleaning the weapons salvaged from the soldiers Jean-Marie had killed. Those bastards might have been greedy and cocky, but they'd been professional. Their muskets and pistols had been well cared for and would need little work to make them useful again, putting San Leandro's men on an equal footing with the French bastards.

"Señor Alvarez from the village wishes to speak to you."

Rafael's hand stilled for a moment before he resumed carefully sponging out the pistol's muzzle. "Please show him in."

Dios mediante, San Leandro's new *alcalde* was someone who would fight.

Rafael's mouth curved slightly, a heady new confidence sweeping through his blood after this morning's blessing and baptism. If the new *alcalde* wouldn't—well, he'd just have to be persuaded, by *vampiro* means if necessary. The French revenge for last night's defeat would have to be met by force, or San Leandro would be ground into dust. They had enough men—and enough arms, with what they'd claimed from the dead soldiers—but only with leadership.

Luis Alvarez limped in on a crutch, his hands heavily bandaged. Rafael's majordomo withdrew, silently shutting the door.

"Señor Perez." Luis bowed very low, balancing himself awkwardly.

"Please—sit down." Rafael rose, laying down the pistol and his tools. *Dios mío*, Luis looked extremely battered. Yet a flame burned behind his eyes, lit by trials too bitter for most mortal men to endure.

"No, thank you. I would prefer to stand."

"As you wish." Rafael waited for the news, hoping they'd found somebody he could reason with.

"The town council has elected you the new *alcalde* of San Leandro," Luis announced baldly.

Rafael stared at him. None of the options he'd considered included this.

"Why? I am a newcomer who knows nothing of your customs! How can I give justice or make laws?" And he couldn't linger in San Leandro after the war with Napoleon was over. He'd never compete with his descendant in such a fashion.

"You rescued us last night from our enemies, as the legend foretold." Luis's dark eyes were as implacable as granite. "You are the only one who can protect us now."

"I could destroy you." Rafael crossed his arms over his chest. *Sabe Dios*, they'd better understand the magnitude of what they were getting into when they asked a *vampiro* to lead them. It would be entirely different than if he advised their own *alcalde*.

"You are our only hope."

"I am not a mortal man," Rafael said directly. "I am a *vampiro*."

"We have guessed that you are not entirely human." Luis shrugged. "It does not matter—and we think it is probably an advantage, judging by last night. God does not hate you, so why should we?"

Rafael took a turn around the room, flicking glances at his startling guest.

Dios santo, Luis was calm. If Rodrigo accepted this, he would rule San Leandro and the surrounding valley like a baron, the way his family had done centuries ago. It wouldn't last forever, of course—only until the war ended. But he'd have a damn good chance of keeping the French bastards away.

He began to smile, thinking about all the tricks he could use. He was distantly aware his fangs were probably showing a little.

"Also," Luis went on, a small catch in his voice, "I would be honored if you would take me into your personal service for the rest of my life. I will do whatever you want, so long as we defeat the French."

Cristo! Could he be telling the truth? He'd already admitted he knew Rafael was a *vampiro*.

Rafael spun to completely face him, using all of his *vampiro* powers to measure every iota of his guest's sincerity.

Truth shone through Luis's mind, as strong as the pain burning in
his hands.

Rafael rocked on his heels, thinking hard.

Luis had no close family left in San Leandro, nobody except some
distant cousins. The loss of his wife and daughters rode him hard,
blinding him to everything except revenge—and the desperate need to
find something that would keep him away from reminders of them.
Serving Rafael would accomplish that.

Jean-Marie was a *vampiro*, who'd be a strong right hand—but
only at night. Rafael would need someone else to stand beside him
during daylight. The best choice would be a *compañero*, who'd be as
strong and fast as a *cachorro*.

He flicked a glance at Luis, still waiting patiently.

"Very well, I will be San Leandro's *alcalde*." He would trust in
God's blessing, delivered by Father Michael this morning, and accept
the mantle.

"*Muchas gracias*, Señor Perez." Luis bowed with a farmer's direct-
ness. "The townsfolk will be greatly honored—and much relieved."

"I will need an assistant, someone who can help me with my household, call out the army, and fight beside me if necessary."

Luis was watching him, almost leaning forward to catch every
word. Desperate hope deepened in his eyes.

"I would prefer someone who can serve me for a very long time."
Rafael chose his words carefully.

"My life is yours," Luis said promptly. "You saved it last night,
and it belongs to you."

"For a century? Or two?"

Luis blinked and swallowed hard. "Yes."

"You will need to drink my blood to accomplish this."

A farmer's lifted brow said Rafael's caution was overly
squeamish.

"Be very certain, Luis," Rafael warned doggedly.

"You are my liege lord, Don Rafael." Luis clumsily lowered himself to his knees using his crutch, closing the discussion. He pressed his hands together and offered them, in the ancient gesture of fealty.

Rafael's throat closed. It was the first time someone had willingly entered his service in centuries without being paid. He wrapped his own hands around Luis's. "You will be my *siniscal*, my seneschal—and my *compañero*."

"I will serve you until the day I die, Don Rafael." Dark eyes met his, shining with complete trust and certainty.

PARIS, JULY 1815

Celeste paced the small drawing room, barely taking in its elegant furnishings. The house was silent, its few servants having disappeared throughout the day, ending with her maid. She was alone and imprisoned by the sun, more effectively than if she'd been caged in a fortress.

The first man who walked in was going to pay for this, after she seduced him into letting her out, of course.

Napoleon had lost his empire and his army a month earlier at Waterloo. He'd be permanently exiled now, of course. France would try to become a monarchy again, leaving little room for Napoleon's most loyal supporters—or the most visible ones, like herself.

Which was why she'd become Talleyrand's mistress, the minister of a thousand corrupt faces, having served every major French administration in the past twenty-five years—including today's restored monarchy.

She'd had more freedom of movement as a double agent, but at least he had interesting appetites in the bedroom.

Horses' hooves pounded over the gravel driveway just before sunset, matched by the dull roar of a heavy carriage's wheels. Talleyrand? But in such a large equipage?

Three people strode up to the house.

Celeste drew herself up and posed coolly in the drawing room, one hand on a chair back. It displayed her bosom quite well, while not having the disadvantages of being stationary in a seated or reclining position.

A man and two women entered the room, their severely tailored garb identifying them as British. Their scent proclaimed them to be *vampiros mayores*—and thus almost certainly impervious to her greatest weapon. *Merde.*

"Monsieur, mesdames." Celeste inclined her head, trying to think. *Mon dieu*, did they know she was a double agent? Were they here to take her back to Britain? Kill her on the spot? Who would help her? *Prosaicos* would be no use, of course. No wise *vampiro* would argue with anything a *vampiro mayor* wanted to do, let alone a trio of *vampiros mayores.*

"Comtesse de Sainte-Pazanne." The man nodded curtly, the women merely stared at her.

Shit, shit, shit.

Well, nothing ventured, nothing gained. She focused her will. *Desire me*, she thought at the man.

He stretched slightly.

Desire me! She pushed harder.

He raised a very lazy eyebrow.

"Stop wasting time, Carleton," one of the women snapped. "You know I abhor spending even a moment in this trollop's presence."

"Sorry, m'dear. I believe she needed to learn her own powerlessness."

M'dear sniffed loudly.

The three *vampiros mayores* circled Celeste, watching her pitilessly. If she'd thought Carleton a possible target of seduction before, his arctic gaze ripped the prospect away from her. "I have served Britain since the reign of the great Queen Elizabeth. Sir Andrew ffoulkes was my *hijo.*"

Breath died in her throat. She couldn't even find the wits to curse.

"Every *vampiro* agent you killed was one of our *hijos*," the other lady said quietly.

Carleton inclined his head, gray eyes assessing her for killing blows. "I'm glad you understand the extent of the blood debt you owe us."

"But we are sworn to follow our superiors' orders," m'dear added, in a tone which left no doubt as to her low opinion of their intelligence.

"Talleyrand has begged mercy for you. Since he's the sole being with any sense in France's government and Britain doesn't wish to see France descend again into anarchy, she chooses to honor his wishes." Carleton could have been reciting a newspaper except for the burning anger in his eyes.

"You must be a far better slut than you look," m'dear commented.

Celeste flushed angrily but reached for the escape hatch. "Then I'll leave now."

"Yes—for lifetime exile," the second woman agreed.

"Exile?" Celeste spun around, staring at her unwelcome guests. "Exile?"

"You will spend the rest of your life in the New World with other followers of the Emperor Napoleon, in New Orleans." Carleton's deep voice rang through the house.

"Why not Marseilles?" From there, she could find her way to England and locate Hélène.

"Remember we can read your thoughts—child." A cold smile curled m'dear's mouth. "Because it's far enough away to never disturb your sister's peace. She's much more important than you are."

"But for how long?"

"Until you die. If you ever try to leave there, we will immediately take great delight in killing you." The second woman was as quiet as ever and just as firm.

Celeste shivered, believing her. To leave France for New Orleans . . .

But maybe New Orleans would be the land of dreams that everyone promised. Raoul's sister and her family had emigrated there in 1802, during the war's brief lull, and were very happy.

Celeste bit her lip, damning the tears welling up. She had to learn to live without Raoul, without visiting the places they'd walked together, without any hope of hearing his voice again even in a dream. Surely ghosts could not cross an ocean.

But her heart ignored her head's dictates, raising up image after image of the man she'd adored. His eager strides to greet her, his laughter when he swung her into his arms, his hot kisses . . .

She buried her face in her hands, realizing yet again how much Raoul was a part of her, down to her very bones.

MADRID, AUGUST 1815

The handful of men stood in a jewel box of a drawing room, whose walls were covered in golden silk embroidered with dozens of golden and silver vines. Overhead, the vines burst into fantastical golden flowers arching over the vaulted ceiling. The tables were golden marble topped by gilded clocks and candelabra, whose rounded forms echoed the floor's sinuous black and gold marble inlays. Great mirrors with gilded, curling frames magnified the room's glory.

It was a setting calculated to impress guests with the majesty and power of the Spanish Crown. After all, if a king could lavish this much money on a very small audience chamber, how much more could he spend on doing good for—or punishing—an individual?

The display would have been more impressive except for its owner's narrowed, suspicious stare and corpulent body. He looked every inch of what rumor painted him to be—the leading police agent and jailer of his country. Ferdinand VII, the reactionary king of Spain, was killing his subjects with a speed and ferocity which surprised even Rafael.

The king was superbly dressed, his coat dripping with ribbons and orders from Europe's great nations. His chamberlain wore livery, admittedly of a very grand style, while the guards at the door were in uniform, their suspicious eyes eternally sweeping the room. The three gentlemen were more simply attired, with black coats and immaculate white linen.

But Rafael and Jean-Marie's clothes came from London's finest establishments, starting with coats from Beau Brummell's tailor. They served as a quiet frame for the Order of the Bath Rafael wore, the greatest honor the British government could give to a foreign nobleman, which he'd earned for his aid to Wellington at the Battle of Vitoria. It was a deliberate reminder of his powerful British friends.

Jean-Marie appeared to be a young man, modestly deferring to his seniors as befitted his age—except for his rapid glances, which missed nothing. He'd resumed the same appearance he'd held for so long as a *concubino compañero*. As ever, the *vampiro* elixir had returned him to the appearance he held in his heart, which was what he'd worn when he'd met his lost love.

He was damn lucky to have lost his gray hair and other marks, although Rafael had heard of more miraculous changes. He'd personally give half his fortune to be free of the scars across his back, evidence of his *creador*'s torture—and eternal symbol of how deeply the agony had burned into his heart.

"Your majesty," Don Fernando Perez began again, modestly enough, "if I may suggest—"

"Suggest? Suggest what? Perhaps an examination of the liberal ideas you expounded as a member of the Seville Junta, while I was imprisoned in France?"

Imprisoned? You went to Napoleon and asked him to take you in! Rafael's eyes narrowed, while Jean-Marie stiffened slightly. *Hid under his apron strings while your countrymen fought and bled and died for liberty in the tens of thousands.*

"I think your successor as minister is the best man to do so," the king continued.

Successor? Rafael didn't quite growl. If the king disposed of Don Fernando as he'd handled all his other ministers, Don Fernando would be lucky to live. The viciousness of his death would be limited only by his enemies' imagination. Don Fernando's brilliance, honesty, and virtue had unfortunately provided him with a multitude of foes.

"Or should he start by asking why your kinsman leads such a large group of militia," the royal brute purred. "Ah, *sí*, now that is definitely something for your successor to question you most thoroughly about. Your kinsman, too, of course."

His deep-set little eyes dwelt with evident satisfaction on Don Fernando's sweating face.

¡Ay, *mierda*, but Don Fernando could have no answer for that question! Only Rafael or Jean-Marie would, because they'd been present throughout the War of Liberation, had led San Leandro's men against the French soldiers. Don Fernando had been in Seville the entire time, working to form a unified, national—liberal—government. The torments those secrets could create for an honest man . . .

The king lifted a languid finger and half-turned toward the door, with his chamberlain and the guards.

If you harm in any way anything or anyone that belong to Don Fernando, now or at anytime, directly or indirectly—you will die immediately. Rafael slammed the thought into the Spanish monarch's skull, branding it into every crevice necessary, refusing to flinch from the sewage he found.

Jean-Marie shifted a hair closer until their sleeves brushed, lending him his energy—and the unspoken cunning of a man born and bred to the Sun King's court, the greatest warren of lethal politics found in Europe for centuries.

Rafael's mouth thinned in rueful acknowledgment, and he finished closing every loophole in the royal rat's putrid thought processes.

Now he needed to take his men far from this brute's reach.

"Your majesty, Don Fernando has been worried about your provinces in Mexico and Texas," Rafael crooned, as sympathetically as possible, when what he wanted to do was rearrange some royal features.

"Particularly in Texas, where that madman preaches independence," added Jean-Marie, who was very careful not to catch Rafael's eyes.

The king did have one consistent passion: retaining his possessions in the New World.

Don Fernando was staring at them both. But he was no coward, and he was quick-witted. "Insanity, your majesty, insanity! Even a provincial must realize Spain is the sun where all light rises and sets."

The royal madman almost preened.

"Don Fernando has greatly aided us in understanding this threat and others like him," Rafael went on.

"Especially with wild Indians so close on the frontier. Why, if settlements like The Alamo were lost . . ." Jean-Marie shuddered dramatically, a motion Don Fernando immediately copied.

"He has so impressed the militia from his lands, which I have the honor to lead," Rafael dared to give a small bow, judging the mood to be more friendly, "that we wish to emigrate to Texas. To fight on behalf of Spain, to keep the peace."

"I presume you'll want a great fortune from me for this endeavor? To be sworn into the army?" The king drew himself up, bringing his guards snapping back into full alertness.

Become one of your officers? And be indebted to you forever? Like hell!

"Your majesty, all we ask is to be sent as private citizens to Texas, where we will form a militia." *And never serve under the command of your army, given any choice.* "I will count it a privilege if I may use my own funds to pay transport for those willing to accompany us."

"You, pay?" A brow shot up.

Rafael nodded, well aware of the likely interpretation. But he'd never keep slaves, let alone force any of his men or their families into indentured servitude to pay for passage. He'd also provide for livestock and household goods. Life would be difficult in Texas for several generations; they'd need to make the best possible start, and he had plenty of gold.

The king clasped his hands behind his back and paced, casting occasional glances at Rafael. Don Fernando managed to remain still, while Jean-Marie was completely serene, if not privately enjoying himself. The chamberlain was barely breathing, and the guards were openly staring.

Finally Ferdinand VII nodded. "You have our permission." He waved his hand as if swatting flies. "We will grant you land to settle your people on."

The fool probably thought he was taking men away from Don Fernando. Didn't he know his country well enough to realize that Galicia had so many people its farms had become too small to support them?

Don Fernando might become the first local landowner whose people could feed themselves from their own farms, rather than seeking employment elsewhere.

Rafael, Jean-Marie, and Don Fernando bowed deeply.

"Your majesty is too generous," Rafael said sincerely. Better that the king had offered the land grant, than Rafael had used compulsion to obtain it. His reconciliation with the church was too new for him to be comfortable with theft, even for the best of reasons.

"He will arrange the land grant's details." A pudgy finger pointed at the chamberlain, who quickly nodded. "You will remain on your lands until *we* are satisfied this is accomplished, Don Fernando."

They bowed again, even more deeply.

A smirk appeared and spread, distorting his coarse features. He left without another word, his jeweled clothing catching nauseating waves of light from chandeliers and sconces.

We'll have to define the land grant's boundaries for them, Jean-Marie commented.

Of course, Rafael agreed. *If you would handle it*—mi heraldo?

There was a stunned pause before Jean-Marie inclined his head. By *vampiro* tradition, only the *heraldo* spoke with the *patrón*'s voice at all times. Given the amount of trust needed to be given, many *patrones* never had a *heraldo*.

Use your memories from those rides with the Comanches. I want as much land as possible.

It will be my pleasure.

Then Don Fernando was on them, his tone biting back incredulous joy. Indefinite exile to his lands, as the Spanish king's last words had commanded, meant safety for himself and his family. San Leandro's remaining residents should be very well protected.

Which left only one loss to tear at Rafael's heart in the New World: Blanche's tomb.

He had to leave, even though it meant he could never pray beside her calm marble visage ever again.

Ay de mi, this departure would feel a thousand times worse than when he'd ridden out of Toledo behind his prince, determined to rid

Spain of a Moorish invasion. Then he'd expected to return, but this time, he'd know the separation was until the end of time.

He'd still love her forever. Nothing and no one could come between them now, not when he still passionately adored her after five centuries.

OXFORD, SEPTEMBER 1815

Hélène counted up bedrooms one more time on her fingers and nodded, satisfied. There were enough to house a coterie of *prosaicos* to support her during peace time. This house's numerous entrances, staircases, and bedrooms made it a perfect "boarding house" for her and a few gentlemen of intelligence. She'd select the first few from the young men flocking back to the university, all of them well seasoned by their wartime experiences. With luck, they'd discreetly refer friends to her after graduation, so she wouldn't have to recruit later generations. She'd have the simplest possible life here, in between frenetic trips abroad to satisfy her Whitehall taskmasters.

She'd use her *vampiro* mind-bending talents to ensure her coterie's silence, of course. This lifestyle was the only way to find a regular supply of intellectually acceptable prey.

Satisfied with the town house's capabilities, she glanced out the dormer window one last time at the sea of church spires and peaked roofs. All in all, there were enough sharp edges here to protect any castle against a siege.

An involuntary snort escaped her at the idle fancy. One would think she considered herself Sleeping Beauty, waiting for Prince Charming's kiss to awaken her from a century-long sleep. Sentimental foolishness, since he was dead and she had to make a new life, no matter how deep the hole in her heart was.

She'd never shared a *conyugal* bond with Jean-Marie, the incredible closeness of emotion and physical sensation which all *vampiros* longed to find. Yet her unhappy heart continued to ache for him as if he'd died only yesterday.

No man, whether *vampiro* or *prosaico*, had distracted her either. Ever since Sir Andrew had died, she'd always had to work with *vampiros* who never dared to relax with her. Lord knows they were no competition for her memories of Jean-Marie.

But here in Oxford, she'd have books and a steady supply of young men for food. Surely one day, she'd learn not to dream of Jean-Marie.

Surely . . .

PART THREE

THE NEW WORLD

TWELVE

COMPOSTELA RANCH, TEXAS HILL COUNTRY OUTSIDE
AUSTIN, TEXAS, MAY, PRESENT DAY

Celeste inhaled deeply, filling herself with Don Rafael's scent. Soon she'd have the man himself inside her again, thank God, and her long crusade would be over.

Leader of the oldest *esfera* in North America, he was probably the richest of all *patrones*. Even better, he was built like a god and could fuck better than a stable of boy toys. Every instant of the Mardi Gras they'd spent together was etched into her memory as sheer sexual perfection. Decades of loneliness finally ended when she'd met her match in sexuality and ruthlessness.

He also trained his men to be both disciplined and sensual, like his beautiful *alferez mayor*—his military commander. Ah, those few hours when Templeton had left his duties and joined them during those marvelous weeks . . .

She'd worked long and hard these past decades to regain Don Rafael's attention. She'd become the New Orleans *patrona* and mastered every other *esfera* between Miami and Memphis, Washington and New Orleans. A mighty *vampiro* army trembled at her slightest whim, led by her enforcer, the former Bayou Butcher who'd escaped from Angola Prison's legendary Death Row.

It wasn't until she ruled the entire Southeastern United States that she received an invitation to visit Don Rafael's Texas home. Now that she stood within two steps of him, *merde*, but her pussy was weeping for him!

They stood outside one of the many long, low buildings at his private mountaintop estate, an isolated place that reeked of animals despite a few gardens and fountains. An enormous group of armed men surrounded them, as was customary when two *patrones* visited each other. They were all his, of course, except for Georges Devol, her devoted *alferez mayor*.

Don Rafael had summarily evicted Beau, her little, blond boy toy before they'd been able to enjoy a ménage à trois.

Pity; she'd wanted Beau to keep an eye on Jean-Marie St. Just, Don Rafael's *heraldo*, chief diplomat, and definitely the same British spy she'd met in Madrid two centuries ago. There he stood, looking so suave with his Gucci suit and impassive expression—except for the glittering eyes, which always knew exactly where she was, damn him! He probably knew she'd been a double agent back then. But he'd never mentioned it to her, and she had more important things to contemplate now. She could have him killed once she and Don Rafael were united.

She'd dressed to display her suitability as an ally, of course—in gold brocade with her favorite ruby necklace emphasizing the deep neckline. God willing he'd quickly ease her breasts out into his big hands and apply his talented mouth . . .

Celeste gulped and reminded herself that Don Rafael unaccountably insisted on carnal relations only in private. He'd have to move to her beloved New Orleans once they were united, of course. The ranch might be comfortable for horses—*merde*, how could he pay so much attention to beasts!—but it didn't compare to the French Quarter for excitement.

"*Mon chéri*, I am delighted to finally visit your home," she purred. She reached up to Don Rafael and kissed him, her mouth and body tasting him fully at last. Unfortunately, the embrace ended all too soon, damn their audience and his aristocratic sense of propriety, which kept him coldly polite.

"Allow me to present my men," he began.

"Ah, *chéri*, forget the formalities for an instant," she interrupted and slid a finger up his arm. Once they were alone, they could resume the passion they'd shared before. "Let's visit alone first, as *patrón* to *patrón*, before we involve anyone else in our *games*."

Ah, the fun they'd enjoyed before with Templeton, who was standing only a few feet away, his face impassive. Surely they could invite him back to spur them on after they'd satisfied their first lusts. Although she couldn't imagine how long it would take to exhaust Don Rafael's well of carnal creativity.

He seemed to stiffen slightly.

"Certainly, madame. The guest house then," Don Rafael agreed and offered her his arm. She accepted it politely, following his lead and restraining herself to the most formal courtesies. Once their alliance was sealed, they could renegotiate trifles like public behavior. She much preferred being able to handle her men when, where, and however she desired.

He took her to a small, dingy building, barely large enough for a single sitting room and a small, upstairs bedroom at one end. A cattle skull hung grotesquely over the mantel, a gaudy flag covered the wall, and a few pieces of rough leather furniture provided the only seating.

What a hellhole. Perhaps they started here so they could destroy the furniture in their passion—or she could shine more in contrast to its absolute shabbiness. The sooner the better to move on.

They were alone, of course. He was, after all, more than five hundred years older than her in the only measure that counted—when a *vampiro* was granted *El Abrazo*. He was more than capable of destroying her in one-on-one combat, not that she gave a damn.

She planted herself in the middle of the leather sofa, patted the seat beside her invitingly, and batted her eyes at him, arching her back slightly to display her charms. Her gold brocade dress was cut low enough to offer her nipples, always one of her most appreciated features.

He hesitated slightly before he sat down at the other end of the sofa. He'd have to get over being such an old-fashioned gentleman soon.

"Mon petit chou," she cooed and scooted next to him, her skin-tight skirt sliding up her thighs as designed.

"Champagne, madame?" he offered, his face tightening—with lust, no doubt. He retrieved a bottle from the ice bucket on the table, behind a small bronze statue. Krug's Clos du Mesnil, a Cuvée Prestige, very expensive and tasty. But who cared about that?

She pouted while he carefully popped the cork. Why was he dodging his increasing hunger by offering wine? "I'd rather talk about us, *mon amour*. Remember the Mardi Gras we spent together?"

"Certainement, madame." His glance flickered sideways at her, but he didn't add anything else.

"The best Mardi Gras I've ever enjoyed," she mused. She toyed with the ruby, running her fingers over it and her breasts, encouraging his memories to return. "You were *magnifique*, a stallion beyond compare, a god among men."

"Surely others have inspired you since then." He handed her a crystal flute filled with the fine champagne.

"Non, you brought me pleasure like no other can," she insisted and tossed back her drink. The expensive vintage mattered nothing compared to the prospect of once again tasting his blood.

Rafael sipped his champagne, his expression unreadable.

"Merci, madame, you flatter me immensely," he murmured. "But enlighten me please. I thought we met tonight to discuss an alliance."

"Exactement, Don Rafael!" *Finally, he spoke directly about unification!* She turned to straddle him.

A hand on her waist stopped her.

What the hell?

"Remain seated, madame, *s'il vous plaît*. Your couturier would never forgive me if anything happened to your magnificent dress."

What? Valentino knew damn well that a ruined dress meant another sale to replace it!

Celeste harrumphed her disappointment but settled back against the cushions. "It's so simple, *mon amour*. We unite our two *esferas* . . ."

He set down his glass, watching her very closely.

Pleased to finally have his full attention, she continued in a rush. "And seal the compact with our bodies, *tu comprends*? We'd be gods, ruling the largest *esfera* in the world. We could conquer every other American *esfera* in an instant and rule the continent inside a year!" She snapped her fingers enthusiastically.

"And the nights, ah, the hours of passion we'd share. *Quelle extase*!" She caught his face in her hands and leaned in to kiss him.

He lifted his glass in a toast, blocking her. She blinked at him, frustrated.

"You flatter me, madame. Men flock to you like bees flying toward the perfect rose, drunk on your beauty. To be your consort is a heady drink, far too much for a simple man like myself."

Why was he being so modest?

"Ah, *mon amour*, don't you see? That's why we'd be so magnificent together! We'd rule everything from the Atlantic to the Rockies, from the Gulf to the Ohio River. And in a year or two, we'd have all of the United States and Canada. Who could stop us?" She ran her tongue over her lips, her nipples pointed and hard against the brocade. *Mon Dieu*, how her blood was pounding. She ran a crimson-tipped finger up his thigh, to remind him of more intimate delights. "And the fucking, *mon étalon*. To have you between my legs again, filling my cunt with your magnificent cock . . ."

"*Non*, madame." Rafael gripped her wrist hard.

"What do you mean? We would rule North America together!" She leaned forward again, desperate to taste his mouth once again.

"No." He put her aside very firmly. "I am honored by your high opinion, but I already have more than I ever dreamed of. I regret I must decline your generous offer; uniting Texas with any other territory is impossible."

She stared at him, her brain finally starting to work. "*Mais*, Don Rafael, don't you desire me?"

"Madame, please remember immense territories have never lasted long among our kind. Content yourself with what you have."

"But I know you want me; every man always has. Why do you keep refusing me?"

"Madame, the answer is no. Neither your great estates nor your beautiful body will take me away from Texas."

Understanding slowly dawned. She threw her champagne in his face and sprang at him, slashing at his eyes. *"Nique ta mère!"*

Rafael grabbed her wrists, his expression bitterly controlled.

Impossible; nobody was cold to her, least of all a coldly formal rage!

She spat curses at him, hissing and scratching, slipping from his grip, trying to slam her knee into his groin. *"Raclure de bidet!"*

He wrestled her to the floor, barely dodging the table. A twist, a roll, and they were in front of the fireplace. He forced her to obey him by lying on top of her, straddling her legs, with her wrists gripped in one of his hands. And always—always!—so damnably cold.

She poured her gift over him again and again, seeking an entry to make him her slave. Nobody had ever walked away from her!

"Soyez tranquille, madame," he insisted, enforcing the command telepathically as well as vocally. "Remember you are the *patrón* of New Orleans."

She stretched against him, rubbing her breasts against his jacket. He lifted an eyebrow but didn't move.

Damn him, how could he say no? Not to her!

She circled her hips against him, making the sexual offering of herself more emphatic. She slammed her gift at him, demanding that he lust for her.

His cock remained as limp as a day-old mackerel.

"Dardillon! You should be hard as a rock for me!" She spat at him, but he dodged easily, his face calm.

He seared tranquility into her mind, pushing anger out of her like a dam locking water from a reservoir.

Logic slowly replaced fury.

"You truly don't want me," she hissed as she stilled under him. He finally released, all too calmly.

She straightened her skirt with angry jerks. Rafael poured her a fresh glass of champagne, which she accepted with a sneer. How dare he be *kind* to her when he'd just insulted her?

She downed it in rapid gulps before she started talking again. "Haven't you ever wondered why I took over New Orleans only after that Mardi Gras we shared?"

Rafael inclined his head and let her speak, his face impassive. What would it take to break through to him? What wouldn't she give to see him hurt the way she did?

And when she thought of all she'd done to get his attention? How she'd become a great *patrona*, just so she'd be a worthy ally for him— the only type of female he'd spend his lifetime with? And what good had it done her?

"I needed that territory so you'd stick around me. Me, *La Patrona d'Esfera de Nouvelle Orléans*! Not just another chick good for only a few weeks," she snarled at him. "And if I can't have you, then by God, I'll dance on your grave." Very happily.

"You can try, madame. But you'll fail."

"And I'll succeed. My assassins have killed more than one *esfera*'s *patrón*." She rose impatiently and began to pace.

Rafael lounged against the fireplace, irritatingly calm. "Their tricks are well known to the least discerning *vampiro*. They will not succeed here."

She'd wipe that bored nonchalance off his face, the bastard.

"Even the best *vampiro* assassin in the world and a *vampiro mayor* at that? The little golden toy who enlivens my bed in gratitude for a place to stay? He'd kill you and a hundred others, just to please me."

"Texas is not like other territories, madame. Even if I die, Gray Wolf will lead the armies of Texas against you. You will regret the day you caused a painted savage to go to war."

The hair on the nape of her neck rose. An Indian leading a war between *esferas*, when very few rules applied anyway? *Merde . . .*

Let Don Rafael and his minions just try it! If he wanted to use Indians—well, she had an army and could find *vampiros*. Plus, there were other weapons that would terrify even him.

She bared her fangs in a travesty of a smile, the ritual start to a *vampiro* duel.

He came to full attention. Good, she had his attention now.

"Or I'll send in my darling Georges to frighten the locals. He would make Texas so hot that *los prosaicos* would destroy you and all your precious *vampiros* and *compañeros*."

"Madame, do not try to alarm me with your talk of assassins and mobs. Texas is too strong for you to take down," Rafael snapped. "Save your strength for where it can be put to better use, such as stopping the river rats that bring drugs and weapons into your great city."

"Don't bother me with your pretty speeches, Don Rafael. We understand each other well enough without them," she snarled and turned for the door. She stiffened when Rafael clamped his hand over her wrist.

"Do not start a war you cannot win, madame, lest you be destroyed by it," Rafael warned, his voice hard. "You are my guest tonight, protected by the laws of hospitality. But if you attack me, then I and my Texans will bury you."

"Damn you, let me go!" She yanked but his grip was immovable. She viciously compared him to the worst forms of life that had ever crawled out of a sewer, or better yet, one of his beloved manure pits.

"You and your entourage are leaving now, madame. If you ever step foot uninvited again on Texan soil, you will die." He forced her to meet his eyes, fury boiling inside him. "Do you understand me, madame?"

"*Oui, je comprends*," she snarled, contemplating her revenge.

He released her slowly.

She nearly spat at him but changed it into an offended snort. She stormed out, striding down the hill toward the helipad and Georges.

Mon Dieu, he would regret the day he insulted her this way. She would kill him and take his precious Texas for her own.

COMPOSTELA RANCH, JUNE 1

Jean-Marie stirred his coffee while he scanned the watch center's monitors, looking for any status changes from the daylight hours he'd been asleep. The room was part of the ranch's underground warren, built to keep *vampiros* safe from daylight, and loaded with every technological device a group of very rich, very paranoid, and very, very intelligent men could want.

Large screens, whose brilliance and clarity would make sports moguls weep, hung just below the ceiling. Underneath them were two rows of workstations, with equally superb monitors and extraordinarily comfortable leather chairs. Men stood or sat before them, conversing in low tones, while they passed on key knowledge to the new shift, clustered into four groups, according to their commander. Luis Alvarez, the *siniscal*, and his men, who watched over Compostela Ranch and its safety. Ethan Templeton and his *mesnaderos*—sworn to protect Don Rafael at all costs—and who also oversaw Texas's military might. Gray Wolf and his men—especially Caleb Jones, his *cónyuge*—who cherished Texas and its people. Finally, his own men, the finest spies and assassins in all of North America.

A raised platform on one end permitted the watch commander to have his own desk, pace, and entertain a visitor or two.

It had originally been built to guard against attacks on Don Rafael and the commanderies by other *patrones*. Here they also watched for any sign that the great multitudes of *prosaicos* had learned about *vampiros*. Those hordes were the deadlier threat, as the Parisian *vampiros* had so painfully learned two centuries ago. They'd made some changes—added technology, changed the mix of personnel, and more—since *la patrona de* New Orleans had sworn a blood feud against Rafael.

Months of vicious war against Madame Celeste had taught Jean-Marie, and all of Rafael's other men, just how quickly life could go from calm to hellish. But that bitch hadn't yet managed to damage *El Patrón*, despite placing a fifty million dollar price on his head. At least he now traveled with presidential quality security, no matter how much he fumed against it.

Today looked to have been fairly quiet. No major incidents; good. Next thing to check was the ranch's arrivals log.

Jean-Marie frowned. *What the hell?*

"Is Don Rafael back from the research center yet?"

"No, sir," the senior watch commander answered, his voice far too neutral. "He left there about five minutes ago."

"Why the devil did he stay so late?" Jean-Marie swung around to stare. "I thought he was just going to drop off a check. You know, make his usual annual donation."

A shrug answered him. "Emilio mentioned he spent considerable time talking to a lady veterinarian," the ex-Ranger reported, his tone implying this was the only fact he could offer.

"Enough to risk trouble on his return, when he's got hundreds of other lovers? Ridiculous." Jean-Marie waved off the proffered explanation and turned to study the map.

Where was Rafael? He needed to be back here before sunset, when Madame Celeste's *vampiro* assassins could take the field against him. Christ, if they lost him now . . .

The two red dots of Rafael's convoy were skimming through the outer pastures. Compostela was located high in the Texas Hill Country, the Alps of Texas, full of roads with sharp turns and surprisingly steep cliffs. It would take time, far too much time for him to reach home—especially by car. That delay needed to be reduced.

Jean-Marie's skin tightened, his instincts almost shrieking to him. He'd always had superb timing, which his swordplay had honed. But becoming a *vampiro* had brought his intuition to knife-edge perfection whenever it spoke to him.

"Get one of the *mesnadero* helicopters ready to launch," he said flatly. He didn't have the right to order them. But his own certainty cut deep into his bones and slashed through his words.

The hard-bitten watch commander flicked a glance at him before turning to the *mesnaderos*. "You heard the man—get that bird ready to roll!"

The *mesnadero* on duty tossed a salute and started talking into his headset, his tone low and urgent.

Jean-Marie set down his coffee cup, absently drumming his fingers while he watched the weather outside on the monitors. Rafael and Emilio Alvarez, a Navy SEAL currently on leave to lead Rafael's daytime bodyguard, could be heard idly chatting over the radio.

The sun still poured sunset's crimson through the skies. If anything went wrong, they'd need *vampiro* instincts aboard that bird to counter Madame Celeste's bastards. Ethan couldn't go, since he was a half-century younger than Jean-Marie and therefore certain to wind up a pile of ash.

Maybe they'd be lucky and this would remain a quiet day. Maybe . . .

"Incoming! Get down, sir!" Emilio shouted.

"Ambush!" shouted Caleb Jones, Rafael's driver. Gunfire, explosions, and—damn, a *landslide?*—filled the watch center from the loudspeakers. The engine of Rafael's big armored Mercedes snarled, clearly fighting for speed.

Jean-Marie's stomach plummeted toward his boots. If anything happened to the man who'd saved his life and given him a family . . .

Not while he was alive.

"RPG, sir, firing from the hilltop," Emilio, Rafael's bodyguard reported. Bullets pinged all too obviously against the windows. "Shit, they've got two shooters in their chopper, too."

Jean-Marie slammed the watch center door behind him and raced for the helipad. Combat's familiar calm slid through him, easing him back into well-known patterns.

Rafael, we're starting one of our helicopters now. ETA five minutes, he reported.

Maldito sea, *no. There's still too much light for you to be outside.*

He barely stopped himself from laughing at his *creador's* overprotective protest. Of course, he was coming to help. But he framed his counter in logic, hoping to keep the argument short.

I've been a vampiro *for almost two centuries, enough to walk in twilight. You need another* vampiro *to fight beside you.*

Mierda, Rafael cursed but said nothing else.

That had gone easier than he expected, probably because Rafael was too busy out there—damn Madame Celeste's treacherous hide! If the only way to stop her from pulling her foul tricks was to kill her, by God, he'd be glad to pull the trigger.

He burst out of the underground complex and into the open. Gardens surrounded him, as was typical for one of Rafael's homes. More importantly, the sun brushed him lightly—warmly.

He hesitated instinctively—but his skin didn't tighten, didn't start to smoke . . . He was still alive two, three, four steps later. Dammit, he could walk in twilight now.

But he didn't have time to celebrate.

His stride lengthened into a run, and men jumped out of his way.

He accepted an MP5 from the armorer waiting at the helipad, yanked the chopper door shut behind him, and nodded to the pilot. Good; he'd be flying with one of Ethan's best *compañero* pilots, who could surely catch any devil Madame Celeste sent.

The other shooter was an excellent *compañero* sniper, thank God, with combat experience dating back to Vietnam. Nobody was a fine shot from a moving helicopter, especially when aiming at another one, which would undoubtedly be dancing across the sky while it tried to take potshots at a speeding car. But Jean-Marie's *vampiro* reflexes should help, as would the sniper's intensive training.

God willing, Jean-Marie's intuition would kick in with some help, too.

They'd succeed; they had to.

The chopper hurled itself into the sky almost before Jean-Marie strapped in. The bird was one of the *mesnaderos'* larger helicopters, one frequently used by SWAT teams. It was fast, maneuverable, and the envy of the few local cops who'd seen it.

As soon as they were in the air, Jean-Marie pulled on the goggles and headset the crew chief gave him. The flight and weapons harnesses went on remarkably easily, a tribute more to their elegant modern designs than his experience. Like Gray Wolf, he was only checked out as a shooter in helicopters once a year, just often enough to accompany Rafael on his more startling excursions.

Success! Now he could open the door, assured he could fire at Madame Celeste's assassins without falling from the sky.

He shoved the door back and braced himself with one hand against the opposite side, the wind whipping at his hair and trying to tear at the edges of his goggles. The bird bounced and jolted sideways in the unpredictable mountain air, making him grunt.

Ah, there was the enemy—an old police chopper, now used for crop dusting by a neighbor. It hung over a strip of narrow, unpaved, mountain road like a furious hornet, stabbing at everything in sight. Dust clouds boiled up in its wake.

But what about Rafael? Were they too late?

He cursed under his breath and looked harder at the road, fighting for glimpses snatched between mountainsides.

Aha!

Rafael's black Mercedes bobbed and weaved through the cloud of dust below, sometimes almost hanging a wheel over the edge, sometimes scraping its paint against the mountain—and always moving faster than even Jean-Marie would have driven.

A channel clicked to life in his headphones. Caleb was humming one of his beloved old songs, Rafael was singing the lyrics, while bullets provided percussion. Jean-Marie rolled his eyes at this evidence of his *creador*'s delight in a good fight.

"Bogey at twelve o'clock low," announced his pilot, a student of old war movies. "Heading for those power lines."

Jean-Marie braced himself as well as he could and cocked his MP5, its readiness echoed with a matching click from his companion's submachine gun. *Die, you bastards, die.*

They dived at the vicious enemy, their own guns blazing. Jean-Marie aimed for the sniper in the doorway, the one closest to Rafael's sedan. Again and again, he fired, timing his shots by his intuition's tap on his shoulder, grimly following his skittering opponent across the sky as best as he could. Short, savage bursts poured from the weapon on the other side of his chopper.

Caught by surprise, the smaller chopper dived to escape. But its blades caught a power line, snapping the metal like twigs. Sparks flew, lighting the sky like fireworks.

The blades' remains kept beating, once, twice, but they couldn't keep the bird in the air. It hung in the sky for what seemed an endless moment. The nose dropped, and it dived into the hill below the road, exploding in a fireball.

Jean-Marie's rage fell away—only to be replaced by an agonizing sense of loss.

He had just proven that he could walk in twilight a few years before anyone had thought possible. But Madame Celeste was still more than capable—indeed, probably eager!—to attack Don Rafael at any time.

If Hélène had been here, she'd have torched those murdering devils in an instant—and he'd have celebrated her success.

Agonizing loss wrenched him yet again, no less painful for the years he'd endured it.

The wind tossed his hair, as if mocking his grief.

He snarled and slammed the door shut on it.

EASTERN SIBERIA

Hélène focused her night-vision goggles, making them drag in every bit of starlight those samples of the latest technology could find. Despite it being high summer and close to the North Pole, where the days were long and nighttime meant the sun circling near the horizon, the valley below was a cavernous black gash.

Deep enough to hide the secrets of an old Soviet bioweapon manufacturing plant from spy satellites for decades. Ordinary bombs wouldn't work against anyplace hidden within this gash in the earth's crust, even if their bearers had made it past the bristling batteries circling the valley. Generations of American and British spymasters had sent their best teams, military and covert, against it. But its brutal terrain and layers of defenses had destroyed its attackers, letting it survive, only to be shut down after the Berlin Wall fell.

A year ago, loose tongues in Moscow attached to hungry men and women had chattered about one of the current government's favorites starting it up again. In a few months, he'd be selling bubonic plague to anyone willing to deposit a fortune in a Swiss bank account.

The only way to utterly destroy such a plant was fire—utterly eradicating every trace from every room and piece of equipment. No chemical cleanser could be as thorough, while bombs would only scattered the pieces across an innocent landscape. Equally important, no Western politician wanted to see anyone in the current Russian government growing rich from this valley's harvest of death. Whitehall had decided to send Hélène's small team in, rather than commandos with thermite grenades.

She was so far away on this rocky slope, none of the old defenses watched her, if Whitehall's penny-pinching intelligence had gotten it right for once. No *prosaico* should be observing this mountain, since only a *vampiro* firestarter could attack the place from here. It was too far for a shoulder-launched missile.

Which didn't stop the skin on the nape of her neck from standing up every few minutes. They'd had a strangely quiet journey here.

At least when she was doing this work, she didn't have time to think about missing Jean-Marie . . .

"Got it," she murmured, finally focusing on one of the ugliest metallic jumbles she'd ever seen. They were lying on a boulder field at the edge of an immense forest. If there were a knife-edged rock that hadn't found her ribs, she didn't know about it. Or one that didn't long to break somebody's ankle.

"Can you see the storage lockers?" Duncan Ross asked. A great bear of a Scotsman and her number two, he was condemned to wear the same brutally uncomfortable body armor she wore. It kept sunlight, mosquitoes, and flies out but ensured that every drop of sweat stayed in. As a *vampiro*, he'd have been far happier shifting into something with teeth—and a thick fur coat to keep the biting pests out.

"Uh-huh. Looks just like the plans." Thank God. If the bastards had done any remodeling, she'd have had a harder time finding the targets, given all the trees and rocks near the plant. "Found the research labs, too, plus the manufacturing plant."

He didn't quite heave a sigh of relief. "Just let me know when you're ready to start, will you?"

"Right." Lots of mosquitoes but nothing larger was stirring—a nasty sign. She'd have been happier if small critters were wandering around, proving no two-legged predators were patrolling other than themselves.

She counted the distant sentries through her glasses as they patrolled, clearly identifiable as brilliant splotches of heat.

One of her bodyguards sat down beside her in wolf form, his tongue lolling out as he tasted the air. She glanced over, and he nodded, giving the all-clear.

The other five members of her team began to give their assurances.

"Ready," she said softly.

She reached out to the most distant, the most buried, of the storage lockers and stirred its molecules into frenzied motion. Faster and faster, hotter and hotter, until metal caught fire and burned like a welder's torch. Damn near as hot as the surface of the sun—thermite grenade hot, like the result of a commando raid.

A second locker and a third, all of them, destroying forever stockpiles of bubonic plague, which had taken decades to accumulate.

"Alarms have sounded," Duncan reported. "Sentries are evacuating the inner core and manning the outer perimeter."

Just as they'd planned back in London. The scientists would probably get away, taking whatever knowledge they held in their heads. Even so, it would be a long time, if ever, before the greedy fools rebuilt that plant.

She grinned and turned her attention to the great vats and piping in the manufacturing plant. A bigger target required a broader brush, a heavier push of concentration until an entire building glowed red, burst into flames, and crumpled into a magma flow of blazing metal which poured over a ravine's boulders.

Even from here they could hear the sirens. Somebody had started firing old antiaircraft guns at the sky.

"Hélène, they're sending helicopters out," Duncan hissed. "They've zeroed in on this mountain as the only location left unprotected."

Shit, they knew about *vampiros*. It was definitely time to leave. But the labs were on the hillside above the plant and the storage lockers. Did she have the right to risk everyone's life? Hell, how many of her missions didn't rate the words *highly dangerous*, if not *suicidal*?

"Prepare to evacuate," she said calmly and moved her glasses one last time. Dammit, the labs were slightly hidden in the smoke. Could she pull it off? If she took out their foundations, dropping them into the manufacturing plant's quagmire below . . .

Ping! Ping! Bullets whizzed past her head. The damned helicopter was making life very difficult.

Duncan cursed.

"Move out," she snapped. One more lab to go . . .

Bullets filled the air. Somebody was shooting back at the chopper.

The lab's wooden struts caught fire, and it began to tumble.

Somebody yelped, the immediately recognizable sound of hard training compensating for a bad wound.

Duncan yanked Hélène unceremoniously onto her feet and raced for the forest, ignoring the rocks that slipped and turned under his feet. Her bodyguard ran beside them, flowing over the treacherous terrain with four-footed grace, obviously holding back his speed. If only they'd let her learn how to shift, she could have done the same. Duncan would have matched her, and they'd be in the woods in no time—without risking her men.

It would be a damned long way back to the extraction point, especially with one man already wounded.

Bullets filled the air around them, singing against the stones and spitting up dust.

She ran faster, praying nobody died on this mission. Wishing Whitehall would let her learn to shapeshift into something useful, instead of treating her like a fragile idiot good for only one task.

Missing yet again, the only man who'd ever treated her as an equal everywhere and anywhere.

THIRTEEN

The Austin Commandery was Don Rafael's original Texas ranch, built after he had enough fighting men to force a settlement deep within what was then hostile Indian country. It still maintained its status as a garrison and a fortress, emphasized by its sturdy buildings and stout limestone walls. Only a few miles from Compostela Ranch and close to Austin, it was now occupied by Ethan's *mesnaderos* and their supporters.

Most of the buildings and their interiors gave clear evidence of the decades they'd been occupied by warriors—longhorn cattle skulls looming from the rafters, the arrowhead collection covering the billiard room's walls, the racks of shotguns and rifles by every door, and more. The walls were plaster or rough-hewn limestone blocks, and the ceiling's beams were clearly visible in most rooms, although the physical comforts were always the latest available—at least everywhere except in the meditation and punishment cells.

Ethan's private quarters reflected his personal taste: a highly sophisticated, very modern mix of architecture, light, and décor where every detail combined into a hard-edged unity. Conveniences, whether technological or hygienic, were concealed behind panels and curtains. Like the man himself, the rooms gave up their secrets grudgingly, although they would obey direct orders from a privileged few, like those gathered here tonight.

Only three of the inner council lounged on the leather chairs: Jean-Marie, Ethan, and Caleb, Gray Wolf's *cónyuge*.

Rafael was with Grania O'Malley, his new lover, whom he'd devoted himself to since they'd first met over two weeks ago. Such fidelity was a shocking display of interest—almost weakness—in a *patrón*, and one that all of his men were working damn hard to conceal from Madame Celeste. Tonight they were tuning personnel assignments so the meeting wasn't, technically, anything he needed to attend.

Caleb was Texas's second-oldest *compañero* and a brilliant geologist, neither of which would have normally qualified him for attendance. He was here as Gray Wolf's alternate, since their *conyugal* bond allowed Gray Wolf to know everything that Caleb saw, felt, or thought. Gray Wolf was in Dallas, picking the brains of dryland farming researchers, one of his favorite passions.

Jean-Marie flicked a glance at Ethan, gauging his temper. Ethan was keying in the last changes to the watch list, his blond hair blazing under the light until he resembled a Renaissance angel. Not a cherubic one, of course, all chubby cheeks and smiles—but the type who stood with a flaming sword at the gates of hell.

They'd first met a year before the Civil War when Rafael had dragged in the young horse thief to learn some badly needed manners. They'd grown to be friends in the decades since, even with Ethan always giving Jean-Marie the subtle deference due an older brother. The former guerrilla had been stretched by this war, as they'd all been, making him a more brilliant fighter and leader.

Even so, Jean-Marie wondered what Ethan wasn't telling anyone. Ethan was seldom talkative, but he didn't usually hide secrets from Rafael or his elder *hermanos*. Recently he seemed to be shying away from private conversations. Odd, very odd.

But not as important as the rapes, suicides, and unexplained deaths plaguing central Texas.

Jean-Marie's phone chimed softly, making his jaw clench, and he automatically hit the ignore button. The unique ring—three descending tones—meant another suicide prevention hotline hadn't been able to prevent a death. A different ring announced when there'd been an unexplained death of a woman. Damn Madame Celeste's two devils and their penchant for feeding on respectable women's terror, which left their victims no peace afterward except in the grave!

"Are we agreed then?" Ethan's right hand thumped the keyboard a few times, closing his entries. Light rippled across the wall behind him and settled into new blocks of text, displaying the new assignments. The great map of Texas facing it glowed in different colors, reflecting the new day and nighttime strengths in various places.

"I still don't like leaving Luis alone. All he's got to back him are some thirty-year-old *compañeros*." Caleb's forefinger stabbed the symbol for Austin. Red-haired and freckle-faced, casually dressed in jeans and T-shirt, he was usually relaxed and ready to joke but not when it came to filling in for his beloved *cónyuge*. Then he worked with an intensity and brilliance that could astonish even Ethan.

"They may be young *compañeros* but they've all got decades of combat under their belts," Jean-Marie countered, summarizing the earlier argument, and came to his feet, unable to sit still.

The death count—whether from suicides or Beau and Devol's murder victims—was now into double digits by his reckoning. If the *prosaico* media caught wind of it and guessed the cause, they'd panic. There'd be hell to pay afterward for all *vampiros*, guilty or not.

"If Madame Celeste is smart enough to try something during daylight . . ." Caleb measured off the miles to New Orleans.

"Which she never has been," Jean-Marie reminded him yet again.

"We'll call in Hennessy's oldest pair of *compañeros* from Dallas if there's serious trouble," Ethan said firmly, sliding the keyboard out of sight.

"It's more important our only pair of *cónyuges* are on the same shift," the *alferez mayor* reasoned. "Gray Wolf has to work nights, which means you're there, too."

Caleb hesitated.

"You know damn well two *cónyuges*, even if one's a *compañero*, are damn near unbeatable in a duel," Jean-Marie drawled, deliberately keeping his voice calm. "With Beau and Devol—Madame Celeste's top two assassins—here in Texas, we need the two of you as our strike team, ready to stop any trouble those assholes might start."

"Shit, I know it's the only way," Caleb muttered, throwing up his hands. "But there's no guarantee we'll succeed, especially if Beau and Devol work together. It'd be different if I was a *vampiro*."

"Giving us two experienced duelists and *cónyuges*—*both* of them with *vampiro* speed and strength? You couldn't wish you were a *vampiro* half as much as I do." Ethan snorted and started double-checking his revolvers. "But it won't happen in time for this fight."

"Takes a minimum of two years to make a *vampiro*," Jean-Marie confirmed, double-checking his knife sheaths in preparation for departure now that Caleb had agreed.

"Yeah—but first, Gray Wolf has to agree to let Don Rafael turn me into a *vampiro*."

Ethan flinched.

Jean-Marie whistled, not quite glancing at the *alferez mayor* out of the corner of his eye. "Oh ho ho, is that the worm in the apple?"

"Yeah." Caleb slammed down his hands, propelling him into movement. "Hell, we're *cónyuges*! He knows down to his bones how completely I'm committed to him."

"But only Don Rafael can create *vampiros* in Texas." Jean-Marie quoted the Texas *esfera*'s first law.

"Yeah—but there's no way in hell Gray Wolf will let me near Don Rafael's bed, even if it's only for a few months during *La Lujuria* while I become a *vampiro*. Despite the fact it'd give us immortality together."

"Shit, you are in a mess," Ethan agreed, coming up beside Jean-Marie. His voice was a shade too hearty.

"I tell you, I'm jealous when I look at some of the couples who've pulled it off—Eli and Sam, Gregor and Anders . . . On the other hand, unlike the fellows who prefer girls—at least I've got hope Gray Wolf will change his mind one day."

Beside Jean-Marie, Ethan was immobile, hard grooves carved into his face.

Jean-Marie winced. Agonizing though it was, at least he'd buried Hélène and knew he'd never find the same heart's ease with anyone else. He wasn't someone desperately in love with a woman. He didn't have to pray Don Rafael would reconsider one of his famously immovable decisions and permit a lady to become a *vampira* in Texas.

NORTHERN SCOTLAND

The small plane burst out of the fog, catching sight of the landing pattern only at the last moment. Hélène automatically planted her feet firmly, bracing herself for the coming steep descent and screeching stop. Despite the decades the British Secret Service had used this isolated station, they'd never bothered to lengthen the runway. Supposedly, poor facilities deterred detection.

Right, just like an empty wallet improved creativity and everyone needed to be toughened up to do a good job. Her mouth tightened.

The plane bounced, and she flung her arm across her sleeping seat mate, making sure he wasn't harmed. But his all-too-even, painkiller-assisted breathing never changed. She sighed, thankful for one small favor.

They'd lost two of her team's eight people during this last mission. No matter what the official report would say, she and the rest knew the true cause—exhaustion. Too many missions, coming too close together, had left too little time to rest and learn the ways of the new enemy. Damn those hard-pushing, shortsighted bureaucrats to hell!

Three of the remaining five had privately told her they didn't plan to reenlist, while the other two were already slated to become instructors. Her team was wiped out—and they'd been the best of the best.

The outcome might have been different if the damned Secret Service still permitted a mix of *vampiros* and *compañeros*, instead of demanding only *vampiros* and *prosaicos*. *Compañeros'* greater stamina and lifespan permitted greater skills and longer missions, as had been proven during both world wars.

And by dearest, dearest Jean-Marie . . .

But, no, the penny-pinching accountants had ruled out *compañeros*, calling their pensions too expensive.

Damn fools. They could have at least looked at how those American *patrones* were using *compañeros* as warriors and future *vampiros*. Texas's Don Rafael, in particular, was a vicious fighter ruling an enormous *esfera*. He'd only incorporate *compañeros* into his men's ranks if they were effective.

She growled under her breath. The plane's engines screamed while it fought to land, echoing her opinion of the bureaucrats.

Duncan glanced sideways at her. Probably wondering why she was visibly angry, instead of her more typical icy calm.

The plane brought itself to a stop, and the lights came up. Its passengers unfolded themselves from their team, silently gathering their duffels with the ease of long practice. Hélène went down the stairs first, expecting to find someone from London to give them passes home. Duncan brought up the rear, using his strength to ease the injured.

Fog wrapped itself around them, barely bothering to reveal an architectural abomination's sullen lights squatting next to the tarmac. Diesel fumes touched the air, along with jet fuel. Somewhere in the distance, waves beat relentlessly upon the land, a reminder of tides' inevitable success.

"About time you made it back." A tallish man, on the shady side of thirty, shoved his thinning blond hair back from his forehead. "There's a coach waiting to take you lot in for debrief. After that, the chief wants to start planning the next mission."

Two of her men groaned, very softly.

Hélène's hackles rose at the fool's tone. Another of those stupid *prosaico* bureaucrats, who thought he was powerful because he was one of the very few who knew about *vampiros*.

It was past time for Whitehall to learn what a treasure her people were. If that meant doing without them for a while, the lesson could start immediately—before anyone else died.

The only sure way to give her team a break was to remove herself, since they were trained to work with her—the rare and dangerous firestarter.

"Any questions?" asked the young bureaucrat, stomping his feet in a futile attempt to warm them.

"What's the magic word?" She smiled at him sweetly.

"What?" His brows snapped together.

"The magic word that will make me want to take my people on this mission."

"What the hell are you talking about? Of course you have to do this!"

"I don't have to—and neither do they. You see, my contract with the British Crown ends when I can walk in twilight—which now I can. So time's up, and you have to *convince* me to accept a new mission."

"That's insane."

"No, that's a fact. You can look it up in your own archives. It gets better, too." Tossing in an American colloquialism was delicious fun—it made his face turn even redder, his neck swell, and her people glow. "Since every team member is trained to work only with one *vampiro*, not as individuals—if I don't go, they don't either. At least not until they're retrained, which takes time." She goaded him a little more. "I'm still waiting to hear that magic word . . ."

He came out of his stupefaction with a roar. "By God, I'll have you arrested for treason!"

"Try it and every other *vampiro* in Britain will come after you, starting with the *vampiros mayores*." That home truth was edged with steel. "Do you have a fine speech for me?"

"Of course not!"

"In that case, I bid you *au revoir*." She bowed slightly, never taking her eyes off him. "Come along, friends, we're taking that vacation they promised us a year ago."

She entered the building's dubious warmth, and the others followed, never looking back at the gobbling bureaucrat.

She'd have to make sure her people were taken care of next, before she rested.

But what could she do after that to heal? Make more money?

She harrumphed softly and barely refrained from rolling her eyes. Nothing had ever distracted her from missing Jean-Marie. She'd even tried the wildest debauchery.

What else was there?

Her beloved house in Oxford and the simple life she led there, filled with books, intellectual challenges, and dreams of sharing her discoveries with Jean-Marie.

For brief diversions, she could go shopping in London. She'd always enjoyed the hunt for the perfect dress, although not as much as little Celeste had. It would at least be better than sitting at home, wishing Jean-Marie was cuddling her again.

Celeste brought the monitors up with a practiced hand. It suited her to let the world believe she was solely interested in power, carnal pleasures, and shopping, while being bored with technology. Only Georges—the one man in the world she utterly trusted—knew how completely she could observe every word and gesture which occurred in her New Orleans headquarters.

She certainly hadn't told Beau just how closely she watched him. He'd already been an experienced assassin and a *vampiro mayor* when he'd emerged from nowhere to help Ivan the Terrible five hundred years ago. All of Russia's subsequent rulers had claimed his services over the following centuries, keeping him hidden in that icebound land until the Berlin Wall had fallen. He'd made his way here a few months ago, claiming remarkable sexual prowess. Surprisingly, he'd had the skills to match his boy toy looks and had soon earned a regular place in her bed—but only when Georges was present. She wasn't enough of a fool to close her eyes near a man obsessed with killing Don Rafael, especially when he quite possibly had the strength and skill to do so. She'd fought too hard and too long for her *esfera*, loved New Orleans too much, to risk it all on momentary ecstasy with a blond slut.

Only Don Rafael, dammit, was worth remaking her world for. The wealthy *patrón* who'd smiled at her on that Mardi Gras and treated her like a lady. And created such surprises for her infinite pleasure. How could she forget what an incredible beauty he'd been in the bedroom? Who else could spend so much time, find so many ways to love a woman's clit with his tongue? Or the positions he knew for taking a woman from behind? *Mon dieu*, she'd never expected to come so hard when not seeing her lover's face!

Who could wonder that she'd called him her stallion and craved him? Measured every other man against him? Dreamed of him for decades?

Until he'd cruelly, stupidly rejected her and signed his own death warrant.

Celeste owned an entire block in New Orleans' Warehouse District, an easy walk from the French Quarter. An enormous, deliberately gaudy casino on the first floor and a nightclub on the second floor lured in hordes of tourists with their King Bacchus theme, providing regular meals for her *cachorros*. Like most young animals, they lacked both taste and discretion. Visiting idiots were therefore the perfect offering, since they lacked the sense to avoid obvious traps like a casino and wouldn't discuss their humiliation after they returned home.

She personally usually looked for tidbits among the world's beautiful people, where they fought for invitations to the private club on the third floor. With both Beau and Georges in Texas, she'd long since exhausted her other *hijos*'s ability to interest her, let alone bring her lusts to a wonderfully hot, angry edge just this side of a murderous rage.

Her fingers flew rapidly over the control panel, keying in commands. The great monitor hummed into life, its green power light reflected in her dressing room's mirrors and the highly polished armoire, where she kept the precious mementos of France.

She'd ordered the fashionable club to be kept extra busy, and her men had done well. Beautiful, half-naked, male and female *prosaicos* sweated to display their charms on the dance floor under everchanging lights. A bar covered one wall, above which shadow dancers flexed and intertwined lasciviously. She could almost smell the musk rising from their audience.

The private booths were immense, the seats actually circular beds barely screened by floor-to-ceiling shimmering curtains. The walls were covered with pale golden woods, on which flashed an ever-changing montage of past Mardi Gras celebrations. She'd removed all photos of the one Don Rafael had attended, of course.

Drugs and alcohol were common, an easy ploy to ensure her *vampiros* were always under her thumb. *Vampiros*, feeding off prey who believed their emotions came from a bottle, were predators eating a weak diet and therefore desperate for a richer meal—like their *patrona*'s blood. They always begged so prettily to come to her bed.

She began to scan the crowd, her long, red fingernails curling over the joystick. Who should she take to her bed tonight—a *prosaico* or a *vampiro*? Or a mixture? Probably several, since she was so very hungry.

"*Quel canon!*" she cooed, zooming in on a stunning blond *vampiro*. He was gorgeous enough to make her forget Beau's attractions for at least a few days, even if his features had more of a knife-edged beauty than Beau's angelic perfection. He was muscular, too, moving with the easy grace of somebody who'd earned his strength through daily work, not conquered it in a gym. He definitely had potential. Still . . .

"But are you strong enough to enjoy my kind of pain, *mon brave*?"

Behind her, Raoul's eyes narrowed from where he watched in her boudoir mirror.

Jean-Marie stood at attention with Ethan, Luis, Gray Wolf, and Caleb in Rafael's office at Compostela, inwardly gagging at just how close the afternoon's attack had come. A woman and her three very young children had nearly died. And for what reason? Because their names exactly matched those of Rafael's long-dead family. The warning that a terrorist would strike Rafael's nearest and dearest whenever he chose could not have been clearer.

It was no wonder that Rafael was furious—but that didn't make enduring his reprimand any easier. Steel shutters covered the windows against the sun, and a small spotlight picked out Rafael's knightly sword above the fireplace mantel.

"It does not matter what you thought, Ethan, or you, Gray Wolf," Rafael continued, his anger still dangerously raw. "The enemy penetrated into the heart of my lands, something you said was impossible. He injured my people—innocent people—solely because of their likeness to me."

"My humblest apologies, *patrón*." Ethan prostrated himself, something he hadn't done in decades. "It will not happen again."

"*Bien,*" Rafael all but snarled, gesturing him up. "And you, Jean-Marie, your networks should have done better than this."

"*Mille pardons, patrón.*" Next time, he damn well would provide advance warning of Beau's approach.

"Take the men away from guarding me and set them to hunting these devils."

What the hell?

Everyone began to talk at once.

"Throwing more men into hunting for Beau will only cloud the waters. *Mesnaderos* are warriors, not spies," Jean-Marie countered, terror for his *creador* and oldest friend boiling up. Dammit, he knew they hadn't done the job Rafael needed by preventing the attack. But this?

"We already have plenty of men hunting for them," Gray Wolf argued, his voice deepening in a rare sign of imminent rage. "To add more men means taking away from—"

"That's a trap! It's exactly what Madame Celeste wants us to do," Ethan shouted.

"Risking yourself like that is foolish, Don Rafael," Luis snarled, directly disagreeing with Rafael for once. "It won't help the *prosaicos* or the *esfera* if they lose you."

Curses spilled into their logic.

"*¡Sí!*" Rafael roared.

They snarled and growled but reluctantly fell silent under the weight of his glare.

Jean-Marie silently berated himself for his own failure, his jaw tightening. He was a diplomat and a spy, not material for a *patrón*. He couldn't help shoulder all of his oldest friend's burdens, especially since they'd never talked as equals. Not with four hundred years between them and those two centuries of torture Rafael had endured.

Nom de dieu, the burdens Rafael carried! It was no wonder the man lost his temper sometimes.

"We must stop them, no matter what. The penalty for failure is death, *mis hijos*. You do not like my punishments—but you will hate those doled out by the enemy more."

A boot heel struck wood floor, instead of carpet, in the great room just outside, and the assembly fell silent in shock. Definitely not one of Luis's well-trained servants—but a woman?

"*Doctora* O'Malley?" Rafael called. "Please come in."

A woman, Rafael's *amante*, perhaps, since the step didn't sound and smell like any of the *prosaicas* from the *comitiva*. But here at Compostela? Impossible.

Everyone inside the office turned to face the newcomer, grabbing for their politest masks.

"*Doctora*," Rafael began a formal greeting.

Still dusty and sweaty, reeking of horse and deathly ill dogs, a tall, red-haired woman tossed her Stetson onto the hat rack, strode past everyone else without a second glance, and wrapped her arms around him.

Rafael choked with laughter and hugged her close, his body promptly curving into a protective, loving embrace.

She'd approached him as an equal, and he'd greeted her as one. Sara had offered Rafael something similar, an affection born of shared decades of pain and companionship. But they'd never been peers, not like this.

For the first time in his long life, Jean-Marie openly gawked. In three centuries, he'd seen his *creador* enjoy the charms of many women, but they'd always been well-polished females. What the hell did this one offer to keep him so fascinated? He couldn't guess.

Ethan's elbow jolted Jean-Marie back into the present, and he edged toward the door with the others.

"Gentlemen, another minute of your time for introductions." Rafael lifted his cheek from the lady's hair.

They stopped and returned to attention, allowing Jean-Marie to discreetly assess her. Beneath the filth, she was a beauty with classic features and brilliant blue eyes.

"*Doctora* O'Malley, may I present to you my *adelantado mayor* and heir, Gray Wolf? You've already met his partner, Caleb Jones."

Gray Wolf bowed, and she nodded politely. Gray Wolf's smile was a fraction warmer than usual with a woman, possibly because she was a *wildlife* veterinarian. His weakness was, as ever, the places and beings of the earth.

"My eldest *hijo* and *heraldo*, Jean-Marie St. Just."

Jean-Marie fell back on the first weapon he'd learned—charm. He bowed, smiling as he would have to his father's favorite mistress. "*Enchanté, mademoiselle.*"

Her eyebrows went up, and she said nothing, simply favored him with a quick jerk of her head. Good God, had she seen through his approach so easily?

"My *alferez mayor*, Ethan Templeton."

"Good evening, Dr. O'Malley."

A very polite greeting from Ethan—and a verbal one at that? What the hell had she done to earn so much respect?

It brought her on the alert, too. She frowned briefly before shaking his hand with all the enthusiasm one would handle an unknown gun.

Rafael's eyes danced but he said nothing.

Jean-Marie studied Ethan, wondering what the hell had been going on. She must have done more than help the Perez family.

"And Luis Alvarez, my *siniscal*."

Jean-Marie turned back just in time to see Rafael's *amante* and Luis smiling at each other as if they were members of the same family. What had he missed?

Luis turned to Rafael. "I myself will go to San Leandro on the Fourth."

Rafael stiffened.

Luis shrugged, his eyes alight while he tweaked Rafael's dictatorial side yet again. "I am the best one to check the preparations, since it must be done in daylight, as you know, *patrón*."

"Very well," Rafael finally yielded. "The children cannot be risked at the picnic."

Luis bowed and turned to go.

"But I swear to you, Luis, as soon as this is over, you will receive *El Abrazo*, no matter what excuse you offer next."

Luis spun, his mouth hanging open in shock at his own bluff being called in return.

Jean-Marie hid his own satisfied grin. Only God knew why Luis had dodged becoming a *vampiro* for so long. It was more than time for Rafael to force an end to it.

Rafael shook his head and hugged *Doctora* O'Malley closer. "*Querida*," he murmured, stroking her cheek. "Will they live?"

"Every one of them will be fine, even the little baby, especially since you gave the hospital a hyperbaric chamber." She kissed her fingertips and touched them to his lips.

Rafael's face softened, allowing Jean-Marie to understand her appeal even more. A lady who was a passionate fighter for the defenseless ones, plus being totally unafraid of a *vampiro mayor*. A very rare and seductive combination, indeed.

"It was carbon monoxide poisoning," she added. "The space heater in the bedroom had been sabotaged."

"It will be a pleasure to destroy those devils," Ethan growled.

Rafael lifted his head, not quite glaring at them. "You have your orders, gentlemen. *Buenas nochas*."

The Texans left quietly, closing the door behind them. They said nothing until they were in Luis's soundproofed office, far away from the main house.

Ethan propped his hip on the desk. "You owe me ten bucks, Caleb, for not believing he was obsessed with her."

"I'd have wagered a hundred times that amount against a display like that." Caleb pulled out his wallet. "Did any of you get a good whiff of her scent? Horse and sick dogs?"

"She earned it while healing others," Jean-Marie pointed out.

"Do you think that's the key to their relationship?" Luis asked, his gaze probing Jean-Marie's expression.

"No. And before any of you ask—no, I haven't seen him like that with anyone else before. Not in three centuries."

And I don't know why.

"If they hadn't known each other for only a few weeks, I'd say they were *cónyuges,*" Gray Wolf put in quietly. "Why else would a *vampiro mayor* relax so completely with her?"

"Impossible!" Ethan snapped.

"But it would explain so much, like why he can't bear to be separated from her," Luis mused. "No *vampiro* can tolerate more than a few days apart from their *cónyuge.*"

"Which would give us two teams of *cónyuges* for duelists, during this war," Ethan commented.

Jean-Marie met his friends' eyes, determination thrumming his veins. "And a far better chance to stop Madame Celeste and her bastards, before they kill any more of those poor women."

Hélène d'Agelet strolled into the private club in Mayfair just after sunset, very pleased with her new Christian Dior outfit. Its crisp jauntiness, from the ridiculous hat to the miniscule purse and the high-heeled shoes, had proven to be exactly what she needed to take her mind off yet another rainy English day. After two centuries of living on this island (except for trips overseas on Whitehall's behalf), she'd once expected to grow accustomed to the weather. But that had never come to pass.

She'd originally diverted herself from pining for Jean-Marie by trying to outspend her salary on clothes. She hadn't succeeded. In fact, she'd become so irritated at the stodgy Britons for continuing to fund her extravagance that she'd learned to make a great deal of money. She still enjoyed fashion more than anything else in Great Britain, except their men. And none of those had kept her attention for more than a few months.

Thank God her team members were doing so well, now that she'd terrified the Secret Service into giving them a generous amount of leave. The bureaucrats had promised not to call her back until her people were ready and had even given her a passport, with a round-trip ticket anywhere in the world. Amazing.

In the main clubroom, a centuries-old hymn to carved wood, old books, and leather chairs, a dozen *vampiros* were gathered around a table, talking excitedly and peering over something with what looked like a magnifying glass, or perhaps a jeweler's loupe.

"Good evening, gentlemen," she said sweetly.

Their leader rose to face her, his expression unreadable.

"Madame d'Agelet." Lord Simon, the current West End *patrón*, bowed profoundly and gracefully, as befitted a duke's son and former colonel. He glanced back at his men, raising a supercilious brow.

They rushed to stand up, looking more like abashed schoolboys than deadly *mesnaderos*. Chairs pushed back rapidly. One fell over. *Vampiros* tried to pretend they'd been behaving like adults, not schoolchildren caught by their teacher.

A glass crashed to the floor. A tall decanter swayed wildly, its golden contents tumbling like an earthquake's barometer.

Lord Simon lifted her hand and kissed it. "Hélène."

The white scar slashing his cheek, courtesy of a Prussian general in the dying days of World War I, puckered when he smiled at her. She'd heard the Prussian hadn't lived long enough after the meeting to count his scars.

"*Mon cher* Simon." She smiled back at him, letting her genuine affection show.

"You look remarkably beautiful tonight. Christian Dior, I would hazard a guess?"

Senses trained by centuries in the deadliest profession came fully alert. Why the devil had Lord Simon, who had no fashion sense, tried to butter her up by mentioning her couturier?

She nodded confirmation, tossing her head so the silly hat's finer points could be seen.

"Please, join us for a cognac. Delamain Très Venerable, *s'il tu veux?*"

A polite invitation, and she'd bet a million pounds he was hoping she wouldn't accept it.

One of the men—a fit-looking fellow, probably one of Lord Simon's SAS recruits—tried to slide the paper off the table and into a leather portfolio.

Hélène promptly lit the ornamental candelabrum at his elbow. He froze, obviously aware that she could have torched him as easily—or the entire house.

"Sounds good," she answered. She enjoyed using Americanisms, just to remind the British she wasn't one of theirs. "Can I have the loupe, too?" She held out her hand and smiled sweetly at Lord Simon.

His eyes narrowed slightly before he gave a resigned shrug and nodded at his underling. He was eighty years old, the oldest of London's current set of *patrones*, while most of his men were the typical ten—to thirty-year-old *vampiros*. He had a good, tough set of *mesnaderos* that no other *patrón* sought a fight with, even if none of his men could stand up to her.

They'd worked together briefly in Occupied France, against the Nazis, and she still remembered his delight in the more outlandish masquerade costumes. She'd been a firestarter on his team of saboteurs, enjoying his creativity in the use of explosives.

But he'd known her long enough to be certain that she wouldn't fly off the handle. So why was he unhappy?

Simon watched Hélène closely, wondering how she'd react to the photo. Whitehall had been almost more nervous about letting it fall into her hands than keeping it in Britain.

Not that he expected her expression to reveal anything. She was notoriously self-disciplined, a vital qualification for a firestarter. Most would-be firestarters torched themselves or their surroundings in split seconds of inattention. But not her, not in two centuries. A good friend and a good lay—but not someone who let anybody get too close to her heart.

It was easier to read her emotions by outward details. When she was happy, she bought books. When she was sad or lonely, she went clothes shopping—especially for nonsensical hats, like the one she was wearing.

He eyed its ridiculous silhouette, wondering how any woman could tolerate such an object on her head. It was far more outlandish than the ones he'd seen at the last wedding he went to.

He glanced at the brandy snifter beside her.

Empty. Damn.

A small sob broke in her throat, and his gaze shot to her face. *Tears?* Bloody hell.

He caught his *siniscal*'s eye and pointed at her snifter, silently demanding a refill. The new glass appeared within seconds and was given to him.

Simon set it quietly down beside her, and she gulped it—*Hélène* gulped it?—without glancing at him.

Minutes passed before she put the jeweler's loupe down.

"Who are the two men?" She tapped the photo, watching Lord Simon.

"One is Jean-Marie St. Just, the *heraldo* of Texas, who I've met before. I assume the other is Don Rafael Perez, the *patrón* of Texas."

A *heraldo*—which made her beloved a master spy and a diplomat, the perfect profession for him. He was still with Rodrigo—no, Rafael—who was the *patrón* of the largest, and probably the richest, *esfera* in North America. They'd done very well for themselves.

And why had Monsieur Perez changed his name from Rodrigo to Rafael? A *nom de guerre*, perhaps? But who cared about him, when she could think about Jean-Marie?

She sternly told her heart to stop frolicking at the absence of Mademoiselle Perez. It was possible, after all, she was missing from the picture, not their lives. It was better to think about more questions than those implications. "Who is the woman beside them?"

A muscle ticked in Lord Simon's jaw. "Madame Celeste, now the *patrona* of New Orleans. She holds most of the southeastern United States."

Hélène gaped at him. *La petite* was a *patrona*? Why on earth would she do that? She'd never shown any interest in ruling and, as a spy, she'd always preferred to work through the men she slept with.

Why was she living in New Orleans? Why hadn't she sought out her older sister in England after the war, if she'd been trapped in Europe by Napoleon's forces? Was she afraid of what the British Secret Service would think of her having been gone for so long?

And what were Lord Simon and his men so worried about? Proof of *vampiro* immortality could spark a *prosaico* outcry and lead to a mob, the one thing all *vampiros* feared. Possessing a picture of a *vampiro* was therefore very unhealthy. But a photo of two *patrones*, especially when one of them was a *vampiro mayor* notoriously thorough about protecting himself? Even one of *London's patrones* could fear for his life under those circumstances.

As for her own reaction, it was entirely possible that Whitehall had warned the local *patrones* to keep her from learning *la petite* was alive, lest she ignore her oaths to Britain and visit her sister.

Her hand tightened on the jeweler's loupe, as if it were a weapon she could hurl at arrogant bureaucrats.

Other questions first, though.

She brought her eyes back to Lord Simon. "How long have they had this?"

"Two years. I warned them you'd be furious."

"Bastards." She smiled wryly, caught despite herself by an old friend's understanding. "They should have told me immediately."

"They were probably afraid of your reaction."

"Or Don Rafael's."

"Agreed. All of these lads have come up against his Santiago Trust before and have the bruises to show for it."

A thought flashed through her head.

"Whitehall doesn't want me to leave, do they?"

He shrugged.

"But I'll just bet they don't want Don Rafael to know about this picture either—or that they've been hiding it from him for two years."

Gasps ran around the room. Someone muttered a soft, vicious curse.

"Do you plan to ring him up?" A gleam of appreciation for the situation's irony lit Lord Simon's eyes.

"No, I'll take it to him, since he obviously knew it was being taken," Hélène announced briskly. "He's known for his courtesy to women so I can do it in safety, which none of you can. I'll tell him it came into your hands recently through a rare prints dealer, offered solely because of your interest in pictures of Mardi Gras celebrations."

Lord Simon started to chuckle. "Whitehall will hate it, but I don't see they have any other choice."

They smiled at each other in perfect understanding.

"You might want to keep your eyes open while you're over there. Don Rafael and Madame Celeste are fighting a rather vicious war, with the lady determined to remove him from this earth."

"A war? Why would they do that?" Hélène blinked. *La petite*'s temper might be fierce, but it had always evaporated quickly.

"She took over the southeastern quarter of the country through war and assassinations, not alliances." The old saboteur's voice conveyed both admiration and warning. "Neutrals aren't being attacked, but that could obviously change at any moment. Many of the European *esferas* have forbidden travel into the area."

Assassinations? Even so, Celeste would never harm her older sister.

But it was far, far more important to be reunited with Jean-Marie first. It was a miracle her shoes were still united with the carpet, when her blood was fizzing so much with joy.

"I'd better be going now, so I can leave for Texas as soon as possible." She began to briskly tuck the photo into the folio.

"Would you care for some company on the drive home?" Lord Simon offered graciously. "I'm sure one, or more, of the lads would be glad to give you an excellent time."

The lads froze, like Cornish game hens in a butcher's window.

She scrutinized them thoughtfully. Lord Simon really did have a fine lot, mostly ex-military, on the whole much stronger and more mature than her usual selection of Oxford college students. They'd all provide an excellent meal. It was even possible one or two could string a sentence together.

Somebody choked. Several others turned pale, as they watched her, as if they expected to be barbecued at any moment.

But she greatly disliked taking the unwilling, even if she needed the meal.

"Thank you, but I've already fed. Perhaps when I return." She kissed him on the cheek.

"Au revoir, chérie."

She chose to ignore his parting comment, muttered so softly even she could scarcely hear it, "I hope it's not *adieu* for you."

Fourteen

Gnats and mosquitoes patrolled the hot summer night, hunting for any bit of flesh gleaming with sweat under the clouded moon. An ancient pickup truck chugged down the long road beside the levee, accelerator hard against the floor. Its driver carefully never looked to his left, into a tangled forest of live oaks and Spanish moss.

He took the turn at the end too fast and spun onto the roadside, tires throwing up a rooster's tail of dust, as they fought to keep him out of the cotton field. A scream of overexerted brakes and a screech of gears returned the pickup to the highway, moving fast amid the spiky remains of a cotton crop.

Rising steep and tall at the roadside behind him, a wrought-iron fence bore formal warning signs to trespassers. It didn't mention its far more brutal electrified brother only a few feet farther back, or the Mississippi River where any fools would be disposed of. Or the extremely high-tech gatehouse inside the woods, whose suspicious sentries would happily shoot first and ask questions later. Alligators prowled the marshland behind that, helping the clouds of mosquitoes and gnats make the long approach into hell on earth for uninvited guests.

Inside those layers of defenses, the estate crouched like an exotic scorpion, whose opponents are more wary of its poison than its shell.

Rosemeade Plantation was quiet on this midnight, allowing the rich scents of jasmine and heliotrope to tease the humid air. Camellia and magnolia blossoms dotted the luxuriant gardens like Chinese lanterns. White columns marched like Greek warriors at the edge of the mansion's two floors. Smaller ones lifted a glass cupola on the roof, almost an offering to Zeus, the god of thunder. All of the chimneys were capped, protecting the house's tinder-dry wood from sparks.

Golden light spilled from doors and windows, their steel shutters left unusually open. A sweeping drive and a huge parking lot showed that the enormous house still offered lavish hospitality, to the right people at least.

It amused Celeste, as it had her predecessors, to maintain Rosemeade as it had been before The War between the States. Back then, Louisiana cotton planters could become millionaires with two excellent crops in a row, and the world had offered its finest goods in homage.

The walls and floors were still the same ancient, highly polished wood, which showcased the great central staircase rising to the cupola. Silk covered the walls and poured from the curtain rods. Ornate wood carvings graced the furniture and accented the high ceilings. Crystal chandeliers and lamps cast dancing reflections across table linens and exotic carpets.

For two centuries, Rosemeade had been the country retreat of the New Orleans *patrones*, ever increasing its reputation for both decadence and impregnability. Celeste and Georges had worked hard to make it invulnerable, proven when they'd successfully fought off multiple attacks by disloyal subjects.

She'd eventually had to purge her realm with Georges's help, in order to stop those rebellions. Six *vampiros* in Memphis, eleven in Miami . . . Those two foolish, blond *vampiras* in Atlanta who'd thought their feminine charms could distract Georges from his allegiance! Once he'd made a particularly bloody example of them, she hadn't encountered any other traitors. They'd had a delicious private party here to celebrate the victory.

But dammit, nothing—nothing at all!—had come together in this war against Don Rafael. He was still strutting like a peacock in Texas, while she was cooped up here in Louisiana, unable to leave her properties to choose a decent meal. This was not the way any of her wars had proceeded before.

She'd given Beau permission, and money, to hunt for a chink in Don Rafael's armor—find someone whose loss would break him. Had he found anyone? No!

Was she going slowly broke, paying for him, extra guards on all her properties, and lost income from her investments? Yes!

Intolerable!

Celeste pushed herself away from the great column and stomped back inside to her bedroom, ignoring her bodyguards. They might be close at hand, but they'd so far proven too young to be useful for anything more than driving a car and shooting a gun.

Her reliance, as ever, was on Georges. Her darling Georges.

She automatically logged in to the videoconference, her mind elsewhere while she snarled at the impassive menu.

"*Cher* madame." Georges's deep voice broke the silence, lingering over the first single soft syllable until it sounded like *shah*.

Unlike other Cajun men who casually addressed almost every woman as *cher*, Georges only gave her that honor, because only she meant sweetness to him. And when he combined two words and called her *cher madame*, it was the very greatest of honors, since he loathed all respectable women. The titles were unforced gifts, too, offered out of his love for her.

Celeste opened her mouth to remonstrate with him and stopped. He had, as ever, been perfect. Ever since he'd escaped from Death Row at Angola Prison, Louisiana's supposedly escape-proof penitentiary, he'd been hers and he'd always been—*perfect* for her needs.

She threw her martini glass against the wall.

"Has something new happened, *cher*?" Georges's eyebrows flew up. He had brown hair, brown eyes, average face, average build—all mixed with the intense viciousness of a starving cobra. Except for moments when they were alone and his gaze shifted to an alcoholic's desperate passion for the only wine cellar in the world.

"Some of my overseas investments have been dropping in value, dammit. I can smell Don Rafael's filthy hand at work."

"*Salopard!*"

She made a very rude gesture of agreement.

"Do you want me to turn my attention to killing the pig, *cher*?"

"No, let Beau be the one to risk his neck. You're my best hope."

Georges nodded reluctant acceptance. Beau's experience as an assassin would be better for this than Georges's past as a serial killer.

"What false trail is that blond chasing tonight?"

"It's the Fourth of July, and Don Rafael has promised to light fireworks at the local celebration." Georges rolled his eyes. "So the famous Russian assassin is crawling through the hills, hoping for a glimpse of the female Don Rafael is supposedly obsessed with."

"Impossible! Even Don Rafael isn't enough of an honorable fool to expose himself and his slut at a public gathering. It would serve Beau right if fire ants devoured his private parts."

"It might be the only way to finally discover a chink in Don Rafael's armor."

"The woman—and destroy her? True, very true." Celeste cheered up, nibbling on a long fingernail. Oh, the delicious ways to have that slut beg for her life while Don Rafael watched!

She beamed at her faithful enforcer, never seeing Raoul's watchful presence in the great pier glass mirror behind her.

"Have you been feeding well, down there in the wilds?"

"Ah, *cher madame*!" An enormous grin split his face. "The fat Texas cows have been pampered for so long, they fire up immediately when I introduce them to terror. Their blood is the finest I have ever tasted."

"Excellent! The unexplained deaths—and suicides?" Georges nodded, his smirk deepening. "Must be driving Don Rafael insane. How are your *bandolerismo* coming, those untamed *vampiros* who will infect Texas and destroy it from the inside like maggots?"

Good, old-fashioned bandits, the bane of every law-abiding *patrón* like Don Rafael. Of course, she'd thrown them out of her *esfera*, too. But they did have their uses at times, like now.

"They're not hard to find, especially since that young Mexican *patrón* started helping us. The difficulty's been getting them into Texas, and I've finished doing that." He straightened up even more until he was standing at attention.

"You've gotten them into Texas?" She stared, her jaw falling open, before glorious possibilities began to suggest themselves. "*Magnifique*, Georges! If I was there with you, *cher*, we'd celebrate for the rest of the night."

She blew a kiss at him, blood humming through her veins. Oh my, the problems she could cause for the sanctimonious Don Rafael now . . .

But first things, first.

"*Cher*, your *bandolerismo* need to investigate Don Rafael's com-manderies, those hidey holes for his men and armaments. Since they're obviously good at sneaking around, your devils should be able to find out—"

"Weak points, watch patterns, garrison size, and so on? Of course, I've already ordered them to hunt those out." Georges eyes shone with excitement.

"Send me the list of *vampiros* and their whereabouts; I may be able to think of other places for them to investigate."

"Are you sure that's safe, *cher*?"

"I'm well able to scent—and punish"—she smiled reminiscently—"anyone who'd dare look at private files on my computer. Nobody'd dare risk their life by sneaking around in my rooms."

"You'll have it immediately, *cher*. Are we finally going to attack the Texans?"

She nodded, her fangs hinting at the traditional preliminary to a *vampiro* duel. She wasn't a shapeshifter, of course; that was for duel-ists, something she'd never needed to become. She'd always done far, far better by selecting a man with the appropriate skills—such as duel-ing, or shapeshifting—and controlling him with sexual hunger. "Ah, *oui*, it's time to start some real trouble, *mon cher*."

They smiled at each other, in perfect accord, despite the miles between them.

THREE WEEKS LATER

Jean-Marie surfaced a mile downstream from Rosemeade, beside Lars. Thankfully, he hadn't encountered another one of the alligators who'd taken a chunk out of his leg the last time he'd visited that hell-hole, just before Don Rafael's duel. That wound had left him with a limp he'd had a damn hard time explaining to his *creador*.

The two swimmers hoisted themselves into their waiting boat, indistinguishable from hundreds of other shabby weekend cruisers used for drinking beer, bragging about fish, and occasionally getting laid. Neither of them said a word until they'd put another five miles between them and any possible pursuit.

The engine purred, the craft's sole sign of wealth. Water rubbed against the hull, a more solid form of the humidity which tried to catch a man's breath. Moss-shrouded trees, and strange calls faded into darkness.

Jean-Marie automatically adjusted his course, following a route he'd known for decades. He'd first marked it during the Texas Revolution to smuggle gold into Texas. It had come in handy during the Civil War for avoiding "Spoons" Butler's occupation of New Orleans. Private negotiations with the New Orleans' *patrones* before Prohibition had strengthened his knowledge of it. He'd hidden his memories after Madame Celeste came to power, of course. She'd heard of smugglers' and trappers' paths through the bayous, but she didn't know where they were. She focused on urban roads, not muddy, mosquito-ridden waters—and, thankfully, kept Georges so busy he didn't have time to hunt down every possible route.

He tossed a can of cheap brew to his now-clean companion. "Think we can get anyone inside the house?"

"If we had a year to spare." Lars settled onto a bench, his eyes

sweeping the surrounding bayou with the same unemotional thorough-
ness as the nearby alligator. "Rice fields are wide open, though."

Apparently satisfied at the lack of immediate danger, he tilted his
head back for a quick taste of the ice-cold beer.

Jean-Marie grunted, wishing he could swill the appalling pap as
readily. "Guess we'll have another look at it, after we take out Madame Celeste's next transfer point for drugs."

He was careful, as always, not to give Lars a direct order. Only Rafael did that; nobody else dared to, lest they trigger a flashback to some
impenetrable hell. It was far better to give him room to maneuver.

"Tomorrow night we'll bust that place." Despite his apparent
calm, vicious anticipation glinted briefly in his eyes. After almost
eighty years, Jean-Marie still hadn't found anything Lars couldn't do
for Rafael. Or wouldn't.

"And we'll call the Feds . . ." Jean-Marie mused, rubbing his finger over the boat's steering wheel.

"*After* the bad guys are disposed of." The faintest possible emphasis
went on the first word, in the equivalent of any other man's shout.

"Of course."

They shared a smile. An unspoken understanding of those details
was one of the reasons they were able to work together. It wasn't the
same type of teamwork he'd shared so many years ago with his beloved Hélène, and God knows he never quite dared to turn his back
on Lars, but it was still satisfying to work with a master craftsman.

Water danced away from the boat under its few running lights, like
ripples in time. An echoing frisson danced through his skin.

Lights rippled over his smart phone, and he frowned. Texas, of
course, but why? He snapped it open. "Yes?"

"I need my *heraldo* back in Texas immediately," Rafael announced
without preamble. "A private plane has left for Dallas, carrying a
vampira."

"Certainly, sir," Jean-Marie answered, quickly considering ways
and means for leaving New Orleans. "Who is she?"

Rafael was silent.

What the hell? Who is she?

Lars was watching him, eyes narrowed.

"Hélène d'Agelet, *mi hijo*," his *creador* said at last.

Jean-Marie stiffened, a wild roaring in his ears like a thousand cascades pouring out rainbows. *Alive, alive, alive* . . . Dared he believe after all these centuries of loneliness?

"She has been alive all these years, but the British Secret Service kept her existence a secret, as their greatest weapon."

He grunted an acknowledgment, his heartbeat pounding in his ears. He'd always avoided England on his travels as much as possible, so it was possible she could have escaped his notice.

Hélène, alive. His love, his only love, coming here . . .

It had been two centuries, so she should be free of her contract with the British. They could build a life together in Texas. Together, forever with his family.

Texas. Rafael's *esfera*.

Molten pain smashed into Jean-Marie's gut and ripped through his lungs and windpipe until he could barely breathe.

How could he have been such a fool as to have forgotten Rafael's rules, and their bitter corollary?

Every *vampiro* Rafael had created in Texas was sworn to obey the laws of Texas, on pain of death. Rafael had always killed any *hijo* who'd dared to turn his lover into a *vampiro*, considering such behavior a threat to his—and Texas's—security. Jean-Marie had always thought him right to do so, since those men's taste in lovers was dubious at best.

He personally followed Rafael out of love, not because he was sworn to Texas. But he knew damn well that if he married someone who wasn't Rafael's *hijo*—or *hija*, impossibility though that was—his only choices were her or exile from Texas and his family.

Merde.

Hélène contemplated the bottle of amber, fizzing Corona Gold beer, crowned by a sliver of brilliant green. Spotlights glowed like lost spaceships in the condensation dripping slowly down its sides. Given the mid-July heat in Texas, even at midnight, ice-cold beer made perfect sense, and she'd always enjoyed a good lager. But a lime wedge? Why would anyone want one of those in their beer? On the other hand, this nightclub felt like a foreign place, so why shouldn't they serve strange drinks?

Formerly a warehouse, the Capital Rose was now the most popular club in Austin for the college-age crowd interested in country, blues, and whatever else hit the marquee. On the inside, vibrant posters covered uneven limestone blocks, while iron beams crisscrossed underneath the tin ceiling. Willie Nelson smiled at Norah Jones from their posters, and Asleep at the Wheel partnered Los Lonely Boys near the bar. Old 97's and Brave Combo prowled above the pool table. Spoon and Steve Earle, Lisa Loeb and Sara Hickman marched up the walls by the upholstered seats. Billiard balls' irregular clack told of pool tables in a back room.

A tall man who would have looked more at home in a pro wrestling arena had been singing a mix of classic Mississippi Delta blues ballads and up-tempo Western Swing dance anthems. Now his deep baritone voice was making love to the Righteous Brothers' hit, "Unchained Melody," helped by the trumpeter from his band's intriguingly Latino brass section. An enthusiastic crowd occupied both the theater-style seats near the stage and the long bar farther away, but only a few of them had trickled into the balcony near her.

After more than an hour here, she still hadn't connected with anyone. Of course, she'd never been good at picking up strangers. She'd rather start with interesting conversation—something intellectual and complicated, like poetry or quantum physics. Her best meals back home in Oxford had always started in her library.

Oddly, she was the only woman here alone. There weren't even any single women at the bar trying to pick up men.

There were certainly enough prime male specimens available—like the blond eyeing her from the bar, or the burly guy at the foot of the stairs. All she had to do was smile at one of them or go down and say hello to someone else. She wouldn't even need to add a little *vampiro* charm.

But here, so close to where Jean-Marie must live? He of the blue eyes, crooked smile, and the wickedly skillful hands whose touch could melt a woman's resolve? Who could think about anyone other than him? Not her, even though she intellectually knew she needed to keep her strength up in order to find him.

Austin was a foreign town and the Santiago Trust kept its secrets very well indeed. She'd learned in London where Compostela Ranch was but that didn't mean its residents would tell her Jean-Marie's location. She'd seen Don Rafael's *vampiros* in Dallas when her private plane had landed from London. They hadn't callenged her, although she was sure she was being followed. It was only a matter of time until they'd accost her and demand her reasons for coming, the usual procedure when crossing an *esfera*'s frontier.

She sighed and reconsidered her drink. At least she was glad to trigger its chemical reactions. She pushed the lime wedge into the bottle with one finger and studied the beer foaming up around it. With a fatalistic shrug, she closed her eyes and took a deep swig of the resulting mixture.

Not bad. In fact, it was probably smoother than the original brew would have been.

She opened her eyes, licked her lips, and started to lift her beer again. But no lights glowed around the bottle's edge, only a single black blob in the center.

She lowered it, frowning. What the hell had changed?

A man was leaning back against the rail beside her, wearing a black leather jacket, black T-shirt, and crisply pressed jeans. His jaw was shadowed by a day's growth of beard, providing a wonderful hint of wickedness. Vivid health shone from his crooked smile and dancing blue eyes.

"Hello, darling," drawled Jean-Marie.

He was *here*?

Her heart stopped beating to be replaced by a million delighted butterflies rollicking throughout her veins. Her drink slipped out of her nerveless fingers and somehow landed upright on the floor.

"Mon coeur," she breathed and caught his face in her hands.

Good God, he looked exactly like the young warrior she'd met at Versailles, not the cynical, world-weary veteran she'd fought beside in the Peninsula. She'd heard *vampiros* could revert to a different image of themselves after *El Abrazo*, if they were comfortable enough with it.

"Are you free from the British?" He yanked her against him, pulling her cruelly—wonderfully—close.

"Hell, yes." Although it had taken her longer than she would have liked to get to Texas. She'd needed to make sure all of her team would thrive with a new *vampiro* after her departure.

"Mademoiselle Perez?" she whispered, trying to observe the formalities while she melted into his grasp, absorbing every beat of his heart through her skin and into her veins.

"She died protecting me from Napoleon's troops," he answered. An indefinable shadow crossed his face, and she stroked his cheek, his beard stubble rasping her fingers in shared pain for all those lost in so many wars.

He caught her fingertips with a kiss and turned away from the stairs, sweeping her with him, and opened a small door cunningly concealed in the ancient wooden planks. An instant later, they were inside and moving swiftly down a steep, narrow stairwell under a single lightbulb's dispassionate beam.

Good Lord, did the Santiago Trust have similar access to every nightclub in Texas?

"Has there been anyone else for you?" Jean-Marie demanded harshly, pausing on a tiny landing.

"Never." Her voice broke, but she managed to smile. Her hands crept up his leather jacket, savoring open zippers catching on her fingers during a hot summer night. Dreams would never include that detail, although they had reminded her of the steady beat of his heart under her palm. "You bastard, I tried everything—and everyone. I even had an affair with another woman, but that only lasted for a day. You ruined me for everyone else."

His eyes flashed, kingfisher bright.

"Thank God." He brushed his thumb over her lips, and she caressed it with her tongue, finding—and remembering—his calluses. His gaze darkened, and he lowered his head to hers.

She met his mouth more than halfway, her joy washing away years of loneliness. Their tongues swept over each other in a hot, wet dance of aching remembrance and anticipation, while their lips matched and melded. She moaned into his mouth, sharing his breath, her arms around his neck. His jacket was supple, echoing the rise and fall of his breath, while the metal stabbed her through her thin T-shirt, highlighting the agony of unfulfilled lust. His starched jeans were a slick armor to rub herself over and against like a cat, desperate to mark her territory, eager for fulfillment. His hands were hard and unendurably skillful when they slipped up the back of her T-shirt.

She nipped his lip, drawing blood, and growled at the rich, sweet taste. More, she needed—she deserved more. "Jean-Marie . . ."

His head came up, his eyes heavy-lidded with passion. *"Mon coeur."* His big hand shoved her disheveled hair away from her face, and he growled in frustration. "Let's go."

They burst out of the nightclub into an alley still simmering with heat. Irregular shadows marked where buildings wove together, while the smaller, boxier shapes of dumpsters and money machines competed for space against their edges, mixed with occasional bicycles chained to poles. A motorcycle stood before them, its black and chrome spotlit by a single brilliant light. Road Star it called itself, and it seemed to pulse with eagerness for the open road.

He unlocked a saddlebag and tossed Hélène a mesh and leather jacket. She donned it willingly, pleased by its evidence of his chivalry. Their matching helmets completely concealed their faces, while echoing the bike's black and silver colors. She was now anonymous to the world—and ready to be a part of him.

She swung herself onto the bike, settling easily onto the pillion seat. Ostrich leather and a backrest? Very nice, indeed, and a far cry from her usual college lad's scooter.

Jean-Marie tightened his leather gloves, giving her an opportunity to ogle him. He'd zipped up his jacket, making it hug his body so he became a true creature of the night.

Her fingers flexed with the need to touch and claim—and keep forever.

He boarded with the same easy grace she remembered so well and brought the black beauty into life with a decisive roar. He glanced over his shoulder at her, the engine rumbling its eagerness underneath them like the look in his eyes. "Ready?"

For so much. She nodded, her knees weak.

He briefly caressed her knee, his leather glove hiding all trace of his fingers. Yet her skin burned and her pulse skittered at the look in his eyes. "Hold on, my love."

He flipped down his visor and brought the Road Star purring down the alley. Their passage along city streets was brief but remarkable for its decorum amid groups of rowdy locals. Amiable men and women filled the sidewalks, frequently inebriated but always talking loudly about music. An occasional policeman patiently eyed the music lovers, who seemed disinclined to cause trouble.

Jean-Marie always stayed in their lane, never threading between the massed vehicles, never doing anything to attract attention. But in each block they traveled, at least one hard-eyed man lifted his head to watch them pass, before turning back to looking amiable amid the music lovers.

Hélène had seen similar men before at coronations and similar functions, ensuring the crowd stayed happy and healthy. The Santiago Trust was obviously out in full force tonight.

She filled her hands with Jean-Marie's chest, letting his steady heartbeat roll into her palms and into her bones. The sweet rise and fall of his lungs broke into a gasp when she toyed with a zipper over his nipple, slowly dragging it up and down. She wrapped her left arm around Jean-Marie's waist and stroked down his right leg to his knee. Hers, thank God, finally he was hers, proven by bone and muscle under her hand, by the pressure of his back against her breasts, by his hips spreading her thighs. Soon, very soon, he'd fill her again, at last.

She hissed in anticipation.

"Remember you have a live mike, Hélène," Jean-Marie crooned in her ear. They balanced on a hillside, facing the highway on-ramp, waiting for the light to turn green. Heat rose from the bike, cooler than that in her blood.

She blushed, hoping he couldn't see her.

He dropped his hand onto her knee, his fingers wrapping around her leg. Waves of hunger rippled through her like rockets, tightening her lungs and making her skin crackling hot and tight. She could have told where his every muscle and bone was, and what they were doing, just by listening to their echoes in her own body.

She dragged in a breath, fighting not to pull him off the motorcycle.

The light changed, and he sent the bike surging forward, jolting her heart into a faster tempo. Soon, very soon . . .

In this world of concrete ribbons, he paid attention only to speed, not hiding in a crowd. The engine roared its approval, pounding rhythmically into her blood, into her lungs, into her pussy.

She fondled his flat stomach and played with his belt, barely conscious of where she touched except it was him, and crooned, singing her own enjoyment. She didn't give a damn who heard, not on this night of nights.

He growled and shifted the Road Star into a higher gear. It screamed when they took a long, curving ramp off the highway and into the thickly wooded hills. Only his skill brought the bike through the tight turns, in the lower gears necessary—despite her fingers playing with the zippers on his jacket and his jeans.

When would they reach his house?

She rocked herself back and forth on the bike, rubbing her jeans' seam against her swollen flesh. She stropped herself against his back, fighting for the perfect position whereby the combination of his superb muscles and bones, plus his jacket, would excite her nipples into truly aching peaks—instead of their current stiff points.

Most of all, she moaned encouragement into the mike, begging him to hurry. "Dammit, Jean-Marie, please!"

"What the hell do you think I'm doing, Hélène?" He sounded as if he'd gritted his teeth when she'd palmed his cock. She smiled privately, pleased he, too, was being driven insane.

They turned into a very proper bit of road, marked by stone walls and signs on either side, and paused before a small, sturdy guardhouse. The man inside leaned out, glanced at Jean-Marie—while she tried to look demure—and rolled back the great gate. He exchanged quick salutes with Jean-Marie when they passed, his sidearm very apparent.

She waved hello, pleased she didn't have to worry about Jean-Marie's household being disturbed by unfriendly types. She didn't want to think about her lover living in an armed community centered on Don Rafael's *comitiva*, a very rare lifestyle in Britain.

Instead she slipped her fingertip between Jean-Marie's belt and his jeans.

He groaned, his stomach fluttering under her hand. "Are you trying to make us crash?"

She wriggled her hips a little closer in answer.

The bike surged forward in response, swooped down the edge of the street, and up a steep driveway. A garage door popped open, and Jean-Marie brought the bike to a screeching halt inside. A half dozen other motorcycles, some classic but all expensive, formed most of the occupants. The latest Ferrari Gran Turismo sports car crouched in the corner, a wildcat ready to run free, next to the more massive bulk of a Mercedes S500, the fastest armored sedan in the world.

Smoke was still rising from the skid marks when Jean-Marie yanked off his helmet. His eyes were hot and deadly with lust, his mouth tightly controlled.

Her hands were shaking so badly, she could barely find the fastenings to her helmet.

Jean-Marie growled something under his breath in a language she'd never heard before and lunged forward. Within seconds, he'd undone her helmet, clipped it to the bike—and tossed her over his shoulder.

She shrieked in surprise and delight.

He fondled her ass, his thumb unerringly finding the center seam and using it to tease her pussy.

She squirmed.

He repeated the caress, lingering to draw out more of her heated cream over her folds and onto her thighs.

She wriggled again and moaned.

Hard muscle rolled under her stomach, and he kicked open the door toward the house, still stroking her.

Dear God, how could he remember so much of what she enjoyed? The slow glide up the long muscles, while teasing her just a bit? Not to mention the absolutely shameless fondling of her pussy, using the seam to masturbate her with her panties. If she'd known simple pieces of cloth could be used that way—well, she might have come naked to avoid being manipulated. Or maybe not, if she'd known she'd encounter him.

The door banged shut behind them, and soft waves of scent reached out to her—lemon and hibiscus, lavender and rosemary, roses and sage, plus others which were exotic and unfamiliar. Water rippled over stones and dripped into a pond. Small insects and birds sang to each other, while the city's noises were impossibly distant. Hélène tried to lift her head for a look, but Jean-Marie chose that moment to knead her ass.

She moaned again, her eyes falling shut. Oh, please could he take her quickly before she grabbed him?

He rolled her off his shoulder and into his arms.

She blinked slightly and tried to form a question.

He stretched her out on a great wooden table, silky smooth and sturdy as a stone altar, nestled within a deep colonnade. Large woven chairs, covered by smooth, supple leather, ringed the limestone walls around it. Overhead, a circular, wrought-iron candelabrum hung below heavy wooden beams holding up long wooden twigs.

What a wonderfully private grotto for making love . . .

Pure anticipation sent fireworks through her veins and put a wicked smile on her face. She wiggled, testing her new throne's potential.

Jean-Marie's eyes flared, and he shrugged out of his jacket, then tore at his trousers. She tugged her jacket open and went for her jeans, fumbling at the buttons. Now—she wanted him now.

He yanked them down to her knees, opening her for him and braced his arms on either side of her, caging her. "Mine. You are mine."

"Always," she returned, equally fierce, and drew a single nail down his cheek. Crimson dripped in answer, enriching the air with blood's wonderful salty perfume.

Their mouths mated, sealing their vow, tasting, devouring what they'd lacked so long. His hands slid down her sides, and he lifted her hips, his fingers harsh yet so very perfect. She arched her pelvis forward, begging silently, and his cock kissed her intimately, delved into her, plunged deep. She shrieked her approval and tightened herself intimately around him.

He shuddered like a lost ship finally coming into harbor. His arms tightened around her for a long moment before he started to move, slowly, then faster and faster. She threw herself onto him, seizing him, greedy for every taste, her every fiber needing proof they were finally together again.

Pulses built into waves, surging toward a crescendo. Fire ran through her veins, leapt from her breasts to her womb, tightened her lungs at the touch of his breath. Everything but him was a blur. All she could see, or hear, or feel was him and his desperate hunger.

He shifted slightly, changing her hips' angle, and tucked her face against the base of his throat. Oh yes, please let her drink from him and taste his magical blood again . . .

He thrust again—and caught that perfect point.

She cried out and tipped into orgasm. Stars burst over and around her, shot up through her spine.

She bit down hard, cleanly, and found his jugular. His rich, sweet, lifeblood flowed into her—brilliant with joy, salty with long-ago tears, complex as the bright flowers of springtime.

Her body locked, convulsed in ecstasy—and she clawed his back, instinct driving her now. Rapture pounded her, ran caroling through her.

Her mate, hers, at last.

He shouted and arched, twining himself around her to take her neck. His fangs pierced her, quick and sharp, like a stab of pure joy—tossing her higher.

His lips closed over her, joining them perfectly at last in three places. He drank, one pounding beat speeding through them both.

A deep pull of his throat muscles tugged at her, sent his cock deeper into her—and tipped him into climax. He jerked again and again, his seed filling her hotly from within while their blood satisfied every hunger of each other's body and heart. Flowing like a river of life back and forth between them . . .

FIFTEEN

Sunset faded from the night sky, revealing the stars. An owl called from the oak and cedar trees blanketing the hillsides beyond the high limestone walls. Fireflies danced in the night air, and a white-tailed deer delicately drank from water rippling down the hillside through a carved channel.

Jean-Marie's garden was so cunningly cut into the hilltop with its terraces and staircases, it was difficult to tell whether humans or animals were supposed to frolic amid the masses of native and Mediterranean plants. Flowers and fruit trees scented the courtyards and stairs closest to the house, before yielding to the forests and thickets bordering the canyon and river edging the compound. Every room had windows offering their own unique view.

Like the rest of his house, the bedroom was furnished in an eclectic mix of Old World and New World antiques. The chests had come from Spain and England, while the bed had been built in St. Louis for the riverboat trade. The rugs were Turkish, the coverlet was a flamboyant, handmade star quilt, and most of the paintings were seventeenth-century Flemish. Museum curators had offered him serious money to break up his collection, and he'd laughed. He'd gathered them together for their memories of good friends and—foolishly, he'd once thought—to amuse Hélène.

She rolled onto her back beside him and stretched lazily, clasping his bed's antique, wrought-iron headboard. It was the start of their second night together, and they still hadn't gone anywhere else. By unspoken mutual consent, they'd spent their time making love, not talking. Everything beyond each other and this moment could wait.

Would he ever be sated? Not of her. Any part of her, from her nimble mind to the blinding rapture of her blood to the smallest portion of her body.

He rolled his thumb over her foot, fascinated by how neatly her toes fitted together. Dear God, she was so damn beautiful with the delicate flush under her satin skin.

He felt, rather than saw, her look down at him. "Still trying to see if they bend in the right direction?"

"You are a *vampira*, after all, whose anatomy deserves the fullest investigation." He gently ran his hand up her leg from her ankle to the back of her knee, finding the strong muscles and tendons under her smooth skin.

"Flatterer." She chuckled, drawing her other leg up and turning onto her side to face him.

He pulled a face in mock dudgeon, teasing her back. She laughed a little harder, and he slid down the bed until his face was even with her hips.

"You left me." Hélène almost sounded like she was pouting.

"Not really." He spread her legs and slipped neatly between them.

"Again so soon?" An air of curiosity, but not raising an objection.

"Why not?"

"True. But you've pleasured me so much, I may not have much to offer."

"Is that a challenge?"

He fluffed her outer lips with his tongue.

"No, just a statement of, ah, fact." She purred, lifting herself toward him. A warm blob of cream slipped down her thigh toward him. He licked it away, and she trembled slightly. *Sweet, very sweet. Oh yes . . .*

"Have something in mind, Mr. Texas *vampiro*?" Her voice was all too husky, and she gently kneaded his hair, while her knees embraced him.

His pulse speeded up, and his skin warmed. Good God, she smelled lovely—musk and sweat, salty and sweet, entirely Hélène as he'd imagined all these years.

"Just a little playing around, my dear firestarter."

His tongue probed into her, delving deep for more of a taste, circling.

He muttered happily to himself and settled down for a feast. If he explored a little more—or maybe if he slipped his finger into her asshole to distract her and please himself . . .

She tugged at his hair, rather emphatically.

"Hmm?" He looked up at her, a bit amused. Sated she might be—but she could still offer surprises. He suspected she'd always find something new to amuse them in bed sport.

"I want to play, too," she announced. Her mouth was bruised with passion, but one hand was tapping on the sheets. "I want your cock."

Lust, which should have been long-since dulled into a pleasant haze, blazed back into life like a desert sunrise. His chest tightened, fireflies of life dancing over his skin faster than the heated sparks outside.

He came up onto his knees over her—and she grabbed his hip, her free hand cupping his balls.

He groaned—and looked down his torso at her. "I had been comfortable," he complained mildly. "And completely willing to stay where I was for hours."

"Are you *refusing* a blow job?" She sounded properly incredulous.

"Are you saying you don't want me to go down on you?" he countered. He kissed the inside of her knee and gently nibbled the delicate pulse there.

"Jean-Marie!" Hélène arched, flinging her head back. Her voice was very husky, and he licked his lips in anticipation of her next reaction. Unable to stop himself, he teased her intimately with his fingers.

"You may have a point," she admitted, panting. "Is this a scientific exploration? I thought we had done with odd behaviors and strange sights when you showed me all those iridescent hummingbirds."

"True—but we're not doing that. We're simply having fun." He slid his hand up her leg, bending it—and levered her onto her side.

"Ah—fun." She dragged the simple word out, investing it with a wealth of sensuality. "You have such wonderful ideas, *m'sieu*—but only when you, too, participate in them."

She opened herself to him, displaying the rich pinks of her intimate flower, bedecked with cream, frilled and heated, begging to be adored. But he couldn't do her justice from a kneeling position.

He laughed at himself for having delayed and dropped down onto his side, facing her.

"Much better," she purred and pulled him closer. She nuzzled the tip of his cock and rubbed her cheek against it.

He chuckled and rested his head on her leg, settling himself for a long bout of simply making love with no urgency to find orgasm.

Damn, how he enjoyed feeling her breath pass through her belly to tease his chest, the changing rise and fall against his nipples. He shifted, wrapping his free arm over her hip to stroke her back, enjoying the tactile perfection of the long, lovely curve of her ass and spine, even when he couldn't see it.

Damn, the delight of hearing her catch her breath if he used his teeth instead of his tongue, or if he licked her to make her skin more sensitive then blew on her, exciting those newly awakened nerves. The sheer bliss of knowing she was here and she was his, every beat of her heart, every flex of her body as she rose to welcome his touch. Just as he groaned under her mouth's enticement, her tongue's delicate flicks and probes, her fingers' spiraling grip.

He wrapped his hands around her thighs, gathering the rich curves of her ass into his hand, opening her. She was curved very sweetly like this, her rump fitting his fingertips perfectly—and comfortably. Delectably.

They matched rhythms almost immediately, at first very simply—a swirl of his tongue over her clit was exactly matched by her hand twisting his cock. They had time to explore, to add more complicated movements—an extra caress here, or a swirl and a stab of the tongue there—but always, always the beat of their lovemaking remained in sync. Passed from one to another like the sound of their breathing, like the musk in the air, the joy in their hearts at simply being together.

His blood began to beat faster, drumming through his veins with her every twitch, every convulsive flex. He stroked her mound, pressing down on it in gentle circular motions to put delicate pressure on her highly swollen clit. Even as fast as a *vampira* healed, Hélène had to be more alive than usual to a man's attentions.

Her hips rolled to greet his hand. Musk clouded the air, blinding their senses.

He slid his hand forward and down, his thumb caressing her pubis, parting her curls. He circled the little bud, using her flesh to delicately caress it.

She moaned again and again, writhing under his mouth, sucking him down more and more strongly. Vision faded before the need to focus only on their hunger.

Ah, the broken little cries she was making, how her hips rolled and bucked under his hand, the trembling in her thighs that told of oncoming orgasm . . .

The hard pressure of seed building up in his balls as if he hadn't come in days, the heady throb of blood through his cock . . .

To know they'd been together long enough, were sated enough he could take his time and enjoy her without rutting like a beast . . .

Her throat tightened around him, pulling him down deeper and deeper.

He thrust three fingers deep inside her eager flesh, finding the sensitive spot he knew—and loved—so well. She convulsed immediately, her thighs locking around his head in rapture's joyous paroxysm.

Her throat tightened around him and pulled him deep, while she simultaneously pressed the sensitive spot between his legs. He bucked hard and came, falling over the precipice into climax so easily that thought meant nothing—and only sensation existed.

He was melting with pleasure, orgasm floating both around and through him, while supple fingers stretched him wide, drilling a pleasure point hidden inside. He rocked back and forth, unable to say where rapture began and ended. But the joy of taking her lover's cock very deep, welcoming it into moist caverns . . .

He fell onto the pillows beside Hélène afterward, with barely enough strength to draw her onto his stomach. Conversation took longer to arrive.

"Did you feel that?" he asked cautiously. What words could he use for describing how it felt to embrace a man?

"Finger fucking me—or being deep-throated?" She drew a tiny circle on his chest before looking up at him, her green eyes wide with wonder. "Who'll say it first, you or me?"

"*Cónyuge.*" He rolled the word over on his tongue and began to grin. Hell, he'd always known he adored her, no matter what it would take to claim her.

"My *cónyuge*," she echoed and leaned down to kiss him. He immediately hungered for her again, his tongue surging into her to discover the tastes and shapes of her mouth. Their lips melded, allowed them to savor the sheer delight of finding and holding their perfect match. His dearest love in his arms.

Hélène came up for air finally, her head pillowed on his shoulder. After all the dreary centuries of being alone, of being regarded with fear and tolerated only because she was a necessary weapon—it was pure bliss to have Jean-Marie as her *cónyuge*.

To feel his contentment at holding her continuously for so long, the joy of his release drumming through her, the shattering tumult of his seed when it bored up through his cock in a white-hot fervor . . . To know all of his sensations, his emotions just as surely as she knew hers in the same instant when she was vaulted to the stars.

Perfection. Especially when thought returned, bringing the realization that they were *cónyuges*, a pair who could share every thought, every emotion, every physical sensation. Who wouldn't want such joy every minute of every day?

Delightful as lying in his arms was, she couldn't resist an intellectual puzzle. "I didn't share your sensations in the kiss. Why not?"

"You were trying too hard." He hugged her reassuringly. "The *conyugal* bond only happens when you completely relax, since it can never be forced."

"Well, that's useless. How can we practice it?" Shit, how the hell could they depend on it in a duel?

"It's why it's so rare," he corrected, sounding abominably calm. "Sometimes it grows stronger during stressful situations."

She snorted in derision and sat up. "That's damn chancy unless we get the SAS or your SEALs to design the training course."

"Hey, I'm the one whose *esfera* has two pairs of *conyugal* duelists, remember?" He gently tapped her cheek. "That gives me some claim to expertise."

She brightened, reminded of her hopes for the future. "Three pairs of *conyugal* duelists, please: Don Rafael and his *patrona*, your *adelantado mayor* and his geologist, and now the two of us. Since Don Rafael and Doña Grania killed the Russian assassin a week ago, he should readily accept another male and female team. That duel's the talk of the European *esferas*."

"Two pairs, my love." Jean-Marie's face darkened, and he rose to his feet. "There are only two pairs of *conyugal* duelists in Texas."

What was he worried about? She was free from obligations to Britain, and she'd come openly and in peace. She'd fully satisfied *vampiro* travel customs. All she had to do now was be introduced to Don Rafael and become part of his *comitiva*, hopefully part of his *mesnaderos*. Plus give him the photo of that long-ago Mardi Gras, as a token of her goodwill.

After all, she was a firestarter, someone who *patrones* had been trying to recruit for years—contract with Great Britain or no contract.

"I'll swear fealty to Don Rafael as soon as we're introduced." Her voice died away.

Her beloved was shaking his head. "It will make no difference. Only Don Rafael's *hijos* live in Texas."

"That's insane. No *patrón* is that narrow-minded!" Jean-Marie shot her a barbed glance, wordlessly reminding her Texas had its own laws. But surely even his *patrón* wouldn't overlook basic military facts. "Wouldn't he want to have a firestarter serving him?"

"You know how often *esferas* usually change hands. A firestarter who wasn't completely loyal to him would be too great of a threat."

She stared at him, opened her mouth to argue—and met blue-steel eyes above a square-set jaw. *Ouch.*

Jean-Marie was reporting someone else's logic, which he wouldn't—or couldn't—change. It made sense, in its own brutally harsh fashion—and she shuddered to think of the experiences which had made its owner so inflexible.

Perhaps another approach might persuade her beloved to act. "What about women?"

If anything, the grooves around Jean-Marie's mouth deepened. "Especially not them, given their small chance of surviving *La Lujuria.*" He held up a finger, forestalling her lunge into speech. "And before you ask about his *patrona*—Doña Grania was forced by the Russian assassin, who planned to use her against Don Rafael."

"Forced into *El Abrazo*?" Hélène crossed herself, her stomach knotting itself in a dozen different directions. When she remembered the mental horrors she personally had endured during those mad days and compared them to what Doña Grania must have gone through . . . "The poor lady."

She began to look for a robe, rather than relive all of her own memories.

"Don Rafael rescued her, since he was her *vampiro primero*, and she's his late wife's reincarnation. Thankfully, their *conyugal* bond survived and they destroyed Beau, the assassin."

"So that ends the war with Celeste, right?" Hélène said hopefully, ignoring Whitehall's veiled warnings about her sister's greed. She pulled on the silk kimono Jean-Marie tossed her and belted it. At least something good had come of that horror, if the Texas and New

Orleans *esferas* were reconciled. Dear Lord, if everyone could be as happy as she and Jean-Marie were.

He snorted bitterly and shook his head. "I wish it had ended the conflict, but it has not. If anything, matters have grown worse. I cannot leave my family while this continues, Hélène." He shrugged, silhouetted against the beautiful gardens and a stone staircase. "After that, I will leave Texas to be with you."

"If we can't live here, where will we go? What will you do?" Her heart turned over and she stared at Jean-Marie, all her fine plans for their future falling into ash.

Dear God, she'd hoped for so much but how could she ask him to give up everything? At least she could ease him by ending the war. "I'll go to New Orleans tomorrow and talk to Celeste. I'm sure if we speak face-to-face, I can find a settlement."

"Why would Madame Celeste talk to you?" Jean-Marie whirled to face her. "She's never shown the slightest interest in negotiating with anyone before, unless there was serious money in it for her."

Hélène swallowed a curse at his words, which had the uncomfortable ring of truth, and tried to sound composed. "She is my sister— Celeste de Sainte-Pazanne."

"Your *sister*?" Shock washed across his face, before he looked back at scenes she couldn't envisage. Finally he studied her again, his expression guarded. "How long has it been since you've met each other in person?"

"November 1808, the day before you and I met in Madrid. She was part of my team, but we were accidentally separated."

"Ah." He made the single syllable sound incredibly significant, and a chill ran through her skin. "The day you nearly died in Madrid."

"That has nothing to do with her." She stared at him, stunned by the disgusting overtones creeping through his words.

"The same team whose *prosaico* was killed by French cavalry, patrolling far beyond their normal range?" His eyebrows went up. "The same French troop who you thought killed your sister." He was watching her very closely.

"Are you telling me she was a *double agent*?" Hélène raised her hand to slap him but he caught it easily, holding her arm to make her look him in the eye.

"No, I'm not saying that—but I wouldn't be surprised to learn it was true either."

"Jean-Marie!" Hélène shrieked and wrenched herself away from him. To gain a *cónyuge* but have her sister's honor besmirched in the same hour was a situation no woman should have to live through.

She stormed into the big living room and began to pace, ignoring the massive stone fireplace and the comfortable mix of carved wood and leather-covered furniture. At another time, she might have asked him where he'd found such superb brass sculptures, or the paintings of horses. But not now.

Not when *la petite* was at risk. She could remember all those long years when Papa and *Maman* had prayed to have another living child. She'd wept so many times when *Maman* was delivered of a child, only to see it gathered to heaven a few days or weeks later.

But then *la petite* was born after they'd almost given up hope. *La petite*, dark-haired and squalling her appetite for life from the moment she came into this world. They'd all loved her so very dearly and they'd vied to make her happy.

How could they be talking about the same woman?

Jean-Marie followed after a moment, clad in jeans, and started making coffee in the well-equipped kitchen.

When she thought she had her temper under control enough to talk, she followed him.

"My sister has always loved me." She faced him from the door, arms akimbo, daring him to contradict her.

He nodded, his expression carefully neutral, and popped the switch to turn the coffeemaker on. "So why didn't she contact you in England all these years?"

"Because she was ashamed of having made a deal for her life, after the cavalry captured her," Hélène hurled back at him.

"It's one possibility." Sympathy, mixed with a bitter knowledge of grief, washed over his face. He took a step, lifting his hand to her.

She instinctively bristled at his unsought sympathy. She'd fought her battles alone for too long to accept help easily. His mouth tightened, and his hand fell back to his side. His gaze returned to its earlier, relentless clarity.

"Still, two centuries of guilt with no word for a loving sister? I'd call it unlikely."

Hélène flinched at the logic in his words. But loyalty kept her stubbornly arguing the same point. "Jean-Marie, she is my only living relative. I cannot believe ill of her."

"Hélène, I have seen her try to kill my family." He looked straight at her, truth naked as a saber in his gaze. "Do not ask me to believe she is entirely good."

Hélène stared back at him, colder than she could recall on any mission. Must she choose between her little sister and her *cónyuge*, between her family and her one true love?

Celeste's "guest" bedroom had never been more beautiful—or more frustrating. Two centuries later, she still enjoyed reminders of Josephine Bonaparte, the great courtesan who'd risen to become an empress. Her bed was an enormous four-poster in the pseudo-Egyptian style Bonaparte had popularized, draped in yards of red silk to hide its many opportunities for tying a man up. Silk wallpaper gleamed behind furniture carved with lions and sphinxes, in a veiled warning to tattlers. Enormous gilded mirrors offered views of whichever *prosaicos* she was enjoying, while the heavy carpets and hidden paneling concealed the men's shouts. Usually of pleasure, of course.

Not one to waste money, she'd also chosen to use its heavy soundproofing for her private videoconferencing center. It was therefore blessed with an enormous monitor and superb sound system, both normally hidden behind a sliding panel. Tonight the monitor was in the open, bleating a plea to buy used vehicles.

Celeste shot a fulminating glare at it and started donning a new dress to distract herself. Versace this time, not Chanel or Armani. Daring, not staid for a *patrona*. Red to make those *prosaicos* know who they should crawl to, despite the damn TV crews stirring them up.

"If that overconfident ass, Beau, hadn't celebrated too soon and turned his back on Don Rafael," she hissed, continuing her previous maledictions against the dead, while she yanked the dress's silk down her arms.

"The Texas cretin would have been butchered," Georges agreed and started carefully hooking her into the exceptionally miniscule example of *haute couture.*

"We'd be sitting high atop his hills, dining on his arrogant, holier-than-thou men." She tapped her foot impatiently, reviewing all the lovely plans she'd had for breaking those oh-so-superior *vampiros.* Beginning with Jean-Marie, he of the always perfectly composed expression. *Merde,* but she'd have enjoyed seeing him beg for mercy.

"At least they've made enough enemies that *bandolerismo* have flocked to us from around the world, begging to help take over Texas," Georges reminded her.

"Locusts." She curled her lip.

"But very useful—and totally under my thumb."

"True." She dragged her nail down his cheek affectionately, making his eyes close in momentary pleasure.

She stepped away and poured herself another glass of champagne, debating whether to punish her sommelier for the second-rate vintage. Probably not, since she didn't give a damn about the stuff, and Georges only drank it for the bubbles. Just another sign of the increasing economies Don Rafael's attacks were forcing on her. Damn, damn, damn!

"You also have your *mesnaderos* and all of your *compañías* from the rest of the Southeast."

Compañías? She'd forgotten about them. Those wonderful groups of *vampiros* from each of the *esferas* she'd grabbed in the Southeast. Hmm . . .

"With them . . ."

"We can attack those Texans on two fronts!" She tossed the champagne bottle to him. He caught it, his yellow teeth flashing.

Raoul watched them silently, invisibly, from a gilded mirror, his eyes narrowed and alert for every detail.

The TV's previous staccato patter died away, to be replaced by a burst of saccharine music.

"And now for our lead st-tory," stammered the announcer, his bald pate sweating under the studio lights.

Celeste sniffed. The network had brought in a third-string news-reader from Iowa after the previous anchors had mysteriously found attractive engagements elsewhere. Freedom of the press had always meant important stories needed to be approved by her first, if you wanted to live in her *esfera*.

"Patience, *cher*. We must hear what they think they know." Georges lifted his glass to her.

"*Think*? Hah! They can't even paint by numbers."

"The governor announced today the formation of a joint task force," the newsman blurted, "with the FBI and Texas Rangers to investigate the string of deaths terrifying the Crescent City."

Celeste's head snapped up. *Joint* task force? With the *FBI* and *Texas*? What the hell was going on now?

A simply dressed, gray-haired woman appeared, wearing excellent pearls as befitted the matriarch of one of the South's greatest political families.

"Damn the bitch." Celeste hissed a string of curses and began to pace. "I haven't been able to touch her since her son was executed for interfering with my *mesnaderos*."

"Do you want her silenced?" Georges offered cautiously, practical as ever. "We own almost everyone else in state government."

"Not yet. She can call Washington privately, which they can't. Plus, the Justice Department wants to investigate all the unexplained law enforcement deaths in the southeastern *esferas* we took over." Her stomach knotted, and she fought to think. If Beau hadn't needed so much blood to prepare for the duel, there wouldn't have been so many killings. She'd always been careful to keep New Orleans clean and quiet, so the tourists would keep coming back. *Damn him!*

"The president has pledged his full cooperation," the governor purred, "and promised to put all the resources of the federal government to work solving these murders."

The camera pulled back, showing the others on the dais. A group of strong, very tough men moved up to flank her. One was tall and very weather-beaten, his eyes all too observant under his white Stetson. The only female among them also wore a white hat but was small and lithe with the poised, exotic stillness of a handmade knife. A foolish man might have been mesmerized by her sensual but firmly controlled mouth.

They were a damn good lot, looking far more dangerous than the usual politician's hangers-on—meaning the governor had finally grown wary enough to demand deeds rather than pretty words from her entourage. Who the hell had that bitch dragged in this time?

"We are lucky to have Ranger Captain Zachariah Howard come out of retirement to lead this joint Texas, federal, and Louisiana task force. The Texas Rangers are bringing what they've learned from the unusual deaths there, while the FBI—"

Celeste hurled a priceless bust of Nefertiti through the screen. White light burst across it, and the governor's saccharine drawl ended abruptly—and satisfyingly. The huge TV shattered into pieces and rained onto the floor, leaving a few bits of electronics protruding from the wall.

Georges straightened up, eyeing her cautiously.

"Stupid slut," Celeste snarled, ignoring the longtime politician's reputation for high personal morals. "I'm putting a million-dollar price tag on her head."

A moment's unhappy silence followed. "That might not be enough, *cher*. Gorshkov of Trenton has provided her with bodyguards."

"Why the hell would a top *patrón* do that?" Celeste stared at her enforcer. "No *patrón* interferes in the inner workings of another's *esfera*, unless he plans to attack it—and Gorshkov is too far away for that."

Georges shifted uneasily, but his gaze remained steady. He was the one messenger she'd never damaged for an unpopular message. "Killing a governor could bring the Feds down on us, *cher madame*, thereby attracting attention to all *vampiros*."

Cursing as she hadn't in decades, Celeste swept champagne and antiques onto the floor. She ground the shards into dust with her foot, consigning Gorshkov and the governor into hell with the fragments.

When she slowed down, Georges pressed a glass of Calvados into her hand. She snorted her disdain for any weakness but knocked back the strong brandy all too quickly.

"Killing her would cost as much as a *patrón*," she remarked finally. "Which takes cash I do not have, dammit."

"I could do it myself," Georges offered, baring his teeth with an anticipatory grin. She smiled at him fondly, remembering all the people he'd destroyed wearing the same expression.

"No, you need to return to Texas and turn up the heat there. Don Rafael and this damn task force deserve to have far too much to think about on that side of the Brazos."

"What do you want me to do first?"

She'd escalate the war to whatever pitch was necessary in order to win. If modern methods didn't work, she'd go back to the old rules, the ones that had worked so well during the Reign of Terror. If Don Rafael caused trouble for her, she'd repay him tenfold.

"Start with the public attack we planned. I want it carried out as soon as possible.

Georges's jaw dropped, and an ugly gray tint suffused his skin. He swallowed hard before speaking. "But, madame, the greatest casualties will be among children—very small children. It could raise passions extremely high, too high for us to predict and counter."

"Exactly what I want!"

He blanched. "But children . . ." he whispered.

"The sanctimonious Texas bastard will either call off his hounds and negotiate with me—or come charging out of his den so we can attack him."

Georges blinked, life and animation seeping back into his face. He flexed his fingers absentmindedly, testing the grips needed for different necks. Celeste hid her smirk at the familiar gesture.

"*Mais certainement, madame*, all shall be as you wish." He bowed low, sweeping his arm wide in a courtier's homage.

. She nodded formally before frowning. "Unfortunately, you'll need to leave immediately to reach the San Antonio safe house before dawn."

He grunted his acknowledgment, his face turning expressionless.

She caressed his cheek. "Remember, the more devilry you awaken in Texas, the faster we'll be reunited."

Delight flooded his eyes. He dropped to his knees and silently kissed her fingertips. A moment later, he was gone, the elevator doors whispering shut behind him in the hallway.

Celeste prowled into her own bedroom, this one mahogany and velvet in the finest tradition of the Antebellum South. A massive four-poster bed held pride of place, matched to a splendid armoire and chests, all carved with stylized sprays of rice. Gold velvet looped and swirled around the windows, heavily fringed with darker gold. The carpet was French and covered in brilliant yellow roses and chrysanthemums. She'd known it was perfect for her the moment she spotted it at the Charleston *patrón*'s home thirty years ago. She'd killed him, of course, to get it.

She opened the hidden bar and poured herself another glass of Calvados, debating whether to snatch a *prosaico* from the casino or use one of her *vampiros* for dinner. Unfortunately, by keeping her *vampiros* young enough not to be a threat, they also lacked strength and stamina in the bedroom.

She curled her lip at the prospect and drank the golden liquid, enjoying its reminder of the apple orchards back in France.

"You should not attack children," a deep voice commented. "You risk pushing your lieutenant too hard, since they're the only beings which melt his heart. Or you might lose your immortal soul."

"Nonsense," Celeste retorted, the fragile crystal raised for another swallow. "Georges is completely mine. No matter what I order him to do, he will always obey."

She poured it down her throat, losing herself in the heady, slightly sweet aromas—and froze. Who the hell had spoken?

She whirled around, searching for the disturbance's source. Her *mesnaderos* could enter within seconds, once she shouted for help. Not that she'd need it.

Raoul looked back at her from within a great mirror, surrounded by an immense gilded frame. His face was that of the warrior she'd glimpsed on that last night at Sainte Marie des Fleurs, but without the wickedly disfiguring scar. His dark eyes were alive with intelligence and worry.

Joy undreamed of, unhoped for, raced through her. She held out her hands to him and took a few tottering steps toward him. "Raoul!" she breathed.

His gaze swept over her, lingering briefly on the meagerness of her dress and the immense glass of brandy.

She flushed and instinctively put the drink down before pride stiffened her spine. "You cannot be real," she insisted. Perhaps he was a phantom, something created by a magician's arts to manipulate her.

"Am I not?" He lifted an eyebrow. "I may not be alive, but I am still on this earth, not a tool of your enemies. Do you wish me to recite the combination for your safe? Or the password to your computer? What about the account numbers for your various Swiss bank accounts?"

"You're bluffing." Celeste drew back, chills running down her spine. No single person knew those items except Georges. Even a combination of her enemies didn't, or Don Rafael would have already used them against her.

"Let me see." Raoul paused, his gaze going slightly unfocused, and began to recite. She stopped him after the fourth tightly held password. *Merde*, what would happen if any of her *mesnaderos* heard him?

"Very well, I accept that you are a supernatural being . . ."

He bowed ironically.

"Who may be the man I once knew as Raoul."

Pity swept over his face. "My angel, how I wish I could bring you joy so you could learn to relax again."

"What the hell are you talking about now?" Temper flushed her cheeks.

"You must trust me again."

"If I'm going to chat with ghosts, why not one of the thousands of others living in New Orleans?" She glared at him, her hands propped on her hips.

"Count me faithful beyond death, as I have sworn before, as I will swear again."

The words rang through the room, bringing echoes of a country lane where two young lovers had pledged themselves to each other for eternity.

Celeste's heart stopped beating, and her legs lost all strength. She caught at the table for support. "Raoul."

"Yes, my heart. I still love you, but I have only recently been given the grace of talking to you."

"Why are you here?" She stumbled forward and put her hands on the mirror, trying to touch him. "It's a bitter joke to be able to see each other but not be together! Damn—"

"Do not soil yourself with blasphemy, Celeste!" Raoul ordered sharply.

She bit her lip and nodded, closing off her recriminations against the Almighty. Her fingers stroked the unyielding glass, aching to find a path through to his warmth. "As you wish, Raoul. But—why are you here? Can you stay long?"

Will I survive if you do? Will I survive if I lose you again? She'd spent so many decades hunting amusements—no matter how dangerous or disgusting—to avoid remembering the awful moment when she'd seen his head shattered. How could she go back on that bitter treadmill again?

"Shouldn't you be in Heaven?" she ventured.

"No." He shook his head, grimacing.

"Why not?" She flared up, instantly protective. "You were an honorable officer."

"Was I? I ordered my men to kill women and children who hadn't harmed them. I helped them to do so, and I made sure we did so very well. We committed sin, Celeste."

"I cannot believe that, Raoul," she insisted. "Not of you."

"Do so and learn from my example." He suddenly seemed decades older. "I have glimpsed the pits of hell and understand the error of my ways. But the Lord has been merciful because of why I sinned, when I thought it would terrify fools into silence, so you and our children would be safe."

"Then you should be in Heaven. You are the best of men, Raoul!" Tears blurred her eyes.

"I must first be purified in the fires of Purgatory, my heart."

She flinched. Purgatory's flames caused suffering which was more severe than anything experienced in this life. How could he endure that for years and years, perhaps millenia to come?

"If you did penance for your sins and came with me to Purgatory, my angel, we could be together for eternity."

An eternity with Raoul? To stand hand in hand with him before the throne of God, united under the light of glory? What ecstasy!

But was she worthy of him? She had committed too many sins to remember, starting by betraying her fellow British agents. And the centuries since, when she'd sought out ways to drive men insane with pain so she wouldn't think about her own screams of loneliness. And the long climb to the top as *patrona*, when she'd ruthlessly killed—or worse—anyone who stood in her way.

How many mortal sins did she have to her name, after all? Hell was for the likes of her, whose very core was destroyed and befouled. Purgatory's fires, however long and agonizing, burned away only venial sins in preparation for admittance to Heaven.

Besides, what did any of that matter when there were tasks left undone?

"No. First I have to bring Hélène, your murderer, to justice."

"Celeste!" His jaw dropped, and he almost leapt out of the mirror at her. "That's fratricide, a mortal sin. There'd be no reconciliation for us. Ever."

"I cannot rest while Hélène's sins go unpunished." She slowly shook her head, her jaw firming. "Do not wait for me, Raoul. I am not worthy of you and will never join you there. The sooner you leave this world, the sooner you will join the saints."

She forced herself to meet Raoul's gaze, while remembering the most bloodthirsty details of the planned attack. Surely it would make him understand how little he should have to do with her.

"*Nom de dieu*, Celeste, how can you even contemplate such a thing?" Raoul grimaced, his hands clenching and unclenching. "Remember everything Hélène did for you, for us while I was alive . . ."

"I told you what I am." She shrugged, keeping her expression masked.

"Perhaps that's what you are—but it's not what you must remain!" he flung back at her.

Her eyes narrowed before she shook her head. Could he be right? Surely not.

"Do not dismiss me so quickly, my angel. There is still confession and absolution—and yes, penance to purify you, too. We still have hope."

"Such optimism is for you, who have a chance to see the gates of paradise, *mon amour*. I have far too much sin on my soul to accompany you. I will remain here and live as I am accustomed to. It is, after all, a very comfortable life." She flung her arms wide, indicating her spectacular room.

He dismissed it without a second glance, his hands flying in one of the abrupt gestures she'd loved so well.

"You still have time, my angel, to think and to act. Do so, I beg of you—for both our sakes."

He blew her a kiss and vanished.

SIXTEEN

Jean-Marie gritted his teeth, listening to Luis detail all the mental health professionals flooding into Central Texas. There were fewer suicides to set his phone ringing—but far more unexplained deaths and outright murders than ever before in history. The Texas media weren't as hysterical as their New Orleans brethren. On the other hand, they hadn't endured two weeks of widespread killings, while two *vampiro* assassins regained their strengths through drinking death energies. That would incense any population and their guardians, including the press.

Reflecting their strained resources, tonight's council meeting was a small one—only Rafael, Ethan, Gray Wolf, Luis, and himself. They were gathered in Rafael's library amid the heavy, leather-clad chairs and towering bookcases for a rare moment of quiet.

Jean-Marie suspected *Doña* Grania had suggested the setting, with its combination of intimacy and masculinity—and its distance from the accumulated memories in Rafael's office. If so, it was yet another example of how much she'd helped him relax since they'd become *cónyuges*.

Maybe it was also a good omen for his mood tonight.

"Anything else, Luis?" Rafael steepled his fingers, his dark eyes alert and steady. Once they would have been narrowed and tense, and he would have been pacing like a caged cougar.

"No, Don Rafael. More are going to New Orleans, of course, plus folk practitioners."

"Voodoo," murmured Ethan.

"And others," agreed Gray Wolf. "Our friends are keeping us informed."

"Excellent. And you, Jean-Marie?" Rafael shifted his gaze, undoubtedly seeing far more than he'd speak of.

"Lars is doing very well in New Orleans." He didn't add—*of course.*

Gray Wolf stirred slightly but said nothing. Ethan's mouth tightened. Luis glanced at Rafael, who nodded approvingly. The Texas *patrón* was the only man present who'd immediately relaxed at hearing Lars's name.

"Yes, he is the only one of us who can say that." Jean-Marie glanced around, spreading his hands in a very Gallic shrug. "Unfortunately, too many people have died in New Orleans and continue to fall in Texas. We need to grow wise very quickly, faster than even Lars can help us."

"Can he tell us how many killers there are?" Gray Wolf asked, bringing his usual ruthless pragmatism to bear.

"We believe the number of *bandolerismo* stabilized at approximately thirty, just before the duel."

"Too damn many," snarled Luis.

"*Verdaderamente,*" agreed Rafael.

"Do you know where all of them are?" Ethan leaned forward eagerly.

"No. Lars is trying to find out, but the information is very closely guarded."

"They must be hiding out as individuals, not in a pack. Without a guide to where they are, it's like looking for dozens of needles in hundreds of haystacks." Ethan smacked his fist into his palm. "We'll find them but it's taking so damn long."

"Take more men off my escort," Rafael ordered.

"No," snapped Gray Wolf. "That's exactly what *she* wants and why *she*'s sent them here. If she wanted to do anything else with them, they'd have already attacked."

Rafael and Gray Wolf glared at each other in a silent argument. The others held their breath, waiting for the result. Only Gray Wolf, the heir, would—or could—have challenged Rafael on this subject.

Even after all these centuries, Jean-Marie would have hated to do so. But maybe, if his *creador* bent a little on this subject, he might be rational about another.

Finally Rafael nodded. "You are probably correct."

Thank God, he was being flexible tonight. His plan might just work . . .

"But rotate the searchers and *mesnaderos* so both remain fresh," Rafael ordered crisply. "Also organize a special strike force from among my *mesnaderos*, in case we have to respond to a sudden attack."

"Have you Seen something?" Jean-Marie asked, caught by a subtle shift in the older man's voice.

"Not an event." Rafael frowned, framing his answer carefully. "Just a troop of men, larger than Ethan's usual *compañía*, which drills very hard. Later, they rush to board my Gulfstream jet."

More than a half dozen *vampiros*? Who needed to go farther and faster than in one of the usual helicopters? Shit.

"It shall be done as you envision." Ethan bowed in his seat before pulling out his smartphone to make notes.

"What else? Nothing? Very well, gentlemen, you have my permission to depart. I look forward to the time when we will not meet every night at this time." Rafael rose, and the others followed, quietly making their good-byes.

Jean-Marie lingered, straightening books while he waited for his moment alone with his *creador*. He wanted to have this conversation in the house's intimacy, when Rafael was relaxed and could scent his *cónyuge*'s presence. Maybe it would make him sympathize with another's plight. Maybe.

*   *   *

Rafael turned back from the door, raising his eyebrows at the sight of his eldest *hijo*. He'd known Jean-Marie had stayed behind, of course, but he'd never seen him twitching with nerves before. He'd have to talk to Grania about this later.

He pulled on an affable smile—so very much easier to do these days, despite the war's worries—and gestured toward the fireplace. "Would you care to join me for a whisky?"

"Thank you," his *hijo* accepted simply, without one of his usual conversational flourishes.

Rafael handed Jean-Marie a glass and was surprised the favored Glendronach scotch didn't bring a release in tension. He took a sip of his own Pikesville Rye and waited, refusing to frown. Whatever the problem, there'd be time to solve it.

Jean-Marie swirled the superb whisky, letting its complex aromas rise into the air, before speaking. He wasn't fool enough to waste time on trivialities.

"You know Hélène d'Agelet, the British firestarter, is currently visiting town."

Rafael inclined his head, allowing Jean-Marie's rush of words to run its course.

"She's staying at my house."

A defensive note? Why? Jean-Marie was the chief *heraldo* and therefore properly entitled to have foreign warriors and diplomats as guests.

"She's welcome to stay in Texas for a week, like all other visiting *vampiros*," Rafael murmured politely. "After that, I'll need to give my blessing for a longer stay."

Jean-Marie squared his shoulders. Rafael set down his glass, his attention well and truly caught.

"Hélène is also the British spy I worked with during the British army's retreat to Corunna."

Dios mío, she was the one he'd relied on so completely? And she was the one woman Jean-Marie had ever lost his head over. Sara's capture of him had been the result of a young man thinking with his cock. Under other circumstances, it would have been forgotten within days. But Hélène d'Agelet had been an entirely different matter, their encounter a true melding of hearts and minds.

To have her come here now, during a war which threatened everything, could only mean the greatest danger.

Rafael searched Jean-Marie's face and found only steadfast loyalty and honesty. He could bore in more deeply, root out every detail of Jean-Marie's days with that female, using his *vampiro* powers and his ruthless ownership of Jean-Marie's psyche, thanks to being his *creador*. But would he learn anything new and useful? Probably not.

Damn. What hold didn't she have on his eldest *hijo*?

"Continue." Rafael's voice deepened to a general's rasp.

"Hélène is also my *cónyuge*." Jean-Marie's voice shifted into the pure music of a chant, joy lilting through it.

Rafael stared, terror chilling his bones. *Cónyuge* for Jean-Marie? What wouldn't this stranger, this greatest of all Britain's secret agents know about him through Jean-Marie? Jean-Marie could name every entrance to this house, the gun vaults, where he and Grania slept . . .

Santísima Virgen, Grania who needed to hibernate at least eighteen of every twenty-four hours! Could he tolerate a stranger knowing where to find his defenseless lady? Let alone someone who was famous as the most ruthless weapon Britain had ever wielded?

Like hell he'd ever allow that bitch near his darling!

He'd never be able to trust Hélène, because he wasn't her *creador*. He couldn't stop her with a single thought, the way he wielded a shield against insubordination, or mutiny, or murder by one of his *hijos*. When he remembered fighting his *creador*, the clang that had roared through his entire body the first time his sword had rung against his *creador*'s, how his blade had sliced through his *creador*'s neck, sending that filthy head bouncing across the room—and all he'd felt was transcendent joy . . .

No *hijos* of his were ever going to have an opportunity to experience that sensation! Especially not when Grania's life was at stake.

"And?" he murmured, hoping against hope for a request he could dismiss without offending his oldest friend.

"May I have your permission to marry her and live here in Texas?" Jean-Marie's eyes came back to him, their kingfisher blue alive with wary hope. "If you ever believe she is a threat to you, *Doña* Grania, or to Texas, you may kill *me*."

Marriage? Permanently bring the firestarter into Texas? If anything went wrong—*destroy* Jean-Marie for another's offense? Impossible. He could no more kill his oldest friend than he could tear out his own heart.

He could feel his body squaring into granite, together with his countenance. "I am sorry but the answer is no. You know the laws of Texas as well as I do."

Jean-Marie's expression shifted into that of a skilled negotiator, offering another bribe. "Perhaps you could make an exception, in light of her value as a military weapon. She is willing to swear fealty to you," he coaxed.

"Others have forsworn their oaths," Rafael remarked, chilled at the thought of trusting such a dangerous stranger.

"You insult her—and me!—by suggesting that," Jean-Marie snapped.

Rafael flung up a hand in silent apology. "I cannot command her fully since I am not her *creador*. In time of war, such as now, any hesitation could become critical," he said, carefully choosing his words.

"I have spent three centuries in your service. If you don't trust my judgment now, those years mean nothing." Jean-Marie's face hardened, and he rose to his feet, a move that Rafael matched. "I became a *vampiro* to finish Hélène's work." His voice crackled with determination. "I am not bound by oaths to Texas. When this war is over, Hélène and I will leave Texas together."

Santa Madre de Dios, must he lose his oldest friend, the foundation of his family? But better that than risk any danger to his own *cónyuge*.

Rafael bowed an icy acknowledgment.

Jean-Marie waited another moment, searching his *creador*'s face.

When Rafael said nothing, he cursed under his breath and walked out, boot heels drumming on the floor like an executioner's march.

Rafael slapped the granite fireplace and cursed, before leaning his forehead against it. Never to play chess with Jean-Marie again, or argue with him about how to improve the breeding program in the Santiago Stud . . .

Soft arms wrapped around his waist, and a tall woman pressed herself against his back.

"You've been eavesdropping," he accused mildly without lifting his head.

You were shouting, his *cónyuge* corrected and kissed his shoulder.

He snorted, half in derision and half laughing at himself. Trust *la doctora*, his beloved wildlife veterinarian with the impressive collection of degrees, to precisely define his previous conversation—no matter how unflattering the term might be.

He turned in her arms and embraced her, resting his chin on the top of her head. Her sweet curls tickled him, bringing a lump to his throat. *Dios,* how he'd missed these simple pleasures.

Have you considered you two seemed to be describing two entirely different women? Grania asked after a long pause, still snugly ensconced against his heart.

Rafael blinked, caught completely off-guard. He'd personally been pondering how best to tempt his adored *cónyuge* into wearing some of the very expensive lingerie he'd ordered for her. Was she putting that splendid mind of hers to work on solving the impasse between him and his eldest *hijo*?

Thank God their *conyugal* link had brought her through *La Lujuria* so quickly. Feeling her insane lust for blood and emotion had shredded his wits nearly to the breaking point. He'd been ecstatic when she'd grabbed the edge of this *vampiro mayor* stability and started healing so quickly, until she was now well able to reason. Like every other *cachorra*, she still needed to sleep often—but those times provided them with excellent opportunities for cuddling.

Grania, querida, *who his lady is doesn't matter,* he reminded her. *Texas law says that only I can create* vampiros.

Yes, yes, I know. I wasn't discussing that. She tilted her head back to look at him, her dark blue eyes quizzical. *But he was describing a woman he'd known and loved for two centuries, while you spoke of a British secret weapon. They don't sound like the same person to me.*

Rafael opened his mouth to argue with her, stopped, and shut it. She waited patiently, any smile discreetly hidden.

Mierda, he'd always been caught by her wisdom, whether it came seven hundred years ago from Blanche's throat or now from Grania.

You may have a point, he conceded grudgingly. He wasn't sure where she was going with that observation. He already knew better than to use their *conyugal* bond to discover things she hadn't offered. *What do you suggest I do?*

Invite her here for a glass of sherry, so I can meet her.

No! he thundered.

She winced and raised an eyebrow.

A thousand pardons, luz de mi vida. He kissed her fingertips one by one until she smiled at him again. He took her to the leather sofa and held hands with her, a pose in which civilized behavior would hopefully come more instinctively.

What if I am right and she is a dangerous weapon?

How many mesnaderos *do you have? How many cameras, hidden weapons—and fire extinguishers? Surely she can't cause any trouble here,* Grania countered. *Trust Ethan and Luis to arrange everything.*

Rafael fumed, unable yet again to find a hole in her logic.

Mi amor, *I alone have no preconceived ideas of her, unlike you and Jean-Marie. You know I have years of experience meeting people at academic cocktail parties. Let me have an hour to form an opinion, as an impartial judge. With you and Jean-Marie present, of course.*

You ask for the world. He filled his eyes with her. *To risk you, even for that long . . .*

Then do not. She brought his hands up to her cheek. *Teach me how to shapeshift into mist, which should be enough protection.*

He froze, his fingers tangled in the silk of her hair. The idea could work. He was a fast enough shapeshifter even a firestarter probably couldn't kill him. A *cónyuge* could teach their beloved through the *conyugal* link how to shift into a new shape. If he gave Grania his own ability to shift into mist, even Hélène d'Agelet shouldn't be able to kill her.

Dios, how he truly hoped Jean-Marie hadn't lost his heart to a conniving bitch.

Very well, we'll invite Jean-Marie and his lady here for a civilized glass of sherry. Ethan and Luis will protect Compostela more thoroughly than when Madame Celeste visited, he gritted, yielding as gracefully as possible.

And my beloved will show me what's in the secret package from Paris, yes? Grania's voice was sweeter than honey.

His gaze shot back to her face.

She peeped up at him through her lashes. It had been one of Blanche's most endearing tricks whenever she'd wished to escape court politics for the privacy of their rooms. *La doctora* had never before displayed any of Blanche's flirtatious mannerisms.

Rafael's heart turned over, and his cock surged in response to her invitation.

Everything shall be as my lady wishes, he responded in mock obedience and swept her up in his arms.

She giggled, just a little, and wrapped her arms around his neck. They kissed enthusiastically, while he commanded the war to mind itself for the rest of the night. Having regained his lady, he would not permit anything to come between the two of them again.

Hélène snuggled closer into the comfort of Jean-Marie's arms in the roadhouse's back booth. He slid a fresh Corona over to her and kissed the top of her head, casting a possessive glance around the bar.

The frowns subsided but didn't quite disappear. She ran a fingernail down her longneck bottle of beer and wondered just what was going on here.

Elmer's Roadhouse served "the best BBQ this side of the Colorado River" and "more beers than anywhere else in Austin." It was a sturdy wooden building, built years ago for function more than looks, and adorned with menus from years gone by. Most of those still seemed to apply except for minor changes in price, judging by the complex spice aromas wafting through the hall and the many meats available—beef, chicken, pork, innumerable sausages, bison, goat . . .

Goat? She shook her head at Texan tastes.

It also boasted of superb desserts, and the patrons argued over those far more than which meat to choose. At least on the roadhouse's respectable side.

The other side was devoted to the bar and its accompanying dance floor. Booths and hordes of cheap tables and chairs provided seating, clearly designed to be easily replaced after a fight. The wall behind the bar was covered with a collection of empty beer bottles, dating back more than eighty years, and backlit to look like stained glass.

The band rejoiced in the safety of its chicken wire screen, which was currently clean although fragrant with beer and tomatoes to her *vampira* nose. During a break, large monitors in the room's corners showed sports games or news broadcasts.

It would have been cozy, with its few ceiling fans patting the air, except for its patrons. For a Saturday night at 11 p.m., there wasn't a drunk to be seen. Even stranger, everybody in sight looked sober. The most popular dances were line dances, where everyone danced in rows without searching out partners—and nobody was alone.

"We're invited to Compostela for sherry tomorrow night," Jean-Marie drawled, slowly turning his bottle of Shiner Bock beer.

"Sherry? To drink *copitas* of sherry?" Hélène blinked at him. "Isn't that very civilized?"

"Do you doubt Texans can be polished?"

She blushed. "Well, I, uh . . ."

"Hmm?" He rubbed her shoulder, his eyes twinkling.

How could she tell him the invitation had unified her two worlds for a moment—the rougher world of action she enjoyed with him and the urbane formalities of peacetime life?

"For a moment, I'd envisioned cocktail parties with Oxford dons, where one drank not particularly good wine but enjoyed excellent conversation."

"I can promise you excellent wine, from the best wineglasses—a Riedel's Sommeliers' sherry *copita*, if you'd prefer?—and pleasant discourse on a range of topics." Jean-Marie's voice was overly casual, while his eyes offered wry understanding of her shock. "A variety of sherries to choose from, of course—Manzanilla, Fino, Amontillado . . ."

"And all from the best *bodegas*?" she queried, regaining her footing amid the language of wine connoisseurs. If she was to drink out of a glass made from over twenty-four percent lead crystal, the sherry itself had to be the very best.

"But of course!" His shoulders lifted in a very Gallic shrug, finished by a swig from his bottle. Through their *conyugal* bond, she, too, could savor the darker taste of his beer. From the largest independent brewery in Texas—in utter contrast to his fine talk of a sherry tasting party.

"I could give Don Rafael the photograph from the New Orleans Mardi Gras at the same time."

"An excellent idea." Jean-Marie nodded agreement. "It would certainly prove you come with good intentions."

The dancers stomped and twisted, advancing and retreating across the floor, every woman within easy reach of another.

Hélène was seriously tempted by Don Rafael's offer. She could wear something very ladylike—nothing seductive or too businesslike. Her green-and-white Oscar de la Renta dress with the matching green silk cardigan should be perfect. It would give her the chance to convince Don Rafael that she was a person who could be trusted, not the living equivalent of a nuclear bomb.

But *sherry*? Mint juleps or whisky she could have understood. Or playing poker or billiards. But not something as extremely polite and associated with the academic world as a fortified wine from Spain. She needed to know more.

"Did he come up with the idea?"

Jean-Marie glanced over at her. "*Doña* Grania asked to meet you."

If anything, Hélène's jaw dropped even farther than it had when she'd first heard the invitation.

Don Rafael, the brutal warrior who'd threatened her with death because she'd been forced into knowledge of *vampiros*—was now willing to let her come close to his most precious treasure, his *cónyuge*? Incredible!

For him to meet her in a neutral setting would have been declaring his trust in Jean-Marie's judgment of her as a reasonable being. For him to yield his prerogative and let his *patrona* choose what risks to take—*Doña* Grania must indeed be an amazing woman to inspire such confidence.

And his *patrona* had chosen to exert her influence on Hélène's behalf. Or more likely, on Jean-Marie's.

Hélène shivered slightly, her chest very tight.

"I'll be honored to accept." She had to clear her throat before she could continue. "I'd like to meet *Doña* Grania. She's a veterinarian, isn't she?"

"A wildlife veterinarian, specializing in owls and other raptors."

"Like eagles and hawks? If she taught him how to shift into those birds during duels . . ."

Jean-Marie's mouth twitched.

"She has?" Hélène sighed enviously. "I wish I knew more shapes. All I can manage is to shift into mist and some birds."

"The British never gave you anything else, not even a wolf to use during a retreat?" Jean-Marie's eyes narrowed.

"No, they said it was too dangerous to let me shapeshift, too. It's too easy to be separated during a retreat." *Instead I held them back and they paid in blood. Dear God, how they paid to keep me safe.*

"Fools. Twice-damned fools." He signaled a waitress far too abruptly.

"But I'm here with you, because of their care." She turned back to face him, touched by his concern.

"Or despite it," he growled. "If you ever had to run for your life from a fire . . ."

Her heart clenched at his understanding of the risks she'd faced. She kissed his cheek, snuggling against him.

"If I meet any of them, I'll kill him," he muttered under his breath and wrapped his arms around her.

She pretended not to hear him and slid her hand up his arm. *The crowd here looks calm. Can we go home now?*

Did you see anybody else in the restroom who was alone? Jean-Marie asked.

No, I was the only single woman. The other women in there were all in pairs, who were clearly watching out for each other.

Same here in the bar. They won't pick up men unless they can stay together—and Elmer's bar is one of the biggest pickup joints on this side of town. He surveyed the room, his jaw setting hard. *Shit*, he hissed.

Even so, it's still quiet here. She nuzzled him behind his ear encouragingly. And that appalling phone of his hadn't rung for the past couple of days. *We're only supposed to stay until ten . . .*

When the nightly news comes on, since they may have sources I don't. He suddenly seemed to have far more lines in his face. *I won't turn my phone off when we leave.*

His blue eyes were as unyielding as a glacier.

Of course not. She held up her hand in surrender, agreeing she hadn't expected him to do that. He'd fulfill his obligations to Don Rafael until he died, no matter what the cost.

He kissed her fingertips, his face softening a bit.

The dancers stomped to a close and spilled off the dance floor. The band gathered up their instruments and quickly disappeared through a hidden door. The TV sets immediately sprang to life above the crowd, racing through ads for any kind of feed, equipment, or clothing a farmer might need.

Ignoring the staccato patter, Hélène slid out of the bar and took Jean-Marie's hand. They started filing out with the others, squeezing between tables and chairs, starting and stopping when people stood up or said good-bye. Others chattered of the day's gossip or the night's plans, or just held on to each other. The stale aromas of sweat and beer filled the air, underlaid with a nameless fear's sour edge.

Jean-Marie pulled Hélène closer against him, his breath very warm on her neck and his body pressed protectively close.

The TV sets shifted gears, the news broadcast's opening bells sounding like the warning of a village's tocsin bell.

"We open with this tragic story from Uriah, a few miles outside of Dallas, where tonight one child and two adults were killed at the famous Uriah Pro Rodeo, when bulls stampeded into the stands," the announcer's rich voice cut in, sounding surprisingly unsteady. An instant later, women and children's tinned screams filled the hall, mixed with men's shouts and animals' bellows.

The entire crowd stopped in their tracks and stared at the horrific scene being reenacted.

An enormous bull had leapt into the stands and was storming along the aisles, trampling or tossing aside any panicked spectators who couldn't escape him. Casually dressed people in Western wear were running before him, leaping over seats, or standing in place—but always screaming. And far, far too many of them were children, battered, bloody, and small.

Hélène's head didn't seem to be connected very well to her body. Jean-Marie's arm was an iron bar around her waist, the only thing holding her up.

"Oh my God," a woman whispered in Elmer's bar. "I grew up going to the Uriah Rodeo." Her voice broke, and she bolted for the restroom. A woman whimpered, while a man began to curse without being reproved.

Bulls raced around the Uriah Rodeo's ring, doing their best to attack the cowboys and men chasing them. "At least twenty people are in critical care at local hospitals," the announcer continued, before his voice was drowned out by sobs and comments on the carnage.

Jean-Marie started shoving their way through the crowd, making a bare pretense of politeness.

Why? Who could have started it? Hélène whispered. *Bulls, especially so many, don't get out of their pens on their own. They must have had help.* She suspected she'd relive in her nightmares the bull charging up the central aisle toward the little boy.

He gave her a quick look of mingled sorrow and frustration. *Who do you think?*

No . . . She slowed, dragging her feet.

See the cowboy over by the bull pen? That's Devol, Madame Celeste's alferez mayor—the most soulless enforcer in North America.

You're seeing phantoms, just because you're in a war with her, Helene retorted instinctively.

Behind her, a woman pointed a finger at the monitor. "See him, Madge? That's the guy I told you about—the fellow we saw yanking the girl out of the New Orleans casino, the brute who the police wouldn't even question. What's he doing in the ring at a Texas rodeo?"

Oh no . . .

Only Madame Celeste would deliberately stampede bulls at a rodeo, Jean-Marie said viciously and slammed into the door, breaking them free into the Texas night.

"That's nonsense!" Hélène spun to face him beside his motorcycle, parked at the edge of the parking lot near the hillside's oak trees. It was an excellent spot for a quiet rendezvous between *vampiros*, should Don Rafael need to send him a message.

He began to yank their helmets out of the saddlebags.

A chill ran down her spine.

"My sister is not a callous murderer!" *Not her, never la petite.*

"She is fighting a war with us. Does anyone else have equally good motivation?"

Hélène stopped, unable to counter his reasoning. "That's ridiculous," she said automatically, her fingers fumbling on her helmet's chin strap.

"And the New Orleans pit boss? You must know Madame Celeste runs the largest, shadiest casino in New Orleans." Jean-Marie tossed her a helmet.

"Who cares if one of her employees gets nasty on his weekend off?" She kept her chin up, refusing to back down.

"Hélène!" He glared at her and yanked off his helmet an instant after he'd fastened it. The *conyugal* bond, which had always hummed with warmth even when they weren't talking, began to turn chilly. "Do you honestly believe a *patrona*'s enforcer would dare to cause this much trouble without permission?"

She stiffened, the icy logic ringing all too true.

"This makes her an accomplice in the murder of one child and two adults, plus who knows how many more will die. Do you believe she's completely innocent?"

Hélène closed her eyes for a moment, thinking back to all she'd heard in London of the war between Texas and New Orleans. Remembering all she'd known, while growing up, of her little sister's sheer determination to obtain what she wanted. And yet . . .

And yet there was also baby Celeste, the infant who'd come after her parents had buried so many other little ones. The adorable child with great dark eyes who'd made slaves of everyone who saw her, who'd cooed and gurgled so sweetly. The laughing playmate and companion who could bargain for an hour to obtain the best silk for her new party dress.

Determined? Yes. Completely evil? No!

"I believe my sister could authorize such an attack as a stratagem of war. I cannot believe she'd deliberately have children killed."

"Hélène!" Anguish and frustration raged through Jean-Marie's voice.

"At least let me talk to her first." She flinched, his pain cutting her to the bone—but she would not, could not, back down.

"No, Hélène, no." He grasped her by the shoulders, a muscle ticking in his jaw. "Can't you see? She's a coldhearted bitch who can't be allowed to live."

"Allowed to live?" Hélène violently shook herself away from him. A spasm of grief twisted his features before his hands dropped away. "I don't believe she's worthy of death. Certainly not on your word alone."

"Wasn't that video enough?" He shoved his hand through his hair.

"Never." She flung out her hands. "I'd have to hear it from her mouth first."

"I can't wait that long." A muscle ticked in his jaw. "Not when children are dying."

Her stomach suddenly started to somersault like a dying satellite. "What do you mean?"

"Her death is the only way to end this war."

"You wouldn't do that, would you?"

She read the answer in his somber face before he spoke. "Yes, I would, especially because I'm probably the only one who can get close enough to her. I'm Don Rafael's eldest *hijo*, which makes me the strongest. Devol will watch Ethan very closely because they're both enforcers. He won't expect me to move against her since I'm younger than she is. I'm just a *heraldo* so I'm the freest to act, since I'm not supposed to be a threat."

Chills were running up and down her spine, making her teeth chatter on a very hot and humid night.

"If you kill my sister, we will have no future!"

"If she kills my family, how can I live with myself?" he countered, a pulse ticking in his jaw.

"Then we are not *cónyuges*." She threw the helmet at him and turned away, half-blinded by tears. What good was falling in love when your beloved destroyed everything you treasured?

"Where are you going, Hélène?" His beautiful voice was ravaged by far too much control.

"To New Orleans and my sister's house." With luck, her presence would keep Jean-Marie from destroying Celeste. Maybe.

SEVENTEEN

For a Sunday night in a popular travel destination, New Orleans didn't have many tourists. And Hélène's heart still lacked the warm reassurance of her *cónyuge*'s presence, just as it had ever since she'd left him in Texas.

Her throat tightened.

She reminded herself she was viewing the Crescent City's beauties undisturbed: the patient mules of the French quarter and their jaunty straw hats; the cathedral's silvery-blue bulk like an invitation to enter another world; the innumerable flourishes of wrought-iron, as if a city playing dice with a swamp needed to somehow remind itself of solidity, however unique; the broad white smiles of its residents, of every creed and race . . .

But there should have been more smiles, just as there should have been more tourists to distribute largesse and evoke those happy beams. But there wasn't, at least not from where she stood outside a deserted coffeehouse.

Instead there were half-empty boulevards and echoing alleys, where sheets of newsprint whispered about dead women and police task forces. Pairs of policemen, in a variety of uniforms, were never far from sight on the main streets, in between the scents of fried oysters, cheap rum, and stale river water. The few people who strode the sidewalks did so briefly and with purpose. But the cars and taxis were very, very busy, flitting from building to building, ignoring streetlights, and dodging near disaster sometimes by less than an inch.

A steady stream of them disgorged their gaudily dressed passengers at Bacchus's Temple, the largest casino in New Orleans. It was located on the edge of the Warehouse District, halfway between a burst of rigid modern high-rises and the French Quarter's ancient cobblestones. Gaudy in its purple and gold, the four-story building was a lavish recreation of an ancient Roman temple, complete down to a great, semicircular portico with columns that covered the entire front. It was designed to attract both attention and awe, while inviting onlookers to enter.

And all Hélène wanted to do was run back to Jean-Marie's garden and hurl herself into his arms. The man she loved. The man who planned to kill her sister.

Not walk into there and face a woman she hadn't seen for centuries, no matter what name they shared. A *patrona* who was whispered about even in Europe, and not kindly.

Surely Jean-Marie had to be wrong, just a little. Just enough for there to be something of *la petite* left inside *la patrona*, someone she could appeal to, negotiate with, stop the war.

After all, the same blood flowed in both their veins. They were Sainte-Pazannes, of the oldest nobility in France and they didn't know how to lose.

She drew herself up proudly and shook her hair out. A streetlamp flashed on it and reflected off a window, catching her eye. Its reflection's golden sliver slid off peeling black letters into the gloom and disappeared into an alley, startling a cat. The feline hissed a warning and leapt away.

Hélène shivered involuntarily before telling herself not to be a fool. If she'd turned back before every mission when she'd been nervous, she'd never have been a spy. She shook herself firmly and set out across the street, her very simple, black silk Vera Wang dress floating behind her.

One day, she would hold hands again with Jean-Marie, her *cón-yuge*, her heart. She had to—or life would not be worth living.

The so-called security guards at the door were *vampiros*, making her raise an eyebrow at that bit of blatant caution. For an inner sanctum, yes—but on a public street? Did Celeste honestly believe *prosaicos* would never learn there were *vampiros*?

She tut-tutted privately but didn't overtly acknowledge them. Let Celeste or her minions make the first move. The fact they didn't made the hair prickle on the back of her neck.

Hélène had to admit her familiarity with casinos was limited to a few in Europe and those in the movies. Even so, Bacchus's Temple seemed extremely ornate and loud. Purple and green were emblazoned across every surface, while every edge and curve seemed to be gilded. Lights streamed across the ceiling in myriad patterns, while crystal chandeliers competed over which could be the most blindingly tawdry. Closely packed banks of narrow machines flashed, beeped, and screamed, according to their mood, while people stared deep into their bowels. Wary, half-naked women moved among them with small trays of drinks. Burly men and even more dangerous women strode brusquely along the carpeted aisles, their badly tailored suits failing to hide electronic leashes.

A plump man with a golden crown beamed from the walls and the ceiling, encouraging everyone to gamble. Judging by the few visitors here, he was as unsuccessful as any other barker in the Big Easy. Less than a quarter of the slot machines were occupied, and there were players at only a few of the blackjack, roulette, and craps tables.

Two dealers were spinning a roulette wheel invitingly at an empty table, its rattle echoing through the half-deserted, high-ceilinged section.

Given the lack of gamblers, Hélène could catch the casino's true scents more easily, without the sharp tang of *prosaico* fear and excitement. She found a private spot by an empty video poker game and sniffed, testing for signs of *vampiros*.

There were a great many young *vampiros* here—not completely surprising, since Celeste had only fully mastered her *esfera* recently. However, she'd taken over New Orleans almost seventy years ago. Ordinarily, a sizable proportion should have been that age. But almost all of them were no more than thirty years old, with most being ten to twenty years. They'd be little more than puppies—high energy, easy to manipulate, but little stamina in a fight. They'd make good troops for conquest but not for a siege.

Hélène had heard rumors New Orleans' *vampiros* were unusually young, but she'd paid little attention, considering it too outré to be worthy of consideration. Why had Celeste kept them this way?

She sniffed again, more deeply, straining for signs of the *prosaicos*.

Alcohol—and drugs, illegal drugs. If Celeste was allowing her *vampiros* to mingle with *prosaicos* who imbibed of such potions, then she permitted her *vampiros* to feed upon *prosaicos* whose emotions came from those false wells. Not the clean, bright taste of passion whose wellspring was the heart, but the sluggish, chemical-born stuff. The old maxim, "you are what you eat," was truer more for *vampiros* than for anyone else—and *vampiros* died fast and young if they fed on drunks, however easy that prey might be.

And such *prosaicos* could die easily while the *vampiro* was feeding because they didn't know if it was a true fantasy or a drug-induced dream.

Shit. Hélène shuddered, her gorge rising fast and hard into her throat. She forced it back, her fingernails digging into her palms. She was on a mission—and peace was worth anything, anything at all, even consorting with the likes of these.

A new odor sifted toward her—*vampiro*, older—and very nervous.

She turned to face him, wrapping herself in a *marquise*'s hauteur, and raised an imperious eyebrow. "Yes?"

"Madame." The plump *vampiro* bowed, his face dripping more and more sweat before her. He was well dressed in a modern Armani suit, which implied Celeste was generous—hah!—or he accepted bribes. "*La patrona* sends her regards and asks you join her for drinks."

A half-dozen *mesnaderos* silently appeared and ringed them, hands very close to their weapons.

Hélène's lip curled. These were some of the missing older generation, with their seventy-year-old wariness and their much greater speed than any of the puppies at the craps table. Of course, none of them were faster than she was—and after centuries with the British Secret Service, she could have torched seven targets in less time than it took to bat her eyelashes.

"My pleasure," she answered, giving him a bare nod and flicking her fingers, gesturing him forward.

"Dear, dear sister. Thank you for coming to visit—you've been far too long in this world." Celeste cast a last, fond glance at the video monitor in her boudoir, before unlocking her small safe. "Unfortunately since you're a firestarter, I'll have to give you a fast death. Otherwise, I'd let Georges play with you for a few weeks before I allowed you to die. Pity."

She hummed happily, sorting through the bottles in the neatly locked drawer. Strychnine, arsenic . . . She'd used them all in at least one city to build up her *esfera*.

"Celeste."

"Raoul?" She whirled around, clutching the small, dark blue bottle of cyanide.

He regarded her somberly from the full-length mirror on the door leading to her dressing room. She could see his entire, lean body from the top of his dark brown hair to the toes of his highly polished boots—and the heavily embroidered uniform donned when he'd taken his officer's commission granted by Louis XVI. Her father would have heartily approved of it, if there'd ever been time to see him in it before blood and revolution had swept over France.

"*Mademoiselle.*" He bowed very formally, mist catching at his outlines.

"Raoul, no! Please stay and talk to me. What's wrong?" She held out both hands, light sparkling on her rings and the bottle.

If anything, his expression became more forbidding, displaying the general he could have become. "Remember I warned you about sin." He nodded toward her hand.

She glanced down, startled, having forgotten all about what she held. The skull-and-crossbones label of deadly poison sneered at her, followed by bold print detailing what would happen to the unwary imbiber. A fast death to *prosaicos* and even *vampiros*, if taken in large enough quantity, as she'd proven before.

Her eyes shot back to him. "But, Raoul, she murdered you. She deserves to die."

"She is your sister, Celeste." His uniform was dissolving into the mist.

"She must die." She pressed her palm against the mirror, trying to pull him through to her. The bottle fell and rolled unseen into the dressing room.

"At what price, Celeste? Your immortal soul—and parting us forever?"

She flinched, started to argue—and remembered she couldn't bargain. Not here, not with him, not with these stakes.

He watched her, a wry smile curling his mouth. "I cannot help you, my angel. Only you can choose to join me now."

His face winked out.

"Damn, damn, *damn*!" She beat her hands against the unfeeling glass.

A chime sounded, and Celeste froze. *Merde.* Now where the hell was the cyanide?

In the next instant, the suite's front door opened, her usual custom since it was so far away from her private rooms. But it was still too damn close for her to spend time looking for the poison. "Madame Celeste, *madame la marquise* d'Agelet has arrived."

Oh crap, she'd have to do without the cyanide for now. Well, she could always kill Hélène a little later—maybe slip the stuff into something fruit-flavored and powdered, the way Jim Jones had done, instead of a good glass of wine.

Or listen to Raoul? No! Hélène was a murderess who deserved to be punished, and there was nobody else who could get close enough to her to do it. Her *mesnaderos* might get close enough to bind her, since the bitch was overly squeamish about harming others, but she'd never let them hurt her.

Besides, according to Celeste's sources at the airport, Hélène had come here from Austin, which was hardly an international travel hub. She must have friends there, perhaps even Don Rafael himself.

Hélène could be a very useful hostage, should those Texas *vampiros* still like her. Hell, they were so stupidly chivalrous, they might be polite enough to protect Hélène, even if they didn't like her. Don Rafael might trade a city or two for the bitch's safe return.

Celeste began to chuckle softly, liking the vision of the handoff at the border under that scenario. Still buoyed, she sauntered down the long hall toward her sitting room to meet her older sister for the first time in two centuries.

Hélène scanned her surroundings once again, pursing her lips. She hadn't called on anyone in a room like this for decades.

The sitting room was designed to impress with its velvet draperies trimmed in gold fringe, heavy Aubusson carpets, and portraits of Napoleonic heroes. The furniture was French from the Second Empire, created just before the American Civil War: heavily carved from ebony and rosewood, upholstered and tufted in silk velvet, which was as opulent to look at as it was uncomfortable to sit on.

The air changed, and she came on the alert, mistrusting the *vampiro* scent coming toward her. Female, more than sated with blood, and sluggish, the usual sign of feeding on the darker emotions such as pain.

La petite posed in the formal sitting room's doorway, superbly dressed in a highly tailored, crimson Valentino suit which emphasized her breasts and tiny waist. She might be wearing a so-called invisible bra, but Hélène strongly doubted it. It was far more likely men's eyes were supposed to follow the ruby pendant down her neckline toward her thighs, and lose all control of their brains. An empress's dress, perhaps—but also a courtesan's. Damn.

The ground shifted under her feet, and ice ran down her spine. But losing Jean-Marie was worth nothing if she didn't treat Celeste as family.

"*Ma chère soeur,*" she cooed and went forward, holding out her hands.

"Dearest sister," Celeste echoed. They met halfway and embraced, hugging each other—quickly—and kissing each other on the cheek.

"To think that you were alive all this time," Hélène sniffled, stepping back. The majordomo had silently disappeared.

Close up, Celeste's scent was even more disquieting, despite her custom-blended perfume.

"Can you forgive me for not having told you? I was so afraid when the French captured me that I lost my head and made a deal." Celeste's eyes were enormous. Tears began to well up. "After the war, I didn't know if you were still alive or how to reach you. I was so embarrassed about what I'd done that when some of my friends decided to come here, I joined them."

She blinked away the threatening moisture and smiled tentatively. Hélène's heart turned over as it always had for her little sister.

"Can you ever forgive me, Hélène? I'm so sorry for disappointing you." Celeste gulped, and tears left silver tracks down her face, badly smudging her makeup.

The poor darling!

"Yes, of course, I forgive you, Celeste. What's important is that we're together now." They embraced again, sniffling.

"Papa and *Maman* would be so happy to see us like this," Hélène chuckled when they broke apart. Celeste shot her a quick glance but said nothing, simply handed her a tissue.

She wouldn't reminisce about family?

Hélène moved to distract them both. "You look beautiful. Valentino, isn't it? And your jewelry is magnificent."

Celeste immediately preened, as Hélène had known she would at any compliment to her attire, and the slight chill in the atmosphere disappeared. "Thank you. And Vera Wang's severity suits your style quite well."

Hélène would have preferred to hear it described as simplicity, but whatever. At least they were on friendly terms again.

"Would you care for some wine? Or something stronger? If you're hungry, I can have one of my men bring a *vampiro* or two up. Or a *prosaico* if you'd prefer."

"Wine please. I'm not hungry at the moment; I'd rather spend time with you." And she'd much rather do her own hunting than drink what came out of Bacchus's Temple.

"Well, let me know when you want a snack." Celeste shrugged, seeming as French as when they'd left Sainte-Pazanne. "There are plenty of men here, and they'll let you do anything you want."

Poor darling, didn't she know the give and take between lovers anymore? She'd once enjoyed that with her Raoul.

Hélène sat down on the sofa, choosing the end closest to the chair clearly designated as the throne.

Celeste handed her a flute of Cristal champagne and seated herself in the massive piece of furniture, accepting its embrace as her due. "To family and the future!" she toasted, lifting her glass high so that bubbles danced in the chandeliers' glow.

"To family!" Hélène echoed. They touched glasses, and the resulting chime rang through the old room, setting off echoes. Crystals danced softly in answer, flashing gently in the old mirrors.

She sipped her champagne, enjoying its predictably high quality.

"How was Texas?" Celeste's voice was silky soft.

Oh dear. Two centuries of experience as a spy had taught Hélène both how to recognize danger and how to control her response.

"Hot." Hélène chose her words carefully. "It's a nonstop flight from London to Dallas, you know."

"And the Texas *vampiros*?" Celeste probed.

"Don Rafael was polite enough to give me safe passage for a week, as is customary, although I didn't stay that long." Hélène met her sister's eyes guilelessly. She was thankful for her slightly older age as a *vampira*, which made it easier to conceal any dissemblance. "Everyone in London is talking about the war, you know."

"English? Bah!" Celeste dismissed them with an angry wave and tossed back the rest of her drink. She refilled it to the brim quickly, making Hélène blink at the casual treatment of a very fine, highly expensive vintage.

Still, Celeste had displayed a slight vulnerability, and Hélène took advantage of it.

"Well, do you want the English mocking American manners? 'Oh, those colonials are having another feud. They're so childish they can't stop fighting, y'know,'" she mocked, adopting an overly stylized upper-crust English accent.

"They wouldn't!"

"What do you think the latest Mayfair gossip is?" Hélène raised an eyebrow and sipped her champagne.

Celeste's face turned a mottled red. She flung herself to her feet and began to pace.

Hélène watched her for a few moments before she twisted the knife a little farther. "Not to mention the Champs-Élysées."

"Paris . . ." Celeste hissed, anger and anguish mingled equally in her voice. "Damn."

She beat her hands on a narrow, marble-topped table, making its golden vases dance. She spun to face her sister, bracing herself against the table's ebony like a lioness about to charge.

Hélène instinctively came to her feet, setting her glass down. If she'd had a gun close by, it would have been under her hand. Or Jean-Marie, her *cónyuge*, would have stood guard at her back.

"Well, the namby-pambies in London and Paris can kiss my ass after I hold Texas and I'm the richest *patrona* in America."

"Celeste . . ."

"No, you listen to me! I'm the *patrona* of New Orleans, and what I say, goes. It's war to the death between me and Texas." An absolute monarch's fixed determination glared from her eyes, vowing destruction to anyone who challenged her.

Hélène bent her head, unwilling to openly agree to a war. Besides, she'd at least made Celeste rethink its merits. She could work later to widen that opening.

"You're welcome to stay with me, dearest sister." Celeste's voice was softer now, almost cooing sweet. "We can talk about old times and the future."

"Thank you," Hélène said and beamed. This had to work. Somehow.

Rafael's office was crowded tonight, with emotions as much as people. His knight's sword hung over the mantel, as a reminder of duty and honor, while his desk hid its high-tech capabilities. Comfortable chairs and a long sofa offered plenty of seating near the round table or facing the wall of windows.

Jean-Marie finished summarizing the other *patrones'* recent messages and took a sip of coffee, stalling in response to his intuition's harsh demand. He'd been feeding on companionship, not lust, since Hélène had walked out. Thin sustenance, especially when taken rarely. Working had been a far better distraction, given the increasingly long list of deaths.

The omnipresent knot in the pit of his stomach tightened yet again. Dammit, when he thought of Hélène being in New Orleans, living under the same roof as Celeste . . .

He yanked his thoughts away from that nightmare and scanned the room again, instinctively checking the only woman present.

Doña Grania was here, her first time at a council meeting. Amazing.

She was clearheaded enough to attend, thanks to drawing on Rafael's sanity through their *conyugal* bond. She'd passed through *La Lujuria* remarkably fast, the time when a young *cachorra* thought of nothing but blood and emotion. Like Rafael's other *hijos*, Jean-Marie found himself treating her with almost more respect than he gave his *creador*.

Ethan seemed to be unduly tense at odd times, often after he'd gone into Austin. Jean-Marie hadn't had a chance to ask him about it privately.

Luis was getting too damn old to still be a *compañero*, at almost two centuries. Jean-Marie hadn't yet spotted a gray hair in the other's glossy black hair. But he knew very well both he and Rafael inspected their old friend at every chance. If they lost Luis to old age before he could be given *El Abrazo* . . .

Gray Wolf and Caleb seemed uncomfortable with each other, almost unduly polite. *Please, God, let them not be fighting about Gray Wolf's refusal to permit Rafael to become Caleb's* creador. Texas needed every pair of *cónyuges* it could get.

Lars slipped in like a ghost and took a seat at the back, sending a chill running down Jean-Marie's spine. He would only have left his post if they needed to plan for the worst possible news.

"We have learned Madame Celeste is gathering all of her commanderies at Rosemeade in two days," Jean-Marie announced flatly, restarting the briefing—and waited for the eruption.

The room broke out into a buzz. Rafael pounded his seat. Ethan's hands tightened convulsively, as if reaching for his revolvers. Luis came to his feet, pulling out his smartphone. Gray Wolf snarled something in his native tongue.

"True?" Rafael asked Lars.

"Yes. Most of her *mesnaderos* will probably stay in New Orleans, though."

"Even so, the commanderies form an invading army who outnumber us," Gray Wolf growled, drumming his fingers.

"What about Devol and the *bandolerismo*?" Ethan snapped. "They're here in Texas, causing trouble now. They're undoubtedly planning to help the New Orleans army."

"I couldn't find out how to contact Devol and the *bandolerismo*, even after I broke into Madame Celeste's comms center in New Orleans." Lars shrugged, harsh grooves of frustration cut beside his mouth.

"Do we know their destination?" Rafael snapped.

"No," Jean-Marie answered, a muscle ticking in his jaw. "Memphis rumor says Madame Celeste will decide after the commanderies are together and she talks to Devol."

An unhappy silence fell.

"Crap," Caleb said, summing up the situation. "Pardon my French, ma'am."

"That's quite all right, Dr. Jones." Grania—or Dr. O'Malley—exchanged nods with him.

"We'll have to destroy the commanderies before they reach us. That's too many men for us to fight here, especially when we don't know where they're going." Rafael started to plan. "Rosemeade's the only possible target."

"An impregnable fortress surrounded by an impassable swamp and hundreds of square miles of terrified *prosaicos*, who'd report a suspicious firefly," Ethan agreed enthusiastically. He'd always wanted to be the one who finally took down the near-legendary torture capital.

"It will have to be a small party," Jean-Marie cautioned. "It's all we can get through on the ground."

"I'll be your sniper." Lars lifted a pair of fingers up.

Which guaranteed the bullets would arrive on target.

"I'll be observer and getaway driver," Jean-Marie volunteered. It would be a relief to get out of Texas with its memories of Hélène—and keep an eye on Lars.

Rafael assessed his two volunteers and relaxed slightly. They knew how to work together well.

So why did Jean-Marie's eyes turn so frozen when he spoke? Grania asked.

What? Dammit, you're right.

"I'm the team commander, of course," Ethan added before Rafael could chase down Jean-Marie's problem.

"If you decide to also raid Madame Celeste's operations in New Orleans, call on the Dallas commandery for support," Rafael snapped, handling the immediate issues. "The Houston commandery has their hands full with the floods from that tropical depression. Remember only the interstate is still open all the way through to New Orleans."

Ethan nodded, his face abstracted.

"Gray Wolf, you'll form a fast reaction force here in Texas," Rafael continued.

"Yes, sir. I'll use the *mesnaderos* and Waco as its basis."

"Good. Luis, you'll muster the daytime version. We'll probably need to bring the *comitiva* in on this."

Luis nodded shortly.

Hell, he'd roust all of Texas if he had to. Any other weapons Madame Celeste might have? Hmm . . .

Grania shot a sideways glance at him but said nothing, either vocally or mind-to-mind.

"What about Madame d'Agelet? Do we know where she is?" Rafael asked.

Jean-Marie's eyes closed briefly. Grania disengaged herself from Rafael and began to inspect his desk.

"Madame d'Agelet entered Madame Celeste's headquarters tonight and hasn't been seen since," Texas's chief spy reported in clipped, emotionless tones.

"In that case, we'll have to assume she'll be at Madame Celeste's side and plan accordingly," Rafael ordered and went to the windows for room to think.

Hélène d'Agelet was both a firestarter—and Jean-Marie's *cónyuge*. Should he order her killed as a danger to his men, now she'd gone over to her sister's side? Or saved, since his eldest *hijo* adored her? Both options were equally impossible.

A muscle throbbed in Jean-Marie's jaw.

"Do you have any, ah, comments, Jean-Marie?" Rafael asked, testing the waters.

"Madame d'Agelet is my *cónyuge*," his eldest *hijo* announced harshly. "The *conyugal* bond disappeared when I told her Madame Celeste, her sister, needed to die."

Rafael froze, fierce pain barreling into his gut. Hélène and Celeste were sisters—yet he was prepared to kill Celeste, to protect his family?

If Rafael ever lost Grania for a similar reason, his life would stop. Had he helped force Jean-Marie into this appalling predicament? If

Hélène d'Agelet had been able to stay in Texas, would affairs have ended differently?

The room was utterly silent. Gray Wolf's mouth was firmly compressed, his hands tightly linked with Caleb's. Ethan's head was held high, his nostrils flared like a stallion ready to fight.

My sympathies, mi hijo, Rafael said finally, unable to find a way through his whirling thoughts.

Thank you. Jean-Marie inclined his head, his blue eyes clouded now, almost gray. "If you'll excuse me, we need to start planning immediately."

He bowed and left the room, Ethan and Lars following close on his heels. The others murmured curt farewells and disappeared.

Grania stretched, her expression pensive. She delicately nudged Rafael's sword with her fingertip, returning it to perfect alignment with the stone mantelpiece.

"What are you thinking?" Rafael queried.

She turned to face him, her eyes contemplative blue pools. "Two days ago, who did Jean-Marie ask to bring into our family?"

Rafael raised an eyebrow. "I don't understand what you mean, Grania."

"Hélène d'Agelet was in Austin then, correct? Jean-Marie's *cónyuge.*"

"*Sí*, the firestarter."

"Who was willing to swear fealty to you, not her sister." His *patrona*'s voice was very gentle.

Rafael winced. *Mierda*, but he could use such a weapon right now . . . "But now she's in New Orleans with my bitter enemy—her sister."

Grania nodded and leaned back against the fireplace. "While you are—"

"Outnumbered and facing an invasion. Plus, my *heraldo* doesn't need to remain in Texas, should he and his *cónyuge* both survive this war." He slammed his fist down onto his sturdy desk. "Could I have been more arrogant? What next?"

"I can understand nightmares, *querida*. But this is life or death."

She caressed his cheek, her eyes dark with sympathy. "Personally, I'm sure you'll figure out how to defend Texas. Afterward, you may need to rethink what makes an acceptable *vampiro*. I'm not sure you can walk away from many more firestarters during a war."

She kissed her fingertips and laid them against his mouth.

He caught her hand and set his lips to her lifeline, shaken to the bone, closing his eyes so he could breathe in her scent like wine.

Did he have the strength to change what had protected him for so long from his nightmares? What he knew would also save his beloved *cónyuge*?

Could he afford not to evolve, if it would help his *hijos* and *compañeros*, plus the people he'd sworn to protect and serve?

He knew only one thing for sure: without Grania, the light of his life, he had no chance whatsoever of finding a path to the future.

Hélène gagged yet again when she reached the hotel's miserable lobby at the foot of the stairs. The desk clerk started to look over at her, and she shoved his attention back to the TV where CNN was yapping about the uproar in New Orleans and Texas.

Damn, how she hated giving blow jobs to total strangers, just to get a little emotion. But at least it was honest lust, unlike that to be found at Bacchus's Temple, and she'd done her best to show a sailor from Venezuela a good time.

She stumbled across the threadbare carpet, the single fan wheezing overhead, and staggered into the narrow street outside. The French Quarter's comparatively fresh air smacked her in the face, laden with wine and a thousand good meals. She smiled faintly and leaned against a locked door, the shallow alcove providing a tiny respite for her recovery.

An instant later, she lifted her hand and flagged down a passing taxi to take her back to the casino. Five bone-jarring, teeth-rattling minutes later in a small sauna guided by a kind man, she was deposited at the casino's front door. She tipped him far too much, overwhelming his speech about being cautious in a strange city.

She had just enough strength to make it upstairs to her room while maintaining a façade of impersonal dignity, despite Celeste's swarm of *mesnaderos* and fawning courtiers. There she collapsed into a chair until the world finally stopped whirling. Her head began to clear, and her stomach gradually settled itself into a calmer pattern.

Her sister had been very friendly today, unlike last night's edgy blend of friendship and defensiveness. Perhaps she'd simply needed time to get over her surprise at Hélène's unexpected arrival. At any rate, they were going to Celeste's country estate tomorrow night to relax. Once they were alone there, she could hopefully persuade Celeste to negotiate an end to the war.

After that, she could return to Austin and rebuild her life with Jean-Marie, please God.

They'd parted in such coldness, never speaking to each other after their bitter argument in the roadhouse's parking lot. Yet when she'd arrived here, she'd found a single, well-wrapped parcel hiding deep in her suitcase, which could only have come from him.

She'd long since killed all of Celeste's electronic spies in the room. Surely she had time and leisure now to see what he'd given her—and the strength, thanks to the hope of a coming peace.

Hélène extracted the package from her suitcase and settled back into her chair to inspect it. A few minutes later found her holding an old, leather-bound journal, approximately two hundred years old by its scent. And probably French.

She'd hunted books for years about the Vendée and her lost childhood, only to find very few. She'd received some offers from American book dealers, suggesting memoirs by minor Bonapartists, who'd arrived in the New World after Waterloo and represented a variety of French provinces.

L de B was stamped on this book's cover in bold letters, with the de Beynac crest in the bottom right corner.

Air whispered over Hélène's neck, as if someone else was watching.

She paused, chilled. Could it be Louise de Castelnaud, *née* de Beynac? A Louise whose maiden name had been de Beynac and was a refugee from the French Revolution? Hadn't Celeste's lover had a younger sister named Louise?

But why would Jean-Marie give her Louise de Beynac's journal? Or did it also contain letters, as many such volumes did?

> *To my beloved Louise, from your brother Raoul, 21 September 1787*

Hélène's hand crept to her throat.

She flipped pages. Louise had kept a detailed diary, embellishing the pages with sketches of her family, flowers, or even places where they'd lived.

Good God, had Raoul truly been that gallant or that handsome? Louise had obviously adored her older brother, judging by how often she'd drawn him and how she'd saved every letter he'd written. First from the academy, the army, and finally from the Revolutionary army.

Those hated, hated Blues.

Hélène whipped the cover shut. She didn't need to remember the agony of those last few months, when she and her parents had been on one side, and Raoul de Beynac had been on the other. Or how it had all ended with her parents' slaughter.

A single sheet of paper flew out like a bird, slapped into her arm, and fluttered onto the table.

Cursing silently, Hélène picked up the letter and reluctantly unfolded it. Now she'd have to read it, so she could decide where it fitted into the diary. Centuries of collecting books wouldn't allow her to let this letter be out of place, when everything else was in such perfect order.

Words rippled across the page, still completely readable despite the passage of two centuries.

> *Outside Sainte Marie des Fleurs, the month Nivôse of the Year II. Ma cher Louise . . .*

A chill ran down Hélène's spine. Why was Celeste writing to Louise only days before Papa and *Maman* had died?

My message is very urgent. Please tell Raoul Papa will come to Hélène's manor near Sainte Marie des Fleurs two days from this date. The English will arrive at midnight to take us all away. As Raoul loves me, please beg him to come with his troops.

Hélène's jaw dropped. Her head spun, yet the damning words remained.

Celeste was the one who'd betrayed their parents to the hated Revolutionary army. Whatever her reasons, she'd known Papa would be arrested and executed. *La petite* was as guilty of patricide as if she'd wielded the musket herself.

Hélène wrapped her arms around her stomach, shuddering.

If Celeste had done that, what other evils had she performed? Had she been accidentally captured by the French in Spain—or had she been the double agent who'd betrayed agent after agent for years? If so, no wonder she hadn't wanted to see England after the war. Whitehall would have happily danced on her grave if she'd given them the chance.

She should have listened when Jean-Marie warned her Celeste was untrustworthy. *Ah,* mon amour, *will I ever see you again?*

Stabbing agony answered her, reminding her of their shattered *conyugal* bond.

She bit her lip and forced herself to think. With luck she could figure out how to contact her beloved before they went to Celeste's country estate.

One thing was certain: Life held no meaning without Jean-Marie in it.

Eighteen

The trailer was dark, allowing all attention to fall on Rosemeade glowing in the monitors overhead. An overhead view and exterior shots rotated on a gigantic wall panel, showing exactly where everything and everyone was outdoors. Dozens of crystalline blobs of light moved across diagrams and photos on another panel, representing the interior. A circle floated among them, converting them instantly into three-dimensional people walking in life-sized rooms. A cacophony of swamp sounds whispered in the background, occasionally replaced by guttural street language overheard from indoors. The only things missing were the humidity and the mosquitoes.

It was far, far better than any video game—and they'd needed decades of watching Madame Celeste and her predecessors to create it, plus live imagery from the planes overhead.

"Looks fun to me," Ethan commented in Jean-Marie's headset an hour after dark. "Sitting there like a nice, white wedding cake."

"Easy target, once you get inside the grounds," Lars agreed. The three of them shared a private channel, while the other teams had their own channels, as well. They were using the latest stealth technology, of course, overseen by Emilio Alvarez, Luis's godson, from where he sat next to Jean-Marie. Emilio's T-shirt was a cacophonous advertisement for a small jazz festival. He'd probably donned it as a reminder to stay inside where he couldn't be captured and become an embarrassment to the Navy—no matter how much that frustrated the Naval Academy grad and motivated him to work harder than ever.

Ethan was circling overhead, high enough that Celeste could neither hear nor see his plane. They'd taken out all of her military lovers this afternoon, eliminating her eyes and ears into local air traffic.

Lars had worked his way in through the swamp the previous night, casually dismissing his encounter with an alligator. He was now watching the main house from the rose garden side, hidden within the tangle of cypress trees and brackish water. Given his camouflaged gear and greater age than Madame Celeste's guards, it was highly unlikely they'd spot him until he started shooting. That was when Jean-Marie would have to fetch him out as quickly as possible.

Like most great houses of its time, Rosemeade had been built of dense wood and designed for natural air conditioning. A great staircase swept up through its center, acting as its heart, and conveyed every breath of air from the cooler cellars to the bedrooms on the top floor. The cupola surmounting the roof vented the house, sucking warm air out.

On this blisteringly hot night, Madame Celeste's almost two hundred *vampiros* had followed the same flow. No *prosaicos* were here tonight, or *compañeros*, just her warriors. They'd parked their cars, vans, and buses on the parking lot between the house and rose garden. After accepting drinks in the small library and music room on the first floor, they'd wandered up the great staircase. Now they milled around on the stairs, the balcony overlooking the first floor, or in the ballroom, gossiping with their friends, challenging their enemies, drinking wines they'd never heard of before or swilling old favorites. All, however, stayed very close to the ballroom, awaiting Celeste's instructions.

Jean-Marie's intuition was silent at the moment, which wasn't nec-

essarily a comfort. It could kick like a mule when it had only one thing
to say in a bad situation.

As befitted a getaway driver, he was currently surrounded by very
fast machinery. His beloved, highly customized Suzuki Hayabusa
Turbo—or Peregrine Falcon—was hidden further back in the trailer,
which was hitched to a semi truck cruising down a back road near
the plantation. It had a compartment to itself, ready to pop open a
concealed door and roar out down a ramp—faster than any other
motorcycle, road-legal car, and many planes.

"Anyone heard from Devol?" Lars asked.

"No, dammit. We've got directional mikes on the house, but we
haven't picked up any traces of him," Ethan snarled.

Jean-Marie's mouth tightened at the news, one of the few strong
sensations he'd felt other than agony over his loss of Hélène. Christ,
how he spent every spare minute plotting how to win her back when
this was over . . .

Ethan was taking Devol's challenge personally, and hopefully, that
wouldn't become a weakness. Texas couldn't afford cracks in her de-
fenders. God knows his own insides were wound tighter than a coiled
rattlesnake, sharp enough to shatter like an overstretched steel cable.
His gut knotted at the image.

He shifted slightly, trying to relax. He needed to, although he
wasn't sure why it was so important to do so before a big raid. Just sit
back and listen to the undercurrents.

"Were you able to get *Baby Mine* loaded?" he asked, returning
them all to the present.

"Oh yeah, that lady is fully packed and flying. One of the Austin
commandery's *compañeros* knew exactly how to make her payload,
thanks to his days in Vietnam." Ethan chortled, immediately restored
to good humor. "She's in the air now and heading this way, right on
schedule. When she gets here, she's going to show these guys how to
party like they've never partied before."

"I've already started things going, too," Lars added. "Just a couple
of well-placed bullets into the right places to set the groundwork."

Which nobody had noticed, of course. Jean-Marie snorted softly, slightly amused by tagging the night's planned events as a party. At least it would be a brief, explosive one for its participants, stopping them from lingering on this earth.

The cursor blinked insolently at Hélène, refusing to allow her admittance into Celeste's PC. Dammit, if she was going to escape, she had to turn off the security system. She'd bet her favorite Cartier diamond necklace Sister Dearest controlled it.

Twenty-four hours under the same roof, and they were still friends, at least overtly. But that sure as hell wouldn't last.

Sounds of a party swirled through the house, reminding her she was outnumbered and outgunned by dozens—even hundreds—of *vampiros*, partying hard in a mansion as flammable as any wood lot. She hadn't seen its like since she fought the Malaysian rebels during the 1950s. There'd been many similar houses there—big, well-ventilated, built of dense, dry timber, just begging to be turned into a bonfire. And, damn, how they could burn faster than anything she'd ever encountered in a more northern climate . . . Which was probably why Celeste had capped all the fireplaces on this showpiece.

But what could the password be for its security program? Celeste was downstairs, going over the final preparations for tonight's gathering with her *hijos*. She probably didn't plan to be gone for very long, so Hélène didn't have time to run a list of common passwords against the system. She needed to guess Celeste's password, based on what she knew of her sister, the *patrona* and murderess.

Well, didn't that just rule her out as an expert, since she hadn't even known Celeste was a killer? She forced back more useless tears and the memory of Jean-Marie's dear face.

Think, Hélène, think. She beat her hands together. Who and what did her sister care about? The standard guesses were names like children, pets, husband . . .

Perhaps a simple variation on her first lover's name, like *Beynac1?*

The screen chimed in welcome and poured icons onto the screen.

An instant's extra curiosity told her a file download program was one of the most frequently used applications. Really?

But she needed to open the door for her escape first.

The old, familiar steadiness dropped over her. Smiling slightly, she tracked down the security application. The same password opened this, and she soon shut down the alarms closest to the house.

She cocked her head and listened, sniffed, for an audience. Nothing. Should she look at what Celeste had downloaded? She gave in to curiosity. A few mouse clicks later, the screen hiccupped, paused, gushed, and abruptly recreated itself as—an address book?

She leaned forward. What on earth?

Roald Viterra. Gerald Hunter, a common enough name but when followed by Yoshi the Fair, it was enough to make any *vampiro* demand protection from their local *patrón*. And even more names and faces, adding up to a horrific *bandolerismo*, every one located in Texas.

Icy cats' feet danced through her spine. If she took this list, Celeste would be furious, probably angry enough for murder. Even so, Texas needed to know how to find these brutes—and she'd already planned to find Jean-Marie, hadn't she?

She scrabbled through drawers and was lucky enough to find a jump drive's silvery rectangle. An instant later, she had it fully loaded with the address book, then threaded onto her necklace and hidden behind the jade pendant. Hopefully, nobody would notice her jewelry didn't lie entirely flat.

She closed the file, covering her tracks, and started to shut down the PC—before stopping abruptly. What the hell was Celeste planning to accomplish with those fiends? Nobody should have that list unless they meant to use them as an army.

The only solution was to destroy the list itself—which would tell Celeste she'd been snooping in her PC.

Hélène's lungs tightened, her pulse drumming a little faster. Was it worth risking her life? Undoubtedly.

Ice rolling over her skin, she commanded the disk to spin faster and faster. A thin thread of smoke slipped into the room and strengthened, followed by the flat stench of burning electronics. The PC was on fire.

She headed back toward her bedroom, pulling on her short tropical print jacket. She was wearing a black bandeau top above matching print Capri pants and fairly stylish comfortable shoes—not what she'd choose for a run through the forest but good enough for sneaking around a mansion. Another minute to change into her jeans and boots, then she'd be out of here, God willing.

The door opened and closed.

Shit.

"Why does my computer carry your stench?" Celeste's voice could have sliced through sheets of steel.

May she not breathe any deeper . . .

"Because you have the best games?" She turned slowly but didn't come all the way back into the room. She was only a few steps from the French doors and the balcony beyond.

"Don't play me for a fool, Hélène." Celeste's ivory skin was sallow with fury. "I know you came back here to kill me."

What? The saving grace of anger ran through her, clearing her vision and slowing time.

"You might cold-bloodedly plan to kill family, sister mine," Hélène retorted, "but I don't. I came to build peace between you and Texas."

"Like hell." Celeste snorted in derision. "The old bull Don Rafael deserves to be blown into ashes, and I'm the *patrona* who's going to do it. Just like I'm the one who's going to finally put you in the ground, gaining justice for Raoul's murder."

"What murder?" Hélène frowned and edged sideways, wondering if she'd ever heard how de Beynac had died.

"You killed him, you bloodthirsty bitch," Celeste snapped. "He came for me at Sainte Marie des Fleurs, but you destroyed him."

Hélène paged rapidly through her memories, looking for forgotten details from a day two hundred years in the past.

"The Blues officer?" she finally ventured.

"The same!" her sister spat. "You destroyed the only man I ever loved, and you will die for it."

"He killed our parents—and you arranged it," Hélène snapped back, forgetting her own danger. "If it hadn't been for you, they'd have escaped to England—"

"If it hadn't been for *you*, I'd have married Raoul and borne his children."

Hélène's skin turned cold at the red rage in her sister's eyes. Were there any stakes higher for a woman than a husband and children?

"Guards!" shouted Celeste.

The hallway door slammed open.

"Shoot her," screamed Celeste. "Shoot her now."

Hélène bolted through the doors, ran across the balcony, and swung herself over the railing, to drop into the ancient camellia garden below.

She slammed a thought into the columns above her, sending a line of flame running over the balcony floor. A fiery curtain leapt up, shielding her from view, and lunged greedily for the floor above.

Shit, just how fast could this house burn?

An instant later, the sprinklers sprang into life, and water poured over the railings like a waterfall, quenching the fire before it had time to do more than scorch paint.

Celeste's bodyguards raced forward, propelled by her imprecations.

Bullets shredded the blossoms and leaves around Hélène. Her *vampiro* speed would only take her out into the open, where they could see her all the better. Where could she go?

Jean-Marie, ah, Jean-Marie, if only you were with me now . . .

Hélène? Jean-Marie's head snapped around. Was he dreaming out of sheer loneliness?

Jean-Marie!

He closed his eyes briefly in thankfulness. His *conyugal* bond had finally reappeared. *Hélène, what's wrong?*

I'm trying to escape, but Celeste's men are shooting at me.

Shit. Never mind that he'd warned her. What now?

"Jean-Marie, what is it?" Ethan's voice crackled into his ears. "You should be giving us the final count of the rooftop sentries."

"Let the aerial observers handle that. My *cónyuge* Hélène is escaping from the house."

He slammed out of his seat so fast the chair fell over, and ran for his bike. Emilio had already departed for it. Like the SEAL he was, he didn't need an explanation, just a call to arms.

Which side, chérie?

The camellia garden, on the east. Her mental voice was equally mixed with relief and desperation.

"On the east. Madame Celeste's men are shooting at her."

Ethan never hesitated. "You'll have to go in after her."

"I'll take my shots early, to distract them," Lars put in.

"Like hell you will!" Jean-Marie objected. "This risk is mine."

"Damned easy shots," Lars countered. "Same places, just a different time. The boys will pick me up before dawn."

"No way—"

"Sounds like a plan," Ethan cut in. "I'll tell the Mustang we're going in early."

Jean-Marie yielded to the *alferez mayor*'s leadership and boarded his bike, cursing the fate that risked brave men's lives. If this got Lars killed . . .

Only way to give you a chance, Lars added over their link as Rafael's *hijos.*

I'll tell the Mustang to hit the gatehouse extra hard, Jean-Marie said viciously. *That should buy you a little extra distraction to get out of the trees.*

Thanks.

"We're good to go, then," Ethan agreed. "You'll have to head straight back for Texas, Jean-Marie. You won't have time to hang around and wait for us here in Louisiana, after Madame Celeste raises the alarm."

"Agreed." He'd known that was coming, as soon as he'd heard Hélène's voice. "You can tell me how you and the boys clean out Bacchus's Temple when we meet again. Good luck and good hunting."

"First one back buys the beer at River Oaks," said Ethan.

"Or whisky at the Lucky Star," countered Lars.

Jean-Marie smiled slowly, feeling family's warmth wrap completely around him. He reached for his *cónyuge.*

Hélène, I'll be coming up the driveway on my motorcycle. You'll have to meet me there.

There was a brief, anguished pause before she answered. *Yes, of course. Just picture it for me, when you get closer.*

That's my girl. A thrill ran through him. She still trusted him, proven by their *conyugal* bond's continuing existence. She hadn't balked at going out into the open where they'd be shooting at her. They had a future, if they made it through tonight.

He put his hand up, signaling his readiness, and brought his Hayabusa snarling into life.

Emilio answered with a matching wave and pressed a panel on the wall. The overhead lights inside winked out, and a single red light began to blink. Five, four, three, two, one . . .

A small door flowed upward, barely tall enough for a man and wide enough for a small car. The night outside was black velvet.

Jean-Marie casually stomped down once, hard. His peregrine falcon burst out of its coop, swooped down the ramp, and alighted on the open road. It was traveling eighty miles per hour before he shifted it into second gear.

Celeste's *mesnaderos* hung over the balcony, spraying the foliage and everything else below with bullets. Rosemeade's expensive sprinkler system had proven as efficient as its makers claimed and had put out the fire very quickly. The guns' noise was deafening, even for *vampiros,* and mixed with the sibilant hiss of cut vegetation and thud of bullets diving into wood and earth. But no yelps or yowls of pain.

It didn't mean that the bitch wasn't alive, muffling her cries of anguish as they killed her. It just meant that Celeste herself would have to go and lead the hunt.

She sniffed—and saw smoke rolling out of her PC's case. It had lost all of its data forever—including the priceless list of *bandolerismo.* Hélène must have found it and had probably copied it, the bitch.

Recreating it meant a single call to Georges—but leaving it in Hélène's hands? Never!

She cursed viciously, slipping back into the gutter French she'd used two centuries ago as an Imperial spy. Life had been so simple then: Kill the British and wait for the chance to kill Hélène. Now she had even more reasons to do so.

She headed for the door.

"Celeste."

She froze, the beloved voice like a knife to her heart. Slowly she turned around and faced the mirror.

Only Raoul's face was visible, haloed in light as if viewed down a long tunnel.

"Be very careful, my angel."

"She can destroy my plans for my *esfera*," Celeste growled.

"She is still your sister."

Celeste gestured violently, too angry to find words. "I have to go. As the eldest *vampira* present, I'm the only one who can catch her scent and find her."

He didn't, quite, sigh. "You still have a choice, my angel."

"Do not wait for me." She looked back at him, her head high.

He inclined his head formally, his dark eyes shadowed.

Hélène was crouched underneath an enormous old rhododendron, quite possibly fifteen feet tall. She'd crept through the garden, concealing herself underneath its brethren and behind equally ancient camellias, taking every advantage of their glossy dark foliage. A single fountain dripped halfheartedly into the gloom, marking the paths' center point. The garden's boundary was marked by a waist-high brick wall, topped by occasional brick pillars with marble globes.

Like many great plantations, Rosemeade's grounds had been laid out in a *T*, with the house at the two bars' junction. The driveway started at the heavy gate and gatehouse, concealed by cypress trees, and curved through the swamp before bursting onto the main approach. It ran up the long main axis to meet the house, with the camellia garden on the east side and the rose garden—its twin in everything but plants—on the west. Here it was flanked by a great expanse of green grass, once used for horse racing, and magnificent live oaks. The entire grounds had been brilliantly lit for nighttime parties, such as this evening's.

To reach the pavement, Hélène would have to vault the brick wall less than two steps away, run across the grass, and meet Jean-Marie somewhere on that barren stretch of asphalt. She'd done her best to minimize the distance, having come as close as she dared to the wall.

She was only a few feet away from the rose garden and apparently downwind of it, too. There was a distinct aroma of gasoline drifting toward her from the parked cars.

Jean-Marie rode his Hayabusa up the highway toward Rosemeade. *Get ready, Hélène.*

On your mark, she answered stoutly.

He grinned, remembering how they'd worked together in the Spanish mountains. Finally they were a team again.

"Three, two," Ethan chanted in his headset.

He whipped his bike around the last turn and turned onto the narrow road, Rosemeade's only weakness. Two centuries ago, it had led to the plantation's dock on the Mississippi River. But the river had moved while the road hadn't. It remained, a short stretch of asphalt pointing straight at the concrete gatehouse—just long enough to suit their needs.

He impatiently brought his bike to a stop and waited. A 1985 Canyon Red Mustang idled just ahead of him, its two passengers' identity hidden by full-face helmets which matched his. Only a racing aficionado might have guessed at the extensive modifications its pristine exterior hid.

"One."

Ethan's number two lifted his finger in a brief salute.

"Go!" ordered Ethan.

Now, Hélène!

The Mustang charged ahead, facing Rosemeade's gate and gate-house. Fire burst out of its left front, hurling a rocket-propelled gre-nade full of high explosive at the gate. The heavy steel shattered under the blast of molten metal, pieces flying into the air and lancing through the explosion's dust.

Barely pausing, the Mustang swerved slightly and fired again an instant later at the gatehouse. The rocket leapt ahead eagerly and smashed into the squat building, tearing it and the *vampiros* within to ashes in a choking cloud of dust and debris.

The twin explosions rocked the air and the ground, sending birds squawking into the air and shaking the sports bike. Their secretive friends would be interested in hearing this report about test firing RPGs from their small, rapidly moving vehicle, its ostensible purpose.

Before the vibrations had fully died, Jean-Marie gunned his bike into the new opening, flashing a quick thumbs-up at the Mustang's crew. God willing he'd reach Hélène before Celeste's men recovered from their shock.

Celeste stood on the front steps, trying to spot her treacherous sister. No sign of her, either sight or smell.

There were, however, lots of *mesnaderos* tramping around with guns, shooting at things and scenting the air with cordite. Most of them were searching the rose garden, having given up on the camellia garden. Two, however, stood beside her, their rifles at the ready.

Her idiot *vampiros* from the commanderies had started to spill out of Rosemeade to watch the show.

Celeste's temper snapped. This, at least, she could deal with. "Damn you, go back inside and wait for me there!" she snarled, slam-ming her order at them with all of a *creador*'s power.

They muttered and obeyed reluctantly, a few slamming doors. Georges had warned her it was risky bringing so many together at the same time, causing dissension and other disloyal feelings to spread without tight supervision. Well, she'd make them pay for their inso-lence in a few minutes.

Now where? The bitch would have to go through the swamp to escape. The journey on this side was the shortest, even if it meant crossing the lawn.

Twin explosions suddenly ripped the air, from beyond the grounds.

What the hell? Celeste desperately held on to the massive column, while the land rolled underneath her and clouds of smoke billowed above the swamp. Dammit, she was being attacked.

A motorcycle's whine sounded within the woods. Hélène leapt out of the garden and began running to meet it.

Maman had hurled herself toward Papa that way at Sainte Marie des Fleurs . . .

Goosebumps ran over Celeste's skin.

Her *mesnaderos* brought their guns up and aimed them at Hélène. Her blood kin. Her sister.

"Be very careful," Raoul had said.

Surely she had time to think, to be more creative with Hélène's punishment.

"No!" Celeste shouted. "I want her alive."

"Madame?" Two bewildered faces stared at her.

"You heard me. Catch her." She snapped her fingers and pointed. The overly honorable bitch would certainly never fry two men who were simply doing their duty.

"*Oui*, madame." They obediently set their rifles on safety and ran.

Celeste went with them, hoping she wasn't being too much of a sentimental fool.

"Almost there," Jean-Marie announced.

"Ready here," Lars agreed.

"*Baby Mine* is turning for her final run," Ethan drawled.

Jean-Marie nodded grimly. Like hell he was staying around for the plane's arrival.

He took the last few corners a little tighter, glad when his knee scraped the asphalt he'd put a full set of armor into his racing leathers. Hélène wouldn't have the same protection, though, on the way out.

He burst out of the forest into the open and immediately drew a cloud of bullets. He hunkered down a little lower.

His darling was running as fast as she could across a wide expanse of green. She seemed a vibrant flower in her colorful clothing, with her hair streaming out behind her. His love, his life, his world.

He opened the throttle a little wider.

Hélène?

Yes, my love?

Run down the driveway, and I'll toss you a helmet.

She never hesitated. *Of course.*

She jumped out from between the great trees and onto the road, bringing her into the bullets' path. Praying hard, Jean-Marie reached behind him, unclipped the spare helmet, and threw it to her.

It flew damn near straight and true, thank God and *vampiro* reflexes, and she caught it. Barely breaking stride, she jammed it over her head and fastened it.

He slammed the bike into a one-eighty and a screeching halt, just before she reached him. She swung her leg over and slid onto the pillion seat, neatly avoiding the back rest and pack rack, locking her arms around his waist. Warmth spread where they touched, despite his leathers.

Ready, mon coeur?

Always. I've got your back, she added firmly.

"On two," announced Lars, his voice dropping into the measured cadence of the true professional.

Jean-Marie launched the bike in second gear this time. He wasn't about to do a decorous eighty before he shifted.

"Two."

Oddly, nobody seemed to be shooting at the moment. Surely it wouldn't last.

"One."

They weren't going to make the swamp in time, with its protective trees.

A thin stream of light threaded the darkness between the flood-lights, heading for the parked cars. Hélène gasped and hugged him a little closer.

The first car blew up, followed by the distinctive, deeper blast of an SUV. A third, fourth, fifth . . .

All of them in a great thundering roll which shattered eardrums and filled the night with black smoke, tongues of flame, and the stench of burning rubber and gasoline.

The bike leapt forward even faster, borne on the fire's edge. They dived into the sheltering forest.

"Clear," Jean-Marie stated, refusing to allow himself the indulgence of a sigh of relief.

"Clear," seconded Lars.

Thank God.

Jean-Marie throttled back a little, taking the curves cautiously to protect his *cónyuge*'s delicate skin.

"*Baby Mine* is coming in now," Ethan observed dispassionately. "Three, two, one . . ."

KABOOOM!!!

The thunderclap started low, deep within the ground, and built up until it shook his bones and the trees like a dog destroying a rabbit. Fire roared into the sky, followed by clouds of thick black smoke laced with Rosemeade's remains.

Centuries of torture, debauchery, and terror had ended in napalm's cleansing flames, destroying hundreds of murderers and rapists. The local *prosaicos* would sleep soundly tonight for the first time in generations.

Hélène squeezed Jean-Marie's shoulder in silent agreement.

Safe at the forest's edge, Celeste stared at Rosemeade's shattered remains without saying a word. Occasions like this when absolutely everything was gone, such as Raoul's death, required planning, not curses. Planning for survival—and revenge.

She'd heard the plane coming—too big for a crop duster, too low for the military flight it resembled—and instinctively dived for cover. The *mesnaderos* nearby had done the same thing, and they were the only ones who'd survived, all three of them. Plus the lot in New Orleans, anyone at her airfield, of course, and Georges.

"Get me a car," she snarled at the *mesnadero* closest to her.

"Yes, madame," he said, almost shrinking in on himself. "But nothing on two wheels or four can catch *that* motorcycle."

She hissed angrily. He flinched but didn't run.

"Would a plane?"

"Yes, madame."

It was something, at least. And she still had Georges.

Dear Georges. Life began to regain its savor.

She flipped out her cell phone. He answered on the second ring.

"*Cher madame?*"

"Texas has destroyed Rosemeade, including all the commanderies' troops and most of the *mesnaderos*."

"Crap."

"You have such a way with words. I'm heading for Hollingsworth's ranch."

Static echoed in her ear, not words.

"It's in Texas, *cher*," he commented finally.

"Just this side of Houston, to be precise—and it's our closest arsenal, other than New Orleans."

"Which the Texans are undoubtedly on their way to raid, even as we speak. I will steal a plane and meet you at Hollingsworth's."

"Excellent. I'm leaving now, before the stupid *prosaico* fire department decides to investigate Rosemeade's demise."

"*Au revoir*, madame."

Nineteen

Jean-Marie brought the big bike off the bridge as quietly as possible. Sand slithered across the streets, overrunning any dirt, and Spanish moss whispered in the cypress trees overhead. The small hamlet's few landmarks included a single traffic light guarding the bridge and a half dozen commercial buildings, all centered on an ancient fish-packing plant—and Dirty Bill's Bikes.

Dirty Bill's was a cross between a junkyard and a bike shop, which could have been one of the biggest in the South if it ever filed any honest paperwork. It was laid out like an old garage, whose big plate glass windows in front allowed passersby to see the tailpipes hanging from the ceiling, swaying like hula dancers in an invisible breeze. An entire side wall held only full-size garage bays, disappearing into the shadows. Cases of parts, racks of tires, both old and new, abounded, sparkling like jewels under an occasional spotlight. Even with all that, most of the cavernous interior was an indoor boneyard where antique motorcycles had come to die, displayed in every stage of agony and dismantling. Out back were acres more of motorcycles' remains, wedged between the bayou and the fish-packing plant's compost pile.

Even if Celeste's plane had been flying low, she was unlikely to spot them here, a speck on the map reached only after zigzagging over back roads and bridges throughout the bayous.

Jean-Marie parked his Hayabusa by Dirty Bill's side entrance, near the office. Hélène climbed down stiffly and took her helmet off, shaking her hair out and gulping in the humid night air.

Thank God she was out of that. She hadn't had time to put it on properly, and her long hair had been crushed inside. She began to finger-comb it out, more interested in watching Jean-Marie clipping their helmets to the bike than discovering their exact location.

He turned back to face her, tall and lean in his black leather. She went into his arms like a homing pigeon, and he kissed her, long and sweet, their mouths relearning each other with every touch and taste, pledging themselves to each other again and again. Heavens, he was delectable, his shoulders' muscles and bones shifting under her hands to hold her closer, his zippers cutting into her to mark her as his . . . Soon, they'd be doing more than kissing. Soon.

"Can you forgive me for trying to destroy your family?" He nuzzled her forehead, his breathing ragged.

"You are my family *now*, the only one that matters." Tears touched her eyes, and she blinked them back. "You were right about her, and I can no longer claim her."

He winced but didn't try to pretend ignorance.

"I'd hoped you wouldn't have to realize—"

"How far she'd fallen?" Hélène shuddered, thinking of Celeste's letter to Raoul de Beynac's sister.

Jean-Marie kissed the top of her head, offering silent compassion. Her heartbeat steadied, his warmth flowing into her, and she smiled faintly. "We can talk later, after you're safe from her vengeance."

"*I'm* safe?" His eyebrows flew up.

"Because you rescued me. I have the names and addresses of her *bandolerismo* in Texas." She flashed the jump drive's narrow silver band at him.

"Shit, no wonder she was chasing you so hard." He whistled softly. "This means we can't rest."

"Were we planning to?"

"Not on this side of the border, no. But you look very tired, and I'd hoped to, cherish you a bit." He caressed her face, his fingers brushing her skin in a foretaste of love.

Her heart melted at the look in his eyes. "I'll be fine, truly. I fed last night."

He raised a disbelieving eyebrow.

She started to stammer something and stopped, irritated at herself. There was no reason, after all, why she should be embarrassed. The fellow had only been food, and she had been separated from Jean-Marie.

"I will personally attend to your needs, *mon amour*, once we reach Texas." Jean-Marie kissed her cheek. "Thoroughly."

She blushed like a teenager.

"Right now, you need to put on the extra leathers. They'll be too big, but they'll protect you so we can leave Louisiana faster."

She raised an eyebrow when he unlocked the office door. "Come here often?" She glanced around the utilitarian space, which seemed focused on posters of bikes and well-endowed women.

"Occasionally—and we always pay in cash. I need to change the bike's tires while we're here. She won't be able to make this run, at least not fast enough, after driving over the gate's remains."

"How long will it take?" Hélène sat down on the small cot and started pulling on the leathers.

"Longer than I'd like. There are only two working roads out of Louisiana right now: the interstate and this back road. We'll have to keep to this route, but Celeste could take the interstate."

"Or she could alert whoever's ahead of us." Hélène contemplated the enormous boots he'd given her, reminded herself she only needed to sit—not walk—and started pulling on socks.

"True, although Ethan and his men are raiding Bacchus's Temple right now. With luck, that's where she is."

"Celeste's never been good at doing what people expect her to."

"Agreed. We're safe once we reach the Houston Commandery." He caught her hand and kissed it, just before she pulled on the first glove.

"Hmm?" She smiled at him, privately laughing at her undoubtedly sappy expression. But nobody had ever treated her romantically before.

"Once the war is over, we can live wherever you'd like. The New Mexico *esfera* is held by Don Rafael's vassal, but he holds to the more traditional customs. I'm sure he'd welcome you."

"You'd be close to your friends," she offered.

He shrugged noncommittally. "Or we could go to O'Malley in San Francisco, if you'd prefer a more sophisticated lifestyle."

"You're very generous, my love." She caught his hands, and he pulled her close, making her feel fragile and feminine inside the clumsy, oversized gear.

"Above all else, I want you to be happy."

"And I you, my *cónyuge.*"

He swooped down to kiss her, and she met him more than halfway, their bodies melting against each other. Would they ever have enough?

All too soon, his radio crackled into life.

"Jean-Marie, do you read me? Jean-Marie, come back."

"Shit," said Jean-Marie with considerable feeling and pulled his helmet on. He keyed the mike, keeping her in the crook of his arm where she, too, could hear. "What is it, Ethan?"

"According to the rats here at Bacchus's Temple, Madame Celeste is flying to Hollingsworth's ranch to reclaim her arsenal."

"Oh hell," she muttered.

She exchanged a long look with her love, both of them having nightmares about how much trouble Celeste could cause with more weapons.

"Yeah, that's just what I said. Did you have a chance to look it over when you made Hollingsworth talk last month, Jean-Marie?"

"Yes, it'd be a good start to World War III. Didn't touch it, though, since we left him in place as a double agent."

"Not much of one, since he's in Aspen with his girlfriend," Ethan groused. "Madame Celeste is in the air right now, and I can't get there before she does."

"Houston's got their hands full with the floods, and you've got Dallas with you," Jean-Marie said slowly.

Hélène began to frantically review a map of Texas in her mind. Were there any big cities close enough to help, other than Houston and Dallas? No.

Celeste and a weapons cache—plus Devol and her very nasty *bandolerismo*?

Hélène's stomach tried to find room for itself in the huge boots.

Jean-Marie's eyes met hers, an honest question in them. He couldn't go in alone, he couldn't leave her behind—his only chance was to do this with her as *cónyuges*. But hadn't they always been a team, no matter how high the price or bitter the task?

She nodded firmly, and he squeezed her hand, his relief and pride spreading through their bond.

"Hélène and I will go. We should be able to reach Hollingsworth's ranch just before midnight."

"You should have a few minutes before Madame Celeste arrives. Don Rafael is flying in with the *mesnaderos*, but I don't have a precise arrival time for him."

"Keep me informed." Jean-Marie cut the radio off.

"Together again, huh?" Hélène tilted her chin up, wishing she'd taken him up on that meal.

"Always." He tapped her affectionately under the chin. "Saddle up, partner."

Jean-Marie stopped the Hayabusa just off the main road, where a gap in the pine trees offered a vantage point, and they dismounted to survey their future battlefield.

Hollingsworth's ranch was more than a century old, originally funded by timber and longhorn cattle, but it had made its real money from oil. A few oil derricks still lazily pumped as a reminder of those days, while a small airstrip hinted at present-day wealth. Thickets of tall pine trees intermingled with stretches of grass, where longhorns grazed in the moonlight.

"*Longhorn* cattle, not something more modern?" Hélène murmured.

"Hollingsworth has ambitions of being an old-fashioned political boss, which means a big ranch in Texas," Jean-Marie answered. "Besides, longhorns are canny beasts and actually quite profitable, as well as romantic."

"Ah." She let the single syllable summarize her disdain for anyone so snobbishly motivated.

The main house was a turn-of-the-century affair, encrusted with columns, layers of white trim, and several turrets. It had been built by an oilman for his three wives and displayed all of their widely varying tastes. It also had plenty of room for gun vaults, walk-in freezers, and other locked spaces. Only security lights were shining now.

"No *prosaico* scent. Hollingsworth must still obey Madame Celeste's order about no overnight staff," Jean-Marie commented.

Hélène raised an eyebrow at him, and he shrugged. "It's cheaper, after all."

"Makes it harder to look after livestock," she countered.

"The only animals here year-round are the longhorns. If he wants horses, he'll truck them in for the occasion."

Hélène rolled her eyes at such niceties and pressed on with their survey. "There's marsh throughout the area, correct?"

"Technically a bayou, which is what's flooded."

They both glanced at the water bordering the road they'd ridden in on. The closer they'd gotten to Houston, the less dry land there'd been. Here it seemed as if ponds and streams penned the cattle as much as fences did.

"So Celeste and her men can only arrive by plane, not car, since this is the only open road."

"Giving us two tasks—prevent the plane from leaving . . ."

"Because we don't want that lot causing trouble in an unknown spot," Hélène agreed vehemently.

"And destroy the arsenal. Or at least stop them from using the arsenal's contents."

"Do you know where it is?" She glanced sideways at him.

"Yes. I was here last month, when we suspected Hollingsworth had betrayed his fealty to us and was talking to Madame Celeste. He became quite chatty after a little persuasion." He offered no details about his methods or the subsequent conversation.

"Hmm." Professional spy that she was, she didn't ask for any such insights. "Do you know the combination to its door?"

"I know what it was, but I'd bet it's been changed since."

A plane hummed through the sky, its engines changing pitch for arrival. Crap. Celeste would arrive early.

Hélène's voice broke the unhappy silence. Was she also trying not to think about the risks?

"Two of us, two tasks. I've only cracked a safe in school, so I'll take the plane. I should be able to figure out how to blow it up."

"Hélène! Dammit, what if that doesn't work?" Horrific visions flashed before his eyes of Hélène caught in an explosion, because she'd had to go too close in order to see. Her skin burnt and peeling away, her voice gasping in pain after inhaling fiery air . . .

"What do you mean, *doesn't* work?" She propped her hand on her hip and glared at him. "Does Celeste have inert fuel tanks so they can't catch on fire?"

"Wouldn't you, if you thought you'd be chased by a firestarter?" he countered.

"Shit." He could almost hear her brain spin. He thought rapidly, racing her to another option.

"We have to stop the plane from taking off," he said firmly.

"How?"

"Use the cattle."

"What?"

"Move them onto the runway after the plane lands."

She frowned but finally nodded. "It could work, but I've been a city girl for a long time. Even when I was growing up, I never herded cattle."

"Just shapeshift and herd them. What shapes do you have, exactly?"

"Owls." She shrugged, looking both embarrassed and irritated. "I enjoy flying."

His eyebrows went up before his face cleared. "Night birds and little use for escape," he summed up.

"Correct. I could learn the shapes during peace time, but they weren't much use for outrunning my bodyguards during a mission."

"Idiots," he dismissed all of Whitehall's staff for the past two centuries. "I can give you a useful shape." It should also keep her out of firing range.

I heard that, Hélène snapped, *but you're right. I can't crack a safe quickly, but I can learn to herd cattle.*

Do you mind?

A little but I'll be fine, so long as you come back to me.

Always. He infused his voice with all the reassurance he could.

The plane buzzed closer, clearly on final approach.

"Go!"

They kissed hard and fast before he ran for the house, taking advantage of every bit of cover. *Tell me when you're in position,* he added. *I'll picture the shape for you then. We'll rendezvous at the motorcycle after you're finished.*

Hollingsworth's ranch slept placidly in the moonlight, yet another boring piece of Texas mud. Celeste couldn't wait to leave, and she'd only been here two minutes.

"Just get the guns and ammo, then come back here. We don't want to spend too long on the ground," she reminded her idiot *mesnaderos.* A quartet now, thanks to finding two more at her airfield. "I'll wait here." She sure as hell wasn't risking her only—only, dammit!—pair of decent shoes by running over this ground.

They nodded and moved faster.

One of them stopped.

"What is it now?"

"Madame, there's a motorcycle hidden in the trees beyond the road. I think it's the one we saw at Rosemeade."

Really? Her eyes narrowed. Forgetting about any disgusting things hidden in the grass, she came to investigate what he'd found. A black and silver motorcycle, barely visible beside the trees and smelling of Jean-Marie and Hélène.

Her hands curved into claws, and she grinned in happy anticipation. There were a hundred, a thousand different ways to destroy those two devils. But she wouldn't give them the easy, fast way out—dying in a cloud of flames atop an exploding motorcycle. Especially since she was certain when time came for the final showdown, she'd have the best weapon of all: Hélène would never have the stomach to fry her younger sister.

"Blow it up," she snapped at the best explosives man among her remaining escort.

"When he starts it?" the fellow asked.

"Certainly not. Use a timer so it will be useless when they return. I want them to know who's responsible for their deaths."

He knew better than to argue with her. He bobbed his head and ran toward one of the sturdy sheds, returning with a wooden crate. He knelt by the expensive motorcycle and went to work, first popping off the fancy trim.

"How do you plan to destroy it?" Celeste asked, her attention caught despite herself.

"Thermite on the fuel tank, madame, contained in a plastic bag and held by duct tape, with my watch as the timer. The bike will be shattered."

"Even better, they won't be able to see the bomb or smell it. Congratulations." She'd commend him to Georges for this.

"Thank you, madame." He bent back to his work with redoubled energy.

Jean-Marie listened intently to the safe's lock, hoping it was still set to Celeste's favorite date. He truly didn't have time to crack it, not if he wanted to help Hélène.

The last number clicked solidly into position on the day the bitch had become *patrona* of New Orleans.

He swung the door open and whistled softly at how much the gun room's contents had expanded since his last visit. If he'd wondered before what he'd do when his Beretta ran out of his ammunition, he sure as hell wasn't worried now.

After he armed himself, he'd change the combination.

After all these centuries, Hélène d'Agelet was back in the countryside with livestock to protect her. If her count was correct, there were more than three hundred longhorns trapped by floods and fencing in this pasture. They were rather closely packed together, all waving horns and long legs with wary dark eyes watching her. No wonder the original Texans had simply turned their animals into the wild and let them wander. These beasts looked as if they could take care of themselves and trample into the mud any human impertinent enough to argue with them.

Amazing—and how very typical of Texas.

She was next to the gate leading to the runway. Once she opened it, all she had to do was run—in wolf form—around the cattle, and persuade them to go through the gate onto the airfield. It should be very easy, as long as none of them decided to kick, or stomp the strange wolf. Or jostle a silly human walking on two legs.

But she would shift because Jean-Marie would teach her. *Cónyuges* always brought each other through.

She smiled faintly, opened the gate, and slipped through to the other side. The plane was on the ground and, so far, none of Celeste's *mesnaderos* had noticed her.

Jean-Marie, I'm ready whenever you are. She glimpsed a small, very well-stocked armory through his eyes and whistled. *Impressive.*

Isn't it? There are enough guns here to arm almost a hundred men. I've changed the combination so this stockpile won't help her.

Naughty boy.

He chuckled. *Did you see how many* mesnaderos *she has?*

Four, all of whom went into the house.

Thank you, chérie; they should be easy enough to dispose of.

She rolled her eyes at his insouciance but put nothing into words.

It's time to show you the wolf now.

I've already loosened my clothes, so I'm ready. She slowed her breathing, easing herself into the place where anything—any form—was possible.

Jean-Marie came fully into her, more clearly in some ways than when they made love. He was a wolf inside her head, entirely a wolf from the tip of his nose to his tail. From the pads on his feet to the tufts of fur atop his ears, the wiry strength of shoulders and hips, the driving energy of legs to run and leap, the sense of smell for hunting, the tail for balance and to talk . . .

And everything he was, she became, too.

She looked up at the fence and sniffed it, her tail swaying her hips.

Good girl, he approved, his pride and relief coming strongly across the link.

She grinned and wagged harder. *Scents are different like this,* she commented, testing their *conyugal* bond. *I hadn't noticed when I was a bird.*

Birds don't smell very much. Wolf senses are increased, just like human senses are boosted in vampiro *form.*

She could hear him perfectly, including his relief, which made him repeat what she'd known, thanks to shapeshifting before.

You can shift back whenever you want to. Just think about mist, then go through that to human.

Right.

That's your biggest risk. You haven't eaten well, and you're exhausted from the bike ride. You've only got one shift in you, and this is it.

Damn, she'd forgotten about that.

I'll be okay. She sure as hell wasn't going to let him worry. *You watch your back.*

Yes, ma'am. Company's coming.

Cold terror ran through her—but not for herself.

Good hunting, Jean-Marie.

And to you, chérie.

*   *   *

Jean-Marie closed the vault silently, unwilling to admit, even to himself, how much he was worried about Hélène. The best thing to do was destroy the bastards inside the house as quickly as possible so he could help her.

The house was full of expensive antiques, including furniture, rugs, and portraits, all witnesses to Hollingsworth's appetite for bribery. The gun room was located off the old library, in what had been the butler's pantry. Hidden behind polished paneling, it was only steps away from the main staircase and the center hall. None of which hid scents from a *vampiro* like himself with two centuries of experience as an assassin.

Two young *vampiros* were trying to sneak down the hall toward the vault, both sounding heavily armed.

Hmm. He dived behind the sofa, providing himself a good view of the gun room's door.

The window suddenly shattered and bullets sprayed the room, grazing his shoulder. He cursed his impatience.

Time shifted and slowed.

Watch out, Hélène! The mesnaderos *know we're here and they're hunting us.*

Understood. You take care of yourself; I'll be fine. Her voice was as icily calm as his own.

A *vampiro* ran for the vault and began to dial the combination.

Jean-Marie came up from behind the sofa and put a single burst into the intruder by the safe. He ran for the door, not waiting to see his enemy turn into dust. Ignoring the bullets, knowing only a heart or a head shot could kill him. Anything else was only pain.

He needed to take out the fellow in the window before he did anything else.

Bullets thudded into his flesh, but he didn't break stride.

He skidded into the hallway and brought up his submachine gun, the very nice MP5 Celeste had contributed to this party.

The shadow behind the shredded curtains started to dive for cover.

But Jean-Marie was faster. He brought the bastard down for good, then turned to hunt the remaining two *mesnaderos*.

Hélène slunk past the cattle, baring her teeth. They eyed her as warily as she did them. Move around, move around to the oak tree, she reminded herself.

Damn, but cattle were huge from a wolf's perspective. They bit, too, or at least they'd tried to, and they wanted to kick her.

Ah, here it was!

Next step: Charge into the cattle and make them head for the gate.

She panted, considering her prospects with the tall, nasty cattle. Decent odds they could break her back with a good stomp.

Shots rang out from within the house.

Better hurry, Hélène; Jean-Marie would need backup or a distraction soon.

She snarled and advanced on the nearest bull.

He lowered his head and swung it, pawing the earth.

She barked sharply—once, twice, thrice—and charged. A last minute dodge and a quick nip won her a mouthful of hide and a furious bellow. She bit the bull's nearest neighbor for good measure before returning to the herd's edge. She harassed another bull, a cow, and a third bull, pushing them always toward the gate.

The cattle milled uncertainly and moved away from her.

She came closer, flaunting her predator's scent, and set her teeth into more of them. *Dammit, move!*

She ran back and forth, barking constantly.

The herd moved away, faster and faster, bellowing their alarm, waving their great horns to ward off danger.

Their only way out was through the gate, and they stormed through it like an avalanche, thundering across the land, moonlight pouring off their horns, mud clots flying up under their hooves.

Yes! Run, you beasts, run! She howled wildly, hurling herself at them and nipping their legs.

The longhorns burst onto the runway and fanned out across it, heads down and running fast.

Yes, spread out! Fill the runway! She dodged back and forth, charging, pushing them into position. Like hell, she'd let them leave a blank space.

But the wider space absorbed their original panic until they gradually slowed down.

Hélène dropped back, watching to make sure they didn't return to their original pasture.

Finally the longhorns were scattered across the big expanse, Celeste's empty Gulfstream jet standing in the midst like a silver mushroom.

A few cows around the edge looked around for intruders. Finding no sign of their tormenter, they dropped their heads and began to graze on the fresh new grass around the tarmac. Others gradually relaxed, too, and the airstrip became their new pasture.

Nobody would land or take off from Hollingsworth's ranch until these cattle were moved off.

Hélène grinned and abruptly sat down on her haunches, panting fiercely. Jean-Marie hadn't been joking when he said this was exhausting. She dropped her muzzle toward the ground, dragging air into her lungs.

She needed a few moments to catch her breath before she went to help him. As a human, of course, even though she'd lose any advantages of wolf form. She was too exhausted, as he'd predicted, to do more than shift back into her native form.

Jean-Marie waited in the hallway, squatting between the chair and table, ready to pounce on the first unwary opponent who came within range. One *mesnadero* was searching the kitchen, while the other prowled the music room at the hall's opposite end.

Come on, lads, it's time to finish this party and hunt down your mistress . . .

A black shadow slipped out of the music room and along the wall.

Jean-Marie fired a single shot, near silent to *prosaico* ears but as good as an alarm to a *vampiro*.

The *mesnadero* dropped immediately, collapsing into a small pile of dust. Jean-Marie ducked into a roll, moving away from danger.

The other came sooner than he'd expected, bursting through the kitchen door and spraying an uncannily accurate hail of bullets.

Jean-Marie twisted and fired, hitting his enemy between the eyes and killing him. Dust drifted from where he'd fallen.

He came to his feet a little too slowly, his hip aching where that last bullet had nicked him.

A quick look established it would heal within a few hours, given some blood, although it would hurt like a son of a bitch until then. He grabbed a napkin from the dining room's collection and pressed it onto the oozing wound, before limping out the door.

Hélène. He needed to find Hélène.

Plus Celeste.

Devol circled the small runway again. He was Madame Celeste's only defender, now those four assholes had gotten themselves killed inside the house.

Where could he set down? How could he reach *cher madame*? If anything happened to her . . .

At this hour of night, landing on a road was not an option, even with *vampiro* eyes.

Crap.

He brought the plane around again, vowing Texas women would pay in blood for any pain *cher* suffered. And God forbid *cher madame* died. Because if she did—if his love, his darling left this earth—he would destroy every *vampiro* in Texas and Oklahoma, no matter what it cost.

Hidden within the woods, Celeste studied Jean-Marie's motorcycle and her sister walking toward it.

Hélène was exhausted, her face very white and her feet barely lifting out of the dirt in those enormous boots. She'd probably shapeshifted, which must have taken a lot of energy.

The duct tape Celeste's *mesnadero* had strapped around the motorcycle barely showed at this hour and distance. Hélène couldn't smell the thermite or see the watch, where it inexorably ticked down the time till this pile of metal became a useless piece of scrap. She didn't seem to have noticed the bomb either.

But Celeste knew to the second when it would go off, thanks to her Rolex watch.

She'd already watched the cattle stampede onto the runway, destroying Georges's ability to rescue her.

She'd heard the gunshots from within the house. Given the number of shots, her men were dead and Jean-Marie was now looking for Hélène.

How many minutes were left until Don Rafael arrived? Not many.

Raoul appeared from behind a tree, strong and elegant in his fine blue uniform.

"I would be glad to fry every *mesnadero* in Texas, spit on Don Rafael's grave, and throw a party to celebrate his demise," she remarked.

"But can you kill your sister, my angel?"

"But then—I find myself remembering when we were children," she mused, her eyes on the bedraggled figure trudging toward her, "and Hélène was the one who covered my meetings with you. Who made excuses for my disappearances to our parents, and invited me to stay with her so you could see me, and bought me pretty dresses to enchant you. Silly little things, really."

"She taught me how to dance so I could make you proud." He stood beside her now, almost close enough that their sleeves brushed. "And gave me my first horse when I entered the academy, as well as later, when I was commissioned."

Hélène was only a few steps away from the lethal machinery now.

"If I warned her the motorcycle was booby-trapped, would she believe me? Or would she think the ploy too obvious and an attempt to catch her as bait for her lover?"

Raoul was quiet, his silence saying more than words.

"I find myself longing for the clean purity of flames, to sweep the dross away before them and let a new life begin." Celeste sighed, wondering where childhood's simple games with her sister had gone. "I'm sorry I've sinned, Raoul. I never meant to make you ashamed of me."

"You could never disappoint me, my angel." His fingers brushed her cheek, and she shaped her lips in a kiss. The scent of cedar and pine teased her for a moment, reminding her of the coming spring. "We will walk through Purgatory's fires and see God's face revealed at last—together."

"Yes." She closed her eyes briefly, finally believing she'd be with him again. "I must go now. I wish there was another way to save her but there is not."

"We will go together, my love," he corrected her gently and held out his hand.

Their fingers met for the first time in far too long. Tears touched her eyes, of joy and agonizing relief.

She smiled at him and raced out of the woods toward the deadly Hayabusa, the Act of Contrition echoing behind her. *I firmly resolve . . . to do penance and to amend my life.*

Hélène trudged toward Jean-Marie's peregrine falcon, too tired to curse the humidity which choked her throat and dripped from the trees. Just a few steps more and she'd reach the rendezvous point, where she could wait for her *cónyuge*. The *conyugal* bond was lovely, but there was something infinitely more comforting about holding him in her arms.

A big body abruptly slammed into her, knocking her down into the road. *What the hell?*

They rolled together over the asphalt, giving Hélène a bare instant to recognize her *cónyuge's* scent and strong body. She relaxed, following his lead, and arrived in the grass at the roadside, locked in his arms.

Two figures sped past, hand in hand. One was Celeste, but the other was wearing—a Blues officer's uniform?

They ripped something off the Hayabusa and ran, heading away from Hélène and Jean-Marie. A soft click sounded and fire leapt from the small packet in their joined hands. It burned, hot and bright—and Celeste and the man threw themselves on it, tumbling down the road, blocking destruction of anything else with their bodies.

Sacrificing themselves . . .

Hélène and Jean-Marie were only a few feet away from the motorcycle. If it blew up, too . . .

BOOM! The two people disappeared instantly, without a sound except for the fire's savage crack and snap. Golden light flared to the sky in a dancing pillar. Heat reached for the sky, almost as hot as the sun's surface, touched only briefly by smoke. The harsh, clean scent of burning gasoline ripped past, remarkably untainted.

But the bike didn't explode, guarded by the distance the two had bought plus the pervasive damp.

"Celeste saved my life," Hélène choked. "After everything is said and done—no matter where the bomb came from—we were still sisters."

"Family," Jean-Marie said with deep satisfaction and pulled her close. She burrowed against him and sobbed, the tears shaking her to her bones.

The fireball exploded into the sky, bright as the sun, hurling fire and smoke along the road and into the forest alongside. Sparks hissed and sizzled in pine trees, and the moon overhead disappeared.

The two people lying in the road vanished under a burst of black, black smoke, deeper and darker than hell itself. More ignoble than the guilt Rafael would carry if Jean-Marie died.

Jean-Marie, his *hijo*, and Hélène, Jean-Marie's *cónyuge*. If they died because Rafael hadn't fought for them . . .

He was out and running toward them before his big Mercedes had fully come to a stop, Grania at his side. He was barely conscious of his *mesnaderos* only a few steps behind; he'd protect his *cónyuge* himself.

Jean-Marie rose and tucked Hélène protectively against his side. He was bloodstained, his face nicked by glass, and his hip carried a bullet to Rafael's experienced eye. She was exhausted, and both of them were filthy. Far worse was their evident caution around him.

An *hijo* to be frightened of his *creador*! No and no and no . . .

Rafael automatically moved to embrace his eldest friend, but Jean-Marie bowed formally, forcing them to stay apart.

Rafael came to a halt, and Grania slipped her hand into his, giving him strength. *Madre de Dios*, his throat was tight with tears, strong as when he'd felt Fernando and Inez and Beatriz die while he was in that foul prison thousands of miles away.

But he could face any trials with his *cónyuge* at his side, his beloved Grania, who was Blanche reborn. Without her, it would always be easier to simply retreat into his old shell and simply demand nobody ever hurt him again.

"Don Rafael, *Doña* Grania, may I present to you Hélène d'Agelet, my *cónyuge* and my fiancée?" Jean-Marie asked politely. Tension thrummed through him, and the dawning of despairing grief.

No. He would not lose Jean-Marie like this. Just this once, he would make an exception. After all, the lady was Jean-Marie's *cónyuge* and therefore a part of Jean-Marie. She was also a firestarter and would be a very great asset to Texas.

Grania flickered a sideways glance at him but said nothing.

"Welcome to Texas, madame." Rafael gallantly bowed over Hélène's hand. "We look forward to forever enjoying your company here as my eldest *hijo*'s wife."

Jean-Marie broke out into a broad grin. "Thank you, *mon père*."

Thank you, he added more privately, *for reaching out beyond past nightmares and welcoming another man's* hija. *I swear to you, we will make Texas proud.*

I know you two will, Jean-Marie. I trust you as I trust myself. Rafael drew them into a hug, letting his body and instincts start learning the new addition to his family.

When they separated, Jean-Marie snatched his *cónyuge* up and whirled her around, both of them laughing like children.

Rafael's eyes were suspiciously damp when he slipped his arm around his own *cónyuge*. *Thank you*, mi amor.

For what? She leaned her head against his shoulder, her soft curls nuzzling his throat.

For helping me face a nightmare and thus giving me an hija. *I have grown much tonight, thanks to you.* His voice was hoarse with tears of joy, even mind-to-mind.

She looked up at him, her eyes shining with all the light in his world. *Together we can face anything, my darling.*

Ethan and Steve's story will be told in

BOND OF DARKNESS
coming Fall 2008
from Berkley Sensation.

You first met them in

THE HUNTER'S PREY

available now from Berkley Heat.

Steve brought her big Ford Expedition to a decorous stop before the impassive gates, gravel shifting under her tires like the butterflies flitting around her stomach. If she'd had any other choice, she wouldn't have come.

Her captain would probably have her up on charges if he knew she was here. Especially if he even suspected she'd brought the case files to a fortress which would probably need every tank at Fort Hood to break down.

To be viewed by the A-number-one suspect in a string of unsolved murders.

No, she was supposed to have sauntered up with another Ranger or, even better, a gorgeous, blessed-by-a-judge subpoena to haul her suspect's ass into town for questioning . . .

No way. Not him. Even if he was the only Texan she knew who could have put those bite marks on a woman's neck—a *vampiro*'s MO.

She slapped the button and sent the window skidding down.

"May I help you, ma'am?" A very smooth voice came from extremely high-quality speakers, not the usual distorted tones. He'd put money into the stuff that didn't show, of course.

Or should she say *they*'d put money into? And just how many men did he surround himself with—and how well could he vouch for every one of them?

One Ranger, one riot. The riot's size didn't matter, since any Ranger could handle any number of bad guys. Every Texan knew that.

Even more, she had to believe Ethan's friends were all good guys— just the way she knew he was.

"Ranger Steve Reynolds to see Ethan Templeton. Please."

The speaker clicked off.

She kept her face impassive and waited, without glancing at the four—no, five!—cameras watching her. Her hands stayed relaxed, easily visible, far away from her pistol. Guns wouldn't do her shit good against Ethan, anyway, given his speed.

She knew—God dammit, she knew every one of those marks from personal experience because she'd begged him to leave them on her. Before she left today, if she left alive, he had to explain exactly how the same bite marks had arrived on all those corpses.

Fifteen years of being his lover, off and on, said he couldn't have done it. She was betting her career and possibly her life on being right.

He had to tell her who'd actually killed those women.

Please, God . . .

Machinery whispered into life like ghosts gathering around a grave. The gate began to slide open.

"He'll see you now."

Author's note

My deepest thanks go to Gwen Reyes, Texas native and longtime participant in Austin's SXSW music, film, and interactive conference and festival, for "founding"—or naming—the Capital Rose nightclub in Austin and "booking" its performers.

I'm hugely indebted to the experts at Yahoo!'s Weapons Info loop for answering endless questions, thinking out of the box, and keeping me on the straight and narrow.

All characters are fictional, as are the towns of Castro Sanchez and San Leandro in Galicia and Texas.

During the British army's retreat to Corunna in the winter of 1808–1809, no roads were open north across the Cantabrian Mountains to Oviedo because of the unusually heavy snows. For Jean-Marie's needs, however, I've invented a smuggler's trail.

The Texas Vampire universe is based on a scientific theory, which I vetted with top animal metabolism and behavioral experts. Every attempt has been made to stay consistent with that theory.

All errors are entirely my own responsibility.

GLOSSARY

Terminology used in the Texas Vampire universe is taken whenever possible from medieval Spanish, supplemented by modern Spanish. The only exception is that *patrones* are given an honorific appropriate to their or their *esfera*'s ethnicity, for example, *don* in Texas, madame in New Orleans, lord in England, and so on.

Adieu. Good-bye forever. (French)

Alcalde. The *alcalde*, the most important official in the Spanish municipality, not only acts as the chief executive in a Spanish town, but also functions as a judge of minor cases and as the head of the *ayuntamiento*, or town council. The *alcalde* not only officially issues laws for a municipality but also holds the authority to arrest and punishes those who violate city ordinances.

Alferez mayor. al-FEH-reth. Military commander-in-chief, overseeing all warriors in an *esfera*.

Ami/amie/amis/amies. Friend. (French)

Amour. Love. (French)

Ange. Angel. (French)

Au revoir. Good-bye. (French)

Bandolerismo. Banditry. *Vampiros* owing allegiance to no *patrón* and living outside the *esfera*'s laws.

Benvido. Welcome. (Gallego)

Bien. Good. (French and Spanish)

Bodega. A wine cellar or storehouse. Because of the distillation process, it's the equivalent of the vintner for sherry.

Bon día. Good day. (Gallego)

Bonjour. Good morning. (Formal) (French)

Buenas noches. Good evening. (Spanish)

Caballero. Knight.

Cachorro/cachorra/cachorros/cachorras. "Cub." Immature *vampiro*, who is unable to shapeshift except to feed.

Certainement. Certainly.

Cher/chère. Dear. (French) However, "*cher*" is a common term of endearment in Cajun French, meaning "sweet," and is pronounced "sha."

Chéri/chérie. Beloved, dearest. (French)

Chou. Cabbage. (French)

Coeur. Heart. (French)

Comitiva. "Retinue." Assemblage of *prosaicos* attached to a single *esfera, patrón,* or *vampiro.*

Commandery/commanderies. Garrison of *vampiro* warriors. A large, stable *esfera* has a commandery in every major city (e.g., Dallas, Houston, Austin, etc.) and also at every major strategic point, such as border crossings. They are rarely staffed by *mesnaderos*, since those are always concentrated near the *patrón.* Usage primarily taken from medieval Spanish military orders.

Compañero/compañera/compañeros. "Companion." Someone who drinks *vampiro* blood regularly but has not become a *vampiro.* A *compañero* always has greater strength, speed, senses, and healing powers than a *prosaico.* The anticipated life span is a century, while surviving two centuries is extremely rare.

¿Comprendes? Do you understand? (The question, using the second personal, informal form of address.)

Concubino compañero. A *compañero* who needs both blood and sexual congress with a specific *vampiro* in order to survive.

Connarde. Idiot. (French)

Cónyuge. CON-yuh-heh. "Spouse" or "partner." Life mate, to whom a *vampiro* is linked by a psychic bond of total trust. The creation of this bond cannot be forced in any way.

Copita. Small glass. Specifically, the tulip-shaped glass used to drink sherry from.

Creador. "Creator." Sire of a *vampiro*.

Dios mediante. God willing.

Don/doña. Sir/lady. (A formal title of respect.)

El Abrazo. "The embrace." The entire process of becoming a *vampiro*.

En clair. Unscrambled, specifically for coded emissions. (From the French)

Enchanté. Enchanted. (French)

Escudero. "Shield-bearer." Squire.

Esfera/esferas. "Sphere," as in "sphere of influence." A *vampiro* territory, which does not necessarily exactly coincide with a present-day geophysical territory. *Esferas'* boundaries are fluid and frequently fought over. The basic concept is adapted from gangster territories during Prohibition Chicago and New York.

Frère. Brother. (French)

Gallego. A Romance language spoken in Galicia, an autonomous community in northwest Spain with the constitutional status of "historic community." In medieval times, Galician-Portuguese was a language of culture, poetry, and religion, used throughout Galicia, Portugal, and Castile. The separation between Gallego and Portuguese didn't occur until the fourteenth century.

Gracias. Thanks.

Gran. Big/great.

Grandpère/Grandmère. Grandfather/grandmother. (French)

Hé. Hey. (French)

Heraldo. "Herald." Herald, who is also a diplomat and a spy. Usage is taken from medieval and Renaissance Europe.

Hermano. Brother. (Spanish)

Hijo/hija/hijos. E-hoh. "Son/daughter/sons." A *vampiro* sired by a specific *creador*.

Je t'adore. I love you; I adore you. (French)

Je vous en prie. Please say yes; I beseech of you. (French)

La Lujuria. "Lechery." The Rut. Upon awakening as a *vampiro*, every *cachorro* will undergo months of insanity, during which their only goal is to obtain blood and emotion.

Mademoiselle. Miss. Traditionally, young (or little) lady. (French)

Madre. Mother.

Merde. Shit. (French)

Mesdames. Ladies. (French)

Mesnadero/mesnaderos. A vampiro warrior who's a member of a *patrón*'s personal guard. Taken from medieval Spanish, for a member of the royal household guard.

Messieurs. Gentlemen. (French)

Meu. Mate, friend, buddy. (Gallego)

Mierda. Shit.

Mozarabic. The Romance languages spoken in Muslim-dominated areas during the Muslim conquest of the Iberian Peninsula. Written in Arabic script and containing many words of Andalusi-Arabic origin, Mozarabic greatly influenced Andalusi-Arabic and vice versa. In some aspects, it's more archaic than the other Romance languages and greatly influenced Spanish and Portuguese. It was spoken primarily by Mozarabs, Iberian Christians living under Muslim domination, who had adopted Arabic language and culture although they never converted to Islam.

Nom. Name. (French)

Non. No. (French)

Oui. Yes. (French)

Parbleu. By Jove. (French)

Patrón/patrona/patrones. The ruler—who is an absolute monarch—of an *esfera*. He is also usually the *creador* of all the *esfera*'s *vampiros*.

Por favor. Please.

Prosaico/prosaica/prosaicos. "Prosaic" or "mundane," similar to the Society for Creative Anachronism's usage. A mortal human, neither *vampiro* nor *compañero.* If he has drunk *vampiro* blood, it has happened so rarely and in such small quantities that it has not affected his everyday life in any noticeable manner.

Puta. Whore. (Spanish)

Quel canon. What a knockout! (French)

Sabe Dios. God knows.

Salopard. Bastard or swine. (French)

Salut. Hello. (Informal) (French)

Santísima. Most holy.

Señorita. Miss. Traditionally, young (or little) lady; the equivalent *"señorito"* means young lord. (Spanish)

S'il vous plait. If you please, or please. (French)

Sí. Yes.

Silencio. Silence. (Instruction to do so, using an informal form of address.)

Siniscal. Seneschal. Responsible for the *patrón*'s entire household and its accounts. The *siniscal* can also call out the *esfera*'s warriors. Taken from fourteenth-century Spanish usage, but rooted in ninth-century Visigothic customs.

Tío. Uncle.

Valgame Dios. God bless me.

Vampiro/vampira/vampiros. Vampire. Someone who survives on emotional energy carried through human blood. Mature *vampiros* can shapeshift to at least one other form (if only mist) and are resistant to telepathic suggestions.

Vampiro mayor/vampira mayor/vampiros mayores. "Elder vampire." A *vampiro* who has lived for at least three hundred years, can walk in full daylight, and drinks less than a quarter cup of blood per day (except in times of great physical need). He also becomes more and more difficult to detect, even with the heightened senses of other *vampiros mayores.*

Vampiro primero/vampira primera. "Primary vampire." The *vampiro* that a *compañero* is principally interested in drinking blood from. The *compañero* becomes utterly loyal to that vampiro, when fed from him long enough. The amount of time needed to form this bond is extremely varied.

Verdaderamente. Truly.

Virgen. Virgin.

Vraiment. Really; truly; veritably. (French)

Photo by Anne Lord

By day, **Diane Whiteside** builds and designs computer systems for the government. By night, she escapes into a world of alpha males and the unique women who turn their lives upside down. Noticing the lack of a husband to keep Diane in line, her Tibetan terrier stepped up to the plate and makes sure that Diane does everything The Right Way—which means lots of walks and dog treats.